I0563306

# Queen Bitch of the Callowwood Pack

Callowwood Pack series, Book 1

Siobhan Muir

Copyright © 2017 Siobhan Muir

All rights reserved.

ISBN: 1-947221-04-3
ISBN-13: 978-1-947221-04-8

# DEDICATION

Dedicated to Tom Keller, who doesn't read romance, but loved the rough draft of this story, and continuously asks me when it's coming out. It's out, Tom! Thanks for the encouragement.

# ACKNOWLEDGMENTS

There are many people who have helped me develop this story and I'm so grateful for their help. Lanya Ross made sure the logic carried all the way through. Natascha Jaffa and Cara Michaels helped me make a kick-ass hook at the beginning, Emily Drew beta read and helped me with the "dreaded" synopsis. Thank you to Geonn Cannon who let me use his surname on the promise of another Callowwood tale with the character as a lead, and to Sharon Sogioka for catching the last minute typos. And of course, thank you to my husband George for his help when I got stuck and his patience when I had to edit for hours at a time. I love you, HB! Great thanks to Kris Norris for creating this amazing new cover that truly captures the characters.

# CHAPTER ONE:
## Waking Up Hungry

*Icy crystalline water on the tip of her tongue...*

*The scream of a dying raccoon with her jaws locked in its throat...*

*The adrenaline rush of blood through her veins as the stag ahead of her bolts...*

*The narcotic caress of the Lady Moon's silver light...*

Julianna Morris jerked awake, her breath thundering in her chest. What the hell was that?

She swallowed hard and scanned her surroundings, trying to make sense of the world. *Am I on the front step?* Scratches and bruises marred her skin through her torn jeans and exhaustion dogged her awareness. She blinked a few times, trying to bring her mind, and her eyes, into focus.

*What the hell happened to me?*

The question didn't help and she rubbed her face, hoping to find clarity. Her glasses were missing and her eyes hurt from the strain.

Groaning, she straightened and dragged herself to her feet. Twigs and bits of leaf litter cascaded around her as she shook her head.

1

*A mad dash through the alpine underbrush after an arrogant rock squirrel…*

Her breath froze in her chest as she leaned against the railing overlooking the parking lot in front of her apartment. What was wrong with her? She stared out at the Fresno suburbs, trying to chase down hazy recollections of hunting in the woods among the scents of pine and other animals. *Real memories or just a dream?* She squeezed her eyes shut and willed the images clearer, but they faded as her mind awakened to the new day.

Pale morning sunlight pushed weakly through the overcast, the warmth threatening, but not full-blown yet. Julianna shook herself and took a deep breath. Something wasn't right, but standing on her front landing balcony wouldn't clear things up. She rolled her shoulders back and faced her door, hoping her apartment might have the answers. The bulging mailbox beside her door offered yet another question. *Didn't I already get the mail today? Wait, what day is it?*

She'd just pulled out the thick bundle of envelopes when her neighbor, Leslie Dunmore, stepped out his apartment door onto the landing. He wore pressed jeans and a plaid button-down shirt without a tie.

"Damn, what the hell happened to you?"

*Excellent question.* "Uh."

"You look dog-tired, and what did you do to your clothes?" Leslie shook his head. "I'm not sure those tears will be fixable."

She glanced down. Her jeans looked like she'd tried to join the ripped-chic club. Stains of some unknown origin marked her shirt, jeans, and skin. None of them looked or smelled good. Leslie sniffed at her and his nose wrinkled.

"Sweetheart, you need a bath, pronto." He waved a hand in front of his beaked nose. "What were you doing again?"

"Survival training," she blurted at last. "I'm working up

to an Iron Man competition of backpacking in the Sierra Nevada in a couple of months. It requires the contestants to trek across long distances, using only what they're wearing and what they can find along the way."

That sounded plausible, right?

"Huh, seems like a terrible waste of good clothes, if you ask me." He nodded to her tattered jeans and his dark ponytail slid over his shoulder. "I don't think they're salvageable, darlin'."

"Yeah, probably not." Julianna glanced down at the letters in her hands. Did one of them say the State of California? "You headed to work this early?"

"It's almost eight on a Tuesday morning. I'm actually late." He laughed, his deep brown eyes crinkling at the corners. "You must have really been out of it if you don't know that."

He didn't know the half of it.

"Don't let me keep you." She dug her keys out of her pocket and unlocked her door, pushing it open. "Have a good day."

"Take care of yourself, darlin'. Maybe a long shower and a bottle of Chardonnay. That'll make everything better." Leslie wore a concerned expression as she closed the door behind her.

*I don't think Chardonnay will be strong enough.*

Dropping her keys on the kitchen counter, Julianna took the mail to her table and slumped into a chair. Her stomach growled, but she ignored it when her eyes focused on the top envelope. The return address bore the official stamp from the State of California.

*Please, please, please.*

She tore it open and scanned the letter inside, her focus sharpening as the words arrowed into her mind. Her divorce from Terence Simmons had been granted and processed. She was a free woman.

Julianna waited for the overwhelming joy and

vindication to flood through her, but all she felt was relief. *Thank goodness it's done.* Anger and grief still swirled through her, but they'd faded to pale shadows of their earlier brilliance. She'd lost eight years to a philandering, manipulative, chauvinistic womanizer. She'd helped him get tenure at UC Fresno in the English Department, and he'd repaid her by sleeping his way through the female professors and half the female students.

*To be honest, it's probably a good thing.* He hadn't been very good in bed. At least not for her. Memories rose unbidden, but not of those boring sexual moments with her erstwhile husband.

*Digging in the soil after a mole. The rich scent of loam mingling with the musky fear of the little insectivore.*

"What the hell is wrong with me?"

Dizziness mixed with fear, and she leaned her head into her hands, trying to get a grip on herself. Paper crackled, and she found her face pressed against the mail on the tabletop. Everything smelled of paper pulp and industrial glue, with a side of woodland debris.

*When did paper millers make everything so pungent?*

She raised her head and scanned the pale rectangles strewn over the surface. Power bill, gas bill, another 20-percent-off coupon from Bed Bath & Beyond. Julianna snorted with tired amusement. She could probably get 600-percent-off with all the coupons she'd received from them. But her amusement evaporated at the sight of her mother's handwriting on a pale cream envelope.

*Oh glory...Dad...*

Her hands shook as she tore the flap and pulled the letter out. It was only a note about the Easter parade scheduled in her hometown of Callowwood, but it was what her mother didn't say that had her hands trembling. Her parents had always participated in the holiday parades, her mother baking goodies and her father coordinating the floats. This year they'd just be spectators. Grief hit Julianna

4

in a fresh wave, and tears leaked out of her eyes, leaving dirty streaks down her face.

Her father had been diagnosed with aggressive lung cancer a year before and her mother's calls and emails had kept her abreast of his condition despite the divorce. They'd tried to fight the cancer with chemotherapy and radiation treatments, but nothing worked. They found the cancer had metastasized into his bones at his last checkup.

"Shit." She dropped her head to the tabletop. More debris rained out of her hair. "Dammit!"

She lifted her head, scowling at the mess. The disarray of her table infuriated her. She wanted to wipe away the frightening words of her mother's letter as if they were written on a dry-erase board. Her hands crushed the delicate paper into jagged shapes.

*What am I going to do now?*

*What are you going to do? Go home, where you belong.*

She hated that voice. It always came out when she tried to avoid some truth. It had always been a part of her, but lately, it had become stronger, like an older, braver sister forcing her to face challenges from which she'd much rather hide. As new tears spilled out of her eyes, a snarl suspiciously similar to a wolf's echoed across her thoughts, and anger swiftly followed.

*Crying will get you nowhere.* It hadn't gotten her anywhere with Terence the Rat Bastard, and it wouldn't help her now. She had decisions to make, plans to set in motion.

But how could she think about going home when she didn't even know what had happened to her last night? Was it only one night?

It couldn't have been. Leslie said it was Tuesday. Three days? Dread curled in her gut. *What if it happens again while I'm with my parents?*

*Holy shit! They'll think I'm crazy and...and...*

The scents of dirt and dried blood filtered into her

awareness.

*I need a shower.*

She shot out of her chair and stomped to the bathroom, slamming the door behind her to keep out the hurt. The stench of the room almost bowled her over. When had her nose become so sensitive? It smelled like her bathroom needed as much attention as her body.

The water helped relax her, but the question of returning home ricocheted against the walls of her mind. Eighteen years had passed since she'd been back to her hometown of Callowwood for anything longer than a week or two. Eighteen years of trying to have an exciting life away from the small town in the middle of nowhere.

She'd found "exciting" all right. With a lousy husband and weird gaps in her memory, she'd had more than her fair share.

Dammit, she still had to go. Dad was dying, and Mom needed her.

*And you need Jefferson,* that older Sister's voice insisted.

The name of the man she'd crushed on since junior high froze her solid.

Memories of Jefferson Lightfoot pushed out the fear and grief, filling Julianna with exhilaration and unrequited need. She thought she'd managed to put the "guy back home" from her mind, but he'd never strayed far from her thoughts. Even now, she could still see and hear him.

He had a rich, gravelly baritone voice that stole her breath. His green-gold eyes had heavy lids so he squinted all the time like a cowboy from spaghetti westerns. He seemed to see all the way down into her soul when he looked at her. Of course, if that were the case, he would've either come to take care of her desires or laughed at her for having them.

Reality smacked her hard, and she opened her eyes, letting the warm fuzzies slip away.

*He didn't want me.*

That hadn't stopped her from wanting him. Or shamelessly throwing herself at him. She hadn't known what "soul mates" were at the time, but she knew he was hers. She'd done everything but strut around buck naked to get him to acknowledge it. Unfortunately, he'd treated her with amusement and affection, completely unaffected by her tight clothes and swaying hips.

Embarrassment still burned in her gut, and she tried to shove it away by scrubbing her body clean. Why hadn't he taken any notice of her? The question had followed her for almost three decades.

*And now I'm crazy.*

Self-recriminations could wait until she'd eaten. *Dad would say nobody thinks clearly on an empty stomach. Awww, Dad.*

Julianna shut off the shower and toweled dry, making herself focus on the here and now. She'd made her decision–she was going home. But she'd keep to herself. She didn't want her weird gaps in time to affect her parents or anyone else in town.

Her stomach rumbled, and she dressed quickly, tracking down something to calm her body, if not her mind. *I need comfort food.* Chocolate and ice cream? No, bacon, sausage, and eggs.

The sun had burned off some of the clouds during her shower, and the waning moon appeared in the open bits of sky to the west. Julianna knew it was waning, knew it viscerally like she knew how to whistle or roll her tongue. She'd become more and more attuned to the moon's phases as her thirty-sixth birthday approached.

*So now I'm a lunatic.*

Hysterical laughter burned in her throat, but she swallowed it as she prepared a large breakfast of eggs, sausage, bacon, toast, and coffee. She sat down at her table, shoving aside the mail, and inhaled the scents from her plate in the weak April sunshine. Soft spring breezes rippled through the branches of the ponderosa pines outside her windows, and she wished they'd scour her heart free of sorrow. Her eyes returned to the moon peeking through the corner of one window, and she sighed.

The moon in Callowwood had always seemed bigger and brighter, a great, silent, comforting presence when things had gone wrong.

*Where is your comfort now?*

Definitely not in Fresno. Julianna's mind returned to Callowwood like a compass needle. Growing up there, the summer days seemed to last forever until the indigo shadows of the mountains stretched across the valley. The evenings had been filled with cricket song, and icy white stars blazed from the inky curtain of night.

It had been perfect.

*Then why did you run so fast and so far?* her Sister's voice asked.

*I needed more than just mountains and stars*, Julianna insisted.

*Bullshit. You ran. You ran from him!*

*Does it matter?* When she went back, she couldn't see Jeff, not with her issues. *Besides, he's probably fat, married, with ten thousand kids by now.* It had been eighteen years. He most likely didn't remember her. *And he certainly hasn't been waiting for me.* She snorted and shook her head with a rueful smile.

Julianna saw Jeff in her mind's eye, his beard trimmed short and his delectable lips grinning at her. She'd wanted to kiss those lips so often her own mouth had grown tired from all the practice in her bathroom mirror. His nose was short and straight, and his brows overshadowed his eyes, giving him a mysterious, predatory look. He'd had short chestnut brown hair, and he'd worn a silver pendant in the shape of a wolf's head surrounded by Celtic knots on a leather thong around his neck. His hands had been small with tapered fingers, but they had fit his body and she had often dreamed of them gliding over hers.

Julianna could feel them gliding over her now.

She heard the tines of her fork scrape her empty plate and blinked. When had she finished all her food? Visions of Jeff had absorbed all her attention and made her ravenous.

*Yeah, ravenous for hot, sexy male.*

*Stop it. He's not mine and never was.* She was sure he'd found someone to marry by now. *I should just forget him.*

But fury rippled through Julianna at the thought of his disregard, and she growled as she stood, yanking her plate so hard the silverware clattered to the floor. She closed her eyes and fumed, her hands tightening on the plate. *It's not fair. He should've been mine.*

What was wrong with her? Why was she still pining over a man who never noticed her interest? *I need therapy.*

*You need Jeff!* her Sister shouted. *You're going back. You can claim him.*

She groaned and stomped into the kitchen, tossing her plate into the sink. She gripped the counter edge until her knuckles turned white and fought the fury building inside her.

*I can't. I'm going crazy, and I have to help my parents. I don't have time for Jeff.*

*Only because you're a coward.*

Why was she arguing with herself? She was going home to help her parents. She'd just deal with the weird problems of the memory breaks as they came. Her dad needed her.

Her stomach lurched, and her shoulders slumped.

Her father's voice, so strong and confident, echoed in her head. *Nobody gets anything done by moping. Pull yourself together and make strides, girl, no matter how small those strides are.*

Using his advice as a shield against her distress,

Julianna loaded her plate into the dishwasher and forced herself to focus on going home. She couldn't just pick up and leave. She couldn't do that to the staff she managed at the B&B. But she could call in sick to give herself a day to regroup.

*Yeah, I don't think one day is gonna do it.*

The phone calls went smoothly enough, especially when she mentioned her father dying of cancer and helping out her mother. Everyone had experienced enough personal tragedy to understand hers. It also helped explain her absence on Monday, though she still couldn't explain that to herself.

She spent the day packing and discarding things she'd always meant to clean out. *Where the hell did I get all this useless stuff?* The fastest way to get her affairs in order was to get rid of most of it. By the time the cloak of night had descended, she collapsed on her bed in her PJs, too exhausted to even think. Sleep took her as soon as her head hit the pillow.

\*\*\*\*

Awareness came slowly, focusing into clarity from the darkness of subconscious. The scents of the evening enveloped Julianna—the heated concrete, burned oil from vehicles, mountain scents of fresh streams and cool trees. Darkness filled the valley, and the lights of the city obscured the stars, but the white-gold disk of the moon showed above the Sierra Nevada Mountains, its glow painting a tingling path of excitement down her body. She stretched her arms up to greet the moon in delight.

She shivered, though not from a chill. Excitement to run filled her body enough to tremble. She turned her gaze to the night-colored world. She'd be warm enough once she started moving. Her strides lengthened into a jog, stretching her muscles. The elation of being outside egged her on, teasing her with scents and sounds she'd never noticed before. When did ponderosa pines start smelling like vanilla? Why hadn't she ever noticed the irises planted in her neighbor's border garden? When had the family of raccoons moved into the trees by the retention pond? She pulled the scents in with great breaths, enjoying their tickling sensations in her nostrils. It was so exhilarating she threw her head back and laughed with sheer joy.

Julianna increased her pace, pushing herself faster until she pelted down the bike trail. The moonlight washed over her, soothing the ragged edges of her life like a balm. Why hadn't she ever noticed it before? It was almost better than sex. Well, better than sex with Terence. *Hell, just about everything is better than sex with Terence.*

Her breath sawed through her chest as a sense of unbalance gripped her. She needed to use her arms more, needed to feel the dirt on her hands. She turned sharply and dove off the path into the bushes, landing on her hands to scramble up the hillside. Branches from the shrubs caught at her clothes, and the scent of moist leaf litter filled her nose. But she couldn't see clearly enough.

Julianna's nose shot out in front of her face, her spine elongated from her buttocks and grew heavy with fur, and her fingers shortened and sprouted claws. Scents became sharper, her vision cleared, and the world intensified. Then the wolf inside her took over, threw back her head, and howled in jubilation at her new-found freedom.

\*\*\*\*

Julianna woke with a gasp. *Holy shit, what the hell was that?* She stared at the red numbers of her clock beside the bed, trying to slow her heartbeat.

Two thirty-seven a.m.

She'd been dreaming. At least she thought it was a dream. It had felt so real.

Was it a memory?

She shook her head hard. *Sweet glory, I* do *need therapy.*

She held her breath, trying to figure out what she'd seen. A clear vision of hunting a lone raccoon surfaced, complete with the scents of blood and fear. She recalled the taste of the raccoon's fury and desperation, and the texture of its fur along her tongue as it fought the grip of her jaws. Then she remembered the sweetness of its flesh as she fed from its warm belly.

Panic and dread swelled with her revulsion.

"Oh my glory," she whispered, horrified. "I'm a monster!"

# CHAPTER TWO:
## Coming Home

Julianna stood beside her mother, Beth, and listened to the pastor drone on about returning to God's side after a life lived righteously. The sun blazed over them, making the air too warm for black clothing, but she ignored the sweat trickling down her back as she waited for the service to finish. Tears dripped down her cheeks from time to time as the grief ebbed and swelled.

Her dad lay in the closed coffin with a flowered wreath on top of it. She knew he was there because of the stench from his rotting body rose with the heat. *Glory, can't anyone else smell it?*

She glanced surreptitiously around at the other mourners. Most of the town of Callowwood had come to pay their respects to a man who'd lived in the community for years. No one wrinkled their noses at the odor untouched by the scents of fresh lilies. She tried to focus on the flowers on the coffin rather than the reek coming from inside it.

*Oh, Dad, I wish you were here.* Grief ripped at her again, forcing more tears down her cheeks. *Those bastards at the factory knew they were poisoning you and they did nothing but pay doctors' bills and funeral costs.* The anger burned almost as hot as the sun overhead and she tried to breathe through it. *Thank goodness you're not hurting anymore.*

At least now she had one less person from whom to hide.

"Are you okay?" Her mother leaned over to whisper the words, her breath catching on her own stifled sobs.

"Yeah, I'm okay. Just pissed and sad, and uneasy."

Beth nodded. "I understand. Me, too." She squeezed Julianna's arm and turned back to the pastor.

*Sweet glory, have I made Mom uneasy now?*

In the two months since her birthday and her unnerving discovery of her ability to shift into a wolf when the moon shone full, Julianna had lived in fear everyone would discover her secret. It had been relatively easy in Fresno where big-city anonymity had shielded her from notice. But at home in her small town where everyone knew her, she'd spent the month holing up in her parents' house, terrified they'd notice the changes in her. She'd avoided going out as much as possible.

*Mom probably thinks I'm some sort of agoraphobic.*

Despite his illness, her dad was still observant and watched her with puzzlement, though he never asked why she was so skittish. She'd tried to be the daughter they remembered, but she moved faster than normal and smelled things before them. She could even scent their confusion, but it only made her more aware of her new differences.

She never told them she could hear them talking quietly in their bedroom at night, even when in the kitchen, noisily washing the dishes to drown out their voices. She tried to laugh off her ability to scent when her mother was sad, or frightened, or amused, or lying. Who knew lying had a scent? She wanted to confide in her dad, tell him everything, but she didn't want him to look at her with fear or loathing, so she'd kept silent.

*Please forgive me, Dad.*

The only response was the wind shifting direction, blowing the death scent away.

Thank goodness she'd moved into the "mother-in-law" apartment over her parents' detached garage. It gave them space to be together in his final days and gave her the freedom to come and go in whatever form she chose without them knowing her secret. Nursing her father had taken an emotional toll, and she'd needed the small apartment as a retreat to regroup for another grueling day.

Now she'd have the time to look for a job, but lacked the motivation. And Callowwood wasn't a booming metropolis by any stretch of the imagination. Other than the Super Walmart between Callowwood and Wipple, and the sleek newer model cars, the town seemed to be caught in a time warp.

At least The Wolf's Den, the bar and pool hall, had grown put in a few big screen TVs to allow the patrons to scream at sports games. She'd considered it as a good job prospect to keep her close to home and her mom except for one problem.

Jeff Lightfoot owned the bar.

Though she'd sensed him in town, she hadn't seen him at all in the month she'd been home. Relief still followed her when she thought of dodging that bullet. What would he say when she saw him? Curiosity matched the relief and she wondered how he'd changed. He was the dream she'd forsaken, but surely, he wasn't as good as she remembered.

*No one is ever as good as we remember.*

*Jeff is.* Her Sister's smug voice pissed her off.

The wind shifted again, and a new scent reached her sensitive nose, cooling some of her ire. Was it streams swollen by spring runoff? Or the earthy scent of rain in the desert? It tasted like a combination of the two.

She wanted to turn her head to chase the delicious smell, but the pastor finished his eulogy, and her mother squeezed her arm before she stepped forward to drop a calla lily on the coffin's lid. Julianna swallowed hard and followed her, resting one hand on the coffin as she bowed her head. *Be well, Dad. I love you.*

She took her mother's arm and moved aside so others could say their goodbyes.

"Well, that's over now." Beth waved at the coffin and mourners. "All that's left is the respects party." She tugged Julianna toward the cars.

"You don't want to talk to anyone here?"

"No, let's just go. There will be enough people wanting to talk to us at the party." Beth shook her head and gave a guilty smile. "It's too damn hot out here. Your dad would've scowled at all of us and shooed us into the shade."

Julianna laughed. "Yeah, he would have. He wasn't into much pomp and pageantry."

"No, he wasn't. It was one of the things I loved about him. He'd get excited over a cheap can of tuna and Triskets, and call it a romantic dinner."

"Please say he didn't do that for an anniversary."

Beth snorted. "No, I didn't let him, but he could make an ordinary picnic special." She choked on the last word and wiped her face with her free hand. "Sweet glory, I miss him so much."

"I do, too, Mom. I'm just glad the respects party isn't at the house." Julianna nodded at a few folks on the way to her Camaro. "I don't think I could stand to clean up after saying good-bye to Dad."

Beth laughed softly. "Me either."

"Are you going to be okay, Mom?"

Beth's silence lasted for several steps, and Julianna worried for her mother.

"I think it will take me a while to get used to being alone in that house."

"Do you want me to move in there with you?"

"No, dear one, you don't have to. I think I should get used to the silence. You're right outside the door, literally, and you need your own space." Beth patted her arm with a watery smile. "You're a grown woman and don't need your mother hanging over you. How will you date?"

Julianna snorted. "Mom, you don't hang over me. And I'm not planning to date anyone for a while."

Beth squeezed her arm. "Don't give up on yourself. You're divorced, not dead."

*I also turn fuzzy during the full moon. Not a lot of guys who'd handle that well.*

They stopped at the car, the burgundy red 2010 Chevy Camaro she'd won from her philandering ex shining in the sun. Julianna couldn't help but smile. She hadn't wanted much from her ex, but she'd known this would hurt him most. She opened the passenger door for Beth.

"Speaking of changing my mind, the town hall was booked for an emergency budgetary meeting this evening." Beth hunched her shoulders and grimaced. "We had to move the respects party at the last minute. It's now being held at the Wolf's Den."

Julianna tried to hide her flinch, but her mother caught it.

"The Lightfoots offered, and I couldn't say no. I know you've avoided everyone, but there was nowhere else to go. You don't mind?"

"No, that's fine." Tension filled Julianna's body as she closed the door.

"I'm really sorry, Julianna. I know you don't want to be social right now."

"No, no, it's okay, Mom. I can handle one party." Julianna took a deep breath and walked around the front of the car.

*It'll be okay. Jeff probably won't remember me. It'll be okay.*

The sunlight and light breeze continued indifferent to

her anxiety, and she tried to let her worries go. She slid into the driver's seat and started the car. Her gaze swept over the cemetery and stopped on a couple standing a little apart from the other mourners. They both stared back at her, and she swallowed hard as a fine tremor shimmered through her body.

One of them was an older woman, her silver hair pulled into two long braids on either side of her head, draping over her shoulders. She had the features of the Paiute Tribe of First Peoples who had lived in Nevada long before it got the name. Though the woman barely came up to her escort's chest as he held her arm, she stood straight and alert.

The second person was Jeff Lightfoot.

"Oh, glory."

He nodded to something the old woman said as his eyes bored holes into Julianna, simultaneously making her blood heat and her heart freeze.

"What? What's wrong, Julianna?" Beth shot her a worried look.

"It's Jeff Lightfoot."

*He's still the same.* Broad unbowed shoulders stretched his suit jacket, which hung over a flat belly. His hair showed no gray in the rich brown, and his face remained unlined around the neatly trimmed beard. *How can he still be the same?* He'd only gained muscle weight as far as she could tell, and her inner voice shrilled a wolf whistle. Her nipples tightened under her black dress, and the scent of her arousal filled the car.

*Damn. How does he do that?*

"Oh, yes. I'm not surprised he's here. Who's he standing with?"

She turned her gaze away from Jeff and quickly checked her rearview mirror. "I don't know. I've been gone too long. You don't know her?" She glanced at her mother, but Beth shook her head.

"She's not familiar to me. Maybe we'll meet her at the party."

"Yes, maybe." But Julianna wasn't thinking of the older woman.

As the only guy in town who'd ever made her hot and wet, Jeff had starred in all her teenage fantasies. Mostly they featured him saving her from bad guys by driving up in his black 1977 Chevy Camaro and whisking her away. As she got older, she'd fantasized about kissing him, feeling his arms wrapped around her, and his body pressed against hers. By the time she'd reached eighteen, the fantasies had become much more graphic and enjoyable, giving her wet dreams and soaked panties.

*Not much has changed, then.*

Julianna strangled a chuckle and pulled the car out onto the road, looking carefully over her shoulder to make sure no one was coming. *Right, and you're definitely not looking back at Jeff and the old woman.* Despite her determined ignorance, she felt their gazes all the way out of the cemetery and along the fence that "kept in the dead," as her father used to say. Now he rested among them. Her tears and sorrow managed to divert her attention from the hard stares, and she focused on driving safely through town to the Wolf's Den Bar.

The bar resided in a squat building taking up most of a town block with a parking lot filling the rest. Dark windows filled with the inevitable neon signs advertised different kinds of beer, from Michelob and Coors to Fat Tire and Moose Drool. Newspaper canisters guarded the glass double doors and a smoking bin/trash can stood a few feet away for the people who were still part of the "black lung club". The Wolf's Den was a non-smoking bar, odd for a drinking establishment, but it'd always been that way. Still, people flocked there from several miles around, including the nearby rural towns.

Julianna parked the Camaro in the shade of a large tree

daring to grow at the edge of the parking lot. She appreciated it now with summer in full swing, but it's shade only provided a little relief from the heat. She threw the car in park and paused, waiting for some sign to get moving.

"Do we have to go in?" Julianna asked.

Beth snorted ruefully. "Unfortunately, yes."

"We could pretend I'd gotten all turned around and ended up driving home instead of here." She didn't sound hopeful, even to herself.

"No one will believe that. You've lived here most of your life." Beth's voice filled with resignation.

"Yeah, I know." Julianna sighed. "Ready to go in?"

"Not hardly."

"Yeah, me either."

She pushed the door open and stood in the oven-heat of the July afternoon. Sweat poured down her back, but not from the heat.

*Take a deep breath. I can do this.* She had. She'd smiled when she wanted to snarl. Laughed when she wanted to cry. *I can get through anything.* She'd endured a lying, cheating husband. This would be easy in comparison.

Somehow, her pep talk didn't alleviate her worries as she took her mom's arm and they walked across the parking lot. The cars from the funeral rolled slowly down Main Street, the hiss of the tires more threatening with their slow speed. She didn't want to face anyone, didn't want them staring, assessing, judging her. She knew there'd be questions. *What are you doing these days? How was California? Didn't you get married? Where's your husband?*

She inhaled deeply to calm herself down, sucking in the scents of hot oil on asphalt. Not only had she failed in marriage, but she'd returned to a town she'd triumphantly escaped, just to get away from a man who'd ignored her. Now she walked into his bar as if everything was fine.

But it wasn't fine.

Her father was dead and she still had to face the man who'd broken her heart. Jeff might not have known what his rejection had done to her, but facing him still soured her stomach. Hell, none of that even covered her peculiar new problem of running four-legged for three days a month.

"Here we go." Her mother muttered the phrase as if bracing for impact.

Telling herself sternly to relax, Julianna pushed open the front doors of the Wolf's Den and stepped through. She gritted her teeth, preparing herself for the curious and judgmental stares she knew she'd face. *Just like at the university faculty mixers.*

The Wolf's Den had never been sexy or stylish, but it had a few quirky accents that gave it flair. The bar top was steel, covered in black lacquer with polished brass rails from Callowwood's first fire engine. The bar stools had red vinyl cushions fraying in spots, but the brass tacks holding the fabric in place matched the rails. Yellow faux-wood panels from the 1970s constructed the stained walls, with enough holes to be reminiscent of Swiss cheese, especially around the dartboards. Old stained-glass lamps hung in various places around the rooms, including over the pool tables and booths on the outside walls, while candles in their red lantern holders sat on each table in the center of the room.

*Like Jeff, this place is pretty much the same.* Instead of the back wall where a juke box had held court, the room opened to accommodate pool tables squatting like tortoises waiting for the days to pass them by. Today, all the tables wore black satin covers in mourning.

"They've done a nice job decorating for the party."

Beth's remarks brought Julianna back to herself and she nodded. She shoved her shoulders back and held her head up as she walked with her mother to the bar, praying no one could hear her heart pounding.

The place smelled like stale beer, sweat, and furniture polish, and homesickness crowded into her heart. Everything was familiar but more pronounced, stronger. New scents of sorrow and anticipation mixed with the *Eau de Bar*, and she resisted the urge to wrinkle her nose.

"Good afternoon, Mrs. Morris. I'm very sorry about Gerry." Richard Lightfoot, Jeff's father and patriarch of the town, took Beth's hand. "If there's anything more my family can do to help yours, you let me know, all right?"

Beth swallowed hard and nodded, tears threatening to spill down her cheeks. "Thank you, Mr. Lightfoot."

"Aw, at this point, you're welcome to call me Richard. No need to stand on ceremony." His deep brown gaze swung over to Julianna and his eyebrows went up. "Ms. Julianna, it's been a long time. When did you get back to town?"

Julianna shrugged. "A few weeks ago. I came to help Mom."

He nodded, the silver at his temples flashing in the lights of the bar. "I can understand that. Will you be staying long or heading out after you get your mother settled?"

"No, I'm back for good." She swallowed hard as he inhaled and his gaze sharpened. "It's good to be home with family."

He nodded slowly as his daughter Tawny, stepped up beside him with wide eyes. "Did I hear that right? Ms. Julianna is home to stay?"

Julianna cleared her throat, shrugging with unease. "Yes, at least for the foreseeable future. Mom needs me and my life had stalled where I was, so I came home."

"That's good. Family's important." Tawny met her eyes and jerked slightly, the nostrils of her beaked nose flaring a moment. She shot a look at her father before she nodded respectfully to Julianna. "We're glad you're home, Ms. Julianna, and I'm very sorry about your dad."

"Thanks." Julianna tried to smile. Surprise bloomed on

the older woman's face, but a real smile peeked out, and Julianna's tension eased a little.

"You're very welcome. Excuse me, please." Tawny waited for her nod and almost bowed back before she went off to help someone else at the bar. Julianna watched her go, trying to understand what just happened.

*Tawny's from the richest family in Callowwood. Why is she acting as if I'm someone special?*

Jeff's younger sister had grown into a beautiful and sultry woman. She was a couple years older than Julianna, but she had the grace held by those mysterious women described in spy novels or seen in lines for nightclubs. They'd been acquaintances when they were younger, but the fragile relationship had ended when Julianna left.

"Don't let me keep you. There are others who wish to pay their respects. Again, I'm very sorry, Mrs. Morris." Richard squeezed Beth's hand once more.

"Thank you." Beth swallowed hard and straightened her shoulders before she turned to face the crowd. Julianna stood beside her, not sure if she offered support or took it from her mom.

Other people greeted Beth, expressing their sorrow and sympathies as they moved toward a booth set aside for the mourning family. The Cutters, who had converted the sawmill into a "fancy" restaurant, gave her mother a quick embrace but eyed Julianna warily.

*What the hell is that about?*

She felt their chill stares and tried to shrug them off, but anger curled inside her. *I can judge myself just fine, thank you.*

The Winthrops greeted Beth warmly, hugging her in genuine sympathy, but there was no such comfort for Julianna. The elder Winthrops didn't even bother to look at her. Cameron, their oldest daughter, stared at Julianna, eyes narrowed with speculation. She tried to smile with bland impassiveness but didn't offer to shake hands.

*What is it about grief that brings out the meanest parts of people? It was my father who died.*

A long line of people, some who'd moved into town after she left and others she knew peripherally through her parents, blurred into one big "we're so sorry and we wish you the best" group. Sympathetic faces and black clothes flowed past her like a river, hardly making a ripple in her awareness. She allowed her face to settle into a vacant, plastic smile, her neck nodding until dizziness threatened. *Glory be, when will it end?*

When Jeff Lightfoot entered the room with his Paiute companion, the bar hushed and the hair stood up on Julianna's arms. All attention diverted to his movements, and she held her breath as he surveyed the room. Only Beth appeared unaffected by his entrance.

Julianna damn near forgot how to breathe. *He's here, now, in front of me. What do I do?*

Her Sister's voice intruded. *Smile, you rabbit, and welcome him.*

*But he didn't want me.* The whine was as old as teenage angst. *He laughed at me all those years ago. How can I face him now?*

*Show him you're strong enough for him.*

Julianna stiffened her spine and raised her chin, willing her guilt and embarrassment away. *I'm strong, I'm old enough, and I've survived a shitty husband.* She met Jeff's eyes, and amazement zinged through her. *Holy shit, he's still gorgeous.*

His green-gold gaze never wavered from hers, though he smiled and nodded to those he passed. His approach was inexorable, and the overwhelming urge to wiggle with excitement made her tremble as a path opened through the crowd. She firmed her stance through iron willpower, but her heart galloped. *He's coming right to me.*

When he reached them, he took a moment to study her and the crowd grew quiet. She held her head up, daring him to insult her or her mother, but a smile slid over his lips and he dipped his head a bit in acknowledgment.

"Good to see you, Ms. Julianna. I'm sorry about your dad." Jeff's rich voice washed over her, damn near breaking her composure.

She wanted to throw herself into his arms and let him take all her cares. Or relieve all her sexual desires. *How does he do that?*

"Th–thank you." She tried to slow her racing heart. How could she be aroused at her father's funeral?

"How are you doing with it?"

"I–I'm okay." *Liar.* "I feel better knowing he's no longer hurting. It was hard to see him suffer when there was nothing I could do for him."

Jeff nodded, his shoulder-length hair sliding over his jacketed shoulders. He smelled like male strength, compassion, and protection. *Does Calvin Klein sell those scents as cologne?* The way he studied her made her want to take his sympathy and wrap herself up in it. Actually, she wanted to throw herself into his arms and sob like a baby until her grief disappeared.

She must have shown something in her expression because he reached out to take her hand. The moment they touched, a frisson of excitement ran through her and the rest of the world disappeared.

Recognition of her soul mate blazed in a moment of clarity, as clear as it had been the day she saw him walking home with Tawny.

*Mine.*

Her head whirled, and for a moment, she viewed him through primal eyes. She saw strength and virility, and a male who could protect her and her offspring. He represented everything she wanted in a male, and she swayed toward him.

*Must get closer.*

Jeff's eyes widened, and he inhaled deeply like his

father had earlier. His grip tightened on her hand, and his arm flexed as if he was going to jerk her into his embrace.

*Yes, yes, give me a hug. Let me rub against you.*

But he came back to himself and his environment, and his arm relaxed into a regular handshake. Disappointment surged through her.

"It's good to see you back in town, Julianna." He'd settled back into the friendly, older brother persona he'd always shown, but not before she caught the fire in his eyes. "I'm sorry this is the way we have to see each other again, but we're all glad you've come home."

*We're glad*, he'd said. Sigh. Ah well, he'd always treated her with absent-minded friendliness. Why should it change now?

*Because I want it to change.*

"It's good to be back." The half-truth tasted sour as he turned to her mother.

The Paiute woman stepped in front of her, assessing her with her deep brown eyes and solemn expression. An unusual ring of dark marks surrounded her left eye like a tribal tattoo.

"Welcome back, wayward daughter." The woman's weathered voice seemed familiar. "I'm sorry for the loss of your father, but I'm glad to see you've grown so much since you were last here. When you left, you seemed so lost, but I see you've found the best part of yourself and I'm happy for you."

Julianna clearly heard the quotations around the word "father" and wondered where this woman fit into her parents' lives. She resisted the urge to frown. *How does she know me?* The old woman's words suggested she knew Julianna had been adopted as a baby, but what was that about the best part of herself?

*Oh glory, does she know I change during the full moon?* What the hell did she say to that? She shot a look around the room and met several eyes. *Does everyone else*

26

*know? Is it stamped all over my forehead?*

"Yes, I—"

But her head began to spin as panic swamped her and her knees threatened to collapse. She staggered to the side, colliding with her mother. The sounds and scents of the bar flooded through her senses, pushing her into a spiral of encroaching darkness.

"Julianna!" Beth tried to catch her, but Julianna outweighed her by at least eighty pounds. "Are you all right?"

She grasped at the threads of consciousness, trying to stay upright and console her mother, but everything slipped away too quickly. Even the confident, strong part of her whimpered in fear as the darkness threatened to take them down.

*Can't fall. Too dangerous.* She struggled to stay vertical, but she couldn't find "up" anymore.

At the last moment, a pair of strong arms wrapped around her as someone dragged her to one of the booths. The scents of the desert after the rain and mountain mornings in summer enfolded her, and her assertive side howled in jubilant triumph. Everything else faded away.

Safety. She'd found it for the first time in years and she wanted to stay.

She heard the murmur of concerned voices, but only as distant reminders of fear. She saw her mother's frightened eyes, but couldn't remember why Beth was upset when everything felt so right.

*I'm okay, Mom.* She wanted to say the words aloud, but her voice didn't seem to work. Beth tried to get her to answer inane questions like "are you all right?" and "do you need to sit down?" *Aren't I already sitting?*

She closed her eyes and settled in wherever she was. in the embrace of whoever held her against his hard chest. She loved his scent and the strength she felt in his body. She'd missed that her whole life, even while with Terence.

Terence's weakness and insecurity made him a pathetic excuse for a male who'd needed reassurance from the females he fucked. This male's strength told her he'd make an excellent protector. She closed her eyes and burrowed into his powerful heat seeping through the layers of their clothing. *Glory, he feels good. I'm so cold.*

A comfortable rumble pushed against her ear where her head pressed against his shirt. It took her a moment to realize he spoke to someone, but the sounds didn't make sense. She ignored the words as she gave into the comfort of resting in the man's arms. It felt right, settled, as if all the pieces of her life finally fit together properly. She finally fit in somewhere. She belonged here, with this male. Excitement shot through her like lightning, both electrifying and soothing, and she sighed with contentment.

"Is she going to be all right?" Her mother's worried voice penetrated the comfortable, settled feeling.

"I think so."

Julianna knew that gravelly voice. It sent little bullets of excitement and arousal shooting through her. The arms around her squeezed gently.

"She's just a little overwhelmed with all the recent events." The Paiute woman's voice soothed, and a warm hand touched Julianna's arm. "She'll come out of it soon."

"She is west of left field, isn't she, Sebrina?" The owner of the gravelly voice sounded hopeful.

*That's Jeff's voice.* Recognition dragged her further out into reality, and she realized she lay in his arms.

"Yes, my son, but we must give her time to understand it fully." Sebrina's voice held caution.

*West of left field? Understand it? What are they talking about?*

Julianna struggled to sit up and get a hold on herself. Chagrin washed through her. How embarrassing to faint at her father's funeral in front of everyone. And now she lay in Jeff's arms.

*Not such a bad place to be*, her Sister remarked.

*Oh, shut up, you're not helping.* She had to pull herself together.

"I think I can sit up on my own now." She pulled out of Jeff's embrace and immediately missed his warmth.

He let her go reluctantly as if unsure of her steadiness, shifting his body over so she could sit on the cold booth bench. She told herself it was better this way. Jeez, she'd swooned like some silly damsel in a Jane Austen novel at the first sight of him. She gritted her teeth and squared her shoulders.

Gathering her courage, Julianna forced herself to stare up into Jeff's green-gold eyes. "Thanks for making sure I didn't hit the floor. That would've been really embarrassing."

He grinned at her, stealing her breath. "Couldn't have that."

"You don't have to sit with me. I think I'll be okay as long as I don't get up."

Jeff stared at her for a long time with an intensity that made her nervous.

"What?"

Before he could respond, Beth appeared at the table with a tall glass of ice water and a small plate of Lily Walters' thumbprint cookies. They were Julianna's favorites, particularly filled with Lily's famous apricot jam, but Jeff's delicious scent overwhelmed them. Beth slid deeper into the booth, effectively sealing Julianna to Jeff's side. She tried not to enjoy it too much. Her mother took her hand.

"I think it'll be okay for us to sit while everyone mills around." Beth nodded to the crowd. "That way everyone can find us and you can rest. It has been a hard year for both of us, hasn't it? Are you going to be all right now, dear one?"

"I will." Julianna tried to ignore the shivers lacing her

body where it contacted Jeff. She took a long drink of water. "I didn't sleep well last night and I'm not used to how dry it is here compared to Fresno. I'll be okay."

"It's just as well," Beth muttered. "I didn't want to stand there the whole time everyone goes over and over how wonderful your father was. I don't think I have the stamina for that."

Julianna felt Jeff stiffen in surprise as she looked at her mother with raised eyebrows.

"What? Why?"

"Because I know how wonderful he was. I was married to him for forty-six years. Hearing everyone else say it only reminds me that he's gone."

"Oh, glory, Mom. I didn't even think of that. Do you want to go home?"

"No, no, it'll be fine." Beth laid her hand on Julianna's arm. "I can take it if I'm sitting down with you." Then her eyes focused on her daughter critically. "You're sure you'll be okay?"

"I'm sure, Mom. Just tired."

Beth snorted and shook her head fondly, but she pasted a plastic smile on her face for the benefit of the oncoming well-wishers. Julianna tried to copy her mother's composure, but the man seated to her left distracted her each time he shifted in his seat.

*Why is he still sitting next to me?* She wanted to ask him, but it seemed rather ungrateful after he'd picked her up off the floor. *He probably thinks I'll keel over again.* He hadn't been so attentive eighteen years earlier. Chagrin slid through her again, but she lifted her head and faced the mourners, grateful she didn't have to face Jeff's assessing gaze.

*Just smile and nod.*

Everyone wanted to say something to her mother or Jeff, but only a few had something to say to her. She had the oddest feeling she was some no-name courtier caught between a king and his grieving friend while the masses came to pay homage. She tried to focus on each and every person who came to the table, catching their eyes and nodding in greeting. Adopted or not, she owned the role of Gerry's daughter, and she deserved the right to be in the "grieving party."

But she'd left. *Most of these folks don't even know me.*

Icy dismay smothered her anger, and she dropped her eyes as grief swelled into the empty space.

*I didn't mean to leave you for so long, Dad. Time just got away from me, and suddenly it was eighteen years later. I'm so sorry.*

Tears slid down her cheeks before she could check their flow while someone told a heartwarming story of her dad. She tried to calm her breathing, but her sobs forced their way out. Jeff shifted at her side and wrapped one hand around hers under the edge of the table. Her eyes closed on the room, and she bit her lip as she felt him lean closer.

"Are you all right?" he whispered, his scent filled with concern.

She shook her head, blindly. "No, my father's dead, and I'm the worst daughter ever."

"Now, I can't believe that—"

"It's true. I wasn't there for him when he got sick. I didn't come home often enough. I let him down."

"But you did come home, and you were here at the end." Jeff squeezed her hand. "That's all that matters. He knew you loved him. Whenever I saw him, he always talked about you with pride."

She opened her eyes and turned to look at him, abashed. "He talked about me?"

"All the time. You might not have been here, but we all knew when you got your degrees. Your dad bragged about the great steps you were taking in education." Jeff gave her a gentle half-smile and wiped the tears off her face with the pad of his thumb.

She didn't know what surprised her more, her dad talking about her to Jeff Lightfoot or Jeff gently smoothing her tears. *I'd have paid a king's ransom for him to do this to me when I was a girl.*

She gave him a tremulous smile and took a deep breath. "Thanks."

"You're welcome."

He squeezed her hand again, and his words gave her the strength to face the rest of the reception with graciousness. Many people told funny stories of her father, and the group laughed heartily. A pattern emerged of a man well-liked and humorous, who gave back to the community and showed his respect to everyone he knew. She hadn't been present for many of the events in her father's life, and it saddened her that she'd missed so much when she'd run away.

*I'm sorry, Dad. I won't run ever again.*

Julianna refused to look at Jeff when her breath began to hitch again, but she felt his support and strength through the hand he still held beneath the table. His scent filled her nose and brought her more comfort. She ached to feel his arms around her again, but she contented herself with his comforting grip. It was more than she'd ever expected.

*Just enjoy him right now.* Sage advice even if her Sister-self growled.

As the stories about her dad continued, several women in the crowd shot venomous glances her way. Their smiles were more aggressive grimaces rather than compassionate gestures. *What the hell is their problem?* She resisted the urge to bare her teeth at them. She hadn't stolen a boyfriend or something equally as heinous. She'd only been in town for a month, and she'd barely been out of the house.

She shifted uncomfortably, willing her fury to settle, but the scent of their enmity nearly gagged her. She tried to focus on the next speaker as she sipped her whiskey after each toast. But the anger in her gut simmered.

"To Gerry." The crowd raised their glasses for the last toast and the mourners shifted toward the buffet.

"Glad that's finally done." Beth sighed. "Are you hungry? I noticed you were squirming a lot there toward the end. I'll get us something to eat, shall I?"

"Oh, Mom, I—" Julianna reached for her, but Beth slipped out of the booth and walked away. "Well, hell."

"Sorry?" Jeff shot her a look of surprise.

Julianna laughed in spite of herself. "Nothing. I just need to use the ladies' room."

He raised his eyebrows, but he released her hand, and she scooted to the edge of the booth. The hand he'd held felt cold without his warmth, but she shoved it away. She didn't need Jeff or anyone to make her feel better. *Well, maybe having my dad still around.* Still, she felt his gaze on her back the whole way to the restroom, and it only encouraged her inner romantic.

Once inside the little room with coral-colored tiles on the floor and walls, Julianna let out her breath and studied herself in the mirror. Life and experience showed in the lines around her eyes and mouth, sorrow making the whites bloodshot. But she could see strength in her face, too. She wasn't without her own skills, but she would like to let someone else handle them for a little while. Someone she could trust. Someone like Jeff.

*I'm pathetic. I should let him go. He's only being nice to me because I'm grieving.*

She used a stall and returned to the sinks to wash her hands before anyone else came in. The last thing she needed was to face one of those angry women. What the hell was up with them, anyhow?

When she returned to the table, Jeff was chatting with Sebrina and some of the other mourners who'd stopped by the table. He never paused in his conversation as she slid in beside him again, but he recaptured her hand. She almost yanked it out of his grasp, uncertain as to why he suddenly felt the need to touch her. But she liked holding his hand, even if his care represented only an illusion, and she left it where it was. She did shoot questions at him with wide eyes, but he just smiled at her absently and continued to discuss the likelihood of a decrease in property taxes in Pershing County.

*Well, all righty, then.*

Her mother returned with some food and settled in beside her. She'd filled the plate with more than either of them could eat, but at least Julianna wouldn't have to get up. Taking a bite of some savory salad, she caught sight of a striking woman with white-blond hair, pale blue eyes, and the figure of a well-endowed fashion model beside the bar. Her stylish black dress fell to just above her knees with a neckline showing enough cleavage to remind anyone else they were of lesser stature. Many men in the bar looked at her wistfully, even some of the married ones.

"Mom, do you know who that is?"

Beth nodded slowly. "Oh, that's Brenda Solaris, Lily Walters' niece from Los Angeles. She's an ad executive, I think."

"Why is she here? Did she know Dad?"

"I don't think so. I think she's here for Lily, really."

Julianna remembered Lily had been Gerry's high school sweetheart. "Lily's broken up over Dad, even after all these years?"

Beth just gave a sharp nod. "They stayed friends."

"And that was okay?"

"It was after I made it clear he was mine for good. She and I even became friends after a fashion. I think she always loved your dad, but she accepted his choice in a mate."

The word 'mate' ricocheted through Julianna, making her shiver. It seemed an odd word choice for her mother to use. She wanted to ask about it, but by then the blonde woman had moved to stand before the table, disdain in every line of her body as she stared at Julianna, anger in her eyes.

The scents of anger and overwhelming disgust flooded over Julianna, and she resisted the urge to wrinkle her nose with distaste. Ms. Solaris switched her gaze to Jeff, and her expression softened into sympathy. Julianna's temper rose again.

"I am so sorry for your loss," Ms. Solaris cooed at Jeff, as if he'd lost someone. "I hope your sorrows will pass soon."

Before Jeff could comment, Julianna raised her chin. "Thank you. I'm sure they will."

The light blue eyes hit her with a bolt of pure outrage before the emotion was smothered by pity, and Ms. Solaris smiled tightly. She returned her attention to Jeff. He nodded just slightly as if acknowledging her efforts. She inclined hers and smiled sweetly before sashaying toward the bar.

*Rival bitch!* her Sister's voice snarled. Julianna couldn't agree more.

Exhaustion hit her like a wall and she closed her eyes to find the last of her reserves. She'd faced her father's illness and death with as much aplomb as she could, but now she felt stretched out beyond endurance. Glory, she was so sick of putting up a front.

"Still okay?" Jeff touched her shoulder.

"Actually, I'm a little tired." She turned to her mother. "Mom, I think I'm going to go."

"What? Why?" Beth's face creased with concern.

"I'm tired, and I just need to be alone." She shrugged uncomfortably. "Too many people around for me."

"Do you want a ride home?" Jeff's voice promised comfort and sweet intimacy, but his expression showed only friendly concern.

"No, thank you, I can drive myself. But can you take my mom home? We came in my car." She began to push her way out of the booth. Her mother moved aside, and Jeff followed, making her heart flutter with excitement despite her fatigue.

"Of course. I'd be happy to do that."

"Thanks, Mr. Lightfoot."

He stiffened with surprise at her formality and pulled her to face him. His nostrils flared as a tremor shifted through her body with his touch.

"Call me Jeff. 'Mr. Lightfoot' is too formal for friends."

"Is that what we are, Jeff?"

He cocked his head, thoughtfully. "I always thought we were. Didn't you?"

*Can we be friends with benefits?*

"Sure."

"'Sure' as in you're humoring me, or 'sure, you guessed it'?"

"The latter."

His eyes narrowed. "But that isn't what you want? To be friends?"

Boldness bubbled up and she lifted her chin. "No, it isn't."

"Ouch." He thumped himself in the chest with one hand. "What do you want, then?"

"Do you really have to ask? I thought it was pretty obvious from my pathetic efforts to throw myself at you all those years ago."

His eyes turned gold as he grasped one hand, squeezing unconsciously. "You were my little sister's friend. It didn't seem right to court you then."

She raised her eyebrows dubiously. "Is that your excuse?"

He laughed. "Not an excuse, a reason. You're still bold as ever, though."

"And I'm still six years younger, Jeff, even if I'm no longer your sister's friend. Has anything really changed?"

"You have." His hand squeezed hers again. "You've

changed a lot."

"Actually, I haven't." She shot him a disappointed smile. "I'm still the same girl who threw herself at you all those years ago. I'm just older."

Julianna pulled her hand free and shook her head, sorrow sliding through her. She wished she was different, more exciting or glamorous. Maybe even statuesque or business-successful. But at the end of the day, she was still Julianna Morris, the girl with the larger-than-life-crush on Jeff Lightfoot. If he hadn't seen it then, why would he see it now? She stuffed her disappointment down deep and smoothed her features, turning to her mother.

"Please say goodbye to everyone for me. I'll see you at home."

"All right, dear one." Beth nodded reluctantly, hugging her. "Take care of yourself and drink some tea. That always helped me when the grief got to be too much."

"Thanks, Mom."

"I'll walk you out to your car," Jeff offered, his eyes still golden.

"You don't have to. You have guests and I remember where I parked."

"These are your guests." He gestured to the people behind him.

Julianna snorted. "Let's be honest. They're here for you and your family, and possibly my mother. They're not here for me. You don't need to take time away from them for me."

"I want to."

She studied him for a few moments, pleased he didn't try to dissuade her. "All right."

He nodded and gestured for Julianna to precede him through the bar. The atmosphere changed immediately. Scents of sharp surprise and anger slammed into her. The hostility returned to the expressions of the younger women when Jeff's hand settled on the small of her back. *Damn, what is so wrong?* She felt the heat and tingle of his touch all the way through her dress, and it buoyed her confidence. She lifted her chin but kept her gaze on the door.

*I can get out of here in one piece. Just a few more steps and I'll be done with this bullshit.*

She barely managed to nod and say goodbye to the people she passed. None of them seemed to care. They headed out the door and into the early evening sunshine, the heat replacing the disbelief she felt in the crowd. Relief poured over her, and she took a deep breath, scenting the hot pavement, the dry wind, and Jeff's protection. She had to find out what kind of cologne he wore. She remembered to get her keys out of her purse as they approached the Camaro before she got caught sniffing him.

"That's a pretty sweet ride." He looked over the car with a sexy smile.

"I got it because of you." She slapped a hand over her mouth.

"Because of me?"

She shrugged uncomfortably. "Yeah. I loved your black Camaro. I thought it was the coolest car I'd ever seen when I was a girl. When I got the opportunity to have this one, I snatched at it."

She opened the door to let out the heated air. At least it no longer smelled like Terence. Her nose had twitched for weeks at the competing scents of his cheap cologne and the feminine perfumes worn by his string of lovers.

"Wow, tan leather interior. Nice."

"Only the best. Never got to see the interior of your Camaro. Was it leather, too?"

"Oh, yeah. Black leather. I loved the scent of it every time I opened the door." Jeff chuckled and shook his head. "I still have that old hunk of junk, but I think this one is sexier."

"You think it's sexy?"

"Very sexy." His look turned predatory. *Remember, he*

*means the car.*

"Good. Maybe you'll notice me now." She met his eyes in challenge.

"I already have."

His answer sent pleasure zinging down her back. *Damn, he's so good at that.* She stiffened her spine and gave him a hard half-smile.

"Good for you. Now you'll get a taste of what I felt." She moved toward the open car door, intending to get in. "Thanks for walking me out."

"My pleasure. It's good to see you again, Julianna."

She wanted to laugh with disbelief, but his words rippled through her hair near her ear. He'd stepped in close behind her, her back to his chest. Heat and arousal flooded through her body, and she shivered at the contact. *Good glory, what is he doing to me?* Her tongue felt like it was swollen too large for her mouth, and she could barely get her breath.

"Goddess, you smell great," he murmured, his hands resting on her hips. "You always smelled good, but it's never been this wonderful."

The sound of his voice pushed lust through her, and she almost rubbed her butt against his groin in appreciation. But her rational mind finally kicked in. *I smelled good before, but he did nothing about it? What the hell?*

"Thanks, Jeff." She pushed his hands from her hips. "I appreciate all you've done for me today. Hitting the floor would've been embarrassing. I think I'll go home for some tea like my mom suggested."

He let her slide into the warm leather seat, but its heat was nothing compared to his.

*Dammit all to hell, let it go.* He was nothing but an arrogant guy who only wanted her because she'd stopped throwing herself at him. *They always want what they can't have.* Terence had been the same, chasing the skirts who seemed more intriguing simply because he shouldn't have them. *Jeff doesn't want me for me. I'm just someone new to chase.* Besides, she had that fuzzy issue every month.

"Get better soon so I don't have to sweep you off your feet again, okay?" His gaze burned just short of smoldering, and she had the sense he'd grab her and seduce her right there in the parking lot if no one else could see them.

She gave him another tight smile. "Right."

He pushed back from the car reluctantly.

"It really is great to see you, Julianna. If you're feeling up to it, we're having a party Friday night at my dad's place, and you're more than welcome to come."

She blinked, her brows coming down. "You're inviting me to a party? Why?"

His eyebrows went up. "Because I'd like to see you again, but in a more relaxed atmosphere. Don't you like parties?"

She wrinkled her nose. "No, not really. There's always some sort of politics going on and subtle one-upmanship." She gestured toward the bar. "Even today. I felt like I was in some sort of competition that I didn't even know existed. It's damn tiring and not really my kind of scene."

Dismay slid across his expression. "Yeah, I hear you there. Seems like almost all my dad's parties are political these days. But I'd really like you to come. We could be the apolitical party together. What do you say?"

She laughed lightly, but some of her unease lifted. Invited to a party by Jeff Lightfoot? The little girl in her did a happy dance. Man, she was pathetic.

"All right. What kind of attire?"

He grinned. "Tawny calls it 'dressy casual,' whatever the hell that means."

"I think I can come up with clothes of that description. What time?"

"Around seven." He leaned closer to her through the open window. "But no one really shows up until eight."

"I'll be there at eight, then." She tried to ignore the pleasure she got from his proximity.

"No, come at seven so Dad can meet you."

She frowned. "I've met your dad before."

"Not like this you haven't," he mumbled, and she raised an eyebrow at him. "It's been a long time, and we'd all love to hear what has happened to you since you left."

*I married a lying, cheating, scumbag, graduated, and now turn fuzzy for three days every time the moon is full. How'd your two decades go?*

Julianna narrowed her eyes at him, trying to figure out what he was up to. But his expression had smoothed into bland friendliness again, hiding his thoughts better than a mask.

"Sure you do," she drawled skeptically.

"Please, Julianna. I'd really like you to be there." He sounded almost desperate.

She wanted to ask him why. Why now after all these years? But she kept her mouth shut.

"All right. I'll be there around seven on Friday. Let me know if you need any help setting up."

"Will do." A slow, sexy grin spread across his face. "Drive carefully now."

"Thanks."

She started the car and backed up, feeling his eyes on her as she pulled out of the parking lot. What the hell was all that about? And why did she feel all tingly when he touched her? Why was he touching her at all? It made her want to jump him, to throw him against a wall and wrap her legs around him until he relieved the hot ache between her legs. Or beat the living daylights out of him, and then jump him.

*Something is really wrong with me. I'm definitely going to need my vibe tonight.*

"Oh my glory! He's human. I've got to stay away from him."

41

Werewolves were supposed to be myths, but somehow, she'd become one. She'd never met any others like her, but with her father's sickness, she hadn't had the chance to look. The legends she'd studied in college were full of shape-shifters, but stories didn't equate reality.

How would she keep this secret? *I can't tell Jeff. I shouldn't go to the party.*

Guilt settled on her shoulders as she drove away from the bar and the man she'd lusted after for years. But she couldn't quite bring herself to call the Lightfoots and decline the invitation.

****

*Mine. Mine. Mine!*

Jeff watched the burgundy Camaro slide away through the sunshine and clenched his fists at his sides to keep from bounding after it. He was fast enough to catch up to Julianna Morris, but it wouldn't be appropriate for the future packleader of the Callowwood Pack to run after a female like a rabid dog.

Protocols had to be followed and appearances upheld.

He tried to remind his cock of that, but the damn thing had a mind of its own, and right now it told him to run after his True Mate, appearances be damned.

"Dammit, calm down." He snarled and pounded his fist against his thigh hard enough to divert his attention from his groin to the pain. "I have to go back inside and face all those bitches and their families."

The idea made him snarl even harder as he ground his teeth.

He didn't want any of them. They might be alpha females, true enough, but most were simpering, self-aggrandizing whelps wanting him only for his position and the prestige it gave them and their families. Every one of them thought she deserved to be the Queen Bitch of the

Callowwood Pack.

*Emphasis on bitch.* He gulped great breaths of air to settle not only his hard-on but also his primal fury.

Pack policies and leadership protocols required him to interview several alpha female candidates for the position of his mate and Luna, the top Alpha female, for the betterment of the pack. It was tradition, left over from a time when Mates were few and far between.

The pack needed a balanced leadership of male and female protection by their Alphas, but the Alpha's True Mate hadn't always appeared. The elders of each pack decided, if the future Alpha's Mate did not appear, the leadership would be chosen by competition, and the future Alpha would choose from a group of likely alpha female candidates who passed a series of tests.

Times had changed. More Moon Singers— werewolves—lived among the humans now and finding True Mates was much easier. However, the tradition of the Luna selection remained in place for the Alphas, and he was bound by his rank to follow it. Before Julianna Morris had returned to Callowwood, the political requirements hadn't bothered him.

Now everything had changed.

Holy First Canid, even her scent beguiled him. The combination of climbing gardenia and heated ponderosa pine forest wrapped around him with sensuous fingers. His hard-on flared again, along with uncertainty. *Why didn't I know she was a Moon Singer before?*

He thought back to all those times she'd flaunted herself at him throughout her high school years. He'd fought his attraction back then while she pranced around wearing cute, tight shirts and pants, sexy summer dresses and flirty attitude. She'd smelled of raging hormones and sweet innocence, but never Moon Singer. Still, it had been all he could do to treat her like another little sister and stay away from her. He'd thrown himself into more cold showers and punishing exercise routines than a high school football team. He'd never been so buff.

Whenever his mind demanded he take her and fuck her hard, he only stopped himself with two thoughts. First, she was too young and not nearly ready for sex, despite her beauty and innocent flirting. Second, she wasn't a Moon Singer. She hadn't smelled like one or acted like one, and her parents were human.

When the hell had that changed?

And when had she become his True Mate?

Jeff recognized it at the funeral, her sweet scent making the odors of the other females seem unpleasant. She'd stepped out of her sexy Camaro with her mother, and her scent had wrapped around him. His body had tightened, and he'd almost grabbed her and claimed her right there. Only Sebrina's hand on his arm had restrained him.

But nothing could stop him at the reception when he caught her as she'd crumpled, holding her protectively against his chest. He'd relished the weight of her soft body in his arms, and he'd wanted to press his nose to her head, inhaling her seductive fragrance forever while he fondled her beautiful curves. Only her mother's worried comments had kept him within the bounds of propriety.

Jeff closed his eyes and remembered the silky softness of her hair filled with her scent. He loved her hair. The dark brown, almost black, tresses would feel erotic as hell draped over his thighs as she sucked his cock, humming and moaning with pleasure against his shaft.

*Damn! Think about something else before you come in your shorts.*

He returned his mind to the reception and how he'd forced himself to tamp down the protective instincts with every other male Moon Singer who got near her. Rage resurfaced and began to deflate his arousal. The females had been as much of a threat, their overwhelming scents flooding his nostrils as they'd paraded past the table. He could barely smile civilly at them. He'd scented their disdain for Julianna, and his Brother form had risen up to protect his Mate.

*Fuck, I'm going insane.*

He'd been told stories of the mating bond before, but the moment he touched her brought them all to vivid life. There'd been no doubt in his mind what he'd experienced, and he'd been unable to leave her side from that moment on.

It killed him to let her drive away now.

His hormones sang like a rabid rock concert crowd, demanding he go find her and seal the bond now, but he held onto himself like a drowning man to a rope. *No, I have to go back inside and socialize as the next packleader.* He had to make it look like he was considering all of them as potential mates.

His Brother form snarled again. *Screw pack politics and protocols. You've chosen your True Mate. Julianna Morris will be your Luna, and all the others can go to hell.*

Jeff didn't want to argue with his Brother, and he took a few more steps toward the street before stopping himself.

*No, no, back to the bar.* He had to let her go for now.

Fury and need warred with his better judgment as he stood panting at the door of his bar. His princess drove away and it damn near killed him. He'd play the courting prince like his father wanted, but his choice was clear. Julianna was his princess, and that was that. He'd been attracted to her for years and now he had his chance. The other alpha females inside meant nothing to him.

Squaring his shoulders and schooling his expression to show bland amusement, he opened the door to his bar and strode inside. It would be a long day, but one thought cheered him as he returned to the posturing females inside. He'd see Julianna at the party on Friday before everyone else arrived. His smile broadened as he faced the wolves in the bar.

# CHAPTER THREE:
## Party Politics

*What the hell am I doing?*

Julianna sighed as she parked her car in front of the
Lightfoots' house, trying to find her party face. It had been
a long week getting used to her dad's absence in the house,
and she wasn't sure she was ready to face more company.
Especially political company.

Despite Jeff's insistence of dressy casual, she couldn't
help but think this party was more important than a simple
get-together. When a young man dressed in a uniform
tapped on her window and gave her an insistent smile, she
damn near jumped. She rolled it down.

"Yes?"

"Are you here for the Garden Party?" The way he said
it suggested its importance. "You're a bit early."

"Uh, yes. I was invited." The inane statement made her
gather her purse and step out onto the drive.

"Nice car." He took her keys with a smile of
appreciation.

"Thank you."

"I promise to take good care of it." He carefully got
into the Camaro and nodded to her before he slowly drove

off to find a parking place.

She shook her head with bemusement. The Lightfoots needed a valet for their party? How big was this shindig going to be?

Taking a deep breath, she moved toward the house along the front walk. The yard looked just as immaculate as she remembered. Sheesh, not even the weeds dared mar the perfection of the flowerbeds.

*Deep breath, Julianna. It'll be fine.* She followed her own advice as she smoothed the flared skirt of her iridescent, peacock green halter dress and pushed the tendrils of loose hair behind her ears. Scents of hot pavement and cool grass filled her nose, and she concentrated on slowing her breathing as she marched to the front door.

*This will be a cinch,* her Sister stated.

*Yeah, right.*

One of the double doors opened at her knock to reveal a woman dressed in a maid's uniform. She gave Julianna a sharp once-over before saying, "I'm sorry, the party doesn't start for another hour, miss."

"Uh, yes, I was invited by Mr. Jeff Lightfoot to meet the family before the party started. My name is Julianna Morris." She hoped her voice held steady despite her nervousness.

Instead of turning up her nose in disdain, the woman's expression shifted and she offered Julianna a warm smile. "Of course, Ms. Morris. Please come in. The family is expecting you."

She stepped back, allowing Julianna to enter. She caught something teasingly familiar in the other woman's scent as she passed. She frowned and tried to remember where she'd smelled it before.

"If you'll just follow me, Ms. Tawny instructed me to bring you to her as soon as you arrived."

"Thank you." Julianna wondered how she'd become an

honored guest in less than a week.

She followed the woman through the house to the backyard, still puzzling over the familiar scent. The Lightfoots had a huge amount of land around their house. Forest hemmed in their yard at the foothills of the mountains and the trees seemed to go on for miles and miles. In the open space before the trees, large white tents stood strung with lights like fireflies on tethers. Julianna stared, entranced.

Tables arranged with at least ten place settings each filled the space beneath the tents, with two long buffet tables set to one side, holding Bunsen burners and rectangular brackets. Serving staff briskly set the tables and arranged dinnerware and centerpieces.

Julianna scanned the people around her with her eyes and nose. She caught scents of food mixed with the distinct musk of predator, but she couldn't pinpoint a single animal beneath the softly glowing shrouds. Tawny appeared out of the crowd of servers, her crimson dress glowing against their black and white uniforms. Her sandy blond hair was drawn up onto her head with a complex series of clips and diamond dangle earrings fell from her ears. Julianna envied her effortless beauty.

"Ms. Tawny, Mistress Julianna Morris has arrived."

Tawny turned, and her face creased into a warm smile. "Welcome, Mistress Morris."

Julianna couldn't help but smile back.

"Thank you, Lindsey." The serving woman nodded and left. Tawny turned her warm smile on Julianna. "I'm so glad you're here. I haven't seen you in ages, and you looked so sad and lost at the funeral. My heart nearly bled for you."

"Thank you."

"I'm glad Jeff invited you tonight. It's such a special occasion, and it wouldn't be right to do it without you, even if you haven't been in town long."

Julianna frowned, unease sliding through her. *Special occasion?*

"Now, you look beautiful. Did anyone tell you? Like a princess already, and you haven't even gone through the ceremony. You'll wow them all, sure enough." Tawny bustled about, straightening a few flowers in an arrangement.

*Ceremony? There's going to be a ceremony?*

"There." Tawny put the finishing touches on the last vase and brushed her hands of pollen. "Let's get these flowers deposited on each table and then you can come in and have a bracing cup of tea with the family before the festivities start."

Julianna took the small vases of gold and white flowers that Tawny thrust into her hands and followed her around to the remaining tables without centerpieces. Tawny chattered on about all the people who'd be there tonight and all the families hoping to get in bed with the Lightfoots because of the succession. She remarked how most of the candidates were as snotty as rich society princesses who thought themselves above all the rest of the pack. but were really nothing more than a bunch of weak puppies.

Julianna said nothing, figuring it was wiser to stay silent than to look the fool. It sounded like a betrothal party for some sort of European royalty, but they were in the middle of Bum Fuck Nowhere, Nevada, and there was no such thing as royalty out there. Succession, society princesses? *What is she talking about?*

Tawny stopped talking long enough to survey her handiwork. The tables gleamed beautifully in the soft lights of the tents. The flowers offered gentle spots of color in an otherwise gauzy white world.

"All done. Come on, Ms. Morris, let's go inside and relax before the rest of the pack gets here. I'm sure we could use just a little down time before we have to play this game tonight."

Julianna paused and cleared her throat. "I think I'm a little confused. Jeff didn't say anything about a ceremony. I thought it was going to be a casual party."

Tawny frowned. "He didn't tell you about his promotion?"

Julianna shook her head. "No. He didn't say anything beyond it being dressy casual."

Tawny snorted. "Men. They always downplay the important things." She shook her head. "It's a bit more than just a garden party."

"Oh glory. Am I under-dressed?"

Tawny's shook her head. "No, no, you look fine. Great, in fact. That shade of green looks fabulous on you, and your hair is perfect. The tendrils next to your face are pure genius."

Julianna gave a half-shrug to hide her unease. "Thanks. My mom helped me do it."

"You look lovely. Come on, let's not keep Dad waiting."

Julianna nodded, trying to keep her disquiet off her face. *Sweet glory, there's going to be some sort of ceremony.* She hoped she wouldn't be part of it. She'd just try to stay out of everyone's way until after dinner and then slip out the first chance she got. *It'll be okay. It'll be fine.*

But it didn't feel fine. She'd missed something important in Jeff's invitation. Her Sister agreed, and Julianna felt her stir with anticipation. Clamping her jaws together tightly, Julianna followed Tawny through the house and hoped she could keep up her cool façade.

Tawny led her to a sitting room at the back of the large house overlooking the tents. The décor had a western motif and the furniture looked like it'd come from a late nineteenth century Old West hotel. Even the lampshades sported fringe. Despite the old-timey air, the room felt warm and well-loved, and Julianna hesitantly stepped across the threshold, concerned she may not be welcome.

Richard Lightfoot sat in one of the wing-backed chairs, sipping something out of a brandy snifter. Though he wore a relaxed expression, Julianna felt his dominance and leadership immediately. A Stetson sat on the decorative table beside him, but it may as well have been a crown. His attention adhered to Tawny as she entered the room, her eyes downcast and her demeanor submissive.

Julianna froze in surprise when Tawny leaned into her father's space and nuzzled him along his jawline. Richard's expression softened, and he rested one hand on his daughter's shoulder, then trailed it down to her wrist, squeezing gently. Tawny's tension evaporated, and she turned to face the doorway. Richard's gaze followed hers, and he inhaled sharply, but his expression flattened. Julianna's unease ramped up, but her breath froze in her lungs at the sight of his son reclining on a sateen couch.

Jeff looked like he'd just stepped out of the wealthy elite of the 1920s, wearing spats, a waistcoat, and a flat hat on his head, but his scent was pure heaven.

*He smells like a mountain morning.* Julianna's heart pounded in her chest and thundered in her ears. *Why does he smell so good?* Terence never smelled that good, ever.

*Because this male is your Mate. It's time to claim him.* Her Sister's voice rose of her heart.

She bit back the urge to snarl and simply reveled in the excitement of being close to Jeff. He was the most beautiful thing she'd seen in a very long time, and her body responded to her attraction by creaming her panties.

Everyone's gaze zeroed in on her as if a claxon had sounded, Jeff rocketing to his feet like he'd been bitten on the ass by a horsefly. His eyes turned to burnished gold, and his expression turned predatory as his shoulders straightened. Richard's eyes narrowed, and he looked back and forth between his son and Julianna as if trying to decipher a hidden message. Tawny gasped in delight and clapped her hands, breaking the spell like a popped balloon.

"Welcome, Ms. Morris." Richard's baritone filled the room, amusement hidden beneath the formality. "We're glad to see you." Was he laughing at her or at Jeff?

"I'm honored to be invited." She dipped her head in acknowledgment of his greeting, but part of her wondered why they were so formal. "It's been a long time since I've been back to Callowwood. I wasn't sure I'd be welcome."

She stiffened when Richard rolled to his feet and reached for her hand to lay a kiss lightly on her knuckles. She thought she heard Jeff groan from behind his dad, and Richard released her hand immediately, taking a short step back.

"You're more than welcome here." Tawny strode to Julianna's side, dropping her head again in that curiously submissive gesture. Her eyes flicked to Richard, who nodded slightly, and she took Julianna's hand. "We're so glad you came early. It's been a long time, and we didn't get to know you as well as we wanted before you left. Come on, sit down. Can I get you something to drink?"

"Please." Julianna let herself be seated on the sateen couch. Warmth left from Jeff's body seeped into her rear when she settled, and his scent enfolded her. She wanted to shiver with delight, but she contented herself in leaning back with just a little wiggle.

Jeff caught her movement, and his smile increased in intensity. "I'm glad you could come. Are you feeling better after the funeral?"

*I'll always feel better when I'm around you.* Sheesh, she had to get a hold of those hormones.

"A little, thanks for asking. It's mostly relief that Dad isn't suffering anymore, but the grief kind of creeps up on me when I least expect it." She grimaced. "I think it hits Mom more often, but she's used to having Dad around, and I've been gone a long time."

"Indeed you have, Ms. Morris." Richard nodded as he relaxed back into his chair, watching her keenly. "Jeff mentioned you moved to Reno after you left Callowwood."

Julianna raised her eyebrows and glanced at Jeff, who smiled ruefully.

"Your dad mentioned it."

*Oh, great.* Had Gerry said anything about Fresno and Terence?

Tawny handed her a cup and saucer, the fragrant tea filling her nose with the scent of jasmine. She immediately relaxed and nodded her thanks. Tawny blushed with pleasure and found a seat in a decorative chair, folding herself into it with the grace of a geisha. A twinge of envy tweaked Julianna.

"Yes, the University of Nevada, Reno was my first choice for college." It was also as far away as she could get from Callowwood and still be in the mountains of Nevada. "Particularly because the program offered pre-college courses in the summer for better placement in the fall."

"Is that why you left right after graduation?" Jeff cocked to one side. He'd sat down on the other end of the couch, and she could feel his heat caressing her across the space between them.

"Yes, I needed all the help I could get with tuition, and their summer 'work-for-school' program provided a tuition waiver in exchange for learning a marketable skill." Julianna ducked her head guiltily and focused on her tea. The tuition waiver had helped, but her motivation had been to escape from Jeff's indifference.

"That makes sense." Richard smiled mildly, but his eyes assessed her with intensity. "What marketable skills did you learn, Ms. Morris?"

"I took leadership and management classes. I thought I'd eventually go into the casino business and manage the staff of a hotel, but business management wasn't my cup of tea. While it did help me pay for school, it just made me antsy for something else." She shrugged. "I felt a little adrift, so I took as many classes in as many subjects as I could to see if there was anything I liked."

"You didn't like leadership or management?" Richard's voice was sharp.

Julianna felt the warning underlying his words. She stifled a frown. *What is that about?*

"I liked aspects of it, but I'm really more of a team player than a lone leader. I prefer to be 'second-in-command', sharing the responsibility but not the one to make executive decisions. I liked working with a partner rather than doing it all myself."

Jeff shared a look with his dad that made ice run down her back. Was her answer wrong? She'd told the truth. Why was she worried if she'd answered correctly? When did this become an entrance interview? She shrugged her disquiet away and sipped her tea.

"What did you finally settle on studying?" Jeff's voice was reserved.

"I chose Native American anthropology, particularly the Nations historically found within Nevada's boundaries."

"Oh? What was your specialty?" Tawny's eyes sparkled with real interest.

"The oral traditions of the Nations around our country. My professor was willing to take me on as his research assistant, even though I wasn't a graduate student. I was second author on the book about the myths and traditions of the Paiute, Shoshone, and Ute Nations." And she was damn proud of her accomplishment.

"That sounds interesting." Richard's expression belied his words. "I assume you graduated?"

Was he just humoring her? She raised her chin with indignation as anger blossomed but clamped down on her temper in the face of his disinterest. "Yes, I did, *summa cum laude*, actually."

"Wow." Jeff raised his brows in appreciation, and pleasure eroded some of her anger. "That's great. What did you do after you graduated from UNR?"

"I worked in the casinos while I figured out what I was going to do next. I took the opportunity to learn tai chi, how to hang-glide, play pool, and play the Irish Tam."

"That's quite a list. Did you learn anything useful?" Richard tilted his head and rested it on his fist as if bored.

Julianna flattened her lips before she said something stupid. What was the old man's problem? Did he think women should just stay home and mind children? Or was he maligning her selection of activities? Who the hell was he to criticize her choices in life? It was her life, dammit.

*Deep breath, stay calm. Don't insult the "big man" in his own home.* She just had to find the right words to tell him he was being a shit and do it with a smile. She thought hard before she responded.

She raised her chin and met his gaze. "I found almost everything taught me patience, persistence, and cadence. None of them were easy to learn, and all of them took discipline and focus. I'd say those two things were the most important."

Richard rubbed his chin thoughtfully with one finger, a half-smile curling his lips. Julianna had the sudden realization she'd passed some kind of test. She resisted the urge to frown. She glanced at Jeff. His smile matched his father's. Did he know what was going on?

*Who am I kidding? Of course, he knows what's going on. He invited me.* But to what? Did everyone meeting this family need to have an entrance interview?

"Have you been in Reno this whole time?" Tawny asked hesitantly into the charged silence.

Julianna wanted to squirm and hide, but she raised her gaze to Jeff's sister.

"No, I got married in Reno then moved to Fresno so my husband and I could both go to graduate school."

Jeff sat up straight, and Richard's chin lifted. The tension in the room ramped up with suppressed fury.

"You're married?"

She raised her eyebrows. "You didn't know? I thought my father would've told you."

Jeff swallowed hard. "He…failed to mention that."

*Really? That's interesting.*

"I was married."

"What does that mean?" Anger filtered into Jeff's scent.

*What the hell does he have to be angry about? That he missed his chance back then?*

"It means I divorced the bastard when he decided I'd served my purpose in getting him tenure because he appeared settled, married." She met Jeff's hot gaze with her own past fury. "Once he'd gotten established, he traded me in for a younger model. Several, in fact."

"That's despicable." Tawny wore horror on her lovely face.

She shrugged as if it hadn't been a painful time. *Which is why I hate these political parties full of lying, secretive people smiling with daggers in their teeth.* "Hey, it's how I got the Camaro." She shot a look at Jeff and inhaled his anger. At her or her erstwhile husband? If he'd just acknowledged her all those years earlier, he could have had that role.

"So he's gone?"

Julianna carefully set her cup and saucer aside. "Yes, he's gone, and I'm done talking about him."

"I can't understand infidelity," Jeff snapped.

Julianna laughed in surprise. "It's a very human trait, particularly of men."

"That doesn't make it right." Her heart warmed at his ire.

"No. I just learned the lesson a little too late, but I'm free of his manipulations now."

"True enough," Richard agreed blandly. "What've you done since graduating?"

Julianna was grateful to refocus on the here and now.

"I worked as a manager at a bed and breakfast in Fresno to pay the bills, coordinating the wait staff with the housekeeping" She laughed at the memories. "The waitstaff were all Chinese, while the housekeeping staff were all Mexican. It was like international relations, and it took a fair amount of patience and compromise. Still, I liked it until I heard my father was dying from lung cancer." She spread her hands. "So I came home."

"What are you planning on doing here now that you've come home?"

She raised her eyebrows, almost laughing in disbelief. Why was it Richard's business? He wasn't her keeper. She nearly told him to take a hike, but something about the way he asked made her think the answer might be important.

"My father's illness took all my attention and energy, so I hadn't considered what to do after." She clasped her hands in her lap to still their trembling from her indignation. "I'd like to continue my research into Native American mythology, but it's more of a hobby right now while I help my mom. I haven't really had time to seriously think about a job."

"Have you thought about remarrying or having a family?" Richard tilted his head.

Two conflicting emotions crashed inside Julianna. *Is he expecting me to be barefoot and pregnant?* Her anger was quickly overridden by fear. *How can I marry someone now that I have the quadruped issue each month?* Sorrow filled in the last little gaps in her awareness and she blanked her expression to show none of it. *I'll never be with Jeff now.*

"No. I'm not sure I'll get married again. Especially now."

She hadn't meant to say the last. Fortunately, her audience thought she meant because of the divorce, not because she'd become some fantastic creature from the very mythology she'd studied in college. *I used to be human.*

"I hope that isn't a permanent condition." Jeff smiled his heart-stopping smile. Julianna wanted to smile back, but her keen sense of loss torpedoed her attempt.

*Oh yeah, it's pretty permanent.*

"Time will tell." Julianna stared at him for a few dizzying moments. *Yeah, if he doesn't mind that I might gnaw off his face when I can't find my favorite chew toy on those full moon nights.* She dropped her gaze to her hands, trying to forget how they shifted into paws.

Damn, it wasn't fair. She'd managed to get Jeff's attention and she didn't have a husband. She just had a little canine issue. She blinked back her tears and tried to smile.

"I know I'd like the opportunity to try." That was the truth.

A slow smile spread across his decadent mouth, and she felt her heart flutter. *Glory, I wish he'd smile at me like that every day.* She'd need new underwear all the time, but she wouldn't mind. *Maybe I'd just go without.*

"Maybe you'll get such an opportunity."

Julianna raised her eyebrows in question at Richard's comment, but he glanced down at his watch and rose. "Looks like it's almost time for the party to start. Tawny, get yourself out there to greet folks as they come in. Ms. Morris, would you mind being a hostess? I know it's short notice, but I think many folks would enjoy being greeted by two lovely young females."

Another dose of surprise hit her system. They were asking her to hostess their party?

"Oh, I don't know. I've been away for so long, I don't really know anyone." Julianna stood and bit her lip, not really wanting to be the center of attention.

"Please?" Jeff's sultry smile burned her in unmentionable places. She wanted to throw herself into his arms, taking advantage of the promises in that smile, but she restrained herself. "It might be something you could get used to."

*What the hell does that mean?* She tilted her head with a frown, but Tawny touched her shoulder.

"Come, Ms. Julianna. Let's open the doors to the pack attending tonight and see if we can't charm the fangs out of them."

Julianna laughed in amused surprise at Tawny's choice of words as they emerged into the hallway. An odd turn of phrase. The older woman walked just a little behind her as they strode toward the front of the house where the double doors stood wide open. Julianna frowned a little at Tawny's insistence of remaining behind her guest. Was it a defensive move or a protective one?

The sight of the valets working overtime to accommodate the arriving vehicles distracted Julianna from her thoughts. Evening warmth wafted through the open doors, carrying scents of hot desert sage and excitement. The dress code for the party may have been "dressy casual", but suppressed excitement filled the scents of the guests. Tawny positioned herself just inside the door and Julianna stood beside her, still too uneasy to be a full hostess. Tawny winked at her just before the first guests stepped in.

Seething with excitement and anticipation, the crowd surged past them, and Tawny transformed into the perfect hostess. She was gracious, friendly without being obsequious, solicitous without being smarmy, and Julianna did her best to emulate her. Most of the people passing treated Tawny with a measure of respect, but their response to Julianna was more reserved. She didn't mind. She hadn't been home long enough to be familiar.

There were a few people she did know. Most of them, like the Winthrops and the Cutters, had attended her father's funeral a few days earlier. Howard and Michelle Cutter brought along their daughters, Tammy and Ashley, both of whom twittered and giggled like teenagers at prom. Both families sauntered past Tawny with regal disdain, taking her greeting for granted. Julianna wanted to smack them all on the backs of their heads, but she smiled coolly, dismissing them as she turned to Bob and Sally Millner. They owned the feed store and were the first guests who seemed genuinely happy to be there. She didn't know most of the others, though she recognized a few more faces from the funeral.

She certainly recognized Brenda Solaris. The blonde woman made an entrance like visiting royalty, complete with someone to announce her to everyone in the house and an unobtrusive bodyguard. She wore a silver gown that looked more appropriate for the Oscars than a Nevada dinner party, with one shoulder bare and a short train behind her silvery heels. A glittering Tiffany headband and bracelets reflected the house lights, and the scent of a perfume, a light, fruity scent reminding Julianna of sun-ripened apricots, flavored the air preceding her.

Despite her added height from the heels, both Tawny and Julianna stood taller than the ad executive. Tawny greeted her warmly with deference, but Brenda's eyes swept past her like she was nothing and fixed on Julianna with immediate dislike and rivalry.

Julianna's first response was reciprocal, particularly after the way Brenda treated Tawny in her own home. The disrespectful action made her straighten to her full five-feet-nine-inches and stare the woman down.

"Sorry, you must've missed Ms. Lightfoot's greeting." Julianna gestured at Jeff's sister. "Welcome to the Lightfoot House, Ms. Solaris. We're so glad you could come." She said it loud enough for everyone in the foyer to hear, and Brenda was forced to stop and acknowledge Julianna's companion.

Fury blazed in Brenda's pale blue eyes, but she pulled out a warm smile and turned it on Tawny. "Oh, I'm sorry. Thank you. I'm very pleased to be here tonight."

"You're very welcome, Ms. Solaris." Nothing in

Tawny's face, voice, or bearing revealed any sarcasm. "Please, enjoy the party. Refreshments are in the gardens out back."

"Thank you." Brenda swept past them regally, her head up and her stride commanding.

Julianna inwardly bared her teeth at her rival's retreating back. She hated "big-fish-little-pond" syndrome. Smoothing her expression, she turned her attention to the next guest.

Before her gaze could focus, her nose caught the scents of wild mountain penstemon and ponderosa vanilla. An odd sense of familiarity enveloped her when she saw the short, slight form of Sebrina entering the double doors. Confusion filtered through her awareness. *Why does Sebrina seem so familiar? I only met her a few days ago.*

Mentally shaking her head, Julianna's jaw dropped as Tawny nearly fell to her knees with reverence and love before the old Paiute woman. Sebrina smiled warmly and patted Tawny's hand at her greeting.

"I'm honored with your greeting, daughter." The tiny quartz crystals sewn into the bodice and sleeves of her dress glittered as she helped Tawny up. "It is good to see you all tonight for such an occasion." She adjusted the geometrically patterned shawl as it slid off her shoulders.

"We're the ones who are honored. This is the first succession party you've been to in a while, isn't it?" Tawny blushed.

"It is." Sebrina's eyes twinkled in the lights of the foyer, and Julianna felt the weight and power of her gaze like a heavy cloak settling around her shoulders.

"Well met, wayward daughter." Sebrina's smile crinkled the crow's feet around her golden eyes. "I'm very pleased to see you here tonight. It's an important night for the Lightfoots and for you, I should think, so it's good you are here. Perhaps you would be willing to escort an old woman to her seat."

Julianna hesitated as she glanced at Tawny. "I'd be happy to, but I have promised to help Tawny welcome the guests, and I can't just leave."

"Oh no, that's fine, Ms. Julianna." Tawny gave her a brilliant smile. "The tide is ebbing, and I can handle it from here on. Please, take Ms. Westwind to her place."

Tawny's reverence caught Julianna's attention, but she filed it away to think on later. "You're sure?"

"Of course." Tawny made gentle shooing motions. "Go on, I'll be fine."

"All right, I'd be honored to escort you to your seat." Julianna offer her arm to the older woman. "Truth be told, you're one of the few friendly faces I've seen coming through these doors, and I'm grateful to stay in your company."

Sebrina beamed with approval. "You're a great flatterer, daughter."

"I can be if I try, but this time, I'm speaking the honest truth."

Sebrina laughed softly with what sounded a little like sorrow. "Yes, I think you are. I said earlier this will be an important night for you, but I think it'll also be a trying one. Have courage, daughter. Remember who you are, no matter the recent changes in your life, and you'll make it through with your honor intact."

Julianna's nervousness increased. Tawny had mentioned a ceremony. Sebrina's remarks suggested Julianna would be part of it. But why? Her jaw clenched as she escorted her companion into the garden tent.

People milled everywhere, and the grounds were awash with all the colors of the rainbow. Pockets of shadow stood beside the colored spots, the more somber color scheme of the males in the group highlighting the females. Sound beneath the tents combined into a muted roar as friends and neighbors caught up with the daily news.

*And I know none of them.*

Sorrow gnawed at Julianna's insides. She'd been gone so long and had missed out on the easy camaraderie of a small town's residents. But a subtle hierarchy among the guests became clear, some commanding instant respect and deferral, others backing down and treating everyone with obeisance. Disgust at their behavior surged through her, and Sebrina chuckled, jerking Julianna's attention away from the crowd.

"Don't be so hard on them, daughter." Sebrina patted her arm. "They know their places and perform them admirably."

"Sorry?"

Sebrina gestured to an older man who quickly stepped aside to allow a younger man to serve himself punch, completely interrupting the older man's task. "He is showing courtesy to the younger man. You will understand this more the longer you stay in Callowwood."

"I'm not so sure. To me, it looks like he's getting railroaded by that young punk, and the youngster should have enough respect to wait for him to finish." Julianna shook her head. "Tell me what I'm missing because that was completely rude. I know there's something going on, but I don't know what it is or what it has to do with me."

"Take me to my seat and sit beside me for a moment. I'll try to explain as quickly as I can before you must play your part in this pageant."

*Shit, I do have some sort of role.*

Sebrina directed them to the table closest to the podium and Julianna helped her into her seat. Reading the place cards, she noted Sebrina shared the table with Richard, Tawny, and Jeff. She spied her own name on a place card beside Sebrina's and was grateful someone had seen to it she'd sit with the few people she knew, even if they were the hosts of the party.

Julianna took her seat and smoothed her skirt in an effort to stave off her jitters. Still, her heart pounded. Her gut told her something big barreled her way, a runaway train of events she couldn't stop. *I'm in such deep shit.*

"Now then, daughter, there's no reason to be so concerned." Sebrina patted her hand where it unconsciously clenched in her lap. Julianna forced it to relax. "I know you've only recently returned to Callowwood, so all of this will be a rude shock, but the timing cannot be helped, and you must do the best you can with what's presented to you."

Julianna gritted her teeth to find patience. "What's going on?"

The old woman settled herself in her chair. "Since you've been home, I've scented the times when you've changed into your Sister form. But strangely, she seems to take control. Is this true?"

Julianna blinked. "My Sister form?"

"That of the Moon Singer, the dusky brown wolf who is the other half of your soul."

Julianna felt all the blood leave her face. "How do you know about that?"

"Don't look so worried, daughter. We all knew your dual nature the moment you returned."

"All?" Julianna repeated weakly.

"Everyone here at this gathering." Sebrina frowned a little, cocking her head to one side like a curious dog. "You're now among more of your kind. Didn't you know? Everyone here is a Moon Singer. You're sitting with the members of the Callowwood Pack, the largest and strongest werewolf pack in the north-central Basin and Range."

The words hit Julianna like thrown stones: *Everyone here, werewolf, your kind.*

She swallowed hard and gripped her chair. *Holy shit! I'm sitting among werewolves.*

# CHAPTER FOUR:
## Candidacy for Luna

Julianna clamped her lips together, trying to avoid throwing up the tea she'd drunk. Suddenly, all of Tawny's remarks made sense. *They're all werewolves.* She clenched her jaw to keep everything down as her hands gripped the edge of the table to keep from falling off her chair. *They know I'm one, too. They knew at the funeral.*

"The whole town?" she whispered.

"Not all of it, but a lot of it. Did you really not know?"

"No, I really didn't know." *Sweet glory, I've been so blind.* "Jeff Lightfoot is one, too?"

Sebrina laughed gently and hope began to bloom in Julianna's heart.

"Oh, yes, daughter. Richard Lightfoot has been the Alpha, the packleader, for the last hundred years and has ruled well, but he's getting ready to step down and hand the leadership to his son."

Julianna's Sister howled with jubilation. *You will claim your male and be his Mate forever! He belongs to you.* Julianna let relief course through her. She wouldn't have to worry about the nights she shifted if she went out with Jeff. But one detail bothered her.

"Jeff is the next Alpha of the whole pack?"

Sebrina nodded with a satisfied smile. "He is. He has been groomed for this position since his birth some forty years ago."

"Isn't that a bit old to take over?"

Sebrina laughed, patting her hand again like an indulgent parent. "Oh my dear daughter, Moon Singers can live a hand of centuries, especially when they're True Mated. Jefferson is quite young to take the reins."

*I'm going to live for centuries?* "I see."

"Tonight is a very special night because, in addition to Jeff's succession, the pack will also begin the search for the Luna."

"Luna? Is that some sort of…Moon Princess?"

Sebrina looked at her shrewdly, her smile full of approval. "In a manner of speaking, yes. The Luna is the female Alpha, the feminine energy that balances the masculine. To be an effective leader, the future Alpha must pick his Luna, the female to rule with him with the Lady Moon's blessing."

Julianna bit her bottom lip as she smoothed a wrinkle in the tablecloth in front of her. "Will the Luna be the Alpha's mate for life?"

"Yes. They are a life-mated pair."

*He is your True Mate. Your male.*

"How is the Luna chosen?"

"In the first days of the Moon Singers, when the Lady walked this world, it was a simple matter of the Alpha finding his True Mate and she would be the Luna."

"That makes sense."

But Moon Singers have become outnumbered by humans, and it became harder for the Alphas to find their True Mates." Sebrina shot a look toward the back of the tents where Richard stood speaking to some other men. "Balanced leadership was still necessary, so the elders of each pack decreed that the strongest alpha females would be presented for candidacy for Luna in hopes that one of them was the True Mate to the new Alpha."

"Wait, wait. You said alpha too many times here. What's the difference between alpha"—Julianna used air quotes—"and Alpha?"

At first, Sebrina looked at Julianna as if she'd lost her mind. Then she lifted her chin in understanding and smiled.

"It is like referring to the president. There are many presidents out there, those of companies or clubs. But only one President of the humans' United States."

Julianna frowned. "Are you saying there are many potential leaders, but only one main leader at a time?"

"That's exactly it." Sebrina beamed. "For Moon Singers, there are many alpha members, but only one Alpha pair. This candidacy party is for the selection of the Alpha female."

"Please tell me the candidates for Luna aren't selected in a beauty pageant." Julianna's eyes narrowed in disgust.

"Of course not. The goal is to find the strongest and most capable female to lead the pack with the Alpha." Sebrina gestured to the colorful female guests milling under the tents. "That they dress their best is one way to show off how they'll be at official gatherings. That's what this party is about. This is where the Luna candidates will be presented to the ruling Alpha and his Successor."

Julianna's eyes followed Sebrina's gesture. "Are all these women being presented tonight?"

"No, only the strongest and highest ranking alpha females."

The older woman pointed toward Cameron Winthrop. She wore a deep mustard-yellow strapless dress with a matching wrap. Her black hair was piled on top of her head in a complicated coif covered in a net of golden pearls. She spoke with several other guests, as regal in her bearing as Brenda Solaris had been in her entry.

"That one is sure to be chosen as a candidate. Her

family has been in this Pack for generations, and her paternal uncle is one of the current Alpha's cadre."

"Cadre?"

"The Alpha's inner circle, most trusted friends and advisors."

"Where is the current Luna? Was that Jeff's mother?"

Sebrina's face grew solemn. "Yes. It was a great loss when she died."

"Is that part of why Richard is stepping down as Alpha?"

"I suspect so. The Alpha does not confide in me now that the Luna is gone."

Julianna tried to remember when Jeff's mother died, but she only recalled Beth recounting the news, not the when or why. She shook her head and took a deep breath. It didn't matter. She had to focus on the here and now.

"If this party is for Luna candidate selection, what does it have to do with me?" She shot a look around the room again. "Jeff just invited me a few days ago. I don't know very much about pack politics or traditions. Hell, I didn't even know werewolves existed until a few months ago."

Sebrina tilted her head. "You've been invited here tonight for two very specific reasons. The first being you're a Moon Singer who has recently settled into the Callowwood Pack's territory. You must swear to uphold their rules and protocols while living here."

"I have to what?" Julianna raised her chin.

"It is for your protection as well as the protection of the pack. Should you be injured by anyone while here, the packmembers will defend and/or avenge you, bringing restitution to your family. The pack will also take responsibility for any injuries you cause and punish you accordingly."

Julianna clenched her teeth around a snarl. "What kinds of punishments?"

"House arrest, wounding, banishment from the pack's

territory. Even death."

Julianna's nails dug into her palms. How dare they tell her how to live? Callowwood was her home. No one had the right to drive her out if she didn't swear to follow the rules of the pack. Gritting her teeth, she closed her eyes and told herself to calm down. She was new to this world of werewolves and just because she was ignorant of the rules didn't mean she wasn't bound by them. Or that the others wouldn't enforce them.

"Fine. I'll abide by the rules. What's the second reason I'm here tonight?"

Sebrina's smile showed satisfaction and anticipation.

"The second reason is you're one of the most powerful alpha females to be born in the last two hundred years in the Basin and Range, making you a prime candidate for the Successor's Luna. You'll be presented as a Luna candidate tonight."

Julianna's jaw dropped and dread filled her gut. She couldn't be a Luna candidate. She knew nothing about being a Moon Singer.

"I can't."

Sebrina frowned. "Of course, you can."

"No, you don't understand. I don't know anything about Moon Singers, their politics, or the protocols governing their pack." Her hands tightened into fists and she wondered if she had enough time to claim a headache so she could get away. "I'm too inexperienced to be a viable candidate."

Sebrina laid a warm hand on Julianna's arm. "You're not as inexperienced as you might think, though you may not know the specifics of the Callowwood Pack. Follow your heart. It speaks to you with the voice of the Lady Moon."

*The only thing my heart is telling me is I'm ignorant and a nobody.*

*Jeff is your Mate and you must fight for him.* Ah, yes,

how could she forget her Sister?

"You already love Jefferson Lightfoot, don't you?"

"What?" Julianna focused her startled gaze on Sebrina's smug face.

"Jeff." The Paiute woman gestured toward the small podium where several people were gathered around Richard and his son. "What does your heart say about him?"

*Let me jump his bones and ride him till he's breathless?* Julianna cleared her throat.

"I get mixed messages about Jeff."

Half of her wanted to throw herself into his arms, rub her body against his as hard as she could, and sink her teeth into his shoulder, never letting him go. The other half of her was furious at his ignorance all those years before. If she hadn't been good enough for him then, what made her good enough now?

Sebrina made a sound of disgust. "Stop letting your mind get in the way of the truth."

"This is the first time I've seen him since I left. I was infatuated with him when I was a girl, but now...I don't know. I don't know him well enough yet."

"Rabbit turds." Sebrina waved dismissively. "You've known him in your heart for decades, daughter. Your infatuation, as you call it, was nothing more than the recognition of your True Mate."

"True Mate. You're supposed to know who your mate is when you're a Moon Singer?"

"Of course. All Moon Singers have this knowledge."

"If that's true, why didn't he recognize me then?" Julianna snorted and shook her head. "If it's obvious, shouldn't it be obvious to both Mates?"

"I don't know what Jefferson felt, but it matters not. It's in the past. But now, you must claim your True Mate and take your place beside him."

Julianna's jaw dropped. "Are you listening to yourself?

The past has created the present. I can't claim him if he's not interested. And I can't claim him if I don't have the capability to be Luna. He needs someone who knows what she's doing, and that isn't me."

"There is no 'can't', only 'won't'," Sebrina stated flatly.

Despite her chagrin, Julianna laughed. "Who are you, Yoda?"

Sebrina's face became stoic, waiting for Julianna to get on with the explanation. She matched the older woman stare for stare, refusing to be cowed. She might not know much about werewolves, but she knew herself and her limitations.

"Why are you so convinced this role isn't yours?" Sebrina raised an eyebrow.

"Because I don't know anything. I don't know the rules, the policies, the hierarchy." She kept her voice level, but it still scared the daylights out of her. "I can barely remember anything from the days when I shift shape. I just shift back with large chunks of my memory missing."

"So you would give up a life with Jefferson simply because of a lack of knowledge?" Sebrina tilted her head.

"You said the Luna is chosen based on the capabilities of the candidates, right?"

"Yes."

"I don't have the capability."

Sorrow bloomed. Julianna would lose Jeff to some other female because of her inexperience. She wanted him, wanted him so bad it made her gut hurt. She allowed her gaze to slide around the room, stopping only when she found him standing near the podium. Just the thought of being near him set her senses on fire.

But she knew she wasn't Luna material, and it killed her. Jeff needed a female who could rule beside him effectively. He needed someone who knew all the ropes, and how to minimize the problems facing the pack today.

She idly wondered if there was a Moon Singers for Dummies book.

"I'm sorry, Sebrina. I don't think I'd be the best choice for Luna."

Saying the words out loud stole her humor, and she bit her bottom lip. Losing Jeff to her inexperience rankled.

"What you think doesn't matter, daughter," the older female remarked, her voice laced with disapproval. "You are Jefferson's Mate, chosen by the Goddess, and he's chosen you as a candidate for Luna. Each candidate will be tested to see her suitability to rule with the Successor, and so shall you be. You must be courageous in the face of challenge and uncertainty."

"As always," Julianna grumbled sullenly.

"Yes, as an Alpha always must."

"I'm not an Alpha."

"But you will be."

Julianna snapped her mouth shut over a snarl. Did she want to be Luna? No, she wasn't here for the job. But she did want Jeff. She always had, even when she'd been too young to attract him. The crowd shifted just enough to allow his face to appear. He'd moved to the side of the tent near his sister. His gaze met hers, and everything stilled.

Recognition flooded through her, recognition of her True Mate, the yang to her yin. Her nipples hardened, and arousal slid down her back, pooling between her legs in hot wanting. Jeff's eyes shifted to gold, and his nostrils flared, even as far as he stood from her. She lifted her chin and smiled a challenge at him as she made her decision. There was no way in hell she'd tolerate any other female touching Jeff. She wouldn't compete to be Luna, but she'd compete to win her True Mate.

"Yes, I will."

She inhaled and relaxed her tense shoulders, presenting the image of a strong, confident woman. Sebrina nodded with approval.

"This is good to see."

"If I really am Jeff's Mate, tell me what's going to happen tonight, in detail, so I can be prepared." If she was going to do this, she'd damn well know what the hell she was getting into.

"After the dinner, you'll be introduced and presented to the pack as a new packmember. You must swear fealty to the current Alpha and agree to abide by all pack rules."

Julianna nodded. "And after I've been sworn in?"

"After this, the candidates for Luna will be announced and presented. I suspect you will be presented last because of your recent induction into the Callowwood Pack." Sebrina eyed her. "Don't be offended by your presentation order. It only reflects your recent inclusion in the candidacy."

Julianna rolled her eyes. "That's not my issue."

"Good. Often, the packmembers are very particular."

She shook her head. "There are bigger things to worry about in life."

*Yeah, like how I'm going to get through tonight when they announce I'm a candidate.*

"You'll be required to socialize a short time before taking your leave of the Alpha. He will offer you a token of his favor, showing everyone that you're a candidate for the Successor's mate. You must always have this token on your person, even if it's not visible, so the pack knows of your status."

"Keep the token on me at all times, okay."

"There'll be seven tests that you must pass to become the Successor's mate, and you must always be on your guard because you won't always know when you're being tested," Sebrina warned. "It's a sign of an effective leader to be calm and courageous under pressure, and what you do when you're being tested will be an indication of what you'll do as a leader."

Julianna grimaced. "No warning of when we're being

tested? Great."

"Like life, daughter. I'll help you and teach you all the protocols of our pack so you're aware of the rules, but you'll only gain the position of the Successor's mate through your own efforts."

"You're assuming I want the position," Julianna pointed out, her guts churning with her anger.

"Don't you?"

"No, I don't."

Sebrina fell silent a moment and just looked at Julianna with her serious gold eyes. Julianna grimaced as she sorted her thoughts.

"I don't want to be Luna, but I do want Jeff, and I intend to be his Mate. If that means I must become Luna, then so be it." She sighed and rearranged the silverware on the table. "I know less about this world than I'd like, and I'm concerned I'll do something wrong before I'm aware of my mistake. I don't know if I could be a very good leader of humans, much less Moon Singers, but it's not in me to give up easily."

A smile creased the old woman's face, and she nodded with satisfaction. "I wouldn't expect it of you. You have a fighter's spirit. You may feel unprepared or uncertain in the position of Successor's Mate, and it is difficult to learn everything in the short amount of time we have, but I'm certain you can do it. You're meant to be Jefferson's Luna. You simply must show it to the rest of the pack so they'll accept you."

*I've only gotten the fighting spirit recently. Eighteen years ago, I ran.*

"I wasn't always so courageous."

"You must walk this path whether you want to or not. It is your destiny. Never doubt your ability to do the job the Lady Moon has set before you."

Julianna shook her head but returned her attention to the tables around her. They filled as the guests took their seats, and she hoped none of them had heard her quiet conversation. She found herself at the court of a king where everyone vied for position and knowledge of one's opponents equaled power. Admitting she knew nothing about this new world could get her dismissed or worse. She smiled pleasantly at the people joining her at the table and waited to see what would happen.

*Breathe slowly and show them you're confident. Confidence is key. They can smell fear.* Literally.

*Yeah, this is where I run screaming.*

Tawny settled into the chair beside her with a delighted smile, and soon all the places had filled but two. Richard strode through the crowd on his way to the podium wearing his jacket and Stetson. Julianna eyed the hat with interest.

*It's a crown.*

Her eyes narrowed when she thought of the interview she'd had with him and his family. Good thing she'd kept her cool throughout it. She suspected they'd been judging her eligibility as a Luna candidate. Would she have lost her cool if she'd known they were werewolves then? Probably.

*And then I would have lost their respect.* She couldn't see Jeff anymore, but she could feel him nearby. His strength and heat tickled her awareness, and she almost rose from her seat to seek him out with the encouragement of her Sister.

*Your Mate. Yours. Go find him and prove it.*

*I'm not going to freak everyone out, or embarrass myself and Sebrina.*

Julianna gripped the table to keep herself seated as Richard began to speak.

"Good evening and welcome, everyone, to tonight's gathering of the Callowwood Pack." Richard's voice flowed over the crowd, full of calm and warmth. Some of Julianna's tension dissipated. "Tonight is a very special evening for many of us, and I'm honored that you've attended to witness it. We have a couple of announcements before dinner, but the bulk of the ceremony will happen after."

A murmur ran through the guests, but no one protested.

"As most of you know, I've been the Alpha for a long time, and it's been a great honor for me and my family." Richard swept the crowd with his gaze. "We've grown as a Pack and as a community, living amongst the humans in peace and prosperity. It's taken hard work and understanding on our part to remain in such peace. Humans aren't always easy to live with." He smirked and the crowd chuckled. "It's a true testament to all of you that there is peace in Callowwood."

Mild applause and another murmur went through the crowd. Julianna nodded. She hadn't known there were so many Moon Singers in this community. She suspected none of the humans in Callowwood had any idea, either.

"However, times have changed and so must we." Richard nodded, a sad smile creasing his lips. "I'm old and old-fashioned, and I've ruled in my times. I won't say I was right all the time, but I won't say I was terrible for this Pack. I believe I've done the best I could in the time I had." He paused as several cheers and hoots of approval came from the crowd, but he held up his hands for quiet. "We're all a product of our times, and when times change, so must we. But it gets harder and harder to see the clear path the older we get. That's why I've chosen to step down as Alpha as soon as my son Jefferson has taken his Mate and whelped his first child."

The crowd cheered louder, and it sounded like a chorus of wolves howling away at the night. Julianna bit her lip, trying to stay calm. The words 'taken his Mate' sent fire shooting straight to her sex, and she shivered at the thought of Jeff taking her anywhere.

"So, tonight, I present my son, Jefferson Mac Lightfoot, future Alpha of the Callowwood Pack."

The crowd roared its approval as Jeff strode up beside

his father. Julianna momentarily lost the ability to breathe as his wide smile flashed at the crowd. She stiffened her legs, clamping them to the seat of her chair to keep from jumping to her feet, running over to him, and throwing herself into his arms. She wanted to breathe in his scent and feel his hard body against hers.

Jeff's eyes zeroed in on her and blazed burnished gold in the spotlight. Her breath caught. His head came up, and his body shifted just enough to suggest he was ready to move quickly.

*Yes, bring it, Mate. Come take me.*

She shivered with reaction to her fantasy, gripping the seat of her chair until her knuckles felt like they'd pop out of the skin.

The energy around her became nearly overwhelming until Richard took Jeff's hand, lifting it victoriously. Jeff's gaze shifted away from Julianna, his face relaxing into easy amusement, and Julianna's rational mind regained control.

*Good glory! I gotta get a hold on that sex drive.*

A mixture of disappointment and jubilation swelled into the space of diminishing arousal. For a moment, Jeff had looked at her with predatory intent, as if he'd devour her with his whole being. But then he looked away. His expression had resumed the bland friendliness he showed the world, and his eyes had returned to their sedate golden green.

*Does he even want me?*

*Of course, he wants you. You're his Mate.* For once, Julianna was grateful for her inner voice.

Relief flooded through her, and her body relaxed. Sebrina and Tawny leaned back out of her peripheral vision, sharing some communication, but Julianna's attention remained riveted on Jeff's presence.

She couldn't look away. She didn't want to. He'd invited her to the party, and she'd take full advantage of his invitation, even if it meant she stared at him all night. *Yeah,*

*I'll just be your friendly neighborhood stalker.* He was irresistible He always had been. And if she was nominated as a Luna candidate, then no one could fault her from enjoying the view of the prize.

"We'll resume the festivities after dinner."

The Alphas waved and sauntered toward their table. She kept her gaze on Jeff, enjoying the way his body moved under his clothes. He was delicious, and she'd savor every little bit she could get.

*How the hell am I going to be able to sit here with him all night and eat?*

*You could always eat him.* The smugness in her Sister's voice damn near made her blush.

When Jeff and his father stopped at the table to pick up their plates, he paused and stared straight at her once more, his eyes back to the molten gold she'd seen earlier. She met his gaze boldly, knowing her nipples pushed against the fabric of her halter bodice like beacons. His nostrils flared, and his jaw tightened, but he retreated to the buffet tables. She watched his ass the whole way until Sebrina pulled her up from her chair.

"Come, daughter. Let's not keep the betas waiting too long." Sebrina patted her arm with amusement.

"What? Oh, yes, of course." Julianna grimaced as she followed the older woman.

Only a few others joined them at the buffet. Brenda Solaris, the Winthrops, and the Cutters, and another young woman she didn't recognize filed in behind them. It took Julianna a few moments to realize Tawny still sat quietly at the table, sipping her water as she chatted with another guest who remained. Julianna frowned. Why were the men eating before Tawny? Wasn't she part of the ruling family?

She almost asked Sebrina about it until her brain kicked into gear.

*Come on, you're dining with werewolves. Think about it.* The "alphas" ate first, just like in a traditional wolf pack, then the "betas", then the "omegas".

The pecking order had already sorted itself out behind her with Brenda Solaris in the lead, Cameron Winthrop and her parents next, Tammy Cutter and her parents, though her sister remained at their table, and the unknown woman taking up the rear.

*Why am I ahead of everyone?*

Julianna watched carefully for protests to her position just behind Sebrina, but though the women glared daggers at her, no one complained, and the line of "alphas" moved quickly down the buffet. She picked carefully through the array of foods, reminding herself to take the choicest items available.

*I have to play this role to be accepted.* Anger burned for a moment, but her rational mind caught up with her, dousing her fury. *Jeff is the upcoming Alpha, and he's worth it. At least, I hope so.*

She filled her plate with rare and juicy meat, some fresh veggies and a roll. Jeff glanced back at her once and smiled with pleased approval at her position in line, warming her a little in the cold disdain she sensed from the others behind her. She smiled back at him before following Sebrina. Her inner wolf snarled at being separate from Jeff, but given her inexperience, screwing up now would hurt worse than taking a subordinate position.

It took her a few moments to realize what her placement in line meant. She ate with the Alphas before all the other candidates. She'd been marked as the favorite.

Dread slid through her. *Could they just paint a target on my back and get it over with?*

*When you win the "prince" and take your rightful place as his princess, you'll be too busy mating to worry about the others.*

Julianna damn near spit the water she'd sipped across the table with her Sister's remark, but she clamped her lips together in time.

"Are you all right?" Tawny leaned close.

"Uh, yeah. No, I'm good. Go ahead." She waved Tawny on with the betas to visit the buffet.

There were far more betas than alphas, but still more people waited before empty plates. Those had to be the omegas, the lowest on the totem pole of packmembers. They'd serve themselves last.

The obvious caste system distracted Julianna from her lascivious thoughts. She hated the unreasoning disdain of the "higher" ranks and the unbalance of the few receiving the best, while the majority picked through the leftovers. The others around her didn't seem to have a problem with it, so she kept her teeth closed around her disgust.

Reminding herself the caste system now applied to her, she waited until Richard and Jeff started eating before she dipped her fork into the food on her plate. Jeff's gaze slid her direction, and his lips curved into a satisfied smile.

*Satisfied because I'm sitting here?* Satisfied because she waited for him to eat? Gah! *Will I have to do that all my life with him? Eat second because he's Alpha?*

She smiled back absently, fighting with her indignation at playing second fiddle.

*That's the way it's done among wolves. And I've been one among them for, what? Five minutes?* She knew so little about his people or her own. Jeff thought she knew how the game was played. He didn't know just what a rookie she was.

Some water went down the wrong way. Julianna coughed hard, and everyone at the table looked at her with concern. She tried to wave them off, gesturing she was all right, but the coughing wouldn't stop.

"Are you all right?" Tawny reached for her, but stopped a few inches from her arm.

"Y's," Julianna choked out, "just tried to prove that you could breathe the O in $H_2O$. Guess the experiment was a failure."

Sebrina thumped her on the back as everyone else at the table laughed at her joke. Good thing she had a snappy comeback. Fear tried to push its way back into her mind, but she ruthlessly shoved it away. She didn't have time to panic.

Evidently, her Sister agreed. *Okay, enough of the pity party. You can freak out later.* She'd just have to suck it up and act like the alpha female everyone thought she was.

The conversation swirled around her and she answered when spoken to, but she hardly knew what she said. She was too busy making sure she appeared relaxed and self-assured. This was supposedly her night. If she appeared a little anxious, that was to be expected. She raised her chin, trying to smile and act confident.

At last, dinner was cleared away by the serving staff and Julianna scented not only their curiosity but their omega status as well.

*I had no idea I could smell someone's rank.*

She smiled at the woman who offered her a choice of coffee or tea and the server ducked her head shyly. Julianna allowed herself to get lost in the scents of rich hazelnut coffee and jasmine tea filling the air beneath the tents. She closed her eyes to savor aromatic splendor and heard a deep chuckle. She blinked her eyes open and stole a look at Jeff.

"I see you like coffee." He grinned.

"Yes, I do. But I've never smelled hazelnut coffee with jasmine tea before. It's a surprisingly good combination." She answered with a self-conscious smile.

"It was my mother's favorite."

"It might soon become mine."

Delight and something more primal flashed through his gaze before Richard touched Jeff's shoulder and they rose.

She blinked as they headed to the podium. She'd been so lost in their connection she'd momentarily forgotten why they were here. Everyone focused on the Alphas in the spotlights. Their eyes glowed like stars, and Julianna wondered if hers would do the same.

*Are we all just wolves in human clothing?*

"Good friends, have you all had enough to eat for the moment? You know how it is. None of us think well on empty stomachs, yeah?" Richard winked out at the assembled and everyone chuckled. "Tonight we have some very special guests who'll be introduced to you soon. But first, we must induct a new member into the pack."

*Here it comes.* She straightened her shoulders.

"Many of you knew her when she grew up with the human population of Callowwood, but she left us to find her fortune in faraway places."

That sounded a lot better than, "She ran away from Jeff because he ignored her."

"She moved to Reno, where she attended UNR and received her bachelor's in anthropology. Later, she moved to Fresno, California, to attend the University of California for graduate studies. She earned her master's in Native American mythology from UC Fresno and has recently returned home to attend the funeral of her human father. She explored many paths and learned many lessons, which she brings home for the benefit of our pack. Please welcome, Mistress Julianna Morris."

Applause erupted, and Julianna rose to her feet, hoping she appeared graceful. When the applause continued, she raised her eyebrows at Jeff, puzzled. His grin broadened, and he beckoned her toward the podium with a subtle wave.

*Smooth. Anything else you can screw up?* Inclining her head graciously to the crowd, she strode to the podium, trying not to giggle nervously. She prayed it wasn't obvious she had no idea what she was doing. Who was she trying to kid?

*Everyone, myself included.*

Jeff's gaze kept her steady, though she hoped he wasn't laughing too hard. He watched her approach with an intensity that stole her breath. It fired up her lust and desire, and she could barely hear the applause over the thunder of her heart. Richard's face remained impassive, but she suspected he saw much more than he revealed.

When she reached them, he took her hands in his and whispered, "This may seem strange at first, but all you have to do is repeat after me and trust that I'm not trying to hurt you, all right?"

*Not trying to hurt me?*

Julianna took a deep breath and smiled. "Okay."

He nodded sharply before releasing her hands to face the crowd once more. "Mistress Morris has come tonight to swear fealty to the Callowwood Pack and to take her rightful place among our people."

His eyes glowing fiercely in the beams of the spotlights, he grasped her right hand and drew it toward his chest. He pressed her palm over his heart and placed his larger right hand above her left breast, making an unbreakable circuit of energy. His strong heartbeat thumped under her hand, and she knew he sensed the clatter of her heart through his. Her eyes widened in surprise. *Holy shit.* The corner of his mouth twitched in amusement, but his voice held steady.

"I, say your full name." Richard's eyes bored into hers, buoying her up with his strength.

"I, Julianna Sarah Morris," Julianna repeated.

"Do swear to protect and serve the Callowwood Pack..."

"Do swear to protect and serve the Callowwood Pack..."

"With tooth and claw, blood and bone, heart and mind..."

She repeated this, feeling the other part of herself rising beneath the surface of her consciousness.

"I swear to hold the People of the Lady Moon sacred and guard their secrets against all enemies, both foreign and domestic. I swear to see to the welfare of the whole pack over that of the individual, but also to leave no packmember unprotected. I swear to defend all the pack's children as if they were my own and to stand shoulder to shoulder with my Mate at such time as I take one. I swear to uphold the laws and protocols that govern the pack and keep it safe in a world of intolerance and fear. I do so solemnly swear as a member of the Callowwood Pack and as surely as my name is Julianna Sarah Morris."

Richard removed his hand from her chest, taking her right hand off his and pulling it to his mouth. She watched him with wide eyes as he quickly bit her finger so blood welled out of the tiny wound. She didn't even move as he licked the blood from her finger before holding her wounded hand loosely in his.

"As the Alpha of the Callowwood Pack and by the blood you have offered, I now pronounce you a full alpha female member of our pack, and welcome you to your people."

A roar went up from the crowd as Richard held Julianna's hand aloft and turned her to face the audience. While the other alphas clapped politely, Jeff's eyes shone with fierce joy, and Sebrina's face held a secret smile. Their jubilation infected Julianna and she grinned, resisting the urge to sprint toward Jeff and throw herself into his arms.

*Just go sit down before you do something stupid.* She forced herself to return to her seat. Her heart tried to beat its way out of her chest, and she could hardly stop her ecstatic laugh.

"Now, the part of the evening that you've all been waiting for." Richard raised his hands to calm the crowd.

His baritone voice sent a shiver of awe through Julianna, followed quickly by the balm of comfort. Instinctive recognition flooded through her, and her tension faded. Soothed by his presence and encouraged by the confidence he showed, she'd become connected by the blood she'd shared with the Alpha. She could look to him as a protector as well as a leader, and relief settled in her gut for the first time that night.

"Jefferson has accepted the position of Successor by right of the Three Tests of Strength, Honor, and Humility, and he was the victor in the Ceremony of Combat."

A cheer went up, and Jeff nodded with his customary half-smile, but his eyes blazed. The air under the tents thickened with anticipation, and out of the corner of her eye, Julianna caught some of the young women in the crowd licking their chops.

*Heh, you can look, but don't touch, bitches. He's mine.*

She blinked and shook her head. *Not yet, he's not.*

"There only remains the necessity of the balance of an alpha pair, the female to his male, that he may have the opportunity to lead wisely and justly. He must have a Mate strong enough to stand with him, compassionate enough to show him mercy, and wise enough to direct his fury. She must be able to bear him pups, and be willing to serve both her Mate and her pack as the Guardian of the Stories."

Julianna looked at Sebrina, mouthing, "Stories?"

Sebrina winked and smiled, but returned her attention to the Alpha.

"Tonight we have five candidates for Luna, and they are among the finest alpha bitches ever to have graced our pack."

Julianna suspected that was said each time a ceremony like this occurred. Of course, they were the finest bitches. He had to stroke the egos of the women and their parents.

"In order of rank, and, ladies, please stand so that we may all see you; Brenda Tiffany Solaris late of Los Angeles, California, now of Callowwood, Nevada."

Julianna saw Brenda rise to her feet from a few tables away with a haughty smile as she pushed her shoulders back to display her generous breasts. A spotlight swung to her, and she shimmered like a star in her silver dress.

*It must be her connection to Lily Waters that makes her the highest ranking candidate.* Julianna spotted her mother's rival beside Brenda. *No wonder Lily didn't challenge Mom for Dad.* He was human and she was Moon Singer.

"Cameron Elizabeth Winthrop of Callowwood, Nevada."

The young woman in gold rose gracefully to her feet, and Julianna had to admit she was a glorious sight in a spotlight of her own. Her smile bloomed quiet and confident, and she stood straight, her bearing regal.

"Mischa Irina Wolensky of Leland, Nevada."

The woman who rose to her feet was very tall and slender. Long red hair hung straight to her butt in a long silken tail gathered at the nape of her neck, falling as straight as the front of her pale blue sheath dress. Her breasts were small, hardly breaking the line of her gown, and her expression had all the liveliness of marble. She was beautiful, like a cold, remote queen ruling from on high, but not a user-friendly leader.

"Tamara Jasmine Cutter of Callowwood, Nevada."

The Cutters' oldest daughter jerked to her feet and straightened her black, sequined top over her tube skirt. She grinned widely from under a mop of thick brown curls held back from her face with a wide, black sequined headband. She twitched and fidgeted in the light, but Julianna could scent her pleasure to be in it.

"And finally, Julianna Sarah Morris, late of Fresno, California, now of Callowwood, Nevada."

A mixture of panic and pleasure swirled in Julianna's gut. She squared her shoulders and rose. She raised her chin, staring at Jeff as the spotlight took away her sight. *Just focus on the goal and you'll be fine.* She hoped she presented the appearance of a confident, serious, compassionate female who'd be the best choice for Jeff's mate.

*That's because you are the best choice*, her Sister insisted.

She resisted the urge to grimace. *Hell, the giggling teenager probably knows more about this whole governing pack thing than I do.*

*Maybe, but she can barely govern herself, a weakness for the pack.*

"The five Luna candidates for the Callowwood Pack."

Applause thundered around them all, and she swallowed hard against the panic/pleasure. She focused on standing still in the spotlight and remembering to breathe.

"Each of these candidates will be subjected to the Seven Leadership Tests of the Luna: Courage, Tolerance, Generosity, Respect/Humility, Honor/Diplomacy, Strength/Calm, and Secrecy."

*And that's when shit gets real.* Sebrina had mentioned the tests, but Julianna didn't understand their significance.

"These tests will be administered without prior knowledge of the Candidates. They will happen wherever and whenever the case may be."

*Woohoo. Pop quiz.*

"You'll be judged on your poise, actions taken, resolutions reached, and character displayed. You must pass all seven tests to be chosen as the Luna, Mate to the succeeding Alpha of the pack. Good luck, ladies, and may the Lady Moon watch over you in the trials ahead."

Applause rose like a wave, and the spotlight finally turned off, allowing her to sink back into the chair as her heart rate slowed. Unexpected testing meant the judges would decide whether she was worthy of leading by her everyday actions.

"Sebrina, what if no one passes the tests for Luna?"

"Then the pack will either search for other suitable candidates from the other packs bordering ours or wait for the younger alpha female packmembers to mature."

"Oh."

Did she really want to be Luna of the pack, to always be in the public eye of the Moon Singer population like the first lady of the United States?

Not really, no. She didn't want the leadership role. She'd always be watched and required to set an example for all the other females in the pack. She hated performing for the crowds, preferring a normal life.

*What about Jeff?* Did she want him that much? Was he worth all this?

She scanned the crowd rising to mingle. Jeff stood beside his father near the podium, speaking with several young males. His head turned, and he met her eyes as if her very gaze called to him. The recognition and attraction were immediate, and she shivered as she fought the instinct to rush into his heady embrace.

*Whoa. Rein it in there, woman.*

*Could you live with the knowledge that another woman got him because you weren't willing to make the effort to have him?* Oh, her Sister could be cruel. *Could you stand to stay in the town where he lives with and loves another woman? What if it turns out to be Brenda Solaris? Could you stand knowing she's fucking him?*

Anger burned through her in a fiery torrent with the thought of anyone, ever, touching her Mate, but she forced herself to smile mildly and accept congratulations from the packmembers who approached her table.

She would fight for Jeff. She couldn't bear to lose him to any of the other women. It'd kill her, twisting pain through her worse than Terence ever had. Her Sister wolf rose up inside her and snarled, *Jeff is yours. Yours. The other bitches better steer clear of him because he is yours.*

*Calm down. I have to set a good example.*

*Growl, snarl, bark!*

She laughed inwardly but kept her expression mild. She might not know all the rules to this game, but she'd learn fast and play hard.

# CHAPTER FIVE:
## Making the Rounds

*Goddess, I hate political parties.*

Boring, full of posturing and false smiles, each party ended with him getting fawned over by the mothers of the alpha bitches as if the laundry list of their daughters' accomplishments would sway him in their favor. All of them were pretty enough, dressed to the nines and elegant, though there was one notable exception. Tammy Cutter looked more like she'd attended her prom than a political evening party. But none of them did anything for him.

Except her. Julianna Morris.

His dick wanted to sing an aria over her.

Julianna was the only bright spot in his entire evening, though she was also a burning distraction. In the den before the party she'd been so beautiful and succulent he'd barely been able to hold himself apart from her. He knew his father had noticed but was too much of a politician to say anything. And when Richard had goaded Julianna, Jeff's outrage and protective instincts had roared a battle cry, ready to take down anyone threatening his Mate.

Despite Richard's efforts to shake Julianna, she'd carried herself like a queen, elegant and poised. She'd passed his father's tests with flying colors. She was definitely worthy of her nomination of candidacy for Luna.

Throughout the party, he'd watched her, trying to keep the others around him from noticing his attention sticking to her too long, but Zach Bushman, his best friend and First beta, smirked knowingly at him a time or two. Zach stood taller than Jeff by a good five inches, but the big, broad-shouldered blond man's personality was quieter, watchful, and downright scary sometimes. Jeff suspected Zach knew the direction of his alpha's thoughts.

At dinner, Jeff had damn near drooled all over himself watching Julianna eat, excited at her placement at his table and the buffet line. Only one person separated them because of Sebrina's sponsorship, and he'd wished Sebrina had moved back one rank so he could feel Julianna's warmth beside him.

At the table, he'd watched her converse with the other women around her, his sister and Sebrina claiming most of her attention. She was regal and confident, though she'd choked on something and blushed furiously over it. Jeff had been thinking lascivious thoughts at the time and fervently hoped she hadn't heard them.

Then she'd lifted her chin and smiled confidently at him, and his insides had liquefied. Damn, but she was perfect. Her eyes sparkled beneath her arching brows, and the tendrils of loose hair around her face gave her a playful look.

*I'd take playful anytime. Want to come home and play with me, sweet lady?*

When she'd closed her eyes and inhaled with a rapturous expression, he thought his cock would explode. How could she make every motion look sensual? Every other alpha female in the pack paled in comparison. He'd wanted to leap across the table and take her right there on the floor in front of everyone, proclaiming her his. That she liked his mother's favorite scent combination of jasmine and hazelnut hadn't hurt, either.

Leaving the table to stand with his father at the podium had been excruciating, but he'd gone. He'd left part of his awareness back with the beautiful female in the blue-green dress that hugged her breasts as lovingly as his hands wanted to. His palms had tingled with the thought. He'd had to clench his fists a few times to keep the other pieces of his sensitive anatomy from giving him away.

Jeff caught his father looking at him a few times, surely scenting his arousal, but Jeff kept his expression bland, and Richard said nothing. When Julianna rose to perform the induction ritual and took Richard's hands, Jeff had gripped the edges of the podium to keep from tearing out his father's throat. His Brother form had screamed outrage at another male, even his Alpha, touching his Mate. Jeff held on, clenching his teeth and concentrating on the crowd around them.

Julianna hadn't looked at him during the ceremony, a blessing in disguise because his control had been tenuous at best. But at the end, her eyes had sought his and he couldn't keep the jubilation and triumph from his expression. She looked like she wanted to throw her arms into the air and dance. But she demurely nodded and returned to her seat until Richard announced all the candidates by name and ranking.

Julianna had been named last because of her newness to the pack, but she'd claimed top rank in Jeff's heart.

"I'm going to go make the rounds," Jeff murmured to his buddies.

Zach nodded but said nothing, his expression watchful as ever. The man trusted very few people and tolerated even less.

Kyle Howler, Jeff's Second beta, grimaced and shook his head. "Good luck, man. Have fun with the matchmaking mommies." He gestured with his clean-shaven chin at the Winthrops' table, his green eyes winking in the light. Jeff didn't have to turn his head to know Catherine and Cameron were burning a hole in his back with their laser gazes.

He'd known the Winthrops all his life, and despite their very well-behaved and groomed daughter, he'd never had more than a passable liking for her. She was beautiful and demure, lovely and elegant, but she was too perfect, too refined and controlled. She had no wildness left, and Jeff needed to play with fire.

Relief had washed through him when his father had approved Julianna for candidacy.

*Thank the Holy Goddess above.* He didn't have to choose between random females.

He shivered with excitement and refocused on Kyle's knowing smirk. "Thanks a lot. I'll be sure to give Ms. Eloise Farkas your respects. I see she's sitting with the Cutters tonight."

Kyle lost his smirk and put his hands behind his back to keep them from rubbing his neck nervously, his tell. He'd pined after Eloise for years, but before he found the courage to ask her out, someone else had proposed.

"Yeah, well, don't go out of your way on my account."

"You sure? I'd think she'd want to know you're thinking of her."

"She's engaged." Kyle's usually good-natured face curled in disgust. "To Scatterstone. She doesn't want anything to do with a lowly beta."

Jeff snorted. "You're about as 'lowly' as I am, Kyle. Plus you're part of the Successor's cadre. That wins you points right there."

"Not in her eyes." Kyle scowled sullenly.

Jeff clapped him on the shoulder. "Don't worry about that too much. It'll all work out."

"Like it did for you?"

Jeff grinned, his thoughts returning to Julianna. "Damn straight."

Kyle just shook his head, but his expression had relaxed into his customary smile. "Go make the rounds. We'll make sure everyone waits their turn properly."

"And Eloise?"

"Yeah, tell her hi for me."

"Will do."

Jeff nodded and left his friends behind, starting the rounds of congratulations for the Luna candidates. He knew Kyle carried a torch for Eloise, but the man hadn't told her in time to stop Tommy Scatterstone, an alpha in rank, from snatching the pretty female up. Jeff suspected Eloise was Kyle's True Mate, but his Second hadn't mentioned anything about feeling the mating heat. Watching him now, Jeff hoped Kyle would come out and claim Eloise before it was too late in the eyes of the human laws.

*Focus, jackass. Quit stalling and get the congratulations over with so you can spend time with your Mate.*

He sighed inwardly and strode toward Brenda Solaris's table, plastering pleasant cordiality on his face.

The pale blonde shifted her body to give him the best view of her voluptuous breasts straining from the top of her dress. She was tall and curvaceous and elegant…and she did absolutely nothing for his libido. Her scent filled his nostrils with sweet apricots, but the smell overwhelmed his nose as if she wore too much perfume.

*A Moon Singer wearing perfume?*

He fought to keep the grimace off his face when she took his hand.

"Congratulations on your nomination, Mistress Solaris." He smiled and nodded.

"Thank you so much, Jefferson. I'm delighted to be included." Her blue eyes raked him over like a delicious meal set in front of her, and he suddenly understood why women hated it when men checked them out that way. It felt invasive.

Jeff returned her look with his bland half-smile. "We're glad you could be here. Good luck with the tests."

"Thank you, Jefferson." She winked, and he retreated from her overwhelming stench of fermenting apricots.

*Just a few more before you can speak to your Mate.*

That only mildly lifted his spirits as he closed on Mrs. and Mistress Winthrop. Both women watched him hungrily, though Cameron's expression smoothed out to a sweet demure smile as he closed on them. Cameron's mother, Catherine, couldn't quite hide her disdain for Brenda Solaris before Jeff reached their table.

"Congratulations, Mistress Winthrop." He extended his hand with only a small fight against his revulsion.

"Thank you, Jefferson. I'm honored and grateful to be here tonight." She inclined her head gracefully.

She tried to make her voice melodious, but it came across breathy to him. He clenched his jaw to keep from reacting with annoyance. Her scent was a mixture of oregano and mint, with a hint of dusty farm thrown in. He admitted it wasn't the worst scent he'd come across, but it didn't make him want to get too close. His cock and libido remained dormant, and he tried to ignore the stench of desperation wafting from Cameron's mother.

"Can we invite you over for dinner next week? We'd love to see you. Cameron recently made the Leland Observer's Hero of the Month with her work with homeless humans." Catherine looked over at her daughter proudly, and Cameron smiled self-consciously, blushing a little.

"Really? That is great, Mistress Winthrop. I'd be happy to come by. Which day would be best for you?"

"Tuesday evening? Would that work?"

"I'll be there. Thank you for the invitation. Congratulations again."

"We look forward to it, Jefferson." Catherine waved heartily.

Jeff couldn't escape fast enough. His heart already

raced as he strode through the tables toward the one female he couldn't live without. At last, he'd be able to touch her, however briefly, and let her sweet scent envelop him. Anything to push away the odors of all the other females desperately sending out come-here hormones. Goddess, if the tents weren't open, it would stink like a brothel inside.

Julianna stood beside his sister, Tawny, chatting with her and two other beta women, Marybeth and Jennilynn Grayhound. The identical twins fulfilled the title except for the color of their clothes, the cut of their hair, and the placement of the dimple in opposite cheeks. He liked the Grayhound twins. They were friendly and jovial, often speaking before they thought, but never unkindly.

He made himself turn his attention back to his duties, no matter how much he wanted to buck tradition and visit Julianna first. *Following the protocols and rankings sucks, dammit.*

When he reached the Cutters' table, he was momentarily distracted by Tammy's twitching. The girl chattered about her pleasure at being chosen as a Luna candidate, but she couldn't hold his attention. She smelled like baby powder and bubblegum, and he could barely make out the individual words in her torrent of speech. He tried to focus, but his hyperawareness of Julianna across the tent kept him barely civil.

"You simply must come to our restaurant for dinner next week," Michelle Cutter insisted as she smiled brightly. She looked like an older, more worn version of Tammy. Fortunately, she wasn't chewing gum. "Are you available Friday night?"

Not if I could help it. "Friday night? Yes, I believe my schedule is open."

"Excellent. We look forward to seeing you. Tammy will have something new to tell you then."

*That she's won the National Gum Chewing Competition?*

"I look forward to it." A flicker of motion to his right made him turn his head. He recalled he'd promised to speak to Eloise Farkas when he saw her cough into her hand. "Ms. Farkas, I hope you're doing well this evening. Mr. Howler sends his regards."

Eloise was a pretty woman, but her expression pinched at his words, and sadness filled her eyes. "Does he? That's nice of him. Isn't he here this evening?"

"Yes, he is."

"Then why did he send you, Jefferson, instead of coming to speak with me himself?"

*Ouch.*

"I believe your fiancé made it clear that Mr. Howler should keep his distance."

Eloise's expression darkened. "Ah, I see. Well, thank you for passing on his message."

"Happy to help." Jeff looked away from the pain radiating from the young woman's body language and recentered on the Cutters once more. "So, I shall see you on Friday evening. Again, congratulations, Mistress Cutter."

Tammy tittered and turned her head to look at him out of the corner of her eye. "Thanks."

He walked away, leaving the bubblegum and sorrow behind gratefully. Jeff wished Eloise had been more receptive to Kyle's message, but he suspected she was more disappointed with Scatterstone's warning than Kyle's lack of delivery.

Jeff tried to keep himself on task with his next destination, but Julianna's scent permeated the space beneath the tents, and he wanted to seek her out like a bloodhound and rub his nose through her fragrant hair. *Stay on point, jackass.* What was the point, again? Oh, yes, greeting all the candidates impartially. Right.

He tried to keep his attention on Mischa Wolensky when he arrived at her table, but it kept drifting to the movements of the peacock green dress wrapped around his

Mate's glorious body.

"Thank you, Jefferson," Mischa said coolly.

Her voice jerked him back to himself. "You're welcome, Mistress Wolensky. See you then."

Jeff had no idea what he'd agreed to, but he no longer cared. He'd done his due diligence and visited all the candidates before his Mate. Now he was free.

His attention never wavered from Julianna as he honed in on her. Just one look at her shot lust straight through his body and her scent drew him like a compass needle. He had to grit his teeth to keep his cock from announcing itself before he arrived at her table.

"I am so happy for you, Mistress Julianna." Tawny clapped her hands as he approached. "You'll be a fantastic Luna. I can see it in you."

"I'm glad to hear you have such faith in me" Julianna smiled wryly.

"Oh, I do." Tawny's face creased into a knowing smile as her eyes caught Jeff standing behind the candidate.

Julianna stilled and slowly turned her head to meet his gaze. Her eyes widened and his body tightened as he caught her scent. It was a combination of the delicate feminine musk he remembered from when she'd teased him as a teenager, and climbing gardenia with a hint of vanilla. His mouth watered, and he was sure his tongue hung out in hopes of tasting her. He watched her nipples harden beneath her bodice, the scent of her arousal filling the air between them.

"Congratulations, Mistress Morris." His voice sounded hoarse to his ears, but he tried to smile to cover his raging need.

"Thank you…" She drifted off, seeking the proper form of address.

"Jefferson."

"Jefferson." She tilted her head a little and gave him her own version of his half-smile. "I appreciate being included tonight. I suspect being nominated as a Luna candidate was all your doing?"

A charged silence settled around them as the other people nearby took in her words with sharp surprise, but Jeff only laughed. He hadn't nominated her. That was against the rules. Fortunately, someone else had seen the potential in Julianna as much as he had.

*Of course, I might be biased by the fact that she's my True Mate.*

"As a matter of fact, it wasn't. I don't know exactly who nominated you, but I'm very glad they did." He almost reached for her hand to bring it to his lips for a kiss, but the reminder of their avid audience aborted his motion.

"Thank you, Jefferson."

"Thank you for accepting the nomination." *Yes, thank you, thank you.*

"My pleasure." Her eyes promised just what kind of pleasure.

He froze in place to keep from lunging at her and dragging her out of the tents and up to his room in the house. Damn…The woman was seductive and all she'd done was stand there, watching him with that challenging look in her eyes.

His arousal roared its approval of her offer, but he clamped down on it, reminding himself they stood on stage. She bit her lip as if she, too, realized they weren't really alone. He fought the urge to lick her mouth. Her eyes flashed with restrained challenge, and her hands tightened on the back of her chair.

"Since I'm so new at this, maybe you can fill me in on what happens next." She whispered the words, her smile amused.

"Nothing." *Smooth, jackass. How about being more vague?* "I mean, nothing more tonight. We're supposed to mingle and talk to the packmembers. But there's nothing more official that needs to be done."

"So technically, you could spend your evening showing the newest packmember around?" She raised her eyebrows, a hopeful smile playing on her lips.

*I want to play with her lips. Both sets.*

He shrugged and nodded, but his customary half-smile felt strained. "I could, but unfortunately, it would appear as favoritism." He grasped her hand and held it in front of him against his belly to convey his sorrow. "I *really* want to, but appearances are everything right now. Do you understand?"

*Please, please, please understand.*

Some of her vibrancy faded as she nodded. "Yes, I understand." She squeezed his hand before letting go. "Thank you for taking the time to explain."

"You are very welcome." He couldn't resist kissing her hand again before he turned and walked away.

Or tried to. He damn near slammed into the chairs of the table behind him, taking a nose dive.

*Fuckin' awesome.* So much for the cool and collected Successor.

Gathering what was left of his dignity, Jeff grimaced and headed for his First, hoping the man wouldn't give him too much grief. Meeting Zach's gaze didn't give Jeff much hope.

He nodded to those he passed on his way and hoped he didn't blush too much. He wanted Julianna so much it hurt, but following the protocols took precedence, even if it was damn near impossible to hide his interest. Zach watched him approach with a smirk and Jeff held back a growl.

"I see you're falling all over yourself with Ms. Morris."

"Shut up." Jeff shook his head. "I just lost my balance."

"Oh, yeah, I can see that." Zach nodded with a grin. "I get the feeling Ms. Morris is gonna have you off balance for a long time coming."

Jeff wanted to argue, but he suspected his First was right.

****

The rest of his evening passed in a blur of people coming to congratulate him and ingratiate themselves to curry favor. While Julianna chatted with Sebrina, Tawny, and the Grayhound sisters, Jeff continued his rounds. He visited with the oldest and respected families, and tried to ignore his Mate's beguiling scent.

*Yeah, good fuckin' luck with that.*

His damn attention wandered every time Julianna's skirt flashed her legs.

He tried to keep his focus on the conversation with old Mr. and Mrs. Trackman, but the acrid scent of anger flooded his nostrils. Often rivalries of lesser members of the pack aired at gatherings like this, but the sharpness of the smell jerked his attention away.

He shifted a little to one side until he could see Julianna. Her body language translated suppressed fury and disbelief. He quickly scanned the area around her to see what might have set her off.

Cameron Winthrop? No, she chatted with her parents and their friends. Brenda Solaris? The woman glared at Julianna but stood nowhere near. What the hell had her so pissed off?

He had the sudden urge to push through all the remaining guests and take her in his arms, soothing her enmity until it disappeared. He'd happily beat the perpetrator into a bloody pulp for her, though she could probably do it well enough herself

She caught his eye and gave him a tight smile, but fury still burned in her gaze. She excused herself from Tawny and the Grayhound sisters, and strode purposefully toward Richard, her expression full of determination. She bypassed the last remaining guests with a sway of her hips that had his cock howling for release, and he gritted his teeth to keep his smile bland.

"Incoming." Zach's whispered warning made Jeff look around.

Brenda Solaris wove through people to reach him first. He would have laughed at the competition, but it seemed the better part of valor to pretend ignorance.

Julianna stopped in front of Richard a heartbeat before Brenda and the other woman checked her forward motion, her eyes flashing with ill-concealed frustration. Julianna's angry scent mixed with disgust and eyes narrowed as her jaw bunched. Jeff clenched his fists behind his back and swallowed a growl. But his Mate smoothed her expression into a version of his bland smile and nodded to the Alpha.

"Mr. Lightfoot, Jefferson, it's been a pleasure." She gave them a sweet smile that didn't reach her eyes. "Thank you for inviting me and inducting me into the pack. I appreciate it, but I have to get home to my mother. Since my father's death, she's been slow in recovering."

Richard took her hand, and Jeff felt his Brother form rear up, ready to attack the intruder touching his Mate. Locking his knees to keep from lunging at his father, Jeff struggled to soothe his Brother, reminding him that Richard wasn't a threat.

*You beat him, remember? And he's touching your Mate.*

*It wasn't a victory. It was a draw. And he's still the Alpha until I'm Mated and she's whelped a child. Calm down.*

Two years earlier, Jeff had challenged his father in Kerstance, the duel for supremacy, and fought him to a standstill in his Brother form. It had been a surprise to all of them. They'd been evenly matched and called it a draw, but Jeff suspected he'd have beaten his father if the fight had continued much longer. Jeff's near victory had caused Richard to reevaluate his position as Alpha, and he'd proclaimed Jeff Successor a week after their Kerstance. The selection process for the Luna candidates began a few weeks later.

"You're more than welcome, Mistress Julianna." Richard patted her hand. "Before you go, I have something for you." He turned and his First Beta handed him a wooden box that held the pack's Luna tokens.

Jeff missed which token his father selected, but they were all the same and clearly stated Julianna to be in the running.

"This token is for you to keep on you at all times. It lets all of our people know you're a candidate for Luna." He set it in Julianna's hand and wrapped her fingers around it. "Take it with our congratulations and gratitude."

She kept her hand closed around the token as she nodded. "I appreciate your patience with a newbie such as me. I'm aware you're taking a big chance on me. I'll do my best to live up to your expectations."

"I'm sure you will." Richard smiled and stood back. "We're happy to have you back in Callowwood. Tell your mother hello for us, and I hope she gets through her grief soon."

"I will, Mr. Lightfoot." She turned her attention on him. "Thanks for the invitation to the 'garden party', Jeff. It was a completely new experience for me."

"You're welcome, I'm glad you came." He wanted to take her hand, but he didn't think he could stop there. "Can I walk you out to your car?"

She shook her head. "No, that's all right. You have your guests to attend to." She shot a pointed look over her shoulder to Brenda waiting with barely contained impatience. "I know my way out."

Jeff stiffened at the anger in her voice and he wondered what he'd done to merit it. She sounded angry with him.

"Of course. Have a good night and thanks for coming." He tried to stuff his dismay down deep.

She nodded and walked away, but his attention followed her even if his gaze turned to Ms. Solaris.

"Go. I'll cover for you."

Kyle's words made Jeff blink. "You sure?"

"Yeah. They're only here for the tokens and approval of the current Alpha. You're good to go."

"Thanks, Kyle."

The crowd focused on Richard and Mistress Solaris as Jeff retreated out of the tents toward the house. He needed to give Julianna a more proper goodbye when they could be alone. His heartbeat kicked up a few notches as he thought of catching her in his house, all alone, and his cock reminded him of its pressing needs.

He found a place to wait and leaned his back against the wall of the hallway. Closing his eyes, he tried to coax his body back into tranquility. Unfortunately, his mind's eye filled with images of Julianna laughing and smiling, along with the flashes of her legs while her skirt swirled around them. His cock only swelled in size.

*Shit.*

He breathed deeply to settle himself, and he caught the scent of his Mate in the main corridor of the house. Lust and excitement surged, and he readied himself for her arrival.

\*\*\*\*

Julianna strode through the house toward the front doors, her fury banked but still smoldering. She gripped her purse in one hand and the token in the other, not sure she'd keep it or hurl it into the bushes. Why the fuck was she required to get someone's approval to leave? She'd rather spit in their faces than beg someone's approval.

As she passed a darkened hallway to her right, a male arm reached out of the darkness and jerked her against a hard body. Rage blazed hot as she crashed into the wall of flesh with an unladylike grunt of surprise. Instinct took over as she slammed her elbow into her assailant's gut. Her Sister's nature surged into the forefront of her awareness and she turned on her attacker with pent-up ferocity.

He yelped as she stomped down on his instep, twisting in his arms. Then she shoved his shoulders back against the wall and slammed her knee into his groin. He collapsed, panting and groaning, when the irresistible scent of the desert rain penetrated her adrenaline rush.

Understanding dawned.

She'd just kneed Jeff Lightfoot in the balls. It would've been funny if she wasn't so angry. His original grip had been sexually domineering, complete with raging hard-on.

"Jeff?" She grasped his shoulders. "What are you doing? Are you insane?"

"What the hell was that for?" He groaned, cupping his crotch protectively.

"Haven't you learned never to grab a woman out of the darkness?" Julianna shook her head as some of her anger drained away. "I lived in the big city for a long time. More than one man tried to take me down. Are you okay?"

"No." He sounded strangled, and she had to hide a smile. "Can't breathe."

"Sorry."

"Damn, woman!"

"Damn, yourself! Why did you try to grab me?"

"I didn't want you to leave yet." He slowly straightened up. His face looked a little gray, but it might have been the dim light. "I wanted to say a more private goodbye, but I think I'm only going to say goodbye to my balls. Shit!"

"I'm not sorry for defending myself." She bit her bottom lip. "Do you want to sit down?"

He nodded, and she slid one arm around his waist, lowering him to the floor.

"Goddess above, you smell wonderful. How did you hide it for so long?" He dropped his head and nuzzled her neck and jawline as she sat beside him. Arousal pushed through her chagrin, tightening her nipples.

"I didn't." She snorted. "I threw myself at you for

years, and you ignored me the whole time, remember?"

"More idiot, me." He chuckled ruefully. "If I'd known you were a Moon Singer, I would've taken you years ago."

Suddenly, rage obliterated all the lustful feelings in her, and she snarled, scooting away from him.

"Taken me?" She growled, pushing to her feet. "You would've 'taken' me? You asshole, am I nothing more than a piece of tail to you? If that's the case, go grab one of those other bitches. I've already experienced being treated like a piece of meat. I'm sure Brenda would submit to you willingly enough, with her tits against the floor and her ass in the air!"

Jeff stilled, and his hands warily covered his groin again as he looked up at her.

"What's wrong, Julianna?"

"What's wrong? What's wrong?" She barely held herself back from kicking him in the ass with her sandaled foot. "What's wrong is that I've joined a pack that doesn't see this"—she stabbed a finger at him sitting on the floor—"as something to be upset about. I want you, Jeff, but I'm not just a piece of ass that any alpha male can use when he's feeling horny. I won't be 'taken' unless I give permission. Do you hear me, Mr. Successor of the pack?"

Julianna whirled and stomped out of the house, leaving Jeff completely nonplussed on the floor behind her ringing heels.

# CHAPTER SIX:
## Interspecies Relations

Julianna dragged herself out of bed the next morning and stumbled into her kitchen to brew some strong coffee. *This shit better hold up the spoon.* She'd been exhausted the night before, but still hadn't slept well after her departure from the party.

Despite her anger at Jeff's "grab-ass" tactics, leaving had been the hardest thing she'd done. Her traitorous body fought her all the way to the valet, aching for more of his touches and scent. Sleeping had been nearly impossible.

*How can I want to screw a guy when I'm so angry with him?*

But it wasn't Jeff with whom she was angry.

*No, it's the barbaric practice of using a female's loss in status as an excuse to get your rocks off.* It had been permissible in the past for unmated alpha males to use the widowed Lunas for sexual gratification. The idea had her completely unhinged. Tawny's explanation infuriated her, but the betas hadn't seemed upset by it. They'd been surprised at her vehement response, and she'd reminded herself she was new to their world, but it still set her rage ablaze.

*It's still ablaze.*

She poured herself some coffee and added cream, trying to use the delicious scents of hazelnut and chocolate to calm herself. If she became Luna, would she just be passed on to any alpha male who wanted her should Jeff die?

*Fat chance in hell! I'll rip their dicks off and feed them to them first.*

No man would "have her" unless she gave her permission. Even if Julianna was no longer Luna, she wouldn't be open for any asshole in the frame of mind to ravish her. She took a deep breath and sipped her coffee. *I'm not a prize, I'm a person.*

Julianna was mostly awake and finished with her first cup of coffee by the time someone knocked on her door. She shot a look at the clock and made sure the Luna pendant was concealed beneath her shirt before she opened it.

"Sebrina? What are you doing here?"

Sebrina looked her over carefully. "I see your Sister has visited you."

Julianna raised her eyebrows. "How do you know that?"

"I can scent her closeness to you."

She shook her head. "I'm not sure if it's her or her anger."

"Either way, this is good because you'll need to be very familiar with her to become all you must. Are you ready?"

"Ready?"

"For your Luna training. You did ask for my help, yes?"

Julianna blinked. "Oh, right. I'd forgotten with everything that happened last night. Just give me a chance to get dressed." She set her mug down on the kitchen counter. "You're welcome to come in while I get dressed."

Julianna threw on a t-shirt, shorts, and corralled her hair

into a ponytail before returning to the kitchen to fill up some water bottles. She didn't believe the fury belonged to her Sister self. At least not completely. It had taken her a long time to realize she was her own person, worthy no matter what her husband did. She'd carry that though her training to be a Luna because she'd be damned before any more women were treated like sexual training-wheels for young alphas.

*Deep breaths. Don't kill anyone.*

She grabbed her keys and stepped out the door with Sebrina. She brought her cell phone just in case her mom needed her. Sebrina eyed the little electronic intruder with mistrust, but she only said, "Vibrate," and Julianna complied.

Sebrina nodded sharply. "Come, we'll go to a place I know and strengthen your acquaintance."

The morning was a perfect midsummer day, and Julianna let her shoulders relax. It had started out cool enough to promise only mild heat when the sun rose higher in the sky. The land seemed to breathe a sigh of relief, releasing high desert scents into the air. Sebrina took Julianna's arm as if she needed support, and she let herself relax into the older woman's experience. Whatever they were going to do that day, Sebrina would take care of her.

When they reached the corner of the road where it turned toward town, Sebrina released Julianna's arm and strode away across the verdant summer grasses of the open space before the sparsely forested hills. Julianna followed her with excited anticipation.

They entered the trees without saying a word, and she felt the shade on her shoulders like a gentle benediction. She tried to take reassurance from the steadfast nature of the forest as Sebrina led her into a small clearing. No one would see or hear anything they did this far from the houses of Callowwood.

"Sit down, daughter."

Julianna dropped to the ground.

"You must be connected with your Sister form at all times to be an effective Luna." Sebrina dropped her chin and held Julianna's gaze. "The other members of the pack will sense this in you and lose confidence in you if you cannot assume her shape with but a thought. Because you've only recently become acquainted with her, this will be harder than if you'd been aware of her from birth."

Julianna nodded, wondering if it would really be that hard. She felt her Sister all the time these days, though she'd never willingly assumed her form.

"Tell me what you feel when you commune with your Sister form."

"I don't know." Julianna shook her head with a frown. "My memories of each time are vague, like scenes from a movie I saw a long time ago."

"I'm not asking what you remember. I'm asking you what you feel when you're with her."

Julianna bit her lip. Emotions surged through her as her Sister allowed some memories to slip loose. She felt fierce joy, release, freedom, excitement, exhilaration, lust, and overwhelming strength, as if she could run forever and take on any enemy. She basked in those feelings for a few moments until she remembered Sebrina waited for an answer.

She recited the list, and Sebrina nodded with satisfaction.

"That's very good, daughter. You instinctually connect with her, and she's willing to answer your call. But we must get you to be more than occasional compatriots." Sebrina crossed her arms over her chest. "You must share this body, no matter what form it holds. While she must lend you her strength and endurance, you must lend her your intelligence and reason so you will both be more formidable.

"Now, focus on more physical feelings." Sebrina stood

in front of Julianna. "Close your eyes. Find the memories of what it felt like to be in your Sister form. So far, daughter, I sense you've only become your Sister form a few times, but you took the back seat. Your Sister is very powerful, but she's too instinctual. She doesn't think enough about what needs to be done to keep either of you safe. You must be her leader, her protector against not only the humans but the others in the pack. It's a delicate balance, and you must provide the direction. You must lead in your transformation from now on. It will keep you and your Sister safe."

"She's stayed safe enough when she took over," Julianna remarked.

"She was not safe. She was lucky!" Sebrina snapped. "It's your job to keep her safe."

*Are you listening?*

*Grrrrr...*

"Focus on what it was like to feel the wind caressing your body, pushing your tail, and fluttering past your whiskers."

Julianna tried to remember what it physically felt like to be a wolf.

"Feel the ground under your paws, your weight completely balanced on all of your limbs. Remember the way the air tasted and the forest sounded around you. Settle yourself in these feelings and memories."

Julianna closed her eyes, settling her mind and body into as much stillness as she could. She focused on what Sebrina described, but her mind slid away from her attempts to analyze the experiences of shifting under the moon. She couldn't access the sensations because the eyes and ears and body hadn't been hers. Instead, her mind served up images of what she might look like in her Sister form, as if she stood outside looking at herself.

*That's not what I look like*, her inner voice sneered.

*I don't care what we look like. I want to remember what*

*it feels like.*

*Why? So you can take more of my time from me? Kiss my furry butt!*

Julianna spun further away from her Sister as anger surged on both sides. Gritting her teeth, she relaxed her shoulders a little and tried again, pushing her frustration away. The memories of her previous shifts began to come into focus, but the wolf resisted being boxed in by her dictation.

*Please, Sister, don't push me away.*

Suddenly a voice more primal than she had ever heard in her head, snarled, *You pushed me away, pushed me down until I had to hide away so you could forget me. You ignored the moon, you ignored the song of Her when She called you. Why did you do this to me?*

The anger and frustration shocked Julianna silent, and her own anger at her Sister's reluctance withered. Had she shoved her lupine half away? Why had she done that?

*There wasn't anyone around to teach me what I was.*

The wolf scoffed. *That's not the full truth.*

Julianna swallowed hard. The truth? She'd been alone among humans growing up, and the instinctual fear of revealing her true nature to them screamed through her. But those reasons were only part of it. She remembered deliberately forgetting the wolf within.

Amazement and chagrin flooded through her. Why had she done that?

A memory surfaced of an orphanage full of children, human children, and being reprimanded for growling and swatting at the other kids like she would her littermates. By the time Beth and Gerry Morris came looking for a child, she'd already suppressed her lupine self to fit in amongst the others. She'd understood that her best chance of finding a family would be to be as human as possible.

Adoption by her human parents brought her to Callowwood, and she'd "remained human" to protect herself from abandonment. Beth was the only mother she'd known. Julianna wanted to be wanted, and kept up the charade to keep her family.

*What happened to my lupine parents?* She'd been adopted by the Morrises when she was a little over a year old. Where were her blood kin? Who were they, and why had they abandoned her all those years ago? Julianna scrubbed her face with her hands.

*I'm sorry, Sister. I was afraid and alone, and no one understood me on the outside. I had to fit in with the humans. I'm very sorry. Please help me remember how it is to be together.*

*No!*

Julianna tightened her jaw. *I can't change the past, and I'm sorry. I understand what and who I truly am, and I need you. I want you to be part of my life, not just someone I know three days a month.*

*You left me alone in the dark. You turned away from me and pretended I didn't exist.*

She grimaced. *I know. I was wrong.*

*I won't let you take back those three days a month ever again. They're mine!*

*I don't want to take them from you. I want to share them with you!* Juliana shouted back, her hands curling into fists. *I want to share every day of every month with you. I don't want to be alone again any more than you do.*

Her wolf half snarled and fought a mental tug-of-war. Her logical brain told her fighting would get her nowhere, but giving up seemed an even less attractive option. Snarls filled the stillness of the clearing as she struggled to gain the upper hand. She saw herself grappling with her darker half in her mind's eye, rolling and snapping with primal fury.

Time ceased to matter as she struggled with her Sister, but eventually humor pushed through the emotional upheaval. Here she was, sitting on the ground, sweating as if she'd run a marathon. She barked a laugh. Why the hell was she fighting herself, again? She owed her Sister.

Her laughter rang out in the clearing and jarred the wolf's resistance. Her Sister's ears flagged and her head tilted in surprise.

*You're right, Sister. I owe you. Take your place as my partner and equal.* She simply surrendered to the wolf side, bowing to her mentally. Her body changed as the lupine surged through her.

Julianna's ears shifted to the top of her head, and sound sharpened into crystal clarity. Her jaw and nose elongated, and her tail lengthened into a thick brush, scraping across the forest floor. Her fingers and toes shortened, and her shoulders slid backward until her chest narrowed. Stifling heat surrounded her as if she wore a heavy, thick coat in the blazing sun, and she opened her mouth to unroll her tongue in an effort to cool down. Then she opened her eyes.

The world had changed significantly. Every detail was sharper. Honeybees buzzed around the few flowers in the clearing wearing sharp jackets of gold and black while the rocks cast knife-edged shadows on individual blades of grass, waving gently in the breeze like green bristly hair. Everything seemed bigger or taller than she remembered. Even Sebrina looked down on her, though her face showed a satisfied smile.

"Very good, my daughter." Her whisper carried like a normal voice to Julianna's ears.

Sounds she'd been ignoring, such as the woodpecker pounding on a tree somewhere nearby or the patter of little rodent feet through the under growth, were as clear as if she'd put on headphones. She inhaled deeply and smelled the rodents and flowers and bees and the deer that had passed through this clearing earlier that morning. Sebrina's scent wove its way into her awareness, a mixture of satisfaction, wolf, and pride. Before Julianna could savor the sights and scents, sharp surprise, sorrow, and regret tainted the air around the Paiute woman, and her smile disappeared.

Quick as lightning, the woman grabbed Julianna's muzzle and turned her head sharply to the right, staring at her intently. Julianna had no idea what Sebrina was looking at, but whatever it was, the woman paled, and her hand shook where it touched Julianna's muzzle.

Julianna whined uncertainly and thought, "What, Sebrina?"

The woman jerked as if she'd been slapped and stared at Julianna's eyes with surprise and disbelief.

"It cannot be," she whispered then, shaking her head in denial without letting Julianna free of her grip. "It cannot be."

Julianna whined again. "What can't be? I don't understand."

"Great Mother Moon, I never thought...to see..."

Julianna's Sister didn't like the scents coming from Sebrina and tucked her tail between her hind legs, trying to back away from the agonized Paiute woman. A whine full of fearful confusion escaped from her chest. The loss of confidence in her inner wolf made nausea rise.

*You must be your Sister's leader, her protector. You must lead in your transformation from now on. It will keep you and your Sister safe.* Sebrina's instructions shot through Julianna's awareness, and she pushed forward, taking the lead from her Sister.

Julianna tugged her head in Sebrina's hand, pulling her lips back to bare her teeth with a growl. The woman held fast for a few more moments, sorrow radiating from her. Julianna's Sister shifted toward panic, but Julianna held on. When she growled again, Sebrina released her, dropping to her knees in the grass.

"I'm sorry, daughter, so sorry!" The woman wailed as she flattened her hands in the grass and placed her head between her arms until her forehead touch the ground. "I didn't understand all those years ago, and I was afraid. Please forgive me."

Julianna waited, her legs braced for flight and her tail low.

*What is she talking about, Sister?*

*I don't know, but this is strange behavior. She is Alpha.*

Slowly, Julianna stretched out her neck to sniff at the back of Sebrina's head. The woman still smelled like sorrow and regret, but new scents of amazement and hope filtered through the morass of discomfort.

"I still don't understand, Sebrina," she thought, cocking her head to one side as she took in the Paiute woman's posture. "Please explain. None of this makes sense to me." She whined again and stiffened her legs to keep from bolting away.

Sebrina jerked her head up and stared at Julianna with such sadness in her eyes. "I'm sorry, daughter. I didn't mean to confuse you." She sat back on her haunches and retreated behind her First People's mask of impassiveness. "You're very powerful indeed if you can speak with your mind alone."

"Why are you so sad, Sebrina? Did I do something wrong? I followed your directions. I don't understand."

"Great Mother Moon, you're more beautiful than I ever expected," the woman murmured to herself, gazing back at Julianna. Then she blinked and shook her head. "No, no, daughter, you've done nothing wrong. You've done very well, and I'm very proud of you. Such strength."

Sebrina's scent had changed again as she levered herself to her feet. Julianna watched the older woman uncertainly, noting her movements seemed a little stiff as if sorrow still dragged at her.

"Now, change back."

At first, Julianna didn't understand the command.

"Go on, change back to your human form."

Unreasoning fear flared to life and Julianna's Sister

locked her will into place, refusing to budge.

*I won't be locked in that hideous upright shape again.*

*Don't be a coward. We're a team, now, remember?*

*We've never been a team.*

*We gotta be one now, or we'll end up dead.*

They fought for dominance again, but Julianna pushed persistently and patiently, offering her Sister self a "seat" in her mind closer to the surface. The wolf gave in with this small concession, and their body changed until Julianna stood upright once more, shaking and panting. The world appeared a little less crisp. It wasn't exactly fuzzy, just less sharp, the sound dampened.

The wind tugged at her clothes and Julianna started. *I'm still wearing clothes? That's weird. Shouldn't they disintegrate or at least fall off?*

"Where do my clothes go when I shift, Sebrina?"

"Into the Goddess' care. She holds them for safe keeping while we are in our true forms then returns them to us when we change back so we will remain hidden among the humans."

Julianna raised a skeptical eyebrow.

"Change again," Sebrina demanded.

Before Julianna could protest, her Sister form leaped forward, swelling into place, and she stood as a wolf almost immediately. Sebrina clucked her tongue in disapproval, and Julianna growled in frustration.

"Change."

Julianna changed back and forth from her human to wolf bodies until she was exhausted. She'd reached a tentative truce with her Sister self, an acceptance of the leadership Julianna could provide in either form. The wolf remained close to the surface of her awareness. Julianna no longer feared to change into her natural shape. The wolf stopped fighting when they turned human.

"Good glory, I'm tired and hungry." She scrubbed her face with her hands.

Sebrina laughed gently. "I'd believe you are. Come, let's go catch our lunch."

"What?" Julianna blinked in surprise, but there was no one to ask except a salt-and-pepper-colored wolf in the clearing.

The creature stood strong and beautiful, despite the white age showing on the bridge of her nose. She had a thick healthy coat, but life had been lived in the body. The ears still perked sharply, and the golden eyes showed no signs of weakness. A ring of silver spots spattered around her left eye. They didn't appear to be a mark of age, but rather a glittering set of beauty marks matching the tribal tattoo on Sebrina's human face.

Julianna studied the wolf for a few moments until the older female growled impatiently and turned toward the exit trail.

"Oh, right." She shifted to her wolf form and followed Sebrina deeper into the woods.

The next hour seemed like a comedy of errors. Sebrina was an expert in hunting, but the best Julianna could do was snag a couple of stupid and slow rock squirrels after she remembered to mentally step back and let her Sister take over. She was so hungry she didn't have time to be disgusted with ripping and tearing at the animal's body. The chase had been exhilarating, and the victory was sweet. Even the hot blood and muscle was delicious.

After their meal, they napped for a short time in the shade of the trees, though Julianna never fully slept. Her ears kept telling her there were too many other creatures around to completely relax. She rested a little, and when Sebrina rose to her feet, she didn't protest.

The rest of the afternoon was spent leaping, literally, in and out of her two forms. Sebrina made her dive into bushes and undergrowth, changing into a wolf as she went. She was supposed to land on all four feet, balanced and in control. The best she managed was a wobbly landing that filled her coat and ears with prickly spines from the shrubbery. Her nose filled with dust, and she ended up sneezing more, which ruined her balance.

She also had to jump over rocks, shift mid-leap, and roll to her feet as a human. Her body looked like it had been on the losing end of a fight with two cats. Scratches scored her thighs and arms, and her hair was full of twigs. She lost the boundary between herself and her Sister. Sebrina's amusement filled her nose and an industrious woodpecker filled her ears while she dragged herself to her human feet once more.

Exhausted and bruised by the time Sebrina took her home, Julianna stood stupidly at her door for a few moments, trying to remember what she was supposed to do.

*Door, there's a door. What happens next? Oh, yes, unlock the door. Right.*

Reaching into her pocket, she withdrew her keys and her cell phone clunked to the wooden deck. It beeped indignantly, and she mumbled a curse as she bent to retrieve it. Every muscle screamed in protest, and she groaned, glad Sebrina had gone home. Leaning her forehead against the door, she used both hands to open the cell phone and saw her mother's text message.

*Have a great day, dear one.*

Snorting with painful humor, she yanked her body upright, ignoring the pain zipping through her tired muscles, and let herself inside. She choked down some cheese and crackers before she dragged herself to bed. She didn't even bother to undress.

Morning came with aches and pains in muscles she didn't even know she had. She shoved her body into some clothes just in time for Sebrina to show up to take her "hunting". She looked askance at the older woman, but soon understood what she meant.

Julianna found herself in her Sister form belly-down in a thicket of scrub oak, watching a pair of cottontails nervously grazing on the summer scrub growing through the tough soil. She crept closer, freezing as the heads of both rabbits came up, only their noses moving. Her hindquarters bunched beneath her as she prepared to pounce, but some scrub jays exploded out of a nearby pinion pine, screaming bloody murder, and the rabbits bolted. She dropped her butt to the dirt with a frustrated grunt.

Her next attempt was on a wily jackrabbit who'd found a comfortable spot in the shade. Sebrina had told her she needed the element of surprise to catch one of the fast leporids. Julianna angled her approach to cut across the most logical path of escape. She slithered forward on her belly, pausing only when the rabbit's ears twitched in her direction.

She gathered herself, took a deep breath, and shot out of the brush. The jackrabbit burst out of its apparent slumber in a cloud of dead leaves and dust. She knew the creatures were fast, but she'd never had to chase one for dinner. The thrill of the chase lent her speed and strength, but the leporid zigged and zagged so fast, she could barely keep up.

She almost had it in her teeth when the rabbit found open ground and began to pull away from her. She pushed herself just a little faster and lunged. Her teeth snapped together on nothing but shed fur and dust. The leporid bolted in ground-eating bounds, and she flopped down in the dirt, gasping for breath.

Soft laughter filled her ears, and she angled her head so she could see Sebrina sitting beside her, her tongue lolling out in an amused grin.

"I told you surprise is needed to catch leporids," she remarked.

Julianna wuffed a sigh. "I had the element of surprise, just not enough." She panted for a few moments. "Damn, those things are fast."

"Then you must be faster. Get up and try again."

Julianna groaned but heaved herself to her feet as Sebrina led her off to the next hunting opportunity.

Despite her fumbling, she still managed to catch a ground squirrel and was surprised to feel disappointment in letting her prey go. Her Sister wanted to eat it once she'd worked so hard to catch it. Julianna agreed, but Sebrina firmly reminded her to release it. They broke for lunch, and she got to eat a cottontail. It tasted so good she swore it was better than some of the fancy meals she'd had in Fresno's high-end restaurants. She even licked the rock clean of the blood and viscera left from her kill.

After lunch, Sebrina insisted Julianna start tracking by learning the sights, sounds, and scents of the other creatures. Sebrina taught her how to see the signs that something, large or small, had passed by through the undergrowth, and how recently. She also learned the warning scents of skunk before she got sprayed, and when a porcupine hid close by. Julianna trained how to track and disguise herself from the cougars and bobcats prowling the hills. She watched coyotes that thought themselves too smart for her to detect and tracked the sneaky critters straight to their dens. Despite their attempts to take her "kills" for themselves, she liked them and knew she could learn from their adaptive ways.

Julianna spent her entire day as a wolf and enjoyed every moment. It was exhilarating to share her Sister's instincts and abilities. She'd certainly scared the daylights out of several cottontails and rock squirrels. Again, she came home that night conscious enough to text her mother and swallow something before she collapsed in a heap of exhaustion.

Two solid weeks of training and getting to know her Sister form continued from dawn until dusk. Her mother looked at her strangely the few times they saw each other and asked where she'd been during the days. Julianna replied she was taking some time for herself to work out, to deal with her grief, and to get her head on straight. They seemed like the right things to say because her mother stopped asking.

Julianna didn't see Jeff, but she couldn't be sure he hadn't visited her home while she trained with Sebrina. If he had, he never left a note and he didn't have her cell number. She admitted to herself she probably would've been too tired to see him anyway. Her body became stronger, and her stamina increased. Muscles she'd never before seen in her arms and legs suddenly appeared in the mirror when she stopped to look.

She'd become a hermit, the pack and the competition for Luna all but forgotten during her training. Even her frustration with Jeff's behavior at the end of the candidacy party dwindled, though it flared at odd moments, especially as the full Moon approached. She worried her Sister would completely take over again, but Sebrina assured her it wouldn't happen. Julianna had come a long way in healing the rift between her human and lupine selves, and her Sister knew it.

With all the time spent training, she grew familiar with Sebrina and her moods. There was something in the older female's eyes each time she looked at Julianna. She thought it was simple pride at first, but it expanded into more than that, a kind of proprietary joy, as if her improvements in the world of the wolf reflected well on Sebrina. She wanted to know why the woman remained so patient with her obvious lack of skill, but she never had time to ask, and at the end of the day, she was too exhausted to care.

# CHAPTER SEVEN:
## Political Wolves

Sebrina looked Julianna over critically. "Today we'll go for tea. Please dress for town."

"Town?" Julianna blinked. "As in around people?"

"Yes. We've done enough physical training. Now we must strengthen your knowledge of pack policies."

"You mean politics," Juliana remarked flatly.

Sebrina shrugged with a half-smile and sat down on one of the chairs on the front balcony to wait.

Julianna turned around and marched back to her bedroom to change. Unease dogged her heels. Being out in the wilds was one thing, but facing people in town unnerved her. She might run into anyone she shouldn't, like Jeff or the other Luna candidates. What if she wigged out? The full moon approached like a siren's song, and her Sister stalked very close to the surface. She swore she had PMS, Pre-Moonal Syndrome, and her temper had grown short.

*Just keep your cool, Sister. We don't need any more weirdness this close to shifting, okay?*

*Humph!*

Julianna pulled her token over her head and held it in

her hand, studying it intently. Each time she looked at it, her heart danced. The token resembled the wolf's head pendant she'd seen hanging around Jeff's neck, carved with a Celtic knot around the outer edge. It was the size of a fifty-cent piece, the silver tarnished along the ridges. Chips of aquamarine filled the wolf's eyes and glittered in the sunlight from the window as she tilted her hand.

Excitement fluttered through her. The token meant she could have Jeff.

*You will have Jeff. He's your Mate.*

*If I pass the tests.*

*You will.*

Julianna slipped the token around her wrist like a charm bracelet and gathered her hair into a ponytail. She glanced at herself in the mirror before she sailed out into the front room and grabbed her keys and phone. At least she looked presentable.

She suspected that was one of the unspoken tests of the Luna. Even the first lady of the United States had to dress carefully when she ran to the grocery store. Shoving her feet into sandals, she paused long enough to grab her purse and lock her door. Sebrina waited outside.

"Are you hungry?" Julianna closed the door behind her. "We could have breakfast with our tea."

"What a good idea." Sebrina offered an ingenuous smile.

Julianna laughed, and they strolled together in companionable silence until they reached "downtown" Callowwood. They passed the post office with the pale pink granite entry steps beside the old Callowwood Hotel and Saloon where it was rumored Jesse James had once stayed. The Rebel gas station next to the Hotel pulled the town back into the twenty-first century with its shiny pumps with digital readouts.

Milner's Grass and Feed still had the hand-painted wooden flower cutouts decorating the front, and the old, dusty pickup trucks mingling with the fancier Hondas and minivans of the Wells Fargo Banking crowd next door. A Smith's grocery store with slot machines just inside the sliding glass doors sat across the street from the Rebel.

The Wolf's Den took up the block between Cindy's Café and the old Sears that still advertised free roto-tiller rentals with the purchase of a 100 pound bag of fertilizer. The Mobil service station with the red Pegasus on top of the white pole shared a parking lot with Landry's Five and Dime—now more like Ten and a Quarter – where Julianna had once found a five-dollar bill caught in a crack in the pavement. The Ranch Drive-in Movie's yard with the huge white outdoor screen edged the empty desert across from a Sonic Burger that seemed to have lost its way from the interstate. She remembered sharing her first kiss with a human boy behind the big white screen after Jeff had ignored her once again.

*He's definitely not ignoring me now.*

Julianna sighed at the quaintness. Reno had been bright and exciting, but she'd missed the familiarity of knowing where all the roads went and who lived on them.

They entered Cindy's Café, run by Cindy Howington and her four sons. Cindy was a heavily built woman who looked as if she could bench press a Mack truck if necessary. Mousy brown hair, held tight to the back of her head in a bun, pulled at her sharp pale blue eyes, making her squint a little. She was stocky and short, but her shoulders were almost as broad as Jeff's and she had large hands that could palm a basketball. Julianna always expected Cindy to have a voice like a bullhorn, but she spoke melodiously, the tones more suited to a singer of ballads than a greasy spoon owner.

"Sebrina, Miss Morris, good to see you," Cindy called out to them as they stepped across her threshold. "Damn, it's been a long time since you were home. How you been, girl? Your mama keeping you busy over in that house?"

"I'm hanging in there, thanks, Cindy." Julianna took the menus from the other woman. She caught the scent of winter nights under the full moon and realized the café owner was a Moon Singer like herself. "I've been trying to get myself together and it's taking longer than I thought. It's hard to live in that place without Dad."

"I imagine that's so." Cindy nodded, her smile fading. "Well, let's get some food into those bellies and everything will at least feel better. Come on, then, I've got a nice booth where you can see the sun and sky, and I'll get you something to drink."

They followed the stocky woman along the windows facing the street, the sounds of happy conversation mixed with the jangle of cutlery against plates. Cindy moved with a remarkably smooth gait as she led them to a booth with real flowers in a vase near the salt and pepper shakers and the box of sugar packets.

Julianna settled into the squeaky vinyl seat and studied the menu while Cindy returned with a little teapot full of hot tea and two mugs. She winked at Sebrina and smiled, then added, "Take your time," before moving away to help some other customers.

Julianna stared down at the menu as the scents of the café enveloped them. Joy and hunger drifted from some of the other customers. Alternating amusement and frustration wafted to her from the kitchen, and Cindy broadcast satisfaction each time the doorbell chimed with someone's entrance. Delicious odors of cooked oil, fried food, and baking bread brought up memories of happier times.

Everything around her reminded her of the Sunday mornings she'd come with her parents to enjoy Cindy's famous brunch after church. Her mother always fussed with her hair, and her father would wink at her when she rolled her eyes and swatted her mother's hands irritably. Though the café hadn't changed much over the years, Julianna felt the loss of her father as she sat with Sebrina in the familiar surroundings.

*Glory, Dad, I wish you were still here.*

Clearing her throat before she started to cry, Julianna chose Bucky's egg burrito with onions, turkey, and Swiss cheese. Sebrina poured the tea, and the soothing scents of hibiscus and orange filled the air inside their booth. Julianna set the menu down and inhaled memories. Her mother had brewed the same tea to calm her down from some horrible nightmare when she was a child.

Julianna waited patiently for Sebrina to speak. She was reluctant to broach the subject of pack politics. She'd hated the politics within the university faculty, and she couldn't imagine they were much different in a Moon Singer pack. To keep her unease at bay, she turned her head to the window and imagined a 1977 Camaro parked in front of the café, Jeff's sexy body emerging from the driver's side door.

"I know you're feeling the Lady Moon's approach, and you don't like politics." Sebrina tapped the table and Julianna jumped in surprise, tearing herself away from her daydreams. "But you must learn what it's like to be part of this world and how to take the lead."

"I know, I know. We all have to live by the rules."

"We do, and they keep us all safe and in peace." Sebrina nodded. "The packleaders must be more knowledgeable in these rules than the packmembers to protect everyone. For example, our people never refer to themselves or others in our community as anything other than…" Her voice lowered. "West of left field when among the humans."

Julianna stared at Sebrina for a moment, trying to see if she was serious. The older woman seemed too refined to say something so odd. A little laughter escaped, and Sebrina gave her a flat look. Julianna swallowed her giggles and smothered her smile, focusing on the flowers next to the salt shaker as she tried to formulate a proper response.

"West of left field?"

"It's a way to speak plainly without alerting the humans to our true natures. You must understand. Under no circumstances can you reveal who and what you are to the humans. It's why you never truly knew the Lightfoots or the Winthrops. They had to keep their natures hidden from you because they thought you human."

That's why Jeff had ignored her all those years. *He probably got tired of the stupid human flaunting herself at him.* Odd that he couldn't smell through the deception. *I guess I'm really good at hiding my true nature.*

"That makes sense."

"This is now true for you as well." Sebrina sipped her tea. "No matter the circumstances, you must not reveal your true nature to any humans in this town, including your own mother."

"My mother?"

Sebrina nodded. "She is human. To reveal our species to her will endanger not only your life, but the well-being of the pack, and offenders are dealt with promptly and permanently."

Julianna's blood ran cold, and she gripped her tea to warm her hands.

"You mean I'd end up dead."

"Or banished, exiled from Callowwood and never seen or heard from again, at least not here. It's not a lightly made decision. Our peace and security depends on the secrecy of every member of the pack." Sebrina's expression grew implacable. "So even when you're threatened or are trying to save someone from something, you must not move faster or be stronger than an average human woman. The reason I stress this today is you'll be tested, daughter, with just these sorts of situations while a candidate for Luna. And you can be tested at any time, any place, when you're not even thinking about the pack."

Julianna bit the inside of her bottom lip to keep from

snarling. With the full moon so close, she had to be careful, but keeping this secret from her mother ate at her. She owed Beth Morris her life. Hiding her true nature seemed like the worst kind of betrayal.

"So I can't tell my mother. That's just evil. What kind of a daughter keeps this kind of secret?"

"The kind who is meant to be a great leader, a leader who protects more than just herself and those she loves." Sorrow filled Sebrina's eyes. "This is also a protection for the humans. Can you imagine the panic they would suffer if they knew they lived among the Moon Singers who are stronger and faster? Think, daughter. How would they react?"

Julianna grimaced. She couldn't deny the truth in Sebrina's words. Just the thought of the Department of Homeland Security getting their hands on a Moon Singer made her want to vomit. Humans were ruthless when they feared something, and she couldn't condemn any of her rivals to that fate.

She nodded. "You're right. It would be awful. That idea scares me more than my inexperience among the Moon Singers." She rubbed the back of her neck with one hand and sighed. "Jeez, I'm so new to this. I could screw it up without even trying. I know how to be human and how to play their games of appearance, deception, and manipulation. But I don't know anything about the pack. I barely understand the hierarchy rules, alphas versus betas versus omegas, and on down the Greek alphabet. I don't know what makes me alpha instead of beta or omega. Is it my parentage? Is it my bearing?"

Julianna shook her head and turned to look out the window with her lips pressed together.

"I hate caste systems. I hate encouraging others to look down on 'lower ranked' people, and I can't stand when people treat others as beneath them. That's sick and wrong, particularly in this country. I believe in equality and that we can be anything we want to be. Does it have to do with birth order?"

"No, daughter, we all simply have our places."

Julianna scowled and Sabrina's gaze softened after a moment.

"You're alpha because you are yourself, because that is your personality. You're a leader, not a follower, and that's borne out by the way you carry yourself."

"I don't always carry myself with confidence and surety." She rearranged the silverware at her place. "I didn't with my ex-husband. And most of these people don't know me. How can they tell I'm alpha?"

Sebrina paused, her thoughts masked. "It's in how you approach life. When a problem arises, do you wait for someone to save you or do you tackle it yourself?"

"I find ways to take care of it, but sometimes I have to ask others for help."

Sabrina smiled. "Exactly. You are alpha. A beta and omega will look to find the leader to do the work."

Julianna frowned. "But that doesn't mean I'm expecting someone else to serve me like a slave. I might lead, but I'm not a queen."

Sebrina snorted. "So you say. But many alphas don't understand how to treat beta and omega members of the pack. They are to be protected and supported, and they'll want to assist you whether you like it or not. It's an honor for them. They're not to be used harshly or treated like servants. Treat them with respect and honor, and they'll be more loyal than anyone could ask."

"But it seems so demeaning."

Sebrina's voice firmed. "They know their places, daughter, and they accept them. If you defer to them, it will confuse and frighten them. Treat them with honor, but don't try to make leaders out of those who are meant to follow."

"I never thought of it that way." Julianna bit her lip.

"Can a lower ranked packmember ever move up in rank? Like can a beta become alpha or an omega become beta?"

"Yes. A beta may become alpha if an alpha member dies, there is no Alpha leader, or they've gained enough experience. A lower ranked packmember may also move up in rank if he or she is given a position of honor or power. For example, the members of the Alpha's cadre are all betas, but they are high ranking betas even if they didn't start out that way. Once they were nominated for the position of the Alpha's cadre, they rose in rank."

"Is there a hierarchy within the cadre?"

"Of course. Usually the oldest and most experienced betas will be the highest ranked within the group."

"So even an omega can be in an honored position?"

"Yes. Despite this, some alphas have a difficult time treating them with honor."

Julianna snorted. "Yeah, I've seen that. Miss Solaris and the other alphas treat the other packmembers like the dirt under their feet." She swallowed the last of her tea with a grimace. "It's so wrong, it makes me sick. But I can see how the betas and omegas see serving the alphas as an honor if the alpha is aware of their own service. They may be lower ranked, but it only makes my responsibility to them more important."

Sebrina just looked at her for a few moments with approval and something else in her expression. Was it pride and gratitude or sorrow and regret?

"It is a wise leader who looks at leadership as service."

"Thanks...I think."

Sebrina gave her a half-smile. "There's a hierarchy among the alphas as well. It's based on age, seniority, and strength. For example, because she's better known in the pack than you and is related to an old Callowwood family, Mistress Solaris is higher ranked. But you're known to this town since you were a child, even if you weren't considered pack until recently. That places you higher than

Mistress Wolensky, who isn't from Callowwood, but well-known." Sebrina ticked the candidates off on her fingers. "You're more highly ranked than Mistress Cutter because you're older and more experienced in life, even if that life hasn't been with the pack. However, Mistress Winthrop is higher ranked than you because of her familiarity with both the pack and Callowwood. But she's below Mistress Solaris because Mistress Solaris is older and has more experience. You must be careful of both these females, daughter."

Julianna nodded and smiled at Cindy as she meandered to their table. "You ladies ready to order?"

"Yes, ma'am."

Julianna ordered the egg burrito, and Sebrina had steak and eggs. Cindy gave them both a smile and said she'd bring back more tea on her next pass.

"Cindy's not alpha, is she?" Julianna watched the café owner stride through the tables to the kitchen.

"No, she is beta."

"But she's alpha in her own household, right?"

"That's correct. To her children, she will always be higher ranked."

"Good thing. Even human mothers don't tolerate their kids mouthing off."

Sebrina laughed. "I'm sure that's true."

"My mother certainly didn't."

Sebrina immediately sobered, and Julianna caught a stronger scent of regret from the older woman. *What does she have to be sorry about?* It wasn't Sebrina's fault Julianna had grown up with humans. Was that why the Paiute woman helped her learn the ways of the Moon Singers, because she'd been raised human?

"Why are you helping me, Sebrina? Why have you gone out of your way to make sure I know the rules of this game?"

The Paiute woman said nothing for a long time, a mask

of stoicism hiding all her thoughts. Julianna scented roiling emotion, but it was so muted, she couldn't identify it. *What is that about?*

Eventually, Sebrina gave her a half-smile and a single shoulder shrug. "You're new to this, daughter, and you must know for what you've been chosen. Also, I sense in you a seeker of the old and honorable ways. You don't tolerate injustice or undue hurt to others, particularly those in your care. This is a good thing and something the pack needs." Her smile widened into a smirk. "Besides, Jefferson Lightfoot is your Mate, so you must past the tests so you can claim him and he can claim you."

Julianna heard the capital "M" on the word mate, and an odd feeling skittered up her back. The combination of excited lust and indignant fear made her shift in her seat. She raised her head and squared her shoulders as if she faced an opponent with whom she had to do battle. The fear made her angry, and she pulled her lips back a little to expose one elongated canine. She didn't remember it catching on her tongue before.

"There won't be any kind of 'claiming' until I understand exactly what this Mate business is all about," She hoped she'd disguised her growl, but being a prize pissed her off.

Sebrina paused, reading Julianna far more accurately than she would have liked.

"Something about Mating distresses you?" She cocked her head to one side. "It's perfectly natural. You don't smell like a virgin—"

"I'm not a virgin." Julianna clenched her hands into fists, willing her voice to drop. Cindy's son Bucky could probably hear them in the kitchen. "But I'm also not willing to just let any male take what he wants from me. Jeff already tried that at the party, and I set him straight in a hurry."

Surprise bloomed across the older woman's face. If

Julianna hadn't been so angry, she would have laughed. "Did you?"

"Yes. Tell me what gives him the right. Tell me why I shouldn't just cold-cock him and be done with it."

"Because he is your Mate."

Julianna lowered her brows. "That's not an answer."

Sebrina sighed. "You're trying my patience. Your Mate has the right because he's your Mate."

*Yeah, my patience isn't intact either.* "And that means what, exactly?"

"It means he is meant for you and only you."

"Great, but that doesn't explain why he has the right to take liberties without my permission."

Sebrina spread her hands. "What liberties? When you're connected to your True Mate, the agreement is there. It's part of knowing who your True Mate is."

"And how do I know that for sure?"

"Among the pack, there was a gift bestowed upon our people by the Lady Moon, or the Goddess, as many now call Her." Sebrina poured them both more tea. "Not only did She give us long life, but She also gave us the ability to sense our perfect Mates, the one who would protect and serve us for all our lives. It works for both males and females because we mate for life. We'll recognize this Mate by our feelings–the need to touch and breed with this person will be almost overwhelming. Some can scent it and recognize it on others as well as themselves, but most just feel a need for physical intimacy that consumes the Mates. They can barely keep from touching and they feel as if they must copulate each time they are near each other."

*Maybe she does know.* How embarrassing if everyone else did, too.

*Good, then those other bitches will steer clear of your Mate,* her Sister quipped.

"Once the process begins, either through a kiss or mating bite or physical loving, you and your Mate's scents will change, and any west of left field person will know you've mated with your True Mate."

Julianna jerked. "I can't even kiss Jeff until I've passed the tests?"

"No. Also, any person of the opposite sex who touches you, but is not your Mate, will smell and feel wrong to you, as if you have fleas constantly stinging or biting." Sebrina grimaced theatrically and shook her head. "For males, I understand it's like static electricity constantly stinging you. It tingles and pulls like little pinpricks. The Mated partner feels a painful charge or the intruder reeks like a junkyard dog. This only happens after the Mates have begun the mating bond that will hold them together for life."

"All this from a single kiss of a male?"

"No, the kiss or bite from your True Mate."

"There's biting involved?"

Sebrina laughed at her outraged expression. "It's not as bad as you might think."

"And once I find this 'True Mate' and kiss him, any other man who touches me will stink and make me physically uncomfortable?" Sebrina nodded. "How long will that last?"

"It's strongest the first year after mating," Sebrina admitted, "but it fades into the background over the years. You'll always feel uncomfortable being touched by a male not your True Mate, but it won't be excruciating after the first year."

"It'll be excruciating during the first year?" *Sweet glory, what did I sign up for?*

"Not necessarily. Everyone is different."

"Great."

"Be aware, your Mated partner will know it when his female is being touched by another male, just as you'll know when he is being touched by another female. There will be no hiding affairs from your Mate. Nor can he hide them from you."

"Well, that's good," Julianna remarked drily. "I'll know when he's fooling around. That's certainly a step up from before."

Sebrina cocked her head to one side, her eyebrows rising. "Before?"

Julianna grimaced and looked out the window, wishing Jeff's Camaro would drive down the street and whisk her away from the ugly memories.

"My first husband regarded me as a steppingstone to better, and younger, things."

Sebrina growled with such fury Julianna jerked her gaze back to the older woman's face. Her expression was stoic as ever, but her eyes glowed with anger and disgust.

"This will never happen with your True Mate, daughter." Her anger seemed disproportionate to Julianna's story, but perhaps the older woman was incensed on behalf of all women left by philandering husbands. Sebrina didn't seem to have a male with her. Maybe she'd experienced something similar.

"That's good." Julianna waved to dispel the tension at the table. "What other benefits are there in having a True Mate?"

Sebrina shivered a little, and sadness filtered into her expression. "Your strength and longevity increases, and you're never alone in times of danger. Your True Mate will know when you need him."

"That's kinda cool. Is that from the mating bond you mentioned?"

"Yes."

They stopped speaking as Cindy brought more tea and their food. She winked at Julianna and nodded to Sebrina then departed to help others. Julianna filtered through their discussion while she picked up her fork. The scents of her food made her mouth water, but her mind kept going back to some of Sebrina's comments at the candidacy party and earlier.

"How do you know that Jeff is my True Mate or that I'm his?"

Sebrina's smile turned smug and knowing.

"This I have known since your father's funeral. Jeff couldn't stop fidgeting, as if he had to get closer to you and hold you as you grieved."

Julianna snorted. "A lot of people are like that."

Sebrina shook her head. "No, this was unique. Also, your scent changes when he's close to you, just as his changes when you're close to him. He hides it fairly well, but not well enough to escape my notice."

"My scent changes?" Julianna grimaced. "That's just a little creepy."

Sebrina laughed. "Not for Moon Singers. But this is why you were chosen as a candidate for Luna."

"Were you the one to nominate me?"

"I was."

Julianna nodded. "Thanks…I think."

Sebrina sighed. "I know this will be a hard time for both of you because he must make it look like he's considering all the candidates. He must treat them with the same courtesy as he does you, but he has already chosen you in his heart. Now you must pass all the tests so he may claim you."

Julianna frowned, and her feminist side rose to the fore. "That hardly seems fair. Why can't I just claim him? He's my True Mate, isn't he? It'd kill him and me if he mated with another female."

"It would be miserable for you both." Sebrina nodded. "But he'll never Mate with someone else, though he will copulate with the successful Luna candidate to pass on the line. He's the Successor, and the female who stands beside him must pass all the tests, even if she's not his True Mate. He will have to turn away from you if you cannot pass them. He'll have to breed with the female who does pass, and Mistress Solaris will try her best to be that female."

"Won't they all?" Julianna shoved food into her mouth to keep from snarling.

"Yes, but I sense Mistress Solaris is different." Sebrina frowned, and Julianna looked up at her, concerned. "You must be careful of her, daughter. She's dangerous to the unwary. She is strong and willful, a worthy rival, but she isn't always direct in her rivalries. She doesn't understand that the pack is weakened by this."

Julianna felt her Sister rush to the surface. "I will pass the tests, Sebrina, because Jeff is my Mate. Mine."

Sebrina jerked back in surprise and shivered. Julianna let the possessive rage burn through her, reveling for a moment in its heat. Brenda Solaris might pretend she was higher ranked or more deserving of the post of Luna, but Julianna would fight for it, and win.

Sebrina said nothing and Julianna turned her attention to the world outside the café. She had to pass the tests and win her place at Jeff's side. But she had no idea how she'd prepare. She let her mind drift as she watched the few pedestrians amble down the road outside.

One familiar walk caught her gaze and she focused on the man striding down main street. While not tall, she recognized the slender build and the long, straight ponytail hanging down the back. *Is that Leslie Dunmore? What the hell is he doing in Callowwood?* She watched her erstwhile Fresno neighbor stepped into Landry's Five & Dime, a frown pulling on her brows. Why was he here?

Cindy came by to make sure their teapot was full, interrupting her thoughts.

"Everything good here?"

"Yes, thank you, Cindy."

She left the bill on the table with a little nod for them to take their time. Julianna wiped her mouth with her napkin and looked up at Sebrina. The older woman watched her carefully.

"I just have one more question."

"Yes?" Sebrina eyed her warily.

"What about sexual needs during this time? His or mine?"

"Sexual needs?"

"Yeah, you know, during the testing. Can he have sex with anyone not a candidate? Can I?"

"No," Sebrina stated flatly.

Julianna wasn't surprised with the answer. "Why?"

"Because it would reflect badly on you as leaders. If you cannot control your sexual urges prior to becoming the Alpha pair, how likely are you to be able to control the pack as a whole? The packmembers would see it as a weakness, and you'd be disqualified as a Luna candidate."

"What about Jeff? Would he lose his Successor status?"

Sebrina's silence filled the booth.

*Dammit, there's a double standard even among werewolves. That's bullshit.*

"Yes, I believe so," the older woman agreed at last. "But it has never happened before. There's no precedent. But I believe the Alpha would be forced to choose a new Successor or continue as Alpha until another male has challenged and won."

"Huh. Thank you for explaining." Julianna reached into her purse and drew out a twenty as her mind churned with her thoughts. "I think I need some time to think on it. Can I see you tomorrow?"

"Of course, daughter."

Julianna squeezed Sebrina's hand as she rose and retreated from the table, waving at Cindy as she headed out the door. No touching or kissing Jeff, no sex with anyone else, and the need to jump the man stronger than it had ever been before. *It's shaping up to be a great summer.*

One thought offered her bittersweet cheer. At least she'd stopped Jeff from doing something he shouldn't at the party. It had saved both their candidacies that night.

# CHAPTER EIGHT:
## Time Management

Jeff ran through the invoice Kyle handed him while the others unloaded the delivery of beer and hard liquor through the back door of the Wolf's Den. Bottles clinked gently in the boxes as they were stacked in the backroom. Jeff usually loved this process of setting up the bar for the night, but the sight of the different microbrew logos couldn't distract him from the ache in his gut.

He refocused on the invoice. Everything looked to be in order, but he never left a delivery to anyone else. He'd learned that from his father. A true leader took responsibility for making sure things ran well. Being aware of problems before they became huge made the difference between a good leader and a crappy one.

"Looks good, Kyle."

"Thanks, boss."

The man looked a little haggard, and Jeff wondered if he'd been getting enough rest. Hell, Jeff hadn't been sleeping much either, not with his True Mate in town somewhere else.

"You all right?"

"Sure," came the terse reply.

"Eloise?"

Kyle sighed, and his shoulders drooped. "Yeah."

"She still engaged to Scatterstone?"

"Yeah."

"That sucks. But I still think it's gonna work out. She wasn't pleased that Scatterstone told you to back off."

"Oh, I can tell. My phone has been so ringing from her calls and texts."

"Just give it a little time."

"Two weeks isn't long enough?"

Jeff snorted. "Not hardly. Scatterstone's probably muddying the waters. But Eloise is a smart woman. She'll see through him."

It was Kyle's turn to snort, but he didn't disagree.

"I'm gonna go up front. You okay back here?"

Kyle nodded, and Jeff left his beta supervisor to do his job. He wound his way through the stacks of beer and liquor boxes, his mind returning to his own dilemma. He usually inspected the boxes but today he strode directly into the bar to find something to keep him busy. He nodded to a few of the "early" customers sitting at the bar. A few others played pool in the back, but the angle of the sun streaming through the windows stated it was too early to have a large crowd.

Which only meant he had more than enough time to think about Julianna Morris and how much he wanted to sink his cock into her warm, snarling heat.

He groaned involuntarily. *Shut the fuck up.*

*You know it's true*, his Brother insisted.

*Yeah, I know, but it doesn't help that she won't talk to me or even see me. Hell, it's been two weeks since she stomped out of the house after crushing my balls.*

*You're her Mate. You must dominate her. She will come around.*

*Oh yeah, that'll really work.* He shook his head. *Didn't you get the memo at the party? Grabbing her was dumb!*

She could kick his ass six ways from breakfast. But he'd give damn near everything for her to do it again. At least then he could see her while she did it.

He'd had plenty of time to get to know the other candidates for Luna. There were endless dinner invitations, "casual" interactions on the streets of Callowwood. Even Mischa Wolensky had cornered him at the Smith's to "discuss" the benefits of going with organic meats rather than those that were commercially processed. He'd met with them all and had been polite, even cordial, but his insides writhed with the idea they'd want him to touch them. He could barely tolerate their hugs. They smelled off, not quite rancid, but definitely not right.

*Only Julianna is right. She's your Mate.*

*Thanks, genius. I got that already.*

Each of the others proudly wore a silver wolf's head pendant the size of a nickel on a leather cord where it proclaimed them as candidates for Luna. Made of pure silver mined from the hills of Nevada, the tokens were antiques, handed down through the Alpha's family for successive candidates. Though he enjoyed seeing the tokens displayed, he wished he'd seen one in particular. Attached to one gorgeous wrist.

Jeff stopped behind the black lacquered bar and wiped down the glasses from the dishwasher so no water spots marred their surfaces. He wanted to snarl and hurl one of them across the room. Goddess, how long would it take for a decision to be made on the Luna candidates? He was going insane, although his insanity stemmed from his need to see Julianna more than the small annoyances offered by the other candidates.

Gritting his teeth, he closed his eyes and held perfectly still, his hands tight around one of the glass coffee mugs. Goddess, he needed Julianna. Staying away from her, pretending he hadn't already chosen his Luna, frayed his control. His temper shortened in direct proportion to his distance from his True Mate, and it hadn't helped when he'd infuriated her at the party. Was that why she hadn't been around? Was she avoiding him?

*Oh, fuck, I hope I haven't screwed up that badly.*

Panic and despair surged through him, but he refused to be swept along in their wake. He didn't know what she was thinking or feeling. He hadn't seen her. He couldn't just let his fears take over. There was still time. No one had passed all the tests yet to his knowledge. His father would have told him if one had. All he had to do was wait for Julianna to pass. Then this farce would end, and he'd have her in his arms.

*And in bed where she belongs.*

Controlling the surge of lust, Jeff took a deep breath and smoothed his expression, opening his eyes. He'd been doing a lot of that lately, especially after the party two weeks ago. Julianna had left him with aching balls and his heart pounding like the Light Brigade riding into the Valley of Death.

*Damn, she was magnificent, even at the cost of my testicles.* Despite the fire in his groin, he'd wanted to pounce on her and screw her to the wall. But she'd sailed out the door and disappeared for the last two weeks.

Two long, excruciating weeks.

She hadn't even come into town, much less the bar, and he was burning for her. He drove past her house on his way to the homes of the other Candidates, always slowing down to see if she was in her apartment over her mother's garage. But the lights were always off, and he didn't dare knock on her door.

The separation was killing him, though being near Julianna was almost worse. She inflamed his senses, and her scent begged him to take her somewhere private and please them both. He hadn't known she was a Moon Singer eighteen years earlier. But it seemed as if he'd been waiting all that time for her to come back into his life, and now she was nowhere to be found. His dick complained he should've fucked her while at his father's house, but he clenched his jaw and tried to think of something else.

He searched the bar for anything that might take his mind off his missing candidate, but nothing grabbed his attention. Everything around him reminded him of her, and he set the glasses down before he broke them.

Sweep the floor, maybe? No, been done. Wash the bar? No, it was clean. Go help stack the boxes in the backroom? No, Kyle and the others would smell his desperation.

Shit.

He threaded his way through the tables and chairs, checking on the candles in the little holders. All were new, and he finally stalked to the front windows to scan the street outside. His mind wished he could see Julianna's sexy body striding through the late morning sunshine, her nearly black hair catching the light, and he put his hands on the windowsill to lean his forehead against the cool glass.

"Where are you?"

As if the Lady Moon had heard him, Julianna Morris strode past the window in sunlit glory. She wore a deep green blouse that hugged her generous curves, highlighting new muscles in her arms and shoulders. Her butt flexed under light blue denim capris, and he wanted to run his hands over her ass to feel if the muscles were as tight as they appeared. Her brown-black ponytail bounced along behind her with each stride.

The beauty in every step she took taunted him with her body's strength. Her magnetism dragged him toward the doors of the bar, his cock hardening as he moved. Damn, the woman had him on a leash, and she didn't even know it.

"Tell Kyle I'll be back in a little bit!" he yelled as he spotted Zach, knocking over a couple chairs in his haste to get out into the street.

There she was, still striding away from him, as tempting as a desert mirage. He threw his dignity to the winds and sprinted down the sidewalk after her, his heart beating way too fast for the short distance he covered behind her.

He'd almost reached her when she spun around and slid to one side, almost out of reach. If he'd been anyone but a west of left fielder, he would've missed her completely. Instead, he stopped like he'd come to the end of his tether and grinned at her inanely.

"Julianna," he gasped. "I, uh, I saw you pass by the bar and wanted to catch you."

"Catch me?" She frowned.

Damn, he sounded like he was trying to round up horses.

"Yeah, you know, catch you before I missed you. I haven't seen you in two weeks and I, uh, well, I just wanted to see how you were getting along since your dad's death."

*Smooth, jackass, just remind her of the saddest day in her life since she got home. Why don't you ask her about her ex-husband while you're at it? Then you could insult her mother and make it perfect.*

"Oh, I'm okay, I guess." Her shoulders slumped.

He wished he could take her home and tuck her into his bed, making sure she got enough rest. When she woke up in his arms, he could fuck her into exhaustion once more. She'd moan and writhe beneath him, and her glorious almost-black hair would fan out over his pillows. He'd run his fingers through it as she sucked his cock, letting the cool strands slide out of his hands to fondle her perfect breasts.

*Man, you gotta get a grip.*

"Thanks for asking," she said, and he jerked back to reality from his fantasy. "I've been trying to come to grips with everything." When he frowned in confusion, she added, "Now that Dad's gone and all that happened at the party. I've had a lot to think about."

His cock reminded him how she'd felt under his hands

that night. "I guess you would. Hopefully, it wasn't all bad, though."

She studied him with her green and gold eyes, and he mentally smacked his forehead for sounding like a complete idiot. Wasn't all bad? She'd kicked his ass and left angry. Was she still furious with him? He felt like a nervous teenager on his first date. Where had his cool gone? Where was the polished Successor? Why couldn't he talk to her like he could to the other candidates?

*Because you'd rather be laying her down on your bed and licking the hell out of her than talking to her.*

*Holy Mother Moon, I am so screwed.*

"No, not all bad, I guess." Hesitancy marred her voice as she shrugged. "It's a big responsibility to be chosen as a candidate. It was more than I expected after the funeral. To be brutally honest, it scares me a little. I've never thought of myself as a leader, and I've never had so many people depending on me to get something right."

"Yeah, I know what you mean."

She blinked. "You do? I thought you were groomed to be Alpha from day one."

"Yeah, I was. But there's a difference between being groomed for it and it actually coming to pass." He shrugged with a rueful smile. "I kinda always thought my dad would be Alpha forever."

"Oh, I know that feeling." Julianna looked distant and strained, lines etching the edges of her full lips. Jeff wished he could wrap her up in his arms, using his strength to protect her from all the things hurting her. She rubbed her neck, and his eyes caught sight of something dangling below her wrist.

*Dear Goddess, is that...?*

Before he could stop himself, he caught her hand and held it between them so he could see what hung from her arm. She yelped in surprise, but didn't fight him as he drew her hand up to his eyes.

Under her wrist, on a long black cord she'd wrapped around it, hung a silver Celtic wolf's head pendant matching his own. The aquamarine chips in the eyes glittered in the morning sun, and he recognized the small notch in the left ear. He'd stared at it for years and years on his mother. The pendant had belonged her when she was Luna, and he'd completely forgotten about it until now.

"Where did you get that?"

Her eyes widened, and she glanced at the pendant quickly before they narrowed in anger.

"Where do you think I got it?" she snapped, jerking her hand free. "It's my token from your father. He gave it to me before you jerked me into a dark hallway trying to rape me into submission, remember?"

"The Alpha gave you that token? But that was my mother's." It seemed the better part of valor to ignore the rape accusation.

Her expression dissolved into chagrin. "Your mother's? Oh, glory, I had no idea. Do you want it back?"

"Back?" He shot her a blank look then jump-started his brain. "No. No, if the Alpha gave it to you, you should keep it until…until a decision is reached." He closed his hands around her wrist and held the pendant against her coppery skin. "I'm just surprised he'd give this pendant to anyone. He loved my mother to distraction. Her death was like a big hole ripped in his world, and he's been harder and colder because of it. Everything he had of hers he kept close. I haven't seen this pendant since her death."

Jeff stopped, swallowing around the sudden lump in his throat. "He must think pretty highly of you to give you this token."

Julianna stared back at him for a long moment of silence, and he damn near fell into her eyes. Tiny brown flecks mixed with the gold and green in the irises caught the light like buried treasure beneath her dark arching brows. How the hell could she be so sexy just standing there? Her skin was soft in his calloused hands, and her scent seared his nostrils until the world fell away. He wanted to wrap her body up in his arms and never let go.

"I hope you think pretty highly of me, too."

He grinned. "I don't think of anything or anyone else. 'Highly' doesn't even begin to cover it."

An amused smile slid over her lips, transforming her from merely beautiful to exquisite. She had an unusual ring of beauty marks around her left eye, but it gave her an exotic air that turned him on. He resisted the urge to pull her against his body and crush her lips with a bruising kiss, but his good sense, and memory, prevailed. Barely.

*I want to kiss her,* his Brother whined.

*Yeah, but I don't want her to kick me in the balls again. She'd at least be close.*

"Good." She nodded sharply. He felt heat bloom in his chest. "It's about time."

He laughed. "Yeah, well, sometimes I'm a little slow on the uptake."

"Better late than never."

"So, are you free this evening?" Not that slow.

"I'm sorry?"

"I'd like to take you out to dinner tonight."

"You would?" Then she glanced around to see if anyone was watching them. "Aren't you supposed to visit with all the other candidates, rather than just me?"

"What do you think I've been doing while you were gone for two weeks?" He threw his hands out in frustration then bit his tongue with a grimace. What was wrong with him? "Sorry. Yes, I have to visit with all the candidates, but I've spent the last two weeks socializing with them, and I haven't seen you once. I figure I have to make up for the last two weeks."

Her smile bloomed again. "Did you meet with the other candidates in public?"

"Actually, we had dinner at their homes, with their

families in residence, so we were definitely not alone."

"Would you prefer to have dinner at my place, then?"

He'd love nothing better, but he knew the mating heat would give them no quarter, and he wouldn't be able to stay away from her. They'd end up with his cock in her pussy, and the whole pack would know it. Probably before they'd even finished.

She saw his hesitation and blushed, embarrassed. "Sorry, I'm still learning the rules of this competition."

Jeff reached out and stroked her cheek with one finger, trying to ignore his body's feverish reaction to her closeness. "I'd love nothing better than to be alone in a room with you, but I'm not sure I could control myself."

"Yes, and it sucks." She shot him a bittersweet smile. "Another time, then."

"Only at your place. Tonight, I'd like to take you out. Still want to go? We could take my Camaro."

Her eyes sparkled as she laughed, and he reveled in the sound. "You will finally take me out somewhere in your black Camaro? I've always wanted to see the inside of that car."

*I've always wanted to see the inside of your pussy.* He had to think of changing the oil on said Camaro before he gave himself away.

"Great, then dinner it is." He hoped his smile didn't look strained. "I'll pick you up about seven o'clock and we'll go to—"

"The Sawmill?"

"Better not. One of the other candidates' family owns that restaurant, and it'd be awkward for them to see us together. It's best to keep the meetings discreet even if everyone knows they're happening."

"Right, sorry, I wasn't thinking." She flipped her ponytail with her hand. "Where would you rather go?"

"How about to Wipple? I know a fairly decent restaurant there that's good."

"What, the Sonic isn't really your style?"

Jeff snorted derisively. "Much as I like burgers, Sonic just doesn't say commitment to me. It says something more like 'I'm a pimple-faced geek who wants to show off his high school girlfriend everyone said he'd never get'. I'm a little too old for that."

She laughed, and he felt his cock harden again. *Damn, I'm gonna have blue balls for a week.* He loved to hear her laugh, and he couldn't wait to make her do it again.

"Okay, Wipple it is, then. Casual or fancy?"

"Casual." He hoped she'd keep on the clothes she wore now.

"Okay."

She seemed to be working up to say good-bye until the evening. Desperate to spend more time with her, he blurted, "So where are you going now?"

"I was going back home. Why?"

"Can I walk you?"

Julianna snorted with humor. "It's not like it's dark or far. I think I can make it. Besides, aren't you at work?"

Jeff shrugged one shoulder. "They can keep the place together for a few minutes without me." He winked at her. "You said it's not far."

She laughed. "Okay, Jeff, you can walk me home. Are you sure you aren't a pimple-faced geek with his high school girlfriend?"

"I won't tell if you don't." He fell in beside her as she grinned. "So, where have you been for the last two weeks? I haven't seen you around town at all."

"I've been hanging out with Sebrina. She's been teaching me about…"

Her voice trailed off, and she turned her head to scan the street ahead. He scented her uncertainty and wished he could reassure her. About what, he didn't know, but he'd move heaven and earth to settle any fears she had.

"She's been filling me in on the events within

Callowwood for the years I've been gone. She's had some pretty interesting stories."

Jeff snorted. "I bet. I'm probably in most of them."

Julianna looked at him with a raised eyebrow. "Not in the ones she's been telling me. Is there something I should know about you, Jeff?"

He widened his eyes in mock fear and put up his hands. "Oh no. No, no. Nothing you need to know."

"Right."

She matched his grin, but it soon faded as she fell back into the thoughtful silence he'd interrupted when he caught her on the street. Her mind was definitely on something, but she didn't wear her thoughts on her sleeve. He frantically searched for something to say to keep the conversation from stagnating.

"So, have you been working since you've come home?"

Yeah, okay, not the best line, but it was all Jeff could come up with on short notice.

"Hmm? Oh, no, but I've been thinking about getting a job to help Mom out with the property taxes."

"A job? What kind of job?"

"I was hoping to find someplace with a managerial position available." Julianna shrugged. "I might as well use the things I learned while in Reno and Fresno to keep Mom and me afloat."

"I think I might be able to help you with that," he heard himself say, though he had no idea where it came from.

"You do?"

"Yeah, I just happen to have a bar that needs a good manager."

She eyed him for a moment. "Isn't that what your job is?"

"No, I'm the owner." *Who is this guy using my voice?* "I oversee payroll and ordering. I need a good manager who can oversee scheduling the wait staff, bartenders, and bouncers, and make decisions on the floor when I'm not available." *Whoever he is, the guy sounds really confident.*

"Don't one of your cadre do that, like Zach or Kyle?"

He shook his head. "Zach oversees security, both physical and electronic, and Kyle keeps track of stock and maintenance. We're all busy."

She bit her bottom lip while she considered his suggestion as they walked. He desperately wished she was biting his bottom lip in passionate lovemaking.

"Are you serious or are you just teasing me? I don't want to come in for a job that belongs to someone else and find out I'm kicking them to the curb. Is this for real or something you just made up on the fly?"

How to answer that one honestly? In truth, Jeff had been thinking of hiring someone to take over some of the duties bogging him down. He got less and less done at the bar with all the other odd jobs cropping up. Scheduling was a big one. But he'd forgotten about it in all the commotion over the Luna candidacy. Now the idea seemed a great one when Julianna mentioned looking for a job.

"I don't have a manager right now," he admitted, "but I've been thinking about hiring one because there's so much to do and I can't be everywhere at once. I could really use the help. So the job is made up on the fly right now, but I do need someone to fill the position. You think you might be interested?"

"I'm interested if it's real." She nodded. "Should I send you my resume and other credentials so you can make it official without it looking like you're just trying to get into my pants?"

Incredulity slid through him. *Did she really just say that?*

*Be honest, you do want to get into her pants,* his Brother quipped.

*Yeah, but that's not why I offered her the job.*
*Oh yeah, why then?*
*To keep her close and see her every day without making*

*it obvious that I'm favoring her over the others.*

"Wow, you don't pussyfoot around, do you?" He laughed.

"Never found a reason to do so."

He snorted. "Yes, send me your resume. It'll help me preserve my reputation as a fair and objective employer."

She laughed again, and his heart swelled in his chest. *Goddess above, I can listen to that forever.* And he would, once she'd passed all the Luna tests, but damn, he didn't want to wait. The sunlight danced over her body, highlighting the curves and hollows exposed by her clothes. The delicate shadow between her breasts called to him, urging him to press his nose to the soft flesh.

He cleared his throat. "In fact, why don't you bring it by in about an hour and I can get you familiar with the way the place runs."

"An hour."

"Yeah."

They stopped at the corner of her street, and everything inside him protested at letting her go on alone. Her scent teased his nose, taunting him to walk her all the way home, inside her door, to tuck her into bed.

"I'll see you in an hour." She held out her hand to him, and he grasped it, fighting the urge to drag her into his arms and kiss the hell out of her.

"And for dinner. Pick you up at seven tonight."

"Yes, dinner, too. I look forward to it."

"Me, too." *Man, do I look forward to it.*

"Good." She retrieved her palm as if reluctant to let go, but she smiled her brilliant smile and sauntered away, her ass twitching in those tight denim capris. His cock rose to attention in salute.

*Down, boy. You have to be a gentleman tonight.*

*Only on the outside*, his Brother remarked smugly.

Shit, he was in so much trouble. Why the hell had he offered her a job in his bar? He'd see her all the time, and he wouldn't be able to touch her. Man, he was so fucked. Despite his penchant for blue balls, Jeff turned to walk back to the bar with an ear-to-ear grin that just wouldn't quit.

**\*\*\*\***

Julianna took a deep breath and grasped the handle to the bar's door. "You can do this. It'll be fine."

She hadn't been back to the bar since the funeral and she didn't really want to face anyone who might think of her as more of an interloper. But Jeff had offered her a job and wanted her resume. *It'll be fine.*

Jeff stood at the bar and looked up with a smile. "Hey Julianna. Thanks for coming in."

She nodded and tried to ignore her excitement. It always flared when he did more than nod politely to her.

"Let me introduce you around."

He introduced her to Zach Bushman and Kyle Howler, his two best friends who worked as Jeff's "right-hand men" at the bar and behind it. Through her new partnership with her Sister, Julianna could tell both were betas, but she sensed given their own place or a little more age and experience, they'd be alphas.

Both of them treated her with respect and deference when Jeff introduced her as the next staff manager.

"Glad to have you coming on, Ms. Julianna." Zach nodded his blond head. "We could use someone with good organizational skills for the staff."

"Hey, I haven't done that bad." Jeff thumped Zach's shoulder.

"You haven't done that great, either."

Kyle watched her with dark eyes full of secrets, but he shook her hand readily enough, palm up. She projected confident authority as they showed her around the bar. The result was immediate respect and probationary loyalty.

Julianna met the waitstaff, a collection of betas and omegas ranging in age from twenty to "forty-five", and mostly women. Sebrina's remark about Jeff's age was confirmed by Kyle's uncle Gary, the oldest barkeep in the Den, still cracking at "eighty-eight", who didn't look older than his mid-forties.

*Is this what I can look forward to when I get older?*

The women staff members watched her without emotion or welcome, but Julianna didn't sense outright hostility. Everyone understood she was on probation until she'd proven she could do the job. No one made any remarks suggesting the only reason she'd been offered this job was because Jeff wanted her above the other candidates, but she read it in the eyes and body language. Even the bouncers, all betas strong and loyal to Jeff, showed reserve, but they remained respectful and just willing enough to give her a chance. Julianna knew she'd have to earn her place.

*I hope that doesn't take too long. If I'm gonna be Luna, I suppose this is a good place to show my leadership skills.*

*About time you got around to accepting your place.*

"So, do you still want the job?" Jeff led her back to the office and settled behind the work desk housing a computer.

She remained standing. "Yes, please. I can see where you need the help and I can think of a couple places where things could be improved. If you're still okay with offering me the job, I'm interested."

He let out a relieved breath. "Thank the First Canid. After we started explaining what we had in mind, I realized what an unorganized mess it is in here."

She grinned. "Yeah, I didn't want to say anything until I got the job, but I have some ideas on how to streamline."

"Great." He rose and held out his hand, palm down. She resisted the urge to frown and shook. "Are we still on for this evening?"

"Yes, if you don't mind going out with your employee."

"Tonight I'm going out with Luna Candidate Julianna Morris. You're not an employee until tomorrow." He grinned.

"Ah, I see. Then yes, I'll see you tonight." She reluctantly released his hand and headed for the door. "Thanks again for the opportunity."

"My pleasure."

Now why did that sound like more than just a pleasant rejoinder?

# CHAPTER NINE:
## Save the Date

Julianna sighed and shifted her weight in her heels as she leaned against the railing in front of her apartment. She listened for the engine of Jeff's Camaro bringing the sexiest man she'd ever met closer to her home. Her nipples hardened with the thought of him taking her out, and she rubbed them to relieve the pressure. She'd stopped by her mom's house after her interview and told her all about the new job and the date. Beth had been thrilled for her, more about the date than the job, but she'd wished Julianna good luck.

Passion and arousal zipped through her as her thoughts returned to Jeff. A mixture of excitement and trepidation bounced in her chest. *Glory, I'm as jittery as a teenager.* She hoped she didn't do anything really stupid tonight, like drop her drink on herself or snort when she laughed. That would ruin the image of a confident Luna candidate in a hurry.

Fidgeting with the tasseled ends of her paisley-patterned silk wrap, Julianna kept her eyes trained on the road beyond the driveway. Would Jeff like what she wore? Did she look the proper mix of demure and hot? She was certainly sweating. She'd pulled her hair up into a French twist and worn actual makeup in hopes of knocking his socks off.

If he didn't knock hers off first.

The sleek black Camaro pulled into her drive, the growling engine soaking her panties with liquid excitement. Her nipples hardened again, and she held her arms still to keep from rubbing them. Her heart skipped a beat as Jeff pulled up and stepped out of the car.

*Oh sweet glory, he's fuckin' gorgeous.*

Jeff had chosen to wear a pair of long khaki shorts and an olive-green Hawaiian shirt with a large leaf print on it in shades of tan and cream. He wore no jacket, but she thought she could see one in the car. Leather sandals covered his sexy feet and she tried not to stare at his legs too long. They were muscular and tanned, the dark hair marking each dip and hollow of his masculine strength. He was built like an athlete in his prime, hard and robust. She shivered at the idea of running her hands over all that exposed skin.

"Wow," Jeff breathed, jerking her back to the present. "You're beautiful."

Her laugh broke free with delighted abandon as her insides warmed to his compliment.

"Thank you. So are you."

"Thanks."

His eyes flared with intense interest as she descended the steps. "No one will see me tonight, though. Everyone will be looking at you. Including me."

Julianna laughed again. He made her giddy.

Jeff strode around the front of the car and opened the passenger door for her, his assessing gaze taking in every detail of her outfit. Before she could slide into the cool, dark interior, he caught her right hand with the token dangling from it and kissed the inside of her wrist, sending a frisson of electricity zinging up her arm. She gasped as his golden-brown eyes watched her intently, a small smile tugging at the corners of his mouth despite his kiss.

"Is that how you greet all the candidates for Luna?" she whispered.

"No." He flipped her hand over. "This is how I greet the others." Then he laid another soft, sensuous kiss on the back of her hand near her knuckles.

The soft brush of his mustache and the heat of his lips liquefied her body. She locked her knees to keep from collapsing and hoped he hadn't kissed the others as sensually. The thought made her growl, but she shifted it into a wistful moan and his lips curled into a delighted smile. She definitely wanted him to kiss her more often and in many more places than just her hands.

He closed his eyes as if tasting a special treat and inhaled deeply. Julianna shivered again, and Jeff's musky, male scent slammed into her awareness, spiced with a hint of arousal. She wanted to pull him into her arms and rub up against him, soaking in the heat of his body and the strength of his muscles. Only the knowledge that she'd hurt their standing in the Pack kept her still.

"Damn, you taste and smell good, Julianna." He back from her reluctantly. "Come on, we better get in the car and go before I drag you up the stairs and into real trouble."

She whimpered as he released her but slid into the seat, trying to still her breathing. Sebrina had been right. The thoughts and feelings washing through her while Jeff held her hand were enough to overpower her civilized mind. And it was only going to get worse from here on out. How the hell were they going to be able to keep their hands off each other now that she was working for him in his bar?

*Sweet glory, I am in so much trouble. The whole pack is gonna know I'm hot for him.*

*Good. That will keep those other bitches out of your way.*

Julianna doubted Brenda Solaris would take any heed.

She swallowed hard and clicked her seatbelt around her with shaking hands. Jeff paused outside his door, cracking his knuckles and inhaling slowly.

*Maybe I'm not the only one affected.* He opened the door and sat in the driver's seat. He looked at her and laughed a little breathlessly before starting up the Camaro. She grinned at him as they headed to the highway.

The drive was tension-filled only because they tried so hard to keep their hands off each other. Julianna held her purse and the door handle with white knuckles. *I gotta get this arousal under control.* She didn't have much hope of that. Her nipples were as hard as stone, and her pussy ached with excitement. It was all she could do to breathe normally.

"Where are we going tonight?" She tried to sound casual, but her voice squeaked until she cleared her throat.

Jeff shifted in his seat and his jaw clenched as he stared at the road. "I thought we'd head to The Macaroon in Wipple. Good food and pretty good service." The muscles in his arms flexed when he shifted gears, and his hands tightened around the steering wheel until his knuckles, too, were white.

"Isn't that the place with palm fronds in their front doors and door men with top hats and tuxedos?" She recalled the place when she attended a friend's graduation party back in the day.

"Yep. They've been there a long time. No valet, but still classy."

Jeff donned a light cream-colored sport coat when they found a parking space in front of the restaurant. He gave her a sweet smile and walked around the car to open the door for her. She took his hand and suppressed the urge to wriggle. When he placed a hand on the small of her back as they walked through the front doors, she felt his touch all the way to her soul.

The maître-d' led them to a table on the back veranda,

and Julianna closed her eyes. She took in the scents of the foods around her, the people enjoying it, and musky scent of Jeff's arousal. Her nose had become so sensitive she could detect the emotional scents of the patrons—fear, nervousness, joy, lust, anger, and curiosity.

*So weird.*

Jeff pulled out her chair and she folded herself into it with a sigh. He sat across from her, his gaze taking in her clothing and cleavage. She tried to focus on the menu, but her mouth watered for something entirely different than the Macaroon's selections.

"Hungry?"

"Very." She licked her lips.

"Do you know what you want?"

"Oh yes." She nodded, but shrugged. "Unfortunately, it's not currently on the menu."

"Oh?" His brows came together. "What's that?"

She looked up at him, met his golden-brown gaze, and smiled slowly.

"I'm not sure what the proper term is, but I think it has something to do with cocks and kittens."

Where the hell had that come from? She'd never been so vulgar on a date before in her life. She almost apologized, but Jeff's eyes sparkled, and he took a deep breath, shivering a little as he exhaled. He reached for his water and gulped down several swallows before he cleared his throat.

"That's a very specialized dish, my dear." His smile turned predatory. "Unfortunately, it's not available tonight, not that I'm not tempted. I think the fare here is far tamer than that. Is there anything else on the menu that looks good?"

Julianna swallowed hard and drank some water herself before her eyes dropped back to the lists of food available. It was hard to think beyond her raging arousal and the scent of his. *Damn, I gotta get a grip.* She bit her lips and chose the top sirloin with roasted red potatoes and steamed broccoli.

"Nothing looks as good as you, but I'll just have to get over my disappointment."

He laughed as the waiter returned and took their order, pausing long enough to look Julianna over with appreciation as he asked if they'd like wine. He was subtle about it, but Jeff's expression hardened and his body tensed.

Julianna raised an eyebrow and declined the wine, trying not to let her nose wrinkle the waiter's stench. *Do they all smell this bad?* Jeff didn't growl, but his eyes followed the young man until he disappeared.

"It's good that he didn't touch you." Jeff bit off each word.

"Yes, it is, for all our sakes. He smells terrible."

"What?"

"Yeah, like moldy cheese and cheap cologne." Her nose wrinkled. "Yig."

He laughed. "'Yig?'"

"You don't say 'yig'?" She gave him a look of wide-eyed innocence.

He shook his head, his lips curling into the sexy smile she loved.

"How about 'wuff'?" She waved her hand in front of her nose with a theatrical grimace. "Cologne is nasty. I didn't even like it before…"

She almost said "before I was west of left field" but added lamely, "Before I came home."

Jeff looked at her for a moment, a small frown creasing his brow, but their salads arrived. Julianna was grateful for a small reprieve. If she was chosen as his mate—when she was chosen—she'd eventually have to tell him about her inexperience as a Moon Singer.

*But tonight is not the time*

"Are you glad to be back in Callowwood?" he asked,

changing the subject.

"Yes, I am." She nodded. "It's nice to see Mom again and all the familiar places in town. Not too much has changed since I left."

"No, we're pretty much in a time warp."

She grinned. "That's what I thought. But I have to admit the best part is seeing you again." She paused, gathering her thoughts. "I honestly didn't think you'd be interested in me. In fact, I thought you'd be married with, like, a hundred kids by now."

He snorted and shook his head. "No, I never found anyone who seemed right. And then there was the whole issue with me being my dad's son."

"Yes, I guess that could make it pretty difficult to choose just anyone."

"I have chosen."

The words rumbled so low she doubted the other diners around her could hear him. But they thundered all the way down to her pussy. His eyes blazed at her as he took a drink from his water glass, but he said no more about it.

Julianna cleared her throat and nodded, trying to still her heartbeat. Unfortunately, the excitement and his scent were revving it up. She wanted to drop her fork and lunge across the table at him, snarling and wrestling to decide who'd be on top. She tightened her grip on her silverware and tried to think about cleaning a backed-up toilet or scrubbing an overly greasy pot, anything to keep her hormones under control.

"Good glory, is this going to get any easier?" she demanded under her breath.

"As I understand it, it only gets worse until we do something about it."

Jeff's jaw and fist clenched, though the rest of him looked calm. How the hell did he do that? She felt like she was going to leap out of her chair.

"And we can't until I've passed the tests, right?"

"Right."

"Shit."

"Yeah." He grimaced and stuffed his mouth full of salad.

"So what do we do now? What do we talk about to distract us?"

"I don't know."

"Well, what did you talk to the others about when you visited them?"

He grimaced and rubbed the back of his neck with one hand. "Mostly, it was all small talk centered around their gratitude for my visit. The mothers pointed out their daughter's most 'attractive' attributes while the candidates preened." He stopped, snapping his mouth closed. "I probably shouldn't be telling you this."

"I'm sorry, I shouldn't have asked. I'm just trying to find something to think about other than…well, you know."

Jeff laughed. "Yeah, I know. I appreciate it, but I think we should stick to more innocuous subjects."

Julianna raised her eyebrows. "Innocuous? Okay. What did you discuss with the others?"

"The most pressing issues facing the group today: development, expansion, membership maximums, and discipline within the ranks." He shrugged as he picked at his salad. "It was interesting to know how they felt the group should be run and what changes they'd make, but each one put her family first. It seemed to be more of a power-play than an improvement."

"How do you feel the group is running? What would you do about those major issues you mentioned?"

He stared at her a moment. "You really want to talk about this now?"

"No, I want to distract us away from the need to jump each other's bones."

He threw back his head and laughed, and some of the tension flowed away. "I like the way you think."

He grinned and launched into his concerns. He never used any words revealing he was the Successor to a pack of werewolves, but she filled in the proper terms. He was amazing, and she realized she had to learn to speak the same way to keep her species safe from human hysteria.

Julianna listened intently and asked a few questions, but she didn't remember much of the conversation. She'd been concentrating so hard on keeping her mind away from the motion of the muscles in his shoulders when he gestured or the way the light danced in his intense eyes. She loved it when she coaxed a smile or laugh from him. He had the endearing habit of rubbing the right corner of his mouth with his index finger when he thought something through.

"Are you ready to go home?" Jeff signed the check and set it aside.

"Yes."

He chuckled. "Have you heard much of what I said?"

"No. Is there going to be a quiz later?" She pushed her chair back and stood.

He laughed. "No."

"Good."

He took her arm as they retreated to the car. Need and desire fired her blood and her Sister whined, but Julianna gritted her teeth and held on. Jeff's tension never eased, either, but he kept his touches tame until they got home. He turned off the car and they sat for a few moments in silence, only the popping of the cooling engine breaking the quiet.

"Thanks for the nice time." She shot him a smile.

"That was a nice time?" He gaped at her.

"Yes." She shrugged. "I like being with you, even if I can't jump you." She grimaced. "If nothing else, it'll make our first time together that much more pleasant."

"Or more desperate," he muttered.

She sighed, resigned. "Yeah, or desperate."

"I was stupid to hire you."

"What?" Her guts clenched. Would he fire her? "Why?"

"Because now I'm going to see you every day, and it's going to kill me." He gave her a pleading look. "How the hell am I going to hide that I want you?"

"Oh." She grimaced. "I don't know. I'm pretty sure the whole damn pack can smell me coming with how wet I am all the time."

He took a deep breath and smiled lazily. "I sure can."

"Shut up." She shook her head. "At least the humans can't smell it. I'd never live it down if my mother found out. Of course, I may not live it down when your sister realizes it."

He grunted in rueful agreement.

"Jeff, does the overwhelming desire for each other mean we're meant to be mates for life? Like True Mates?"

He glanced at her quickly before turning his eyes back to the world outside.

"I think so. I've never felt it before for anyone, even when I was young, dumb, and full of myself. I was a horny teenager like the next guy, but I was never unable to control myself. I'm having a helluva time around you."

His honesty amazed her. It was refreshing and unnerving at the same time. *I should probably reciprocate.*

"Because I was raised by human parents, I never learned about this thing called the mating bond until Sebrina brought it up." She fidgeted with her shawl. "What do you know about it?"

He raised his eyebrows, but nodded. "I guess that makes sense. Your folks wouldn't have known about it."

"Nope."

"Well, what I know about it I learned from things Dad mentioned and from watching other packmembers go through it." He paused, rubbing his chin. "The males get all twitchy and aggressive, like they are gonna put you through a wall if you go anywhere near their woman. And the females get even more standoffish with every guy but their Mate, as if you suddenly stink or are wearing the wrong clothes. Both the males and females get more touchy-feely, like they just can't stop touching each other, and they smell like mixtures of each other for a long time after they Mate."

"That's what Sebrina told me. But what about love?"

She grimaced apologetically when he stiffened. "I know the L-word's the worst thing to hear on a first date. But have you noticed if the pairs seem to love each other? It can't just be lust and sex, can it?"

"I don't know. I don't think so. The ones I've seen really care deeply for each other, and there's been no infidelity because it's just impossible, or so I've been told." Jeff shrugged. "Dad said that touching another female after he Mated with Mom was like wearing gloves made from nettles. Mom died in a car accident fifteen years ago, and he hasn't gone near another female since, although he says it's easier the longer she's gone."

She stared at him, aghast. "You mean he can't take pleasure from anyone else, even now?"

"I don't know. I didn't ask" He grimaced. "I hope not."

"Glory, me, too."

Silence filled the car as they both ruminated, the crickets singing in the night air. Julianna felt overwhelmed, not only with her attraction for Jeff, but with the repercussions of it once she'd mated with him. If she lost him for some reason, sex would be awful, something she'd never considered. And she'd be damned if she'd let some horny alpha male use her for sex.

But there was no way in hell Julianna would give up. Even if their relationship ended up being short, she wouldn't give up the opportunity to have it.

"That won't scare me off, you know." She turned back to him with a smile. "I'm still going to pass all the tests, and I'm still your Mate."

Jeff caressed her with his eyes and his smile. "Good."

He got out and walked around the car to open her door, but stepped out on her own. He took her hand and led her up the stairs to her front door.

"Thank you for taking me out tonight." Glory, she ached to ask him for more.

"You're welcome. I enjoyed it." He rolled his shoulders in his jacket. "Well, most of it."

"Yeah. I guess I'll see you tomorrow."

"Tomorrow?" A blank look crossed his face.

She smirked at him and winked. "All day and most of the night. I start at one, don't I?"

He paused, his eyes clouded with lust, until his memory caught up. "Oh, right. One o'clock, yes, that's the time you start, right."

"I'll be there." She stepped close and wrapped her arms around him in a hug. A long, hard ridge of flesh pressed against her belly.

His arms squeezed her tightly, and he buried his nose in her neck, inhaling deeply.

"Good night, my sweet Lupine. I'll see you tomorrow."

"Good night, Jeff. Thanks again."

He reluctantly let her go, and she made herself turn and unlock her door before her body overrode her mind. She hadn't missed the sign of his arousal, nor the scent of his desire, but she forced herself into her home. She locked the door behind her as much for her own sake as his.

She needed to keep her distance, even if neither of them really wanted to. Julianna kicked off her shoes and trudged to her bedroom, cursing up a blue streak. How the hell was she going to remain aloof? She stripped and fell into bed, her body too hot and lusty to put on her t-shirt. Her nipples tightened, making her groan.

*Good glory, how am I going to pretend I don't want him at work?*

# CHAPTER TEN:
## Spicy Dreams

Julianna woke with a start and opened her eyes, lying still and listening hard. What the hell was that? Something had jerked her out of sleep, but her ears picked up only her thundering heart.

The hair on the back of her neck twitched. Silver moonlight painted wide strips of light on the floor of her room, making the shadows seem deeper than usual. She took a deep breath to calm down, but it hitched as a dark shape drifted across the carpet and paused at the foot of her bed.

*Oh glory, what is that and how did it get in?*

The creature stood on its hind legs and shifted shape from wolf to man with the sounds of straining muscles and cracking tendons. She inhaled in surprise and caught the scents of warm summer night and mountain streams. When he'd shifted completely, he leaned on his hands at the foot of the bed, his golden eyes blazing in the hot darkness.

*Where's the AC when you need it?*

Julianna's heartbeat kicked up higher, but not from fear. "Jeff? What are you doing here?"

"I came for you." His voice rumbled deep into her

breast bone and she inhaled his arousal.

"You didn't wear clothes?" It was an inane question, but having him naked in her bedroom had short-circuited her brain.

"I don't need them tonight." Jeff pushed onto the bed and crawled up over her body, trapping her beneath the covers. "Not for what I have planned."

The moonlight caressed the hard, naked muscles, and cream flooded her pussy in a delicious rush. His cock hung stiffly below his belly, the flared head pointing straight at her. She wanted to run her tongue over the slit weeping pre-cum. She tried to pull her arms out of the bedding, but he held her still. She whimpered and writhed in an effort to free herself.

"What's wrong, my little Lupine?" Arousal roughened his gravelly voice. "Is there something you need?"

"Please, Jeff, let me touch you," she whispered.

"Not just yet." He leaned forward and nuzzled her neck. "Ah, Julianna, you smell so damn good."

The sensations of his nose and breath against her skin shot pleasure straight to her core, and her nipples hardened. She moaned and arched her back, rubbing the taut nubs against the sheets as she sought relief.

"Oh, glory, Jeff. What are you doing to me?"

"What I've wanted to do from the moment I saw you at the funeral." He stroked his tongue down her throat onto her chest. He peeled back the blankets enough to expose her breasts and sat back to look at her in the dim light. "My, my, my. You sleep naked, lovely Mate. How lucky for me."

Jeff grinned and the flash of his elongated canines set her Sister to growling with approval. The growl erupted from Julianna's chest and she shifted her shoulders, making her breasts jiggle. His molten gaze riveted to her swaying nipples and his grin faded into intensity.

"I want you, Julianna. Here. Now."

He dropped his head and took her lips, thrusting his tongue between them as if he had a right to be there. Her squeal of protest ended in a long moan when his taste hit her tongue. Earthy, male, and so dominant, his flavor exploded in her mouth and sent cream flooding between her nether lips.

Julianna tilted her head to take more of his wicked tongue, wriggling harder until she worked one hand free. She speared her fingers into his shoulder-length hair and held his head where she wanted it while their tongues battled for supremacy.

He pulled away and stared at her, his chest rising and falling with each breath. The aquamarine eyes of his wolf pendant winked at her and she imagined it nuzzling her pendant when they came together, like True Mates.

Mates...mates, why did that thought make her nervous? Wasn't there something about the pack she was supposed to remember? Jeff pulled more of the blankets away and licked the soft skin on the undersides of her breasts. Her thoughts splintered and scattered, but she held onto one shard of warning.

"But Jeff, what about the pack and the tests?" Her Sister barked, *Are you crazy? Don't make him stop.*

"To hell with the pack and the tests." He pulled the covers away from her mound. "You're my Mate, chosen by the Goddess, not some political pageant. And I've waited for you long enough." He buried his nose in the hair of her mons. "Oh, Goddess, your scent is fucking amazing."

The sensation of his beard hairs dragging against her nether lips nearly shot her into orbit and Julianna fisted the sheets to keep from launching off the bed. When he stroked his tongue over the hood of her clit, she keened an ecstatic wail as stars exploded against her eyelids. Pleasure swamped her mind and the wet heat of his mouth melted her core.

"Oh, glory, Jeff. Do that again."

He chuckled and sat back, yanking the bedclothes off entirely. She growled at him and wiggled her hips in invitation, and he cocked his head with curious intensity. She reached out with one hand and grasped his hard, jutting cock, rubbing the pad of her thumb over the head slick with pre-cum. He hissed with pleasure as she sat up and slid her other hand around his hot, tight balls.

"I love the feel of your sack in my hands." She dropped her gaze to watch his cock twitch in her grip. "I love knowing it's mine to touch, mine to savor."

"Oh, it's yours, all right." He growled, grinding his hard flesh in her hands. "But I came for more than just your hands, my little Lupine."

Jeff gently disengaged her from his hard cock and wove his fingers through hers, pushing her down. He pinned her hands to the bed and shoved his hips between her thighs, spreading them wider. Then he paused, staring at her with glowing golden intensity.

"Do you want me, Julianna?"

He dipped his hips and rubbed the head of his cock along her outer lips, teasing her with his tempting heat.

"Oh, glory, yes, Jeff. I want you so much." She rocked her pelvis to increase the pressure, but he pulled away and she groaned in frustration.

"I can scent your sweet, dripping pussy, and my Brother is demanding I take it. Should I tell him no?"

"No, Jeff. Take my hungry pussy. Feed it your hot cock." Julianna rolled her hips again and growled, taunting him with her needy slit.

He growled back at her, his eyes blazing, then swung his hips back and slammed his cock home, balls deep. She screamed with the erotic intrusion and her arousal burned through her body. Her fingers tightened on his as he withdrew achingly slow, dragging his scorching shaft along the underside of her clit.

Jeff paused again.

"Do you want more?"

"Yes. Don't stop. Ever."

"Rub your clit for me, little Lupine."

Jeff released her hand and guided it between their bodies until her fingers pressed against her little hood. She met his gaze with surprise.

"Show me how you take pleasure in your sexy body."

Julianna strummed her clit, massaging the hard nub as he dragged his cock back past her fingers. Slick juices made his skin smooth and she reveled in the slippery texture.

"Yes, that's it." He pushed in a little harder. "Keep rubbing, Julianna."

Pleasure built within her with the combination of her fingers on her clit and his hard strokes within her pussy. Shots of fire flared in her awareness, pushing her closer to orgasm then dying back.

"Good glory, Jeff. Harder, please."

A growling laugh erupted from him before he thrust in again, his cock shoving deep into her clenching heat. When he pulled back the next time, he didn't stop. The slide of his cock against her clit and lips drove Julianna higher toward her release. She ripped her hand away from her clit and clamped it to his hard ass, holding on.

She writhed beneath him, meeting his thrusts with her own, until they pounded each other in a frenzy of delicious torment. Julianna moved her hand and dug her fingers into his heaving shoulders, savoring his shifting muscles and undulating motion.

She looked up into Jeff's face and his eyes blazed golden fire at her, his teeth bared in sexual intensity. He looked so primal, so dominant, so male. Her orgasm slammed into her and she gasped.

"Yes! Yes, Jeff! Yesssssss!"

Ecstatic bliss flooded through her mind just as he pounded twice more and let loose a roar of release. Hot jets of cum filled her pussy, drenching her with sweet, slick moisture as his body tightened above her. Julianna bounded away into the stars with her Mate, joy and intense pleasure trailing in her wake.

"I knew you'd be perfect, Jeff." Julianna squeezed his fingers and grasped nothing but sheet. "What the—?"

She sat up and looked around, her heart pounding once more. Her room above her mother's garage was empty, the silence broken only by her panting breaths. The scent of sex perfumed the space around her and her pussy juices soaked the sheets between her legs.

"Oh sweet glory. That was only a dream?"

She dragged a hand over her clenching pussy, rubbing her cream into her lips.

Damn, it had felt so real. She giggled and lay back in her bed, trying to catch her breath. She listened to her heart hammer against her ribs as she thought about her sexy dream lover. Just the memory of him riding her hard had her pussy clenching with erotic aftershocks.

She closed her eyes and tried to slow her breathing, inhaling the scent of sex. Could she detect a little of Jeff's scent in the room? *Nice try, Morris. He wasn't really here.*

Her rational mind finally clicked back into place, and relief trickled through her.

*Thank goodness, he wasn't really here. We would've been in so much trouble.*

She snorted and rolled onto her side, wrapping the sheets around her. Snuggling deeper into her bed, she chuckled with wicked amusement.

*But he can visit again. I don't mind. Really.*

\*\*\*\*

Jeff sat up with a gasp, his cock at half mast, straining the sheet. A sticky sheet.

*Shit. What the hell?*

He looked around his room, but everything remained quiet and still. Where was Julianna? He'd seen her so clearly. He inhaled deeply, trying to catch the scents of the room. But the only smells were that of his dirty laundry in the hamper and his own release in the sheets of his bed. His heart thundered in his chest from dread. Dread that she'd been there. Dread that she hadn't.

He dropped back to the mattress and let out a breath he hadn't known he'd held.

*Thank the Goddess she's not here.* He let out a groan. *Damn, she's not here.*

It had only been a dream. A fucking hot dream, but just a dream. Despite his understanding, he could still taste her sweet cream and smell her aroused scent. The memory of her hot pussy clamped around his cock made the wily anatomy rise for a second round.

*Oh shit.* How the hell would he be able to work with her and keep his cock on a leash? *I'm so fuckin' screwed.*

He grasped his dick and massaged it a few times as he rolled over and moaned into the pillow. The competition for Luna couldn't end fast enough.

*I need Julianna.*

Too bad he had to wait for her to prove her worthiness. He wanted to roar. To hell with the archaic rules. Julianna was his True Mate, like his mother had been his father's. He shouldn't have to jump through hoops when she was here, in town, and they both knew it.

He screamed into the pillow, fury, frustration, and sexual need like a hot ball in his gut.

He wanted Julianna. He wouldn't tolerate the touches of any other woman. *She had to pass the tests. Otherwise I'm going rogue.*

Fortunately, no one had passed any of the tests yet, but time would tell.

*Doesn't matter.* It would be Julianna or no one. Decision made, he rolled over and settled back to sleep.

# CHAPTER ELEVEN:
## Testing Begins

Julianna's first day on the job went rather well, though her mother dropped by the bar. She'd been surprised and nervous, not only because of the species difference, but also because of the wet dream. She'd worried everyone could scent it on her, but Jeff and his friends hadn't seemed to notice, and greeted Beth warmly. She promised to stay out of Julianna's way, and watched her with a big 'proud-mama' smile. Julianna blushed but focused on the job at hand.

*Nothing like having your mom check up on you like it's your first job.*

She learned the rules and schedules quickly, and even managed to iron out some of the previous snags affecting the smooth operation of the bar. Jeff and Zach took turns for the morning shifts as barkeep, so Zach could have some time off as well. He returned as head bouncer in the evenings.

The other three bartenders–Laura Thomas, Gary Howler, and William "never Bill" Phillips–all worked the evenings, rotating the weekends so everyone got a chance for bigger tips. Laura and William were human, as were four of the waitresses, but all the bouncers were west of left field. Julianna wondered what they did for security on the nights of the full moon.

The four west of left field waitresses were omega members of the pack, but they held their own with the humans and the other patrons. Most of the bouncers were beta, though one or two of them were omega, and deferred to the others. They stood up to humans without any trouble.

She coordinated with Zach to make sure the bouncers rotated. Julianna liked all of them. Most belonged to Jeff as part his cadre, a group she didn't understand well. They had their own ranking within the group, and the other bouncers outside the group deferred to them, regardless of rank. Despite their size and strength, all were intelligent and sharp, and treated her with respect and deference.

On her third night at the bar, a young alpha and his beta friends got a little too worked up. Woody, a younger omega bouncer, moved in to escort the young man and his rowdy friends outside so they wouldn't disturb the rest of the bar. Julianna saw Woody gesture in his careful, polite way to encourage the offenders to leave. But the scent of the alpha's anger and disdain carried all the way across the bar, and the hair on the back of her neck rose. The other patrons around them scented it, too, and edged away from the burgeoning confrontation. Julianna wove slowly through the crowd, watching the exchange very carefully.

"Gentlemen, let's take the discussion outside." Woody waved politely toward the door.

The young alpha sneered at him, flipping him the bird and turning his back. "Fuck you, omie."

Woody's jaw clenched, but he stood his ground. "I must insist. You're disturbing the other patrons. Please take this outside." He crowded the alpha and his friends, using his body to move them toward the door. Julianna was impressed with how "cool" his scent remained.

"What are you gonna do, carrion dog?" One of the

alpha's friends stopped in front of Woody.

Another snorted with derision. "Nothin'. He doesn't have the balls for it, stupid omega."

"Time to go, gentlemen. You've had enough." Woody took it all stoically and pulled the chairs away from the table to allow the party room to move away.

The alpha and his friends shook in inebriated fury and turned on Woody, snarling and shouting drunken curses at him. *Aw hell, this is totally gonna suck.* Julianna slid past the other patrons, waving toward Zach. The blond man wore his usual mask of impassiveness, but anger glittered in his eyes as they approached the growing conflict.

They'd almost reached to the table when the alpha took a swing at Woody. *Oh, shit.* The omega bouncer ducked and caught the alpha's hand, using the momentum to swing it around the other man's back and pin it there. The alpha screamed in rage and tried to throw him off, but Woody held on and shoved him toward the door. The group of betas leapt at Woody, but Julianna's sharp whistle aborted their motion, and Woody froze.

"Hey!" Julianna shouted into the startled silence. Even the players at the pool tables looked up in surprise. "What's all the shouting about?"

The young alpha jostled in Woody's grip, but the omega bouncer didn't let go.

"Lemme go, you mangy cur!" he bellowed, still struggling. He shot a venomous look at Julianna. "He's got no right to hold me like this."

Julianna looked over at Woody and nodded slightly. The bouncer released the young alpha and stepped back out of reach.

"He's let go. You want to fill me in on what's going on?" she drawled blandly.

"The problem is that stupid asshole grabbed me and dragged me toward the door for no damn reason!" The young man's shout corresponded with a finger stabbed in

Woody's direction. His friends muttered assent.

Julianna raised her eyebrows. "Is that the way you saw it? Because I saw my bouncer ask you to leave politely, and you took a swing at him in response. I think he has every right to escort you to the door. However, if you're willing to go under your own power, he'll merely watch your back until you're outside."

The young alpha snarled. "He had no right to touch me or any of us. He's only an omega."

Anger curled in her gut, but she nodded. "He's definitely an omega, but he was doing his job. You were causing trouble and disturbing others. How 'bout you make it easy on everyone and head on out to sleep it off?" The young man glared at her, seething, as she gestured toward the front doors.

"Who are you, bitch, to tell me what to do?" he sneered, his body bristling with cocky rage. "You might be the newest bitch in town, but you're nothing. You can't tell me what to do or where to go, so you can just fuck off!"

*Oh, you little jackass.*

Julianna narrowed her eyes, but took a deep breath and considered her next move. Drunk as a skunk and feeling his oats, the young idiot was in no condition to fight more than one bouncer. They'd have him and his friends out before he knew what hit him. *And my own ego isn't that fragile.*

She shot him a tight smile, but a low growl filled the silence, and she shivered. The base animal inside her screamed in panic, demanding she hide from the oncoming deadly predator.

Jeff stalked toward them through the crowd. His face was composed and looked even mildly amused, but Julianna scented the fury rolling off him in waves. Excitement zinged through her at the sight of his furious beauty, and she inhaled shakily.

*Sweet glory, he's fuckin' sexy.*

"Is that any way to talk to a lady, Bobby?" Jeff's voice

remained deceptively calm.

He stopped next to Julianna and cocked his head like a curious wolf. Bobby swallowed hard and held very still.

"I'd appreciate it if you kept a civil tongue while in my bar. I don't tolerate insults to my employees, and this lady is the bar manager." Jeff raised his chin. "She's in charge of the bar. What she says goes. You been making trouble tonight, Bobby? Did you take a swing at one of my bouncers?"

Bobby took a breath to say something, his expression rebellious.

"You better give me the truth because I'm in no mood to listen to stories." Jeff crossed his arms over his chest. "Start with what really happened, and you just might be welcome back here."

Bobby glared daggers at Juliannna until Jeff's words sunk in through the alcohol soaking his brain. His eyes widened and he shifted his gaze to Jeff's forbidding presence beside her. Whatever he saw there killed his belligerence, and the color washed out of his face. His head dropped into a submissive position as his eyes slid to one side, no longer challenging either of them.

"I'm sorry, J—" Bobby stopped and swallowed hard when Jeff growled, dropping his head lower. "I'm sorry, Mr. Lightfoot. I'm not myself tonight."

Jeff raised his eyebrows expectantly.

Bobby cleared his throat. "I'm sorry, Ms. Morris. I think I'll take your advice and go home."

"Good choice, Bobby," Jeff said. "I'll tell your dad hello the next time I see him."

Bobby's face, already white, paled even more. Apparently, his father still held sway at Bobby's household. The young man nodded jerkily, retreating backward, never turning his back. A few loose chairs toppled to the floor as he and his friends fled.

Julianna let out the breath she didn't even know she'd

been holding as she watched the other patrons regroup and relax. Jeff clapped a hand to her shoulder.

"Nice job."

She shot him a smile, trying to ignore the pleasure of his touch. "Thanks. Are they always such jackasses?"

He shook his head. "No, but some have bought into the idea that alpha means 'boss', rather than 'leader.'"

"He's gonna make a shitty boss, that's for sure. I wouldn't work for him."

Jeff's lips curled into a sexy smile. "I'm very glad you work for me."

Julianna took a deep breath to keep from pulling him into her arms. "Me, too. Although this waiting crap sucks."

"Yes." He nodded and removed his hand from her shoulder. "I'm gonna go see if they need help behind the bar. Again, great job."

She nodded and watched him go before the sounds of the doors closing caught her attention. Woody returned after escorting the little assholes outside. He paused, his gaze calmly sweeping over the room, but she could smell his unspent fury. This close to the full moon, he'd held back admirably well.

Catching his eye, she gestured with her head toward the back of the bar, and he followed her, his strides stiff and sharp. He refused to look at her, and Julianna's frustration rose until she remembered an omega wouldn't challenge an alpha by looking her in the eye.

"Nice job, Woody. You kept your cool and held your ground. Good work."

"Did you think I wouldn't?" he snapped, still not meeting her eyes. When she raised her chin, he added quickly, "I'm sorry, Ms. Morris."

"In answer to your question, I never thought you couldn't do the job for which you were hired." She stuffed her anger down deep. "On the contrary, most men wouldn't take a verbal assault as calmly as you did, and I was both impressed and pleased with your performance."

Woody breathed out roughly, staring at her chin to remain submissive despite his greater height.

"Forgive me, Ms. Morris. Those taunts were hard to take." His hands clenched into fists and released. "I've worked hard for this position and earned my place. I didn't mean to take my frustration out on you. It won't happen again."

"Good." Julianna nodded. "I don't enjoy being snapped at any more than you do. Why don't you take a five-minute break to let out some of that frustration and then come on back in to finish your shift."

As he turned away, she added, "You're a better man than he is, Woody."

He paused with his body turned three-quarters away from her then nodded sharply before he left the bar through the back. Julianna bit the inside of her mouth thoughtfully but turned her attention back to the crowd. Hopefully, the rest of the evening would be calm. She didn't see Jeff anywhere, and disappointment bloomed. She knew it was probably for the best. He couldn't show her favoritism, and she couldn't push him up against the wall and kiss him.

*Yep, definitely better that he's not here.*

Her neck prickled and she scanned the room. The other bouncers and Zach watched her impassively. As she caught Zach's eyes, he inclined his head respectfully. The tightness in her shoulders eased a little, and she took a deep breath. *One test passed, even if it wasn't for Luna.*

Zach came up to her near closing and touched her elbow. "Can I talk to you a moment?"

"Sure, Zach." She set down her things. "What's up?"

"I wanted to thank you for sticking up for Woody." His voice wasn't as deep as Jeff's, but she sensed quiet authority in it all the same.

"You're welcome. Woody did his job well in a difficult situation. I told him so."

"Thanks for that. He's lowest ranked, but me and the guys try to watch out for him. He's a good guy."

She nodded. "I think so, too. The patrons had better listen to him, regardless of their status."

"After tonight, they will. Your backup gave him a status boost."

"Yeah? Good. He deserves it."

Zach gave her one of his rare smiles and turned away to help close up. He was younger than she'd thought and quite handsome when he dropped his stoicism. She grunted softly to herself as she marked down a few changes to the schedule and left it in the office. She grabbed her purse and her keys, and headed for the door.

To her surprise, one of the bouncers peeled off from the others and followed her outside. He didn't say anything, but his expression was watchful and protective without being oppressive. She didn't scent any resentment in him, and she thanked him when she got into her car. He nodded, closed her door, and stood back while she drove out of the parking lot. She smiled to herself, both amused and grateful to have someone watching her back.

**\*\*\*\***

For the next two weeks, things remained quiet at the bar. When the full moon rose into the sky over Callowwood at the end of the first week, Sebrina came and took Julianna out into the mountains north of town. Julianna had wanted to fight her, but the wolf inside her recognized Sebrina's superiority, and she followed reluctantly behind after calling her mom to let her know she'd be gone. They stayed away from town for three days, running as wolves to continue Julianna's education, and Julianna learned that all the candidates, not just her, had left town to keep the competition impartial. The call of the Lady Moon was too strong to fight their natural urges, so the candidates were removed from the proximity of the Successor to keep it fair. Julianna agreed it was probably wise, but her Sister wasn't pleased.

Julianna resumed her morning training with Sebrina before she went to work, alternating mornings with Beth for breakfast. Beth had started to heal from her grief, and her smiles, while still bittersweet, came more frequently. She commented on Julianna's physique, and Julianna told her she'd been "running" every other day to reduce some of the stress weight she'd gained after Gerry's death.

"Is that the only reason you're getting in shape?" Beth had asked, a smug twinkle in her eye.

"What are you really asking, Mom?"

"How did the date with Jeff Lightfoot go?" Her mother had smiled innocently.

Julianna laughed and said, "It went fine." Beth looked pleased.

With Sebrina, Julianna learned the protocols on how to deal with the hierarchy of the pack, which alphas came after the Alpha Pair, the order of betas and omegas, and how to know which omega was higher ranked than the others. It was complicated, and Julianna hoped she'd get it right when it counted. It had to do with age, experience, familiarity within the pack, length of residency in the "home range", and services rendered to the Alpha.

"Sweet glory, I don't think I'll ever keep everyone straight." She'd rubbed her face with her hands as Sebrina just smiled faintly.

"You'll pick up on it eventually, daughter."

After the protocols, including who was served first at a "state" dinner and how each visitor was greeted at the door, Sebrina told Julianna the Stories of the Lady Moon and the First Canid. Julianna was intrigued, not just because these were the creation myths of the Moon Singer People, but also because they were great teaching stories, with morals, adventure, love, and deep understanding of how to integrate several kinds of people living together.

Her favorite Story was entitled "The First Canid."

"In the time before we knew our places beneath the sun and stars," Sebrina began patiently, her hands working a beading loom, "the Lady watched over all the Peoples with Her opalescent eyes, but Her favorites were the Wolf Peoples because, though they were vicious when hunting, they were true to their natures and kept the other Peoples from overpopulation.

"One of the Wolf People was called Ho'a'tote, Thinks Before He Eats, and he was a magnificent wolf. He spent much of his time observing the other Peoples around him, learning from them, discovering new things about them, and trying to understand points of view other than his own. His family and friends thought him odd, but harmless, so they tolerated his presence among them without fuss.

"In those days, the Lady walked among the Peoples, bestowing blessings, healing hurts, and keeping the balance of life. One day, She noticed Ho'a'tote watching the Beavers building their dam to hold back the water in the stream. At first, She thought he was hunting the Beavers, so still did he lie there, so patiently. But when he didn't move for hours and hours, through many moments when the Beavers would've been easy prey, She realized he was doing something else and stopped to ask him.

"'Ho'a'tote, what are you doing?'

"'I'm watching the Beavers building this dam,' he replied in a fascinated voice. 'I think they will stop up the water to make a pond and it will benefit all the Peoples because it will make it easier to drink the water.'

"'Why do you watch them so carefully? Are you hunting?' She asked.

"'No, I'm trying to learn how they do it so my People may do it in other streams and have enough water when the world becomes too dry in the summer. It also makes a good way to cross the stream without getting wet.'

"The Lady looked at Ho'a'tote, who'd gone back to watching the Beavers. She shook Her head and went on Her way. But a few days later, She found Ho'a'tote staring up into a tree, watching a little tiny bird flit in and away.

"'What are you doing, Ho'a'tote?' She asked again.

"'I'm watching a Bushtit making her nest for her little ones," he replied, his attention never wavering.

"'Why, Ho'a'tote?'

"'I'm trying to learn how to construct a safe place for me and my children to stay when the weather turns foul. The Bushtit knows how to build such a protective place.'

"Again, the Lady shook Her head and went away. Sometime later, She found Ho'a'tote on the coast, watching the water most carefully. She followed his gaze and found Sea Otters smashing clams on their chests with rocks.

"'What are you doing, Ho'a'tote?'

"'I'm watching Sea Otter using rocks to get to his food,' the wolf replied. 'It's a very smart use of his strength. The rock does his work for him.'

"Later still, the Lady found Ho'a'tote watching Raccoon pick through berries for her meal after washing her hands in the stream.

"'Tell me, Ho'a'tote, why you want to learn these things?' She said then. 'You are a Wolf. You have claws and teeth and are able to run fast to catch your dinner. Why do you wish to learn these other skills of the other Peoples?'

"Ho'a'tote left off looking at Raccoon and said simply, 'I want to learn everything I can. The more I understand about others, the better I can live with them, in balance and harmony. I don't want to give up my own skills, but I don't wish to be limited by them.'

"The Lady cocked her head and asked, 'What would you do if you had such an expanded understanding?'

"'I would protect my family,' he answered solemnly. 'Learning about others, their strengths and weaknesses, protects us all, strengthens us all. It keeps the balance and encourages harmony.'

"The Lady considered. 'Very well, Ho'a'tote. I shall grant you your wish to be more than just Wolf. I will give you a form so you may fit in with the Human People, who have all the skills you seek and share this land with you. However, there's a price to be paid. You must wear your Wolf skin three nights of every month when my Eye is full and watching you. Your People may be born in either form and will keep that form until they change into adulthood. Then they will be free to shift shape at will.'

"Ho'a'tote jumped up and danced in gratitude for the Lady's great blessing. But the Goddess raised one hand in warning.

"'You must keep the knowledge of your special abilities within your People, Ho'a'tote. If the others see these gifts, they will not understand and may try to harm your People. Choose your confidantes carefully. Some will understand, others will only fear what you are.'

"The Lady sang a song of Change, and Ho'a'tote shifted from being only Wolf to sharing the shape of the Human Peoples. He was much colder in his human shape, but he had hands with which to manipulate tools to make a new coat and a warm shelter. He harnessed Lightning's Fire and made friends among the Human People, bringing peace.

"His strength and wisdom pleased the Lady, and She offered his People one more gift, the gift of the mating bond, the knowledge of our True Mates. Ho'a'tote mated with a glorious she-Wolf and she became his Luna, the Guardian of the Stories. The children of this Alpha Pair inherited their father's ability to shift shape as promised, and thus began the Moon Singer People.

"Ho'a'tote is remembered as the First Canid of our People, the First Alpha of all the packs in the World, and we offer our prayers and blessings to Him for His wish to become more than just Wolf."

There were other stories, of how the hierarchy was established and why, of the Luna and her role in the pack, of the Stances and the Kerstance, the ritual of succession, of the reasons for keeping the People hidden from the humans. Julianna learned them all.

"Sebrina, are all the other candidates learning these stories?" They went for a walk through town, the sun already warm.

"I don't know, daughter," the older woman confessed. "Each of them should have heard the Stories since they were children, but I don't know if they know them. Many have forgotten the old ways and the First Canid. His teachings should have been carried down through the generations, but I've seen fewer and fewer who remember them or the blessings bestowed upon our People by the Lady Moon."

"But isn't it important that the Luna of the pack knows the Stories? Didn't the Alpha say the Luna must be the Guardian?"

"He did, and he may believe that, but it has been a long time since a Luna was here to recite them, and an even longer time since the need for the knowledge has been enforced." Sebrina shook her head. "I see our pack pulling further and further away from the old ways. Some change is good, like making the Kerstance non-fatal between father and son. But forgetting the teaching stories and the beginnings of our People can only bring hardship and despair."

"Will I be tested for knowledge of the Stories?"

"Not directly. They are teaching Stories, and their value lies in understanding their underlying meanings. Using their examples in your responses to events in your life is the best way to show your knowledge of them."

"Right," Julianna grunted, and let it go.

# CHAPTER TWELVE:
## Making Friends

Julianna's interaction with the women of the Callowwood Pack increased in frequency with her candidacy. Many of the beta females sought her out, grateful for her approachability. Eloise Farkas, a friend of Tawny's, invited Julianna to her bridal shower with a shy smile. She was engaged to Tommy Scatterstone, a low-level alpha who worked as a building and carpentry contractor.

"I'd be honored if you'd come, Ms. Morris." Eloise brushed back the edges of her white-blonde hair with a hesitant smile. "I heard what you did for Tommy's brother, Woody, and he suggested I invite you."

"Oh. Thank you. But, um, if you're only doing this because your fiancé suggested it, I'm okay with not going." Julianna wiped down the bar before grabbing a glass for ice water. "It's your party. You should invite who you want to be there."

A blush rose in Eloise's cheeks. "I *do* want you to be there. You're the nicest of all the candidates, and Tawny speaks highly of you."

Julianna nodded. *High praise from everyone but Eloise.*

"Oh dear, I'm not saying this right, am I?" She shook her head and rubbed her hands over her face. "Please come. I'd like you to be there and I'd like to get to know the woman everyone is talking about. At least, everyone I respect."

Julianna nodded. "And some you don't, I suspect."

Eloise grimaced. "Yes. Everyone is talking about you, but I'd like to know the real person."

"Not just for political gain?"

Eloise shook her head. "No, not just that." She smiled and Julianna laughed.

"Fair enough. When and where will it be?"

The party was held at Nadine's Salon and Day Spa in Leland, a small square building with an overhanging sign, and a covered porch around the front door. The place smelled like shampoo, fried hair, and nail polish, but Julianna also scented feminine satisfaction and contentment.

Tawny, JenniLynn and MaryBeth Grayhound, and Julianna were the only packmembers invited. She chatted with the other women, grateful for the invitation.

"Thank you for inviting me." She gave Eloise a wide smile as they waited in the foyer of the salon among the potted palms and ferns. "It's nice to get out with the girls to be pampered every now and again. I haven't done this in a very long time, nor had many friends with whom to do it."

Eloise chuckled. "I'm very happy to have you with us. It'll be nice to talk to you when no one is posturing for a "better rank" in the pack." She sighed. "The politics get tiring, especially among the females during a Luna race. And I figured you're new to the pack. It's pretty lonely at first."

"Haven't you been in the…" She shot a look around at the human attendants. "Group all your life?"

"Yes, but not this one." Eloise took over her jacket and set down her purse. "My family became part of

Callowwood when our old Alpha died and most of the members moved away. We used to live in a very small town, smaller than Callowwood. The change was really hard at first."

"Wow. Your old Alpha didn't have any heirs?"

Eloise shook her head and lowered her voice. "No, and the humans were taking over. It wasn't very safe for us." She shrugged it away. "I'm glad you've come home to Callowwood. From what I've seen and heard, you're the only candidate who could actually take on leadership without losing herself to the position."

"Losing myself?" Julianna hung her coat beside Eloise's.

"Yeah, you know." Eloise raised her chin to look down her nose. "It's all about me. I'm the most important. Bow down to your true master."

Julianna laughed. "Oh, that. Yeah, I'm not really into all that. In fact, I didn't even know I'd be a Luna candidate until that night."

Eloise blinked. "Really?"

"Yeah, I kinda had to hit the ground running." She shook her head with a grimace. "I hope I didn't look like a complete and utter fool standing there among people who'd been doing this... you know, for all their lives."

"You could've fooled me. I'm pretty sure you fooled everyone else, too." Eloise winked. "For what it's worth, I hope the Successor chooses you." She shrugged. "The others just don't feel right for our pack."

Julianna studied the other woman for a few long moments in surprise.

"They don't 'feel' right? How?"

Eloise grimaced and scanned the lobby, her shoulders hunched.

"I can't really explain it. My father says I'm just being silly, but I keep feeling like the other candidates are too worried about themselves and what they can gain than they are about the pack as a whole." She shook her head. "Those kinds of folks make lousy leaders."

Julianna nodded. "They do. I hope I'm better than that. To be honest, I wouldn't be needed as a leader if there wasn't a pack to be governed. Thanks for the insight."

The bride-to-be blushed. "You're welcome, Mistress Morris."

"Would it be possible to call me Julianna? This "mistress" stuff makes me feel like I'm on some sort of pedestal, and it's kinda lonely." She winked.

Eloise studied Julianna for long moments, her light blue eyes introspective. Julianna's respect for the beta female increased exponentially. "You don't make a good statue."

"Right?" Julianna froze her face into a blank look. "I don't think I'd be very majestic." She snorted when Eloise laughed.

"Not with that look."

Julianna chuckled. "Thanks for the reality check so my ego doesn't get too out of hand."

"Anything for a friend."

Julianna stopped as warmth rolled through her. "I'd like that a lot. You have no idea how much that means to me." She hadn't realized how alone she'd been until Eloise offered friendship.

A warm smile creased Eloise's lips. "You're welcome to it. We can be outsiders together."

"Deal." She matched Eloise's smile.

"Come on, you guys. No more politics tonight." Tawny appeared with a big smile. "It's time to celebrate and have fun."

Eloise shot Julianna a look and rolled her eyes, making her grin.

The Grayhound sisters appeared, chattering a mile a minute. The energy of the party shifted away from current issues to frivolity as everyone giggled and laughed like teenagers at the mall. Eloise laughed with the others, but her smile was tinged with sorrow and her scent held hints of worry and unease.

The atmosphere at the spa was festive, and all the women seemed to be enjoying themselves. But Eloise still broadcast sadness, and it grated on Julianna like an off-key piano. She settled beside her new friend for their pedicures.

"Hate getting your nails done?" Julianna shot a look at Eloise.

"What?" Eloise laughed. "No, it's okay."

"Then what's bothering you? I can read it in your face." Actually, she could smell it, but the humans were listening. "When is the wedding again?"

"Two months from this Saturday." Eloise kept all her attention on her feet.

"Are you looking forward to it?"

"Of course."

"Please contain your excitement. I'm not sure my heart can handle it."

Eloise laughed. "Am I that obvious?"

Julianna bit her lip. "Well, the little black rain cloud over your head might be a hint."

Eloise sighed. "I am looking forward to the wedding. Tommy's a dream come true."

"Right. I see that."

Eloise snorted, a rueful smile curling her lips. "It's not him, though. My older sister, Nora, is supposed to be my maid of honor, but she's missing."

Julianna blinked. "Missing?"

Eloise nodded. "She hasn't been seen for weeks, and no one can get a hold of her."

"Have you checked her social media accounts?"

"Yeah. She hasn't been online at all, which is weird." Eloise shook her head. "My whole family is out of their minds with worry. I mean, what could've happened to her? She's too strong for a rapist or a kidnapper to get a hold of, and she never goes this long without contacting people."

Julianna reached out and squeezed her hand, heedless of their newly painted nails. "When was the last time anyone heard from her?"

"Four weeks."

"Was she planning on taking a trip or maybe visiting friends somewhere?"

"I don't know. She never said anything to me about it."

"What's your sister's name?"

"Nora Farkas." The surname sounded like *far-kash.*

Julianna rubbed her chin. "Have you talked to Richard Lightfoot about it?"

Eloise shook her head. "We didn't want to trouble the Alpha with something so trivial."

"It doesn't sound trivial to me, especially when she doesn't normally do this."

Eloise bit her lip. "I don't want to jump at shadows. What if I tell him and she shows up?"

"Then it's all good." Julianna shrugged. "She's part of the pack and she's missing. The Alpha needs to know about it." She paused. "If you'd prefer, I can mention it to Richard or Jeff Lightfoot."

Eloise frowned. "No, I think I should do it. I know the most about it."

Julianna nodded. "If you want, I can go with you when you do it. Have your back and all that."

Eloise raised her eyebrows. "You'd do that for me?"

"Anything for a friend." Julianna winked. "Just let me know when and where, and I'll be there."

"Thanks so much." Eloise's eyes filled with grateful tears.

She squeezed Eloise's hand once more. "It's going to be okay."

Eloise gave her another long look. "Do you really believe that?"

"Yes. I know it."

The bride-to-be would have said more, but the twins

burst in from their massages full of enthusiasm. Laughing and giggling, they pulled Eloise up to her feet and whisked her away to a special couch where she could open the few gifts piled at her side. Julianna followed more slowly, her mind caught up on Nora Farkas.

She was glad to be included in the bubbling excitement and laughter, and she smiled as the others exclaimed over the gifts. Everyone was relaxed by the time the evening drew to a close. Julianna shared smiles with Eloise, hoping her confidence in the Lightfoots wasn't misplaced.

"I think I'm going to head out." Julianna rose and collected her jacket. "It's been fun, but I'm tired and I gotta work tomorrow."

Eloise rose with her. "Thanks so much for coming along, Julianna." She smiled as the others exchanged wide-eyed looks. "It was nice to hang out with you. Let me walk you out."

"Thanks." They headed for the front doors of the salon. "Hey, let me give you my cell number. If you ever need to talk or shoot the breeze, or you need a wingwoman, you can call or text."

They exchanged numbers and Julianna impulsively hugged the other woman. "It's going to be fine. We'll find your sister, I'm sure of it."

"Thanks. I needed to hear that. Have a good night and drive safe."

Julianna nodded and stepped out the door. The heat of the summer night enveloped her, and she took a deep breath. She liked being with the women, but sometimes Tawny and the twins were a lot to take in.

*And what the hell happened to Nora Farkas?* It was scary to think someone could kidnap and keep a Moon Singer.

Julianna strode around the corner of the salon toward her car, gripping her phone to text Jeff. But the scent of the night changed, and the hairs on the back of her neck stood up. She paused and inhaled deeply through her nose. The stench of malice and excited men pushed away all her other thoughts, and her canines elongated in her mouth as a growl worked its way up from her chest.

*Incoming.*

She waited for her eyes to adjust to the limited light and listened hard. Only one street lamp cast weak light over the vehicles parked beside the salon. The wall to her left was solid cinder blocks with no doors or windows to break its concrete monotony. *So no witnesses.*

Five men of varying size materialized out of the dark and closed in on her. Julianna slowly rotated her back against the wall, grateful none of them had gotten behind her.

"Hey, little girl. What are you doin' out all alone?"

She clenched her jaw and shoved her phone in her purse. *Not a little girl, assholes.*

Four out of five were taller than she, but they all outweighed her by at least fifty pounds. She smelled alcohol and cigarettes on them, but their motions were sober.

*Why couldn't I get the really stupid bad guys my first time out?*

If they'd been drunk, she could've kicked the shit out of them and they wouldn't notice her speed or strength.

"What, cat got your tongue?" One guy sneered at her. "I got a better use for it." He grabbed his crotch.

Their leering expressions made her hackles rise, and her canines elongated again, but she kept her lips tightly closed. She'd have to be careful not to give away her species. She wondered if she could keep her secret without allowing these men to hurt her.

*Like there's any choice.* Thank goodness she'd learned tai chi. If she just sped up the moves a little, she'd be able to defend herself enough to either get to her car or back into the salon.

"Aw, she's shy. We're gonna have to convince her to play."

Julianna kept her eyes on all of them as she threw her purse strap over her neck and cinched it down tight. She took deep even breaths and settled her body into her "readiness meditation." Her heart thundered in her chest, but she relaxed her shoulders and waited to see what they'd do first.

"It's a little late for someone like you to be out alone." The bald one tipped his head. She could see edges of a tribal tattoo when he nodded at his buddies. A single silver ring hung in his right earlobe.

"I'm not alone." She watched the others peripherally. "My friends are coming out any minute now."

"We'll be long gone by then, little girl." He stepped closer with an evil smile. "You just come with us and do it real quiet, okay?"

"Sorry, can't help you with that one." Julianna gathered her energy to move. "I'm not known for being either cooperative or quiet."

"Now, don't make this harder on yourself than it has to be," he cajoled. "You know you're outnumbered and outclassed."

Humor uncurled inside Julianna and leaked out in an unladylike snort. "I got nothin' but class."

Irritation spread across their faces, and someone darted toward her. She heard and smelled him, twisting away. She locked her hands together and swing back, slamming her elbow into his gut. He bent in half over her arm, grunting painfully. She shoved him backward until he tumbled into his fellows. The stench of his cigarette breath burned her nostrils and she resisted the urge to gag as she dropped to a defensive crouch. The fallen men struggled together in a cursing heap.

Part of her stopped in amazement at what she'd just accomplished.

*Woo-hoo! Did you see that?*
*Focus! It's not over yet.*
*Right, right.*

The adrenaline of a fight zinged through her system, but she breathed slowly, waiting for the other men. They appeared taken aback at her move, but their expressions hardened, and one closed in to throw a punch at the side of her head. She ducked and shoved both hands into his chest as she focused her chi through her arms.

*Not too much strength, not too much.*

Despite that, her blow hammered him hard enough to knock the breath out of him when he hit the ground. He flailed and wheezed, landing just within the spill of light from the windows of the salon. Julianna hoped one of the women saw him, but her attention was diverted when someone new grabbed her left arm.

This man stood shorter than her and smelled like burnt onions. Julianna shifted her weight into him, surprising him into loosening his hold, and shook off his grip as she kicked the side of her foot into his ankle.

She spun in a pirouette when he collapsed with a cry of pain and found herself nose to nose with Baldy Tattoo. He had blue eyes that widened as she threw her arms outward, removing his leverage, and brought her right knee up to nail him in the balls.

He saw her move at the last second and shifted so she thumped his thigh. But she drew one hand back and threw it forward so the heel of her hand crashed into his nose. He grunted in surprised pain and released her, his eyes tearing.

Julianna twisted sideways to get around him and heard the downed men get up, still cursing a blue streak. One lunged at her and met her foot with his throat. He choked and dropped to the side, clutching his neck. Julianna tried to ignore the triumphant howling of her Sister as she looked around to see where she was.

The windows and the door of the salon were to her left.

She took a chance and bolted for them, but one last grab by a determined thug caught her arm. She used his stationary presence to swing around and smash the heel of her left hand into his face, dancing backward to slam into the door. With the last of her adrenaline strength, she shoved it open using her legs.

"Dial 911!" She scrambled into the room as the receptionist looked at her in amazement. "Dial 911. I just got attacked by five guys out here. Call the police!"

The woman scrambled to do so as the other women cried out in dismay.

"Oh my Goddess, Julianna, what happened to you?" Tawny demanded as she took a deep breath, taking in the scents of fear and men.

"I just got attacked by five guys out there in the parking lot." She pointed back at the doors. "I just managed to get away. Thank goodness I learned tai chi."

"You got away by using tai chi?" Eloise asked skeptically, looking out the windows.

"It's slow kung fu. I just sped it up. It's still a martial art."

"The cops are on the way," the receptionist said then, and Julianna slumped down in a chair by a potted palm, well away from the windows.

"Good." Julianna closed her eyes.

"You didn't kill anyone, did you?"

Julianna opened her eyes to meet Eloise's concerned gaze.

"No. I pulled my punches."

"Oh, thank the Goddess for that." She slumped down next to Julianna. "You would've been disqualified from the candidacy."

"For killing someone bent on hurting me?"

"For killing a human."

Julianna shook her head. "I made sure they were hurting, but not dead."

Eloise hugged her. "I'm really glad you're okay."

"Me, too."

The Leland PD showed up a moment later, and Julianna wearily rose to meet them. They'd caught two men because they couldn't breathe enough to run. Each woman had to give a statement, and Julianna told her story four times before she met Detective Mark Cannon.

"Can you describe your attackers, Ms. Morris?" Det. Cannon had "old" brown eyes and a very careful smile as he showed her his badge. Julianna smelled the wolf in him and more of her tension fled.

"It was too dark. I only got a good look at one of them." She shook her head. "He was taller than me, say about six feet in height, had blue eyes, a single silver ring in his right earlobe, and some sort of tribal or flame-like tattoo on the back of his bald head."

"Did he have any facial hair?"

"No."

"How much did he weigh, do you think?"

She frowned. "Two hundred, two ten. He was strong and hard, not fat at all."

"Can you describe any of the others?"

"One guy was shorter than me and smelled like burnt onions. He should have a limp 'cause I kicked him in the ankle pretty hard. Two of the others had goatees, and they all smelled like alcohol and cigarettes, like they were hard-core smokers." She paused, searching her memory. "None of them moved with any sort of martial arts training. Oh. Baldy Tattoo smelled like overly sweetened fruit, like apricots."

When Det. Cannon raised an eyebrow, she retorted, "That's what it smelled like."

He nodded, a small smile quirking one corner of his mouth. "How many of them were there?"

"Five of them."

"All male?"

"Yes."

"Thank you, Ms. Morris." He put his notebook in his jacket pocket and handed her a card. "Here's my card. If you remember anything else, please don't hesitate to call me. You're free to go home now."

"Thanks…Uh, Detective Cannon?"

"Yes, ma'am?" He turned, the lights from the salon catching red highlights in his dark hair.

"Do you do any work with missing persons?"

"Missing persons, ma'am?" He frowned. "Is someone missing?"

"Yes. And she's a little west of left field."

He froze and scanned her a little more intently as if seeing something he hadn't before. Understanding stiffened his body as he took a few steps closer to her.

"Come with me, ma'am." He gently drew her outside to the parking lot, away from the other officers investigating the scene. "Are you one of the candidates for Luna in Callowwood?" He gestured to the wolf's head token on her wrist.

Julianna studied him, her gut churning. She couldn't see or smell anyone near them who might overhear, but caution screamed through her mind. The conversation could easily get her into trouble.

"Did you come to Mr. Lightfoot's selection party?" She raised her eyebrows. "I didn't see you there."

"No, I was on duty that night and couldn't get away."

"Ah." She nodded. "Too bad you missed it. It was quite a shindig. Perhaps you'll make the next one."

He smiled, sadness pulling at the corners of his mouth. "I hope I get the chance."

Julianna wondered at his sadness, but she shoved it away. "So can you help me?"

His expression filled with chagrin. "I'm not sure I can. Is there really someone west of left field missing?"

She nodded with a grimace.

"Does Mr. Lightfoot know?"

"I don't believe so."

"He's the man to talk to first, see what he suggests." Cannon scanned the parking lot around to make sure they were alone. "He might contact me or someone like me to look into it." His smile held admiration. "But if you remember anything else about tonight, please give me a call."

"Of course."

He nodded to her then backed away, only showing his back when he approached the rest of the cops still milling around. Before he turned, he winked and nodded again.

Julianna let her breath out in a sigh. *Glory, that was close.* Given her position as Luna Candidate, she hoped she'd passed a test by talking to the detective. *I didn't give anything away.* She turned and collided with her car with a grunt. She leaned against the warm metal and glass, smiling a half smile. *Sneaky bastard, he knew who I was from the beginning.* Must have been a test.

Hiding her true nature from the humans was exhausting. She unlocked her car door and dropped into the seat, leaning her head back against the seat.

*This is what it's going to be like for the rest of my life, isn't it?*

*You're always going to have to be careful what you say and to whom,* her Sister offered.

"Dammit." She shoved the car into gear, her mind churning with the events of the night.

Who were those guys? Were they just out to cause trouble, or did their assault have something to do with the Luna candidacy? There'd been enough of them to take down a normal woman. *I'm probably just being paranoid.*

Julianna hadn't come to any useful conclusions about anything when she pulled into her driveway. A black Camaro rested to one side, and Jeff waited at the foot of the stairs, his feet braced shoulder-width apart and his arms crossed over his chest.

"Shit-oh-dear." She swallowed hard. "Tawny must have called him."

She a deep breath before advancing toward the stairs and the man waiting for her. His hair hung loose around his head and shoulders, his expression haggard. When her door closed, his head came up.

His lips compressed into a flat line and his jaw bunched with tension as he studied her. He took a few deep breaths, and she knew he was scenting her attackers as well as her own emotional state. She tried to keep calm, but his presence and his concern brought up the shock reaction she'd been fighting all night.

"Are you all right?" His rich voice opened the floodgates.

"Oh, glory, Jeff!" She threw herself into his arms.

"Shh, shh, it's okay now." He wrapped his whole body around her. "You're safe and home. It's okay."

The tears poured out of her as if someone had opened up a valve somewhere. He kissed her hair and held her as she wept against his chest. She wept out her fear and confusion over discovering her true species. She wept in relief she'd survived an attack by five men bigger than she was. And she wept for the frustration of having to stay away from the one man she wanted over everyone else–the one man to whom she wanted to give herself to completely but had to hold herself back. She never wanted him to let go.

At last, the flood of emotion ebbed, and Jeff whispered, "They didn't hurt you, did they?"

"No, but I hurt them a little."

"Did you? Any of them dead?" He sounded amused.

"No." Julianna growled. "I pulled my punches."

"Good." He squeezed her before he pushed her back to look into her eyes. "I don't think I would've had the restraint. I would've killed them for attacking my Mate."

His seriousness made her shiver. "But you're fine?"

"Yes, just a little wound up from the adrenaline rush." She closed her eyes as Jeff wiped the remnants of her tears away. "Tawny called you, didn't she?" When he nodded, she nodded as well. "I'm glad you're here."

"Oh, my sweet Lupine, there's no way I could've stayed away." His smoky, sexy tone reminded her of her dream. "I just wish I could be a little more here for you." He smiled his wickedly sexy smile, and she knew she'd pass the tests just to see it directed at her each day.

*You were 'here' for me the other night. Sigh.*

"Can you walk me up and come in for some…coffee or something?" She was half afraid he'd turn her down, half afraid he wouldn't.

He hesitated, his expression frozen.

"Please, Jeff. I don't really want to be alone right now, and my mom won't understand."

A tender smile creased his lips, and he nodded. He took her hand and drew her up the stairs, his attention razor sharp and watchful, as if he suspected someone might be waiting. He allowed her to unlock the door, but he went in first and checked all the rooms in her small apartment.

*He's thorough.*

Her Sister growled. *Protective.*

She dropped her purse on the table and switched on a light in her small kitchenette to fill the teakettle.

"No coffee?" Jeff locked her front door and returned to her kitchen table.

"I decided it would keep me awake too late, and I'm already hyped up on adrenaline. I thought chamomile tea would work better." She shrugged. "I can make something else for you if you'd like."

"No, tea is good." He shook his head and muttered something under his breath.

"Sorry?"

"Nothing. I just prefer coffee in the morning." His

smile looked a little strained as he sat down. "Tea's fine." He crossed his arms over his chest. "So, are you going to tell your mom about tonight?"

Julianna sighed. "No. It would just make her worry for no reason. I'm okay, physically, and if this has to do with being a Moon Singer, it's best she doesn't know."

"Why do you say that?"

"What?"

"That it's about you being a Moon Singer."

Julianna paused, frowning. "I don't know. Something about it made me think it was a setup, like those guys were supposed to take me out."

"Sabotaging your tests?" Jeff raised an eyebrow.

"Yeah, that sounds pretty far-fetched, doesn't it?" Julianna rubbed her eyes. "It's probably just my adrenaline-crazed imagination."

"I'm glad you're all right." His jaw clenched as his anger rose in his scent. "I'd have killed them."

She snorted. "You'd have to know how to hide the bodies."

"I do."

Those two little words made Julianna shiver. He sounded primal, dangerous.

*He is dangerous.*

She leaned against her kitchen counter, and the reality of his presence, here in the light of her kitchen, hit her broadside. Jeff matched her perusal with his own, the anger giving way to arousal as his heated gaze slid over her body.

She wanted him with all her heart and soul. She wanted to feel him on top of her, beneath her, pounding away at her body as his lust took over. Could she ever get him to completely lose control or did he have built-in safeguards against that kind of behavior? What would it be like to kiss his lips and feel his tongue tangle with hers?

*No kissing, remember? Can't start the mating bond this early.*

Her Sister form ignored her thoughts because she found herself suddenly bending over him, her eyes locked with his. He hadn't moved, but his hands on the arm of her kitchen chair were white-knuckled, and his eyes blazed with hot molten gold.

"I–I'm s-sorry—"

She tried to pull back, but one of Jeff's hands shot out and grabbed the back of her head, hauling her down to meet his kiss.

*Holy First fucking Canid!*

Jeff's kiss was the most wonderful thing she'd ever experienced. It was soft and hard, sweet and sultry, gentle and demanding, and so damn sexy.

Julianna let herself fall into it with a soft moan of relief, tilting her head to the side to fit her mouth with his a little better. He tasted of sweet desert rain and male lust, all scorching heat. His hot, slick tongue caressed her lips, and she opened her mouth to let him plunder her. The erotic drag of his tongue against hers drove heat straight to her pussy, and he gave his own moan of delight when her scent changed.

Hard arms closed around her as she dropped to her knees between his legs and he jerked her hard against his chest.

She drowned in his kiss, his taste, his scent. She never wanted it to stop. This was what she'd been waiting eighteen years for. This was the taste and scent she'd dreamt of all the years away from Callowwood. Now that she'd gotten a sample, she'd be damned if she'd let it go. She desperately wanted him to go much, much further than "first base."

"Oh, Goddess, Julianna, we have to stop." He groaned, pushing her away from him. Red tinged his cheeks and his eyes unfocused, his breath coming out in heaves as his hands kept her from getting back to his lips.

"What? Why?"

"Because I won't be able to stop at kissing you." He panted, shaking his head as if to clear it. "I should probably go."

"Oh, glory, Jeff. Please don't go, not yet." She gripped his hips. "I need you to stay a little while. Just till I fall asleep. I'm so wound up and spooked from what happened tonight that I really need you…just for a little while. Please?"

He stared at her a long time, his chest still heaving as he tried to catch his breath. His jaw bunched, and he shook head again.

"Please, Jeff," she pleaded, dropping her head onto his thigh. "I need someone to hold me and to tell me it'll be all right. You're the only one I can let near me these days. We're both adults. I won't let you go any further than just holding me, for both our sakes. But I really need someone to lean on."

She ignored the voice warning her it was already too late after that kiss.

His hand settled on her hair and stroked it gently. Julianna didn't care that she'd just had it styled at the salon. Feeling his gentle touches more than made up for the mess, and she closed her eyes. She wanted to be here forever, but she'd take tonight as a sample.

Jeff sighed. "You're pushing my control, Julianna."

"I know," she agreed softly. "But this is the best excuse you can have to see me alone. Just tell everyone I'm distraught over the attack and I need someone to make sure I'm okay. I won't let us have sex, Jeff, but I really do need you to stay for a little longer." She raised her head to look at him.

He opened his mouth to reply, but the whistle of the teakettle sang shrilly into silence. She reluctantly rose to take it off the heat, afraid he'd take the chance to leave. *Please don't go.* He didn't move as she poured hot water into a mug, her hand shaking enough to spill some of the water.

"Don't burn yourself." He rolled to his feet and took the kettle from her, setting it on the stove with a sigh. "I really shouldn't stay." He sounded weary. "It's a small town, and everyone will recognize my car in your driveway."

Julianna steeled herself for his retreat. Her heart dropped into her feet, and disappointment crashed over her. She could barely breathe, but she nodded. *It's probably better.* She dropped her gaze to her steaming cup of tea, seeking comfort in the fragrant heat.

"But you're my Mate." She looked up at him in surprise and he shrugged. "And I can't walk away if you really need me to stay. It's just not in me to leave you distressed."

Tears started in her eyes. "I need you, Jeff."

He sighed again then held out his hand to her. "Come on, then. Get your tea and we'll put you to bed."

"I don't need the tea."

She dumped the mug in the sink and grabbed his hand, following him into the bedroom. He switched on the light. The sight of him in her room made her heart thunder against her ribs, and she recalled the dream. *This time he's really here.* A delicious shiver cascaded down her back, but she firmly told herself to calm down.

Damn near impossible when he seated himself on her bed, positioning the pillows behind him to prop himself up. Her mouth went completely dry, and she suddenly wished she still had her tea.

He looked perfect against the white and purple comforter. She could imagine him lying there completely naked, waiting for her with a sexy smirk on his face. Right now, he looked stressed and tired, but he gave her an encouraging smile, and she shook herself back into reality.

"I'm going to change," she choked out, clearing her throat. "I can't stand the scent of those bastards on me."

"I'll be here."

*Thank goodness.*

Julianna grabbed a tank top and light PJ pants and darted into the bathroom. She'd never stripped so quickly in her life, but tonight she couldn't get out of her clothes fast enough. Though she removed her bra and panties, she made sure she was modestly covered when she returned to the bedroom.

Jeff hadn't moved at all, but his eyes heated when he saw her. The same heat zinged down her back and wet the place between her legs. Julianna damn near threw herself on top of him and kissed him again, but she reminded herself she'd promised they wouldn't have sex. Her hands fisted until her nails pressed into her palms.

"Come to bed, darlin'," Jeff drawled with a tired, crooked smile. "Let's tuck you in and let you get some rest."

He held the bed sheets up, and she looked at him with raised eyebrows. The space he offered was against his body, between his legs. Granted, he still wore his clothes, but getting between his legs had been a dream of hers for so long she was momentarily confused at the opportunity to do so.

"You coming?"

"Are you sure it's safe?"

Jeff laughed and nodded. "It is tonight. I promise."

Rather than fight it, she slid into the bed between his muscular thighs and laid her back against his chest as he wrapped his arms loosely around her. His arousal reminded her of his very real attraction, but he made no move to force the issue.

"Thank you, Jeff. I've been waiting forever to be right here."

"Oh, my sweet, beautiful Lupine, it's my pleasure." He kissed the top of her head. "Now, you get some rest, and I'll be right here."

"Okay."

He reached up and turned off her bedside lamp,

snuggling her against him with a sigh. Julianna meant to stay awake and appreciate the comfort, the strength, and the immense contentment she felt being in his arms. But the events of the last few months caught up with her and dragged her beneath the edge of sleep within moments.

## CHAPTER THIRTEEN:
### Politics and Gossip

Jeff grimaced as he looked at his phone in the morning
light. Ten messages, eight texts, and two voicemails.
*Doesn't anyone have anything better to do with their time?*

He'd woken up to find Julianna snuggled up against
him, her head on his chest, her left arm across his belly, and
her left leg draped over his thighs. They still wore all their
clothing, and his hands rested in PG places. Despite the
discomfort of sleeping in his clothes, he rested content with
his situation.

And then his phone beeped at him imperatively with a
new voicemail.

Shit.

He hadn't meant to fall asleep with Julianna, but his
exhaustion, paired with her soft breathing and sweet scent,
had overpowered him, sending him into dreamland. He'd
intended to do as she asked—watch over her until she slept,
then get up and leave her so his car wouldn't be seen in her
driveway the next morning.

That plan had been blown straight to hell.

He rose carefully out of the bed and softly kissed his
Mate on the cheek, making her smile in her sleep. The

smile tightened his chest, and he knew he'd lost his heart to this woman. The mating bond made him lust after her, but last night's attack had brought home just how much he loved Julianna Morris. The thought of her hurt had damn near suffocated him, and he hadn't calmed down until he saw her step out of her car. Even then he'd had to hold her.

The phone beeped again, and Jeff grunted in disgust.

"Yes, I know. I'm coming."

He gathered his phone and his keys and headed out the door, locking the bottom lock behind him. Once he sat in his car, he checked the voicemail and text messages before he started the engine.

Most of the texts originated from Zach and the other bouncers who'd seen his car parked in the Morris driveway. The first voicemail came from Tawny. She'd noticed his car was missing when she got home and wondered where the hell he was.

The second voicemail was from his dad, telling him in a tight voice to get his ass home. They had to talk. Jeff suspected his father had heard about his location from someone and steeled himself. Why the hell did he feel like a kid caught with his hand in the cookie jar?

He drove to his father's house like he faced the hangman, and probably to a lecture, given the messages he'd heard on the phone. He parked the Camaro in its customary spot beneath the large cottonwood tree shading the driveway and got out. *This is gonna suck.* He'd kissed Julianna, so his scent had changed, but he hoped it could be forgiven. *Because I don't regret it.* He took a deep breath before he walked to the kitchen door to let himself in.

The looks Etta and Lindsey gave him. Etta, their cook, had been mooning over his father for years since his mother died. Lindsey, the housekeeper, kept the household running like a Swiss watch, everything in its proper place and at its proper time, and he'd definitely been out of his proper place.

Jeff nodded to the two women. "Where is he?"

"The office." Lindsey's lips tightened and she ducked her head.

*Uh oh. If Lindsey's walking on eggshells, I'm in real trouble.*

He swallowed his unease and made his way through the house to his father's office. The door stood closed, and Jeff took a moment to shake his head and straighten his shoulders. Then he opened it.

Richard sat behind his desk, his attention drawn to the doorway, though his hands still rested on the keyboard of his computer as if he'd been working on emails or some other form of correspondence. Jeff met his gaze and strode over to the wet bar to pour some of the coffee from the silver coffee pot left on a tray. The door clicked closed behind him.

"Thanks for coming so quickly." Heavy irony marred Richard's voice.

"I came as soon as I got the message."

Richard nodded as he leaned back in his chair. "Where were you last night?"

"Come on, Dad. Let's not pussyfoot around. Just be honest."

"All right." He assumed his Alpha persona, and Jeff's guts clenched in dread. "Why were you at the Morris place last night?"

"Tawny called me from Leland and told me Ms. Morris had been attacked by five men in the parking lot. I drove to her house to make sure she was all right. She arrived just after I got there."

"And...?"

"And nothing. She asked me to stay to make sure she was okay. She didn't throw herself at me, and I didn't take advantage of her. I tucked her into bed, and that was that."

"But you stayed all night."

"Yes, I did. I didn't intend to, but I guess I was more

tired than I thought." Jeff shrugged and drank some coffee. "I fell asleep watching over her, and nothing happened. I'm still wearing my clothes and so was she when I left this morning."

"Dammit, Jeff." Richard growled as he rose to his feet. "The whole damn town knows you spent the night with Ms. Morris. I'm gonna have the families of the other Luna candidates all over my ass because of it. Couldn't you just stay away from her a little longer?"

"That's all I've been doing, Dad." Jeff carefully set the coffee cup down to keep from throwing it against the wall. "I have been staying away from her, but when Tawny called, there was no way I could just let Julianna come home alone. Nothing happened, and I accidentally fell asleep. It wasn't my intention, but there it is. We didn't have sex." He stomped to the window, trying to curb his anger.

"That's not what people around here are going to think, especially the other Luna candidates. Hell, I've already had calls from the Winthrops and the Cutters about your car in her driveway."

"It doesn't matter what anyone else thinks." Jeff growled as he shoved away from the window. "She's a candidate for Luna, just like the others, except she doesn't have anyone else to comfort her except her human mother, who doesn't know what we are. Julianna was attacked. I couldn't just leave her there alone all night. So I stayed and held her. Nothing else happened. We didn't overstep our bounds."

"But that's not what people will think. Dammit, this is a political thing now!" his father shouted at him. "You have to pretend you're being objective, no matter how difficult it is."

"I couldn't stay away from her even if I wanted to." Jeff shook his head at his father's wary expression. "She's my Mate, Dad, and she was in distress. I couldn't walk away from that. She needed me, and I was there. I didn't do anything to consummate the bond, and you can smell that for yourself. But she begged me to stay until she slept, and I couldn't say no. I was just too tired, and I fell asleep with her. I had to stay. Don't you see?"

Richard stared at him for a long time, his face hard as stone. But his expression softened, and he nodded. He dropped back into his chair and rubbed his hands over his face.

"Yeah, I do, Jeff. It was the same way with your mother. I couldn't turn her down for anything." He paused, thinking again. "You're sure she's your Mate?"

"Yeah. I knew it the minute I saw her at the funeral."

"Dammit," his father grumbled, but there was no heat in it. "That complicates things, but I'm glad you told me. I had a feeling she was when we interviewed her before the party. That's why I gave her your mother's pendant. I was right?"

"She's my Luna, Dad." Jeff nodded firmly. "Whether any of the others pass the tests or not. Julianna's well on her way to passing all of them anyway, but no matter what, she'll be my Luna. I can't stand to touch or be around any of the others."

"I know." his father agreed solemnly.

"Do you? Because it doesn't matter to me if she's passed the political tests. She's my Mate, and I won't mate with anyone else." Jeff raised his chin. "I'll repudiate being Alpha to make sure I mate with Julianna."

"You can't."

"I can. I won't choose anyone else when my Mate is here. Someone else can be Successor in my place. Julianna is it for me."

"You'd give up your place in the pack just to mate with her?"

"Yes." Jeff had never been so certain in his life.

Richard sat silent for a while, a thoughtful expression

on his face. Jeff had the feeling there was a lot going through his father's mind, but the old man had always been good at keeping a poker face.

"All right." Richard nodded. "There's no denying the Lady's grace with regards to Julianna being your Mate. But no matter what, you have to keep up the appearance of impartiality."

"I'm not impartial. Pass or not, Julianna is my True Mate. I won't go against the Goddess in this."

"I understand, but you can't tell anyone she's your True Mate. We'll have rebellion in the pack." Richard sighed. "However, it has been long enough to narrow the field of candidates you're considering."

"Meaning?"

"Meaning, you don't have to pay court to all of them. You can pick one or two besides Ms. Morris to offer your attention. Mistress Cutter's behavior is just this side of immature and Mistress Wolensky doesn't interact well with the packmembers."

"But, Dad, even the others just—"

His father held up a hand. "I know, Jeff, but we're still in a political game here, and you have to keep up appearances until Ms. Morris passes the tests."

"You do understand this is just a show, right?"

"I do. The reports I've been getting indicate Ms. Morris has passed Courage, Generosity, Strength, Calm, and Secrecy. She only has to demonstrate Tolerance, Respect/Humility, and Honor/Diplomacy to pass. Then the problem of balancing personal with political will be moot."

"She'll do it, Dad."

"I know she will. Still…"

Jeff looked up at his father with a raised eyebrow.

"While you can't influence how she reacts to things, you can always put her into situations that'll allow her to pass the last few tests so you don't have to struggle so much."

"What are you saying?" Jeff narrowed his eyes. "Are you saying I should set her up?"

"Not at all. I'm just saying when a situation occurs where she can demonstrate her skills, you can always encourage her to take the lead."

"That smacks of interference."

To Jeff's immense surprise, his father made a noncommittal sound and tossed his head from side to side slowly.

"Holy shit, you're serious."

"How badly do you want her, Jeff?"

Jeff laughed in disbelief, but he felt like he'd choke.

"Bad enough to let her get this on her own," he confessed. "If I do this for her, she'll never know if it was her merits or my pull. She'll pass, but I gotta let her pass without my help. She's my Mate. I can't take this from her."

Richard didn't say a word. Jeff slowly realized that he, too, had just passed a test. How could his father do something so underhanded? But in a game this serious, Richard had to be certain of all parties. He had to be certain the future leaders would play by the rules and keep everything fair.

"She's my Mate, Dad, but I won't sabotage her chances. But if she doesn't pass, I can't pick one of the others. I'll have to step down." Jeff rubbed the back of his head. "It's killing me not touching her. I swear I did nothing more than a friend would've done in my place last night."

Richard snorted with derision. "And it was so easy to resist her."

Jeff laughed humorlessly. "Hell no. It was excruciating and damn near impossible. But she made us honorable. She did nothing to provoke either of us to break the rules."

*Well, mostly.* Richard wouldn't agree about the kiss they'd shared.

"Not this time," Richard admonished with a knowing look. "But the moon approaches full again. You'll have to be a hundred times more careful when both of you are full to bursting with Her Song."

"I know." Jeff sighed. "I just hope she'll have passed the tests by then. Otherwise, I'll have to leave town for a few days."

"You can't."

"I'll have to. My control is good, but not when my Mate is there in all her Lupine glory and baying for the Lady Moon. I won't be able to stop myself." He shrugged. "We'll have the choosing ceremony that night, like it or not. I can't be around Julianna in her Sister form and stay away from her. I just don't have the strength."

"She wasn't here last month. Sebrina took her out of town."

"It was a good thing." He'd missed her so much he'd had to fight the urge to search for her.

"Hopefully, it won't come to that." Richard rubbed his eyes. "Which of the others are you going to keep up pretenses?"

Jeff wrestled his mind back to the discussion at hand.

"Ms. Winthrop and Ms. Solaris. Since they're the only viable contenders, anyway."

For the pack, not for him. *How the hell am I going to pretend I'm still interested in either of them?*

"Good enough." Richard wasn't fooled by Jeff's cool façade.

"Great."

"Don't worry, Jeff. This will all get resolved soon, and we'll be able to make a decision."

"I've made my decision." He shrugged. "The rest is just window dressing."

"Jeff—"

"No, Dad. It's Julianna or I step down." He'd made his decision. The question remained whether or not the pack could accept it.

\*\*\*\*

Julianna slipped into the bar later that afternoon and tried to ignore the stares peeling the clothes off her back. She sighed as she stowed her purse and keys in the office.

*You gotta love small towns.* Everyone knew everybody's business, and if they didn't, they'd just make up a story to make sense of it.

Jeff had spent the entire night, and elation rippled through her. He said he'd stay only until she fell asleep, but he'd been there in the morning to kiss her good-bye before stepping out the door.

She wanted more of that, though she doubted she'd get her wish. Now tongues would wag about why he'd stayed and what they'd done together. She suspected the patrons believed they'd had sex, but neither her nor Jeff's scents had changed at all, despite their kiss.

*I guess Sebrina was wrong. His kiss didn't start the bond.*

Everyone should know they hadn't mated, but some folks refused to heed the facts. Julianna tightened her lips before she screamed in irritation. It was no one's business but her own whether or not they'd had sex.

*Small town politics suck.*

Squaring her shoulders, she stepped out of the office and made her way to the main room of the bar. *Sink or swim, Morris.* Once again, she walked amongst the wolves. Julianna hoped her calm poise would dissuade the gossips.

When she returned to the main room, she smiled and greeted Zach behind the bar. He studied her intently and scented her then frowned. She raised her eyebrows at him, waiting for his appraisal.

"Afternoon, Zach." She raised her chin when he said nothing to her. "How's it going?"

"Good, Ms. Morris." He lowered his voice. "You don't smell like him."

"Like whom?"

"Like Jeff."

"Why would I?"

He hesitated, and she tried to curb her disgust.

"Do you have a real question for me, Zach?"

"We know he stayed there all night, Ms. Morris." Zach gave her a hard stare.

"That wasn't a question, but I'll answer it anyway." She scowled. "Yes, Jefferson stayed at my house all night. It's not really anyone's business, but he came to make sure I was okay. I guess he fell asleep when the night went too late. He didn't intend to stay."

"That's not what the rumors are saying." Zach wiped down the bar, his eyes on the few patrons in the taproom. "Rumor has it he's chosen you over the others because you're the newest candidate in the pack, and we can smell his interest every time you're around."

Julianna snorted as she unloaded the dishwasher beneath the bar. "Who's the source of these rumors?"

Zach shrugged.

"So you're going to believe the rumors over one of the people in them?" She shook her head. "I thought Moon Singers could smell when people were lying."

"We can."

"Well, then. Rev up that nose of yours and listen up." She met his gaze. "Jeff and I didn't have sex. It's no secret we care about each other, but neither of us would jeopardize the tests. Am I lying?"

Zach shook his head.

"Fabulous. As for whom Jeff's chosen, you'll have to ask him." She winked.

Zach snorted with humor, and his lips quirked into a small smile.

"You know, you should smile more often. I know

Tawny has noticed the few times you do. I think she keeps a running total in a notebook."

"She told you that?"

"No, but I've caught her scoping you out every time she comes into the bar. Just thought I'd mention it."

She shrugged and retreated to the pool tables, checking on the condition of the chalk cubes and pool cues. Zach watched her progress through the bar. *Yeah, chew on that for a while, and leave the gossip alone.* True enough, Tawny only had eyes for Jeff's head bouncer and Zach stood straighter and taller when she came to the bar.

The afternoon passed without incident, though she kept getting looks from most of the west of left field patrons. She suspected they'd come to the bar just to see if the gossip had merit.

It had been a close call last night, but she and Jeff hadn't overstepped their bounds and her scent hadn't changed. Acting guilty would only encourage the small-minded humans who couldn't scent the truth for themselves.

*I did kiss him pretty thoroughly, but I fell asleep almost before my head hit his chest.* She felt a smile curl her lips. Expert in loopholes. *Oh yes, I am.*

Gary came in to take over bartender duties from Zach and custom picked up around five-thirty. A few humans arrived, but the bar filled with west of left fielders intent on scoping out the alphas. Most of them gave her a narrow-eyed once-over, sniffing surreptitiously, but she shrugged it off as small-town politics. Her scent protected her.

When she saw Eloise and Tommy Scatterstone come in, she waved at them and strode over to their table.

Tommy was a dark-haired, dark-eyed young man built like a pro wrestler. He had broad shoulders, a wide barrel chest, and biceps as thick as Julianna's thighs. Julianna buried her revulsion as his eyes wandered over her physique and his smile curled with lascivious arrogance.

His scent sharpened into cloying interest.

"Good evening, Eloise, Mr. Scatterstone."

"How are you tonight, Ms. Julianna?" Concern filled Eloise's eyes and she rose to give Julianna a hug.

"I'm okay. Thanks for asking." She stood back. "I should've texted you when I got home, but I was pretty wrung out."

"I can imagine." Eloise squeezed her hand. "I'm so sorry that happened at my shower. Did you, uh, well…" She grimaced. "Did you tell Mr. Jeff about my sister?"

*Her sister?* It took her a few moments to reconnect the dots. "No. Crap, I completely forgot. Thanks for reminding me. I'll talk to him tonight."

"You were a little too busy last night, eh?" Tommy leered. Eloise gasped in dismay, her face blooming scarlet.

Julianna turned her full attention on him as she lost her smile. "What do you mean by that, Mr. Scatterstone?"

"Uh, well, everyone's talking about how Mr. Lightfoot spent the night at your place." Tommy's leer lost some of its wattage.

"It seems they are." Julianna turned her attention back to Eloise. "I'll make sure Mr. Lightfoot knows about your sister tonight."

"Thank you, Ms. Julianna." She leaned closer. "I'm really sorry about Tommy. Usually he has much better manners."

"I'm sure." Julianna nodded, resisting the urge to curl her lip.

"I wanted to ask if you'd heard the news." Eloise's eyes lit up.

"News?" She hoped it wasn't more rumors about her and Jeff.

"Yes, the candidates for Luna have been cut to three."

Her heart beat a fearful tattoo in her chest. Had their night together disqualified her? "Really? Do you know which three?"

"Mistress Solaris, Mistress Winthrop, and you."

Relief slithered down her spine. "Wow. Did you hear why the others were dropped?"

Eloise shook her head. "I think Mistress Cutter was just too young and inexperienced, and Mistress Wolensky was too withdrawn."

"Huh. Well, I certainly wish them the best."

"Yeah, right." Tommy smirked, and Julianna let a little frown crease her brows.

"To gloat over someone else's misfortune is small-minded and mean-spirited, Mr. Scatterstone. The only way I can gain this post is through my own merits, not the failings of my fellow Candidates."

"Good Goddess, Tommy. You're being rude tonight." Eloise scowled and stepped away from him, her scent filling with chagrin. "I'm really sorry. He's been listening to all the rumors, when he gets something in his head, he won't change it for love or money."

Julianna raised her chin. "And what do you think about the rumors?"

"I think you'd tell me or I could smell if they had any truth." Eloise met her gaze steadily.

Julianna smiled. "Good answer. Thanks again for checking on me. Call if you need anything. You folks have a good night."

She turned and moved swiftly away from their table before she lobbed a glass of water at Tommy Scatterstone. She hoped he learned better manners before his wedding or Eloise dumped him.

Shaking her head, she slid behind the bar where Gary produced drinks like an automaton. She smiled at him and loaded the dishwasher with the used glasses from the sink. He inhaled deeply through his nose, but tried to do it unobtrusively. Julianna shook her head and said nothing. If he wanted the story, he'd have to ask. Gary gave her a quick look and his own smile, but kept his mouth shut.

*He must've gotten his answer.*

The rumor mill had to be working overtime if Tommy's leering remarks meant anything. Thinking of Scatterstone reminded her she needed to speak to Jeff about Eloise's sister.

"Hey, Gary, has Jefferson come in yet?"

"Yeah, I think he's in the office."

"Thanks." She finished loading the dishwasher before she headed to the back.

Julianna knocked on the door before she turned the knob and pushed it open. She came to a hard stop when she realized who stood inside. The noise in the bar had disguised the shouting and screaming going on in the room, but it stopped immediately with her appearance.

Tammy Cutter whirled around to give Julianna a look of surprise that quickly morphed into venomous anger.

"Oh, excuse me." Julianna grimaced. "I didn't realize you had a meeting."

"That's all right, Ms. Morris," Jeff said. "What did you need?"

"I'd like to speak to you about an important matter when you have a moment."

"I'll find you when I'm done here."

"Thank you. Again, excuse me." She backed out of the room and closed the door. "Oh boy, that can't be good."

Shaking her head, she heard the screaming take on a new volume behind the door and deduced Ms. Cutter had taken issue with being dropped as a candidate for Luna. Of course, her screaming only confirmed she wasn't ready for the position. Julianna quickly retreated into the taproom.

Julianna helped Gary behind the bar when the orders began piling up. She cleaned blenders, switched used dishes into the dishwasher, and made sure full bottles had been stocked behind the bar. Kyle improved their efficiency by hauling more from the back. Julianna kept her attention on helping Gary and the waitresses as business increased, subbing for bathroom breaks and breathers.

"Hey, Ms. Morris, this order is supposed to go to one of the pool tables and I gotta pee really bad," a waitress named Lucy announced as she bounced in place a little.

"Sure, I'll take it. Which table?"

"Fourteen, all the way in the back." Lucy sidled toward the bathroom.

"All right."

Julianna grabbed the tray of drinks and threaded her way toward the pool tables. Heads turned, and she could almost read their thoughts. *Cheat, hussy, gold-digger*. She sighed and resisted the urge to grimace. The exercise in stoicism wore her out.

*How does Jeff do this all the time?*

As she approached Pool Table 14, a frisson of unease slid down her back and a sense of wrongness intruded on her thoughts. She carried the tray of drinks to the little table beside the pool table and unloaded them, but she kept a wary eye on the players.

"There you go, gentlemen. Enjoy."

Julianna turned away to go back to the bar, but someone stepped into her way. Tall and broad, the man wore an old LA Raiders ball cap turned backward, and dark sunglasses. A leather cord hung around his neck with a pewter skull and crossbones pendant, and a single silver hoop pierced his right ear.

She wouldn't have recognized him from his looks, but the scents of apricots and male maliciousness identified him.

"Let me pass, sir." Her heart rate kicked up.

"Now, don't be so quick to leave, little girl," he drawled in a bad Texas accent. "We'd all like a pretty lady to stay and help us play."

"I really have to get back to work." Julianna tried to move around him, but his arm shot out and grabbed hers, halting her.

"Oh, come on, sweet thing, stay awhile."

"No, I can't. Let go of me."

"But we haven't finished with you." Her eyes snapped up to his face as he pressed something cold and hard against her side. "Now, now, don't you scream. You don't want to cause any trouble."

*I don't want to cause the trouble?* Why did men always expect women to be quiet and take their shit?

Anger thundered through her veins as she considered who'd set this up. Had Lucy been in on it? She'd asked specifically for Julianna to take this order to the table in the back where none of the bouncers could see her. *Why are these guys so determined to mess with me?*

Julianna focused on relaxing her body, but everything remained taut. She desperately wanted to throw Baldy Tattoo into his buddies while she pummeled the shit out of him, but she didn't think an average human could avoid the knife, even with martial arts training.

Fear trickled into her awareness as her Sister growled with the realization that she'd have to let someone rescue her. She faced her hardest test and could only hope Gary noticed she hadn't come back before these three humans did anything really stupid.

# CHAPTER FOURTEEN:
## Impartiality

Jeff ran a hand over his face and tightened his ponytail with a grimace. Damn, Tammy had been a little bitch about being dropped as a candidate.

Ironically, her screaming fit in his office this afternoon only underscored her unsuitability for Luna. She had a lot of growing up to do, most of which he'd prefer to miss. With a vocabulary full of "likes" and "totallys" and four letter expletives that didn't accurately describe how she felt, she reminded him of a bad '80s movie. The idea of mating with her made his stomach curdle. She was too much like another little sister he had to tolerate until she needed a swift kick in the ass.

He'd given her a verbal smack-down, and reminded her of her place within the pack. She'd snapped her mouth closed and bowed her head as the full power and chill voice of the Alpha fell on her. He'd called her parents to let them know they needed to discipline their immature daughter. She'd been mortified and apologized profusely, bringing the whole episode to a much welcome end.

It'd been a long day with everyone eyeing him with either lecherous approval or scandalized disdain, but he'd kept his typically half-amused face on, refusing to show any guilt. He thanked Julianna for that. She'd kept them from doing anything disastrous. Her interruption of Tammy's tirade had been a bright spot in an otherwise frustrating shift, and he intended to find out why she needed to talk to him. He surveyed the taproom, but he didn't see her.

"Hey, Jefferson, did Ms. Morris find you?" Gary asked when he appeared.

"Yes, but I was in a meeting. Have you seen her?"

"Yeah, she took an order to Pool Table 14."

"She's taking orders now?"

"She does it when one of the waitresses needs a break. Lucy had to pee, apparently."

Unease raised the hackles on Jeff's neck. "There's Lucy. How long ago did Ms. Morris take the order?"

Gary frowned and shook his head. "I dunno. We've been hammered."

"That's okay. I'll go find her."

Gary nodded, but his frown remained.

"Zach," Jeff called on the little walkie-talkie he carried when in the bar.

"Yeah, boss?"

"Send Leo, Thomas, and Woody to the pool tables. We may have a situation brewing at Table Fourteen."

"Done, boss."

Jeff ignored the looks he received as he strode toward the pool tables. Everything seemed serene enough, but a small knot of tense people clustered around one of the tables. The scents of anger and fear wafted over the crowd. Too many people blocked his view to see what was going on, but Jeff's unease intensified. He spied Leo and Woody slipping through the shadows along the side of the pool hall, faces tense. Thomas wound his way through the tables to Jeff's right as he closed in on the crowd.

His unease shifted into full-blown fury when he stopped

at the back of the small mob. A large man in an old Raiders ball cap and black tank top held Julianna pressed against him, but she didn't look happy to be there. Jeff's canines elongated at the sight of another male touching his Mate. He didn't understand why she didn't pull away until he caught a flash of silver pressed to her side and scented her frustration and fear.

He took a deep breath through his nose and more scents flooded his awareness—the big man's malice, the excitement of the crowd around them, and a curious scent of apricots. He ignored them all as he watched two other men position themselves behind and around Julianna, hampering her escape even if she tried to bolt.

The guy in the ball cap told Julianna they had some unfinished business to discuss. *Not if I have anything to say about it, asshole.* Jeff's rage swelled. One look at Ball Cap's swollen nose and blackened eyes sent pride shooting through him. These were the bastards who got a taste of Julianna last night when she kicked their asses.

"What's going on here?" Jeff stepped out into the circle of light, burying his fury behind his bland expression.

Julianna's body relaxed, and she shot Jeff a look of relief so profound his fury crystallized to a diamond-hard ball within his chest. This close to the full moon, it would be difficult to keep himself from killing the bastard touching her.

Ballcap glanced over and snorted a little at Jeff's shorter stature. "Nothing you need to worry about, Shorty," Ballcap shook Julianna a little. "This little bitch and I have some business to discuss. So you can just fuck off."

Jeff widened his smile to show his canines. The scent of apricots assaulted his nose, an oddly feminine scent. Who was he to judge?

"Yeah, that's not gonna happen." Jeff caught Woody's and Leo's eyes and nodded toward Ballcap's cronies while he and Thomas moved in on the human holding Julianna.

The two bouncers dipped their heads in acknowledgement and melted into the shadows behind the other thugs. "You need to let the woman go." He raised his chin. "Now."

The crowd around Ballcap drew back a little, the scent of their unease spilling into the space. Ballcap's monkey brain must have caught on because his gaze darted around with the withdrawal. He searched for his compatriots, but they'd disappeared. Ballcap lost a little of his bravado, and fear seeped into his scent.

"Look, she owes me money. We had a deal."

Jeff shook his head as the rancid scent of the lie hit his nose. "Yeah, I'm not buyin' the shit you're sellin'."

Thomas eased up behind the human. "And since this is my bar, you get to let go of my employee, and I'll let you walk out of here on your own two feet."

Ballcap twitched with that little announcement, but his expression remained hard and arrogant.

"But I got business—"

"No, your business is done."

*He's touching your Mate! Kill, kill, kill!* Jeff's Brother snarled beneath his calm façade.

*Be patient. We might have the opportunity.*

"Let the woman go and get out."

"You want her? Come and take her!" Ballcap shouted, pushing Julianna hard with his knife hand. She gasped and fell, and then all hell broke loose.

Thomas grabbed Ballcap from behind while Jeff launched himself at Julianna with a snarl. Ballcap let out a choked exclamation and dropped the red-bladed knife onto the floor. Jeff heard it fall, but lost track of it as he caught Julianna while the man tried to fight the constriction around his throat. Thomas kept squeezing until he slumped unconscious in his arms.

"Julianna!" Jeff didn't know how to hold her without hurting her.

"Oh, glory, Jeff. It really hurts."

"I know, sweetheart." Sweet Goddess, there was blood everywhere. *Why isn't she healing fast?*

She moaned as he lifted her, and his heart constricted in fear. He couldn't lose her. Not when she'd finally come home to him. The scent of her blood and fear sickened him, but he clenched his teeth and prayed for control.

He pivoted on the balls of his feet and carried her through the bar to the office, the crowd parting to let him pass.

"Hold on, Julianna! It'll be okay." He laid Julianna on the couch, rolling her so he could look at her injury.

Zach appeared in the open door. "The cops have been called, and the assholes are detained. The big guy is still out."

"Good. I can't get anywhere near them or I'll kill them. Get Gary in here. He was a WWII medic. She's been stabbed."

"Shit!" Zach disappeared from the doorway.

Gary appeared before Zach had gone more than two steps. Jeff's First followed him back in, closing the door behind them.

"What happened?" Gary asked in a cool, professional voice.

"She got stabbed in the side with some sort of short-bladed knife," Jeff reported.

"Okay, let's see what the damage is."

Gary spoke conversationally, but every muscle in his face hardened. He peeled back Julianna's shirt to expose the wound in her side, and Jeff tightened his hands into fists. Blood oozed out of a two-inch puncture as she breathed, staining her clothes in an increasing arc.

*I'm gonna kill him!* His Brother form howled with fury. *He touched my Mate!*

"Get me some scissors," Gary ordered, and Zach jumped to obey, rank forgotten.

They cut away her shirt, and Gary probed the wound

gently with his fingers. Julianna moaned in pain again, and Jeff clenched his jaws to keep from biting something. But Gary's expression relaxed a little.

"It's a shallow puncture and clean. She won't have any trouble healing." He sighed. "But you'll have to get her to change. The damage will only be minor if she changes soon."

Jeff's guts clenched again. "I can't do that."

Gary raised a doubtful eyebrow.

"She's a candidate for Luna. If I'm near her when she changes this close to the full moon, it could be considered a breach in protocol." *Not to mention my desperate need to mate with her.*

"Jefferson, someone has to get her to change or she could suffer much worse damage." Gary taped a gauze bandage over her side.

The door burst open, and everyone tensed for battle. Jeff only relaxed when Tawny and her best friend Eloise flew into the room. The ladies stopped as if hitting a wall and all the blood drained from their faces when they spotted Julianna.

"Oh Goddess above, is she all right?" Tawny dropped to the floor beside her brother.

"She has to change into her Sister form." *Why does my voice sound frightened and desperate?* "I can't do it because it'd be a breach of protocol, but she could be in real trouble if she doesn't shift soon."

"Okay, then." Tawny briskly got to her feet. "I'll do it."

"You can't, Tawny." Eloise touched her friend's shoulder.

"Why not?"

"You're part of the Alpha's family. It'd look like favoritism." Eloise shot a look at Gary. "Can she be moved?" Gary nodded, and Eloise leaned down, gently scooping Julianna into her arms. "Get the door, would you please, Zach?"

Jeff scrambled to his feet as Zach held the office door wide, almost yanking it off its hinges. He followed the ladies as they headed to the door leading to the loading dock. His mind swam with the fear of Julianna's mortality

*Hold on, Julianna. Hold on for me.*

Zach held the loading doors open, but caught Jeff before he went through. Jeff snarled, but Zach held his ground. "You have to be impartial."

Eloise slid past them and gave him an encouraging smile. "Thanks, Mr. Jeff. Can you please tell Tommy that I won't be coming back tonight? I'd appreciate it."

There was no way in hell he could tolerate the arrogant Scatterstone tonight.

"I'll do it." Tawny smiled as Eloise nodded before she disappeared into the night with the woman he loved.

Jeff swore the world spun in a gut-wrenching spiral. *Holy Goddess, please help her heal.*

He stood there in the doorway, trying to calm his raging emotions. Fear burned a hole through his gut, and he swallowed repeatedly around his heart lodged in his throat. If he hadn't been clear how he felt about Julianna that morning, no doubt remained now. Love was the only thing that could hurt this much.

"Come on, Jeff. We have to go back inside." Tawny patted his shoulder, her eyes full of empathy. "Julianna's gonna be fine. Eloise is the best trauma nurse in the clinic. She knows what to do."

Tawny laid a hand on his shoulder, her scent full of compassion. He shuddered a sigh before he turned and stalked back into the bar. He clenched his jaw and swallowed hard to keep in his rage. He'd get some answers about those bastards. Why were they stalking Julianna? It stank like a setup, and someone knew about it. He just had to determine who. He'd start by asking that little bitch, Lucy.

\*\*\*\*

Julianna woke in pain and itching discomfort as if she wore the wrong skin.

She kept her eyes closed, but someone shined a flashlight into her face and whispered, "It's time to change into your Sister form, Julianna. Shift, return to the wild part of yourself. The pain will go away if you go to your Sister. It's time."

*Sister...why does that term seem so familiar?* Confusion reigned, but her needs pushed through the morass of emotion, and she shifted her attention to them. She wanted to run through the silver moonlight on all fours, racing the wind and singing to the Lady in the sky above. But something hurt. *Why is there so much pain?*

"Julianna!" the person barked sharply. "You must change. It's time, and you have to help yourself. You must shift."

She groaned. *I'm so tired. Can't I do this some other time?*

A snarl tore through the air close to her ear, and she jerked in surprise. Anger quickly followed, and her Sister demanded release. Her mind filled with memories of the wind in her coat and the sights and sounds of nighttime serenading her.

Her body slowly changed shape, and everything seemed fine until agony ripped across her awareness like lightning. She screamed, and it turned into a howl of pain when she fully shifted into her Sister form. She panted as the pain ebbed, lying on her side with her head on the ground. *Holy Goddess above, why do I hurt so much?*

Someone whimpered next to her, and she slit her eyes open to look around. A silvery white wolf with brown eyes stared back at her, worry stamped on every muscle. The wolf's tail lowered, and her ears flattened. She licked the top of Julianna's head in supplication and whined a little.

Julianna just lay there and breathed. It felt better just to stay still. She urfed to tell the other wolf she felt better, but exhaustion stole her energy, and her fear faded away. The white she-wolf backed up a little way from her and lay down with her head between her front paws, watching her carefully. Julianna closed her eyes and bounded off into the comforting darkness of sleep.

# CHAPTER FIFTEEN:
## Rights of Passage

Julianna woke to find herself in a bed, but not hers. The room smelled of furniture polish and jasmine. *This isn't home.* She'd never used furniture polish in her life.

Vintage wallpaper in gold and white stripes covered every wall, and an antique vanity with an oval mirror showed an addle-pated woman with crazy hair staring back at her. A single white closet door and an old maple bureau filled the space on the wall across from the bed. White cotton sheets tangled with her legs under a brightly-colored patchwork quilt. The window to her right allowed the sun to shine its light through the gauzy curtains, billowing from the breeze coming through the opened pane.

*Where am I and how did I get here?*

Scouring her memories, she recalled being at work when Eloise told her the news about the candidates. Ms. Cutter had been in the office with Jeff, and then...Julianna frowned as she tried to think.

Images of a drink order, pool tables, and Baldy Tattoo flashed across her mind's eye. The human had threatened her and stuck a knife into her side. Her memories became confused after that. Had Jeff been there? She thought she remembered his face bending over her, his eyes wide with anger and fear.

*But that can't be right. Jeff's never afraid. Is he?*

Sense memories of pain and light pushed to the forefront of her mind, along with a white she-wolf.

Eloise, in her Sister form. What was she doing there?

Julianna remembered Eloise staying with her, but then the memories ended. Now she rested here.

Julianna scented Eloise in the air of her room. Where was she, exactly? Wriggling her body out of the tangled sheets, she sat up, bracing her arms behind her. Two things became very apparent.

First, she wore nothing, right down to her sockless feet. And second, she felt no pain in her side, not even tenderness from an injury. Julianna paused, thinking hard. She distinctly remembered getting stabbed. Puzzled, she threw back the covers to look down at herself.

Nothing showed on her side between her ribs and the swell of her hip. No scar, no redness, not even a thin white line to show a wound. Her skin covered her body whole and smooth.

Julianna stared at herself for a few moments, her mind racing with the implications of what she saw. Or rather, what she didn't see. No marks of any kind scored her skin, not even the old scars on her knees from skinning them as a kid. She leaned back in the bed and pulled the sheet back over her body, mulling everything over.

*Nice to know some of the myths are true. Werewolves do heal crazy-fast.*

Julianna had turned her mind to what she needed to do next when the door opened and Eloise entered with canvas bag over one shoulder and a breakfast tray in her hands. Bacon, sausage, eggs, hash browns, a bagel, and a glass of water filled the tray, and Julianna's mouth watered with the scents.

"Oh, good, you're up." Eloise smiled and nodded to

her. "How are you feeling?"

"Good," Julianna croaked, and grimaced. "Hungry, but better than I expected. How did I get here?"

"I brought you home after you shifted into your Sister form. You fell asleep and couldn't hold the form for long, but shifting helped you heal." Eloise grimaced. "Of course, you already know that. I've brought you some breakfast and a change of clothes from your place. Your mom heard about the bar fight." She rolled her eyes. "Damn small town gossip. She brought you the clothes. Do you want to eat or get dressed first?"

"I'd prefer to get dressed, but I'm too hungry and it smells way too good." Her eyes never strayed from the tray. "Just give me a T-shirt and I'll eat before I take a shower."

"Right."

Eloise handed her the bag of clothes, and Julianna found one of her comfy t-shirts, as well as panties, and her denim capris.

"Way to go, Mom." Julianna pulled the shirt over her head. "Did she give you much trouble?"

"No. She knows I'm a trauma nurse at the clinic, so she was okay with you staying here while I kept an eye on you."

Eloise handed her the tray without comment, but Julianna scented unease from the other woman.

"What's wrong? You look like you're afraid I'll bite your head off or something."

"I have something to tell you, but I don't know how." Eloise sat poised, looking ready to bolt if Julianna made any sudden moves.

"Just tell me straight out and we'll go from there, okay?"

"Okay."

Eloise watched Julianna eat for a few moments more before she opened her mouth again. "After your mom dropped by, I asked her to keep an eye on your while ran to the grocery store for some supplies. Ms. Solaris happened to be there and she looked pretty pleased with herself. I didn't dare say hello because I don't think she likes me very much, and being beta, I can't really just walk up and talk to her."

Julianna tried to hide her grimace, but her mouth flattened. Eloise didn't appear to notice.

"She was talking on her phone to someone and she said it had to be done that night and in a place no one would see anything. She complained that they hadn't gotten it right last night, and this was the best time to take care of it. Then she said, 'I don't care if you ruin the dumb bitch, just get rid of her.' She said to call her when they'd done it and hung up."

The food turned to dust in Julianna's mouth, and a chill slid down her spine.

"She hadn't seen me yet, so I stepped back out of sight and tried to figure out how to get out of the store." Eloise fiddled with a ring on her right hand. "She walked around for a little while longer and saw me in the checkout aisle. She didn't say anything to me, but when she stood behind me in line, I got a scent of her perfume. I don't know any Moon Singers who wear perfume because it messes with our sensitive noses, but she wore a fruity scent, like apricots. It was strange."

"What did you just say?"

"What? That it was strange?"

"No, before that. What did she smell like?"

"Apricots."

"Damn." Julianna lost her appetite as her mind made connections. "Have you told this story to anyone else?"

"No, I had to get back here last night to relieve your mom. I haven't seen anyone else since then."

Julianna nodded. "I have to talk to Jeff and Richard Lightfoot."

"What, now?"

"Yes. Your story is more important than you know."

Julianna set aside the tray and scooted out of the bed, her mind racing. Could Brenda Solaris have organized the attacks on her? Would she really be that underhanded? She combed her fingers through her hair and pulled it back into a messy ponytail with the hair tie Eloise gave her. She jerked on her capris and found her shoes.

"Can you give me a ride to their place? My car is still at the bar."

"Of course." Eloise led the way out of the bedroom of the cute one-bedroom cottage.

"Oh my glory. Did I take your bed?" Julianna stopped, chagrin pulling her mouth down. "I'm so sorry."

"No, don't worry about it. You needed it and I didn't mind." Eloise patted her shoulder. "It was an honor and my job to make sure you were comfortable."

"You're sure? I really appreciate you looking out for me."

"I'm sure. I was happy to do it." Eloise gave her a real smile.

"I'm…I'm very grateful." Julianna rubbed the back of her neck. "I don't know if I could've done it without you."

"You're welcome. Come on. We'd best get you over to the Alpha's house before it gets much later."

Julianna caught Eloise's sleeve. "I mean it. Thanks for helping me when I needed it."

Eloise smiled as she dropped her hand on Julianna's. "That's what friends are for."

"Yeah." Julianna nodded with her own smile.

They loaded into Eloise's car and drove over to the Lightfoot place. Julianna hoped she wouldn't get into trouble visiting the Alpha before the conclusion of the Luna competition, but this was too important to keep to herself.

"Thanks for the ride. I really appreciate it. Come in with me."

Eloise bit her lip. "I'm not sure I should."

"Yes, you should. The Alpha needs to hear your story about Ms. Solaris." Julianna nodded and added a grin. "Besides, I need a ride to my car afterward."

Eloise laughed. "So I'm just a chauffeur."

"Exactly." Julianna grinned.

"Oh, fine. The things I do for my alpha friends."

Delight filled Julianna as they went up to the door and knocked. The housekeeper recognized her and let them in, directing them to the dining room. Jeff and his dad sat talking over breakfast. Sunshine from the windows gilded everything, including Jeff's hair and the muscles of his arm as he buttered some toast. Julianna had no idea such a mundane task could be so sexy, but Jeff's motions sent cream straight to her pussy, and she exhaled in a soft sigh.

He turned his head and his eyes blazed with hungry intent when he saw her.

"Julianna." He rose to his feet. "I didn't expect to see you so soon. How are you feeling?"

"Better than I expected." She approached the table with Eloise in tow. "We have some news we'd like to share, if that's all right, Mr. Lightfoot."

"Of course, Ms. Morris." Richard nodded with a smile. "Would you care to sit down?"

"Thank you, Alpha." She nodded to him courteously. Jeff jerked out the chair beside his, and she sank into it with a smile. "Thanks. I'm sorry to interrupt."

"Not a problem," Richard said. "What's this news you have to share?"

Sitting before the Alpha, all Julianna's initial suspicions seemed a little more far-fetched, and she hesitated to blurt them out. Could she really accuse Ms. Solaris of trying to take her out of the competition? What proof did she have?

She cleared her throat. "I've been thinking about what happened last night and in Leland, and I think they're connected. I recognized the men last night as the ones from the salon, but after the first night, I can't understand why they'd come after me again. Especially when I, well, kicked their butts."

Jeff snorted, and Eloise gave a shy smile as she settled in the chair beside Julianna.

"It just seems strange that they'd keep coming after me." Julianna frowned. "Eloise Farkas, my friend who gave me a place to rest, told me about an experience she had last night that made me think it might have been a setup."

"Oh?" Richard focused his gaze on Eloise. "What happened?"

The blonde woman swallowed nervously, but she reiterated her story to the Alpha. Julianna watched Jeff's expression grow colder and harder with each word. Richard's face showed nothing at all. She curled her hands into fists to keep from throwing something in her fury while she waited for the Alpha to speak.

Richard sat quietly for a few moments more, "What makes you think Ms. Solaris was speaking about you, Ms. Morris?"

"Eloise said Ms. Solaris wore perfume, the scent of apricots. It's the same scent I smelled on the man who attacked me at the salon and last night in the bar. The scent wasn't part of him. It was on him, like he'd come in contact with someone wearing it. And the scent is distinctive."

"Is there anyone who can verify that?"

"I can." Jeff raised his hand. "Ms. Solaris wore that scent on all the occasions I met with her, and I smelled it on the man in the bar last night, too. I thought it strange that a man would smell so fruity, but he's human." He shrugged. "I didn't make the connection until now."

"You said there were five men who attacked you at the salon." Richard tapped the table with one hand. "Did any of the others smell like apricots?"

"No, just Baldy Tattoo."

"Baldy Tattoo?" Richard raised an eyebrow.

Julianna grimaced. "That's what I called him in my head because he didn't introduce himself. He was bald and had a tribal tattoo on the back of his head that stretched from ear to ear."

"I can verify that, too," Jeff said. "Thomas removed the ball cap last night after he incapacitated Julianna's attacker, and he had a shaved head and a spiky tattoo on the back."

"Did you see any of the other men last night who attacked you at the salon?"

"No, Alpha, but I did see him with two friends. The Leland PD got two of the five attackers at the salon. I can only assume these other two were part of the three who got away."

"Why were you anywhere near these men last night?"

"I took a drink order to the pool tables for a waitress who needed a break." Julianna frowned. She recalled her unease at the time. "I thought it must have been a setup when I realized who the men were. Did anyone talk to Lucy?"

"I did." Ice filled Jeff's voice.

"What did she say, Jeff?" Richard raised his eyebrows.

"She said the man in the Raiders cap offered her a large tip to have Ms. Morris bring the drinks back to the table."

"And she didn't think that was strange?" Eloise blushed when they glanced at her. "Sorry."

"She said with everyone gawking at Julianna last night because of the rumors going around town, she thought these guys just wanted to see the source of the gossip."

"Should we do something about her, Dad?" Jeff settled his arms on the table

"Who, Jeff?"

"Ms. Solaris. Are these events grounds for disqualification?"

Richard shook his head. "We have no proof that Ms. Solaris did anything unless the tattooed man says something to implicate her. We just have a scent and a suspicious one-sided conversation."

Julianna drummed her fingers on the table. "We have no proof. But that might not be a bad thing."

"What do you mean?" Richard tilted his head.

"If Ms. Solaris is the one behind the attacks, she thinks she's gotten away with it, and it should make her overconfident. She might make a mistake that'll expose her manipulations." Julianna shrugged. "At least, I hope that's the case."

Jeff growled. "I don't like playing games that allow her to do more."

Julianna nodded. "The problem is she has to condemn herself. We can't do it for her. Hopefully, she'll get caught or try to bribe or manipulate the wrong packmember. I won't play her game by her rules. Now that we're aware of her involvement, we can guard against it better." Julianna paused and turned her attention back to Richard.

"Alpha, I won't challenge Ms. Solaris over this. I have too many other things to worry about that are more important. But I wanted you to be aware of the direction of my thoughts in this matter."

No one said anything for a few moments after Julianna's statement. Eloise squeezed her hand under the table and winked. Jeff wore his customary amused expression and Richard looked at her with calm attention.

"What if she tries again, Julianna?" Jeff tapped the table with one finger.

"I'll be vigilant and ready to call for help if the situation gets out of hand, but I won't retaliate until I have proof that Ms. Solaris is behind all these events." Julianna raised her chin. Anger and frustration welled up inside, but she crossed her arms over her chest to hold them back.

*I really do want to be Luna.* Julianna wanted to win the competition on her own merits, not because she exposed a fellow candidate as a cheat. And she wasn't convinced Ms. Solaris had done anything. Something about the two attacks didn't ring true. *There's something I'm missing.*

"You could always let the rest of the pack know that you've lost respect for Ms. Solaris," Jeff said into the silence. "You know how rumor spreads through this town."

"Jeff." A growl underlay Richard's voice.

"What?" Jeff tried to look innocent. "Julianna is my Mate, Dad. Ms. Solaris should be punished for her actions. I wish I could kick the crap out of her myself and send her back to LA. I think the pack should decide if Ms. Solaris is so deserving of her rank and status."

"You can't interfere, Jeff."

"I won't." Jeff offered his customary half-smile. "I leave that up to Eloise's discretion." He shot a look at the beta woman.

Julianna shot a look at her friend. "What do you think?"

Eloise blushed. "I'm honored that you all think to ask me, but I don't have any more proof than you do. There's a lot of circumstantial evidence—I learned that from those cop shows on TV—that seems to point to Ms. Solaris. But I can't say for sure if it's her."

"A wise and measured response, Ms. Farkas." Richard nodded.

"Thank you, Alpha." Eloise's blush deepened.

Julianna beamed at her friend. "I have to win this on my own, through my own positive actions, but it's good to have folks who back me up."

Jeff shifted a little in his chair until his thigh brushed hers under the table. "We definitely want to back you up." The subtext that ran through her head was, *against the wall of my bedroom.*

"Thanks, Jeff. It's just so messed up with everything that's happened. I mean, I've had rough times, but I've never been a target before. It's unsettling."

Richard nodded and gave Jeff a look she couldn't interpret, but she wrangled her mind back to the present. Eloise had given her a place to stay. It was time to do as she'd promised.

"But my problems aren't the only reason we needed to talk to you." She shot a smile at Eloise. "Ms. Farkas mentioned to me that her sister Nora has been missing for four weeks without contact of any kind."

Richard's expression settled into thoughtfulness as he switched his gaze to Eloise. "Is this true, Ms. Farkas?"

The blonde woman nodded, her blush returning. "Yes, Alpha."

Richard's brow creased in a frown. "Does your sister normally do this sort of thing, disappearing for a while?"

"No, Alpha. This is out of character for her."

"I mentioned it to Detective Cannon of the Leland PD and he suggested I bring it to your attention." Julianna squeezed Eloise's hand again.

"Exactly right." Richard nodded. "Thank you. We'll get on it right away, and I'll be talking to your family, Ms. Farkas."

Elois nodded and stood. "Of course. Whenever is convenient. Thank you, Alpha."

Julianna rose as well.

"Can you join us breakfast?" Jeff gestured to the table.

"I—Thank you, but Ms. Farkas is my ride. My car's still at the bar. I need to get home and check on my mom, anyway." She smiled, wishing she could do more. "I'll see you at the bar for my shift tonight."

She and Eloise nodded to the family and headed out to the car, both breathing a sigh of relief as they got in.

Julianna laughed. "That went pretty well, I think."

"Yes, it did. Thanks for mentioning my sister. I think the Alpha will actually do something about it." Eloise threw the car into gear and pulled out of the Lightfoots' drive.

"I know they will, and I'm happy to help. It's scary to think a Moon Singer can go missing."

"It is." Eloise nodded. "Almost as scary as the idea that

Ms, Solaris is trying to sabotage your bid for Luna."

"That's the thing. I don't know if it really was Ms. Solaris." Julianna frowned. Something about the events at the salon and the bar seemed off. Everything pointed to Brenda as the mastermind behind the attacks, but Julianna didn't take her for an insecure bitch.

"You don't think it was her?" Eloise raised her eyebrows.

"Without concrete evidence, I can't point fingers or make accusations. But I swear I'm missing something." She shook her head. "My gut's telling me someone else is pulling all the strings and calling the shots from behind the scenes."

She had no reason to suspect anyone else in this mess, but the feeling of a hidden player just wouldn't go away.

"What if there is another person trying to make it look as if Ms. Solaris is trying to take me down?" Julianna's mind projected the scenario forward. "If this person engineered my failure and didn't get caught, one of the other candidates would have a better chance of being chosen as Luna."

"Okay, so who would benefit most from having you drop out of the competition?" Eloise stopped at a traffic light. "There are still two candidates, Cameron Winthrop and Ms. Solaris."

"That's true. I haven't heard anything about Cameron misbehaving or acting out. Brenda would still have to contend with her if I failed."

"Yes. Do you think it's one of their family members? Someone who thinks they have a better chance against one another without you in their way?"

Julianna shook her head. "In this game, everyone's looking at me and Brenda as primary rivals. No one else appears to be in the top rank. But who'd have the most to gain if I failed and Brenda got accused of manipulating it?"

Her thoughts splintered as her phone pinged with a text

message. She pulled the little device out and opened the message.

**Call me as soon as you get home. I have something important to tell you. Jeff**

She raised her eyebrows but texted him an affirmative back before putting the phone away. *That's weird. I wonder if he already has news about Eloise's sister.*

"Everything okay?" Eloise pulled the car into the parking lot of the bar.

"Yeah. I think so." *Maybe Jeff needs to tell me something about the Luna competition.* That wasn't a happy thought. "Can I ask a favor of you, Eloise?"

"Sure. What?"

"Are we supposed to dress up really fancy for the Luna ceremony? I've never seen or been in one so I don't know."

"Oh, yes, I think it's considered a black-tie event." Eloise threw the car in park. "Why?"

"I don't think I have anything to wear. Well, nothing formal enough. Can you come with me this afternoon and help me find something worth wearing in front of the whole pack?"

Eloise grinned. "Of course, I'd be honored."

"Good. Thanks." Julianna nodded and opened the car door. "Thanks so much for last night and giving me a ride. I really appreciate it."

"That's what friends do. You've helped me so much, Ms. Morris, I'm terribly grateful."

"It is what friends do, and they also use first names." She pointed to herself with a raised eyebrow. "Repeat after me: Julianna. Julianna."

Eloise laughed. "Ju-lee-aahh-nah."

She grinned. "Very good! You get a treat." She laughed as she stepped out. "I'll text you when I'm ready to go this afternoon. You really don't have any plans?"

"No. I've taken leave for the next week while we figure out what's going on with my sister." She shook her head and sighed. "This is the first time I've felt like things are moving in the right direction."

"It's going to work out. I know it. So I'll see you this afternoon."

"Okay. Talk to you then."

She watched Eloise drive off as she clicked open her car and sat in the driver's seat. Eloise's gentle teasing made her smile, but Jeff's text worried her. What was so important when she'd just seen him?

Shaking her head, she turned on the car and headed home. Hopefully, her mom didn't notice that she hadn't come home last night. *Oh, who am I kidding? I never got away with anything as a teenager because she always knew.* Not that Julianna was a teenager now or had to report to her mother. But the small-town grapevine had probably already told Beth that Julianna had been in a bar fight. *Yeah, how am I going to explain that?*

Hopefully, Beth hadn't heard she was stabbed, but gossip mongers loved that kind of stuff and Julianna didn't have much hope. She pulled into her driveway and found her mother waiting for her at the bottom of her steps.

*Aw hell, here we go.* Before she got out, she sent Jeff a text to confirm she was home. Taking a deep breath, she pushed out of the car and faced her mother.

"Hi, Mom."

"Don't you 'hi mom' me, missy! I heard you got into a fight at the bar." Beth rose to her feet, every inch the mother she'd been growing up.

"It wasn't really a fight—"

"Don't hand me excuses. I heard you were assaulted. Are you all right? You weren't hurt, were you?"

"Yes, I'm fine. No, I wasn't hurt, just a little bruised. Jeff and the bouncers at the bar helped make sure I was okay." That was close enough.

"Oh, glory, Julianna." Beth yanked her into a hug. "When I heard you'd been assaulted, I panicked, and then you didn't answer your phone. Worse, you didn't come home. Where were you?"

"Deep breaths, Mom. You're going to have a heart attack." Julianna grasped her mother's shoulders. "I'm sorry about the phone. It wasn't on me and after the assault, I just wanted to lay down. My good friend Eloise took me to her place to crash because I was in no condition to drive." *That's an understatement.* "She kept an eye on me and brought me back to the bar this morning to get my car." She grimaced. "I'm sorry I didn't call you or text you back last night."

"Oh my goodness, Julianna." Beth hugged her again. "I was so worried. Please don't do that to your old mother again."

"I promise to be better about answering my phone." *Because I can't tell you Moon Singer business.*

"Good. Now, have you eaten? I can make you breakfast." Beth looked her over critically, her gaze focused on her clothes. "Dear sweet glory! Is that blood?"

Dammit, she'd forgotten the clothes she'd worn the night before still had the marks of where she'd been stabbed. She scrambled for something to say just as Jeff drove up in his Camaro, parking beside hers in the driveway.

Julianna's heart fluttered and a goofy grin curled her lips as he bounded out of the car.

"Oh, thank goodness, Jefferson. I'm so glad you're here. Can you please talk some sense into this young woman? She needs to tell her mother when she's in trouble instead of letting me hear about it through the town gossip." Beth crossed her arms over her chest. "Do you see this? There's blood on her shirt."

Jeff frowned and scanned Julianna with his sharp gaze, inhaling as he took in her clothes. Then his face cleared and he nodded. "Oh, yes, the blood. Right. That was from the guy in the bar. Julianna broke up the fight and he bled on her. It's not her blood."

She blinked at his bald-faced lie, but couldn't argue. They couldn't tell her human mother about her increased ability to heal without exposing Moon Singers.

"That's not her blood? But her shirt's torn."

"Yeah, it got ripped when she tried to get the men apart, but one of them bled all over her after they knocked her down." Jeff nodded with a good-natured smile.

Beth narrowed her eyes, unconvinced, but she switched her gaze to Julianna. "Next time you'd better call me before I hear it from the gossips."

"I promise, Mom."

"Good. Are you sure I can't make you breakfast?"

"Nope. I'm good. Thank you." Julianna hoped her mother would be mollified by Jeff's explanation, but Beth wasn't stupid.

"All right. I'm going to work on the garden and get it ready for harvest to work out my worries. If you need me for anything, text please." She gave Julianna a stern look.

"Yes, ma'am."

Her mother nodded and headed back to her own house, her scent filled with relief and satisfaction. Julianna let out the breath she hadn't known she was holding and shot a look at Jeff.

"Thanks for the backup. So what was so important that you had to come over?"

A grin lit up his face as he took her hand. "Let's go into your place and I'll tell you."

She followed him up the stairs and unlocked her door before they headed into the living space. "Do you want some coffee or something? I need to eat eventually, but coffee might be enough to stave off the hunger."

"You haven't eaten? Why didn't you join me for breakfast?" Jeff scowled.

"Because I didn't want to be accused of influencing the Alpha's family or taking bribes or anything else political."

She shook her head. "Besides, I couldn't eat in front of Eloise. That's rude." She shrugged. "So what's so important?"

His eyes grew heavy with his arousal and his cock pushed against the front of his black canvas shorts. He padded across the room to her, his green-gold eyes alight with desire and fierce joy.

"Mine," he growled, lust filling his voice.

"Seriously, what are you doing here, Jeff?" She backed up, fighting her own needs in the face of his intent. Thank the Goddess she still wore clothes. "You know you can't be alone with me until I pass the tests."

"It doesn't matter now." She raised an eyebrow at him, and he grinned. "I'm here to offer my very special, personal, congratulations on passing all seven tests."

"Wait, I passed? Why wasn't I told?"

"I'm telling you now." He leaned in to kiss her cheek near her ear. "You've passed all the tests, and now you'll be my Luna." His lips teased her arousal, scorching her from the inside out. Each kiss elicited a sigh, and her knees tried to melt out from under her.

"Doesn't some sort of announcement or ceremony have to happen so the pack is aware of my success?"

His kisses drugged her mercilessly, but she held on to her wits. She refused to screw everything up now that she'd come so close to winning the man of her dreams. She squeaked when he bit her earlobe. What had she been asking about again? Oh, yes, official ceremony.

"Yes, there is." He lifted her shirt and filled his warm hands with her breasts. "It'll happen in two days here at the house. The whole Pack will be here to see it."

"Oh, Goddess, Jeff." She moaned as he massaged her breasts with his hands. He ducked his head to lick her skin. "But isn't that a Friday night? Won't the loss of revenue—"

"The bar can handle a little revenue loss."

"Wait, don't we have to stop? The others will know

when we're standing up in front of them that we've done this." She gasped as he pulled one nipple into his mouth and suckled gently. "Oh my glory, that feels good."

He chuckled around her nipple and sucked a little more before he stepped back and pulled her shirt over her head. She met his gaze with her own desires heating her blood, the wash of lust shutting down her thinking. But she fought her Sister's arousal with determination. Sebrina's warning about pre-ceremonial sex brushed through her mind. She didn't want Jeff to lose his position of Successor because he'd succumbed to his hormones.

"You have to stop, Jeff." She ignored her body's screaming protests and stepped away from him. "I won't lose you because we've jumped the gun. You could lose your position as Successor—"

"That's never happened before."

"There might not be a precedent, but there's always a first time." She held him at arm's length, and he leaned against her hands. "I am your True Mate, but I won't lose my candidacy because I've fucked you early. Do you hear me?"

"Such language from the future Luna of the pack." He *tsked*, a predatory smile creasing his face as he pushed her toward her bedroom. "I might just have to spank you for being so naughty."

*He's lost his mind.*

Jeff's grin only widened at her incredulous stare. He herded her into the bedroom, but she twisted sideways away from the bed, her heart pounding in her chest. She wanted him to chase her. *No, no, no. I have to get away before we get in trouble.*

With a yip of excitement, he caught her hand and used her momentum to drag her back into his arms as she pivoted. Triumph filled his expression until Julianna bent her knees. Her intent to escape backfired as she slid down his body, leaving her face level with his bulging crotch.

They both froze.

The scent of his arousal enveloped her, and her Sister whimpered with desperation.

*Please, let me just taste him a little.*

Julianna stared at his hard cock pressed tightly against the fly of his shorts. Jeff looked down at her, his face flushed, his eyes wild. His chest rose and fell, stretching his shirt against the hard muscles she ached to touch. His beauty and power filled her with rampant desire to submit to his dominance. Her smile widened. She'd tease and torture him, but she would get her way.

Sliding her hands up his thighs, she pressed her breasts against his knees and he trembled with surprise. She grasped his belt buckle and released the belt with a hiss of leather. Her fingers pulled open the top button and slowly eased the zipper down until his shorts hung loosely on his hips.

"What are you doing?" Jeff panted, bracing his legs far enough apart to keep himself upright. His eyes blazed with scorching lust.

"I'm compromising, as any good politician must." She shoved his shorts and boxer briefs over his ass and down to his ankles. His cock pushed forward, gently thumping her nose. "I'll give you pleasure to relieve the edge of your need, and you'll wait to fuck me until after the choosing ceremony. Deal?"

She rubbed her tongue around the rough edge of the head of his cock, and he shuddered.

"Oh, Holy Goddess."

"Deal?" She stroked the skin of his balls with her nose.

He whimpered and nodded vigorously when she licked from the base of his balls all the way up the shaft to the head. Then she sucked his cock into her mouth, massaging the tip and enjoying the feel of the hot, smooth skin on her tongue. He tasted the way he smelled, like the desert after the rain combined with musky, aroused male.

She tightened her lips around him and pushed her head down. His cock slid deeper until the tip pressed against her throat.

She swallowed.

"Oh, sweet Goddess!" He groaned and fisted her hair.

Julianna dragged her tongue and lips back up his shaft, pausing only to suck on the head before she pulled back and nuzzled his balls. The soft sac drew up tight against his body, but the muscles relaxed a little as she stroked them. Jeff's scent changed around his scrotum, becoming more earthy and wild, and she reveled in it. She dropped teasing, wet kisses on the crinkled skin and wiry hair, laughing when he grabbed her head and thrust his cock back into her mouth.

He moaned his pleasure as she moved her head forward and back, matching his slow thrusts. She slid one hand up under his shirt along the line of hair rising from his groin, and the muscles of his belly contracted. Each stroke of her lips over his taut cock hardened him more, filling her mouth with his earthy taste. She increased the pressure, scrubbing her tongue-tip over the sensitive spot just behind the head.

Jeff growled and thrust faster. He threw his head back, his eyes closed in furious concentration. The muscles of his chest bunched under his T-shirt as his fists opened to hold her head where he wanted it. Julianna dropped her hand to the base of his cock and held his hip with the other as he shuttled in and out of her mouth.

"Your mouth is heaven, Julianna." He met her eyes with his molten gold gaze.

She growled around his cock, and he grinned in ecstatic amazement.

"You like taking me, my sweet Lupine?"

She winked at him and tightened her grip on the base of his cock as she tickled the ridge of his head with her tongue. He groaned and closed his eyes, tipping his head back on his shoulders once more as he slammed his hips forward. The room filled with the sounds of his rasping breaths and the wet slide of skin against skin. He reached his peak as his cock turned to stone in her mouth, and his belly contracted with his building pleasure. Fierce triumph made her Sister howl, and her body wept in sympathetic arousal.

"Oh, Goddess, you're gonna make me come."

Julianna wanted to swallow down his seed, but some sane part of her made her pull back and finish him with her hand. The change in venue didn't make a difference to him. He let loose with a roar, thrusting the last few times as his release shot out over her hand, scalding her skin with its erotic heat. She reveled in the scent of sex and satisfaction, both hers and his. This was her Mate and her male. And she gave him enough pleasure to elicit a roar.

Finally, he stopped with his eyes still closed. Julianna rested her head against his hip and tried to catch her own breath. Jeff had been magnificent in his pleasure, even better than in her dream, and she wished she could have felt his release in her throat.

"Thank you."

She tilted her head to look up at him and met his eyes. They'd returned to their green-gold glory, but they brimmed with gratitude and relief.

"My pleasure."

"Not yet, but I have plans about that." He reached out and lifted her to her feet, straight into his arms. "Thank you for thinking beyond the satisfaction. You probably saved us a world of hurt."

Julianna delighted in the warmth of his body against her naked chest, but her own arousal snarled in the background like her rabid Sister.

"Only in the eyes of the pack."

Jeff's relaxed amusement faded into concern. He slid one hand up her neck to cup her face, tilting it to lay a soft kiss on her cheek as he inhaled her scent.

"Oh, my little minx, you're too devious for your own good." He growled with amused satisfaction. "I can scent your arousal. You're burning with it, aren't you?" He chuckled, dropping his hand to her peaked nipples. "I can help you with that, you know."

"Oh, I'm counting on it. But after the ceremony. Now, I have to take a shower."

He grinned. "Me, too. Let me help you with that."

"We can't have sex, Jeff."

"What definition of sex are you working from?" he countered, leading her into her bathroom. "I mean, didn't we just do something defined as sex?"

He stole her breath as he slid back her shower curtain and adjusted the water to the proper temperature. Then he drew her shorts off her hips and threw his shirt to the floor. The muscles in his back and arms flexed in a symphony of motion, the view flooding her pussy with erotic cream. She sagged against the bathroom door, fighting her desperate need to throw herself at him. As if sensing her needs, Jeff reached for her and pulled her into the tub under the stream of hot water with him.

"You never answered my question." Jeff slid his hands and lips over her body.

"What question?" Her breath hitched when his hands followed the flood of water down her belly to her mound.

"Your definition of sex." His fingers dipped between her lips, sliding through her cream. "Mmm-mmm, you're wet."

She grinned. "I'm in the shower."

He chuckled and rubbed his thumb against her clit. "Not that kind of wet." Then he pressed a finger into her tight cleft, and she gasped. "This kind of wet."

"Oh, glory, Jeff!" She arched her back to push his hand deeper.

"That's it, my little minx. Ride my hand."

Julianna groaned and rocked her hips against his thrusting finger, seeking relief from the overwhelming lust and desire. Jeff pressed her up against the wall of the shower, the cold tile against her back making her squeak in surprise. He grinned at her and inserted a second finger, stretching her tightening pussy.

"Come on, sweet Lupine, let me give you pleasure." He scraped his teeth along the cords of her throat, and she whimpered, thrusting her hips harder against his hand.

The scent of sex and lust filled the shower space, and she felt like she'd explode. He moaned at her neck when her pussy involuntarily clamped down on his fingers, and he thrust them harder into her. Thick steam clouded the glass door when she reached her peak. She dug her fingernails into his shoulders as her body ruptured with pleasure. A wail of rapture escaped into the noise of the shower and he caught the tail end of it by sealing his lips over hers.

Jeff's hard arousal pressed against her hip, and his tongue danced in her mouth, branding her through the bliss soaking her mind. His kiss was brutal with his fierce joy and desire, but he slowly pulled his hand out of her clenching slit and reverently rested it on her thigh.

"Goddess, Julianna, you're so beautiful when you come. I've never enjoyed watching an orgasm as much as I just did with you. You're magnificent."

"Thank you. I so needed that."

He chuckled again as he drew her away from the wall. "I'm happy to provide any pleasure you ever need. All you have to do is ask."

"Oh, believe me, after the ceremony on Friday, I'll definitely be asking you for everything."

He did nothing more than touch and kiss her, but she knew he held back only because she'd asked. The hard cock between his legs assured her he wanted more.

Jeff's mesmerizing gold-brown eyes flared with desire,

but he didn't say another word while he washed her body with great care and gentleness. Julianna's joy cascaded through her, building momentum and fury until she felt she'd burst. His sweet intimacy touched her heart in ways their mutual desire never had. His cock rose to half-mast while he smoothed soap over her breasts and ass, but he kept his hands soft and his touches practical.

He turned her to soak her hair, and she bent her head beneath the spray, reveling in the slide of his hand over her back and buttocks. Pulling her out of the water, he filled his hands with shampoo and rubbed it into her hair. He attended to her ablutions with an aching tenderness that melted her heart.

*Maybe he feels more than just lust.*

When he rubbed his hands softly over her swollen nether lips, cleaning her release and the scent of feminine arousal, she acknowledged the shift in her own emotions. She'd always loved Jeff on some level, but her feelings had deepened from an immature crush to something stronger during the testing period. She'd found real love under the infatuation.

Her heart bloomed with comprehension, and she wanted to scream with excited joy. Instead, she whirled around and threw herself into his surprised arms.

"Thank you so much, Jeff."

He laughed a little uncertainly. "You're welcome to whatever it is I've done now."

Julianna pulled her head back to look up into his eyes. "You've given me pleasure without getting us into trouble."

"I told you it all depends on which definition of sex you're using."

She laughed and squeezed him harder. "I see that." She leaned her head against his shoulder and closed her eyes. "I love you, Jeff."

He froze under her hands, and his breath caught. "You

do?"

"Yes." She hoped she hadn't made a mistake. "I really do. I think I always have. It just came out as lust and attraction. But that's not all I feel."

Jeff pushed her back and lifted her chin with one hand so he could meet her eyes. His wet hair hung in tendrils around his face and water droplets made glassy constellations on his cheeks. She searched his eyes for any emotion, but he wore his typical half-smile that hid everything. She wished she could read his thoughts as he laid a tender kiss on her lips.

"That's not all I feel, either," he whispered at last. "Come on, let's finish up."

Inwardly, she sighed in disappointment. He said he felt more than lust, but perhaps it hadn't grown into love.

*Yet,* her Sister said.

They rinsed off quickly, and she tried to enjoy it, but his lack of declaration bugged her. He watched her, following her hands as they dried her breasts, belly, and thighs. She smiled and let him look. A sense of power and sexiness filled her, and her worries faded a little.

Julianna wrapped her towel around her, and they retreated to her room in a companionable silence. The silence held while they dressed, but the looks they warmed her heart. She licked her lips to wet them, and his nostrils flared as his eyes blazed, his gaze following the tip of her tongue along her mouth.

She tried to take comfort in his obvious attraction, but her heart insisted attraction wasn't love. *Does Jeff only like me?* He could simply consider her a fuck-buddy, a friend with benefits. The mating bond seemed to be based entirely on hormones, no matter what Sebrina had said about soul mates.

She ripped a comb through her hair fiercely, and Jeff's eyebrows slid toward his hairline in surprise.

"Are you all right?" He stopped behind her, his own

hair mussed from drying with the towel.

"Yes. No. Ugh. I don't know. I think so."

She buried the heels of her hands in her eyes and tried to calm herself down. *Getting angry now is a complete waste of energy.*

"Hey, what's wrong?" He pulled her hands away from her face. His eyes searched hers for a few silent moments. "Come sit down on the bed and tell me what's going on in that head of yours."

Jeff sat down facing her with one knee drawn up. "You smell of fear and anger, but for the life of me, I can't figure out what you'd be mad about. Did I hurt you in the shower?"

How was she supposed to answer that?

"I'm sorry, Jeff." She picked at the hem of her shirt. "I'm just feeling a little overwhelmed by the change in status. You know, from candidate to…whatever I am now." She ran a hand through her brutally combed hair and tried not to wince when a finger caught a recalcitrant tangle.

The silence between them stretched, and she glanced at him. His body appeared relaxed, but she knew he could move with lightning quickness if he chose. The weight of his gaze made her fidget, and she tried to still her hands, and her heart.

*I don't want my love to go unrequited, especially if I'm supposed to mate with him for life.*

"You're my True Mate, and after the ceremony on Friday, you'll be the next Luna of the Callowwood Pack." Jeff frowned a little, uncertainty in his eyes. "Isn't that what you want?"

"Yes."

"But?"

She sighed and looked across the room, searching for something on which to pin her gaze.

"What, Julianna?"

"I want more." She bit her lip. "I want it all. I want your

heart, your love."

A huge grin spread across his lips, and he lifted her hand to place a sensuous kiss against her knuckles.

"Oh, my sweet lady Lupine, my heart has been yours since your father's funeral." He gave her a half-shrug. "You looked so sad, but you stood strong and you held your own against all those bitches who tried to snub you."

Julianna raised an eyebrow, and he nodded. "Oh yeah, I noticed. You didn't need me to protect you, but you didn't shove me away. I counted my lucky stars that I got to sit next to you and feel your body against mine where I've wanted it for years."

*See? I told you.*

*Yeah, shut up. I want to hear this.*

"In the last few weeks, being without you has been excruciating." Jeff grimaced. "I know it comes across as the simple desire for you to warm my bed. And believe me, I really want you to do that." He gave her a look full of wide-eyed desperation, and she laughed.

"But I also want you around me all the time. I want to share my life with you, Julianna. I know being the Successor makes dating hell. Believe me, I know." He ran a hand through his hair. "But you're here now, and you've passed all the Luna tests. I want you. Hell, I've wanted you since well before I should have. I only avoided you because I thought you were human."

He stopped then and frowned a little, and dread skittered through her. "Speaking of which, how did you hide your Moon Singer self? You even smelled human."

Julianna pulled her hands out of his, wrapping her arms around herself. Jeff let her go, but his frown deepened and trepidation settled into a leaden weight in her stomach.

What could she tell him? Her story seemed stupid when she thought about it now. If she told him she'd only discovered her Sister form a few months ago, would he see her as a fraud and a cheat, leading everyone on? He hadn't told her he loved her, only that she'd gained his heart. Would that change with the truth?

*Best to do it now before he chooses the wrong female.* Julianna tried to ignore the stab of fear and pain with the idea of Jeff mating with another woman, but her guts twisted.

"You know I was adopted by the Morrises, right?" She tugged the bedclothes straight for something to distract her.

"Yes."

"They're human."

"I know."

"I was too young to know what that meant. Them being human while I wasn't. But I learned pretty quickly that human children didn't play like I did. When I got in terrible trouble at the orphanage, I realized something was wrong." She rubbed her knees with her fingers. "I suppressed my Moon Singer tendencies to fit in. I started acting different and ended up thinking and acting human. I didn't realize there was any other way to be until a few months ago."

She raised her gaze, but he wore a closed expression, a stoic mask like his father's. Unease stabbed her, and she rose from the bed, wishing she had armor against the coming loss.

"I didn't learn I was west of left field until just after my thirty-sixth birthday. I don't know why it happened then. Maybe it was because my old life had fallen apart and I had to start over." Misery nipped at her thoughts as she leaned against the dresser. "When I got back to town, I didn't even know I wasn't the only one. I thought everyone here was human, and I'd have to hide from them. And from you."

Tears gathered in her eyes, but she held them back. "The night your dad gave me the token, I realized how many Moon Singers lived in Callowwood. I hadn't had a clue you were all wolves while growing up. Everything I know about being west of left field I learned from Sebrina over the last couple of months. I'm a novice, Jeff, a rookie."

She sighed and shook her head, staring at her toes. "I can understand if this disqualifies me from being Luna. No one wants a leader who's inexperienced at being her true self. I've learned a lot and tried to put everything into practice without giving away how ignorant I am. But I'm bound to make a mistake at some point, and that mistake could get someone in trouble. Mainly me."

Silence filled the room for several breaths. Her heart sank, and ice settled into her veins. *I've lost him.* But she couldn't lie to him about this. He needed to know how pathetic she was.

"Let me get this straight." Jeff crossed his arms over his chest. "You came home to Callowwood despite learning you're actually west of left field, with no idea that the pack was here. Then you were picked as a Luna candidate, passing all seven of the tests for Luna on this little knowledge?" She nodded. "Holy shit, Julianna, do you know how amazing you are?"

"What?"

"Most rookies would've panicked, run, or just refused to be a candidate." Jeff rose and sauntered across the room to her, grabbing her shoulders. "You've been thrown to the wolves, literally, and still managed to come out on top. Disqualified? Hell, no! I think that makes you far and above the best candidate for Luna."

She searched his face for clarity, and his intense expression softened.

"Julianna, you're my True Mate, whether you learned about it when you were a kid or last Tuesday. The other requirements were put on you by the pack, and you passed them with flying colors." He brushed her cheek with his fingers. "At the choosing ceremony, I'm going to pick you as my Luna, even if the others have passed the tests. You're my Mate. I love you as you are. Your ability to adapt on the fly only makes you more desirable as a Luna, not less."

Jeff kissed her so sweetly a little sob escaped. Relief poured through her right along with the arousal, and she nestled into his embrace. He wrapped her in his arms and held her against his chest, the soft thump of his heartbeat in sync with her own.

"I love you, Julianna," he whispered against her hair.

"Really?" She winced the moment the words left her mouth.

He chuckled and drew back to look her in the eyes.

"Yes, really." A stupid grin stretched her lips, and he laughed again "Now, I better get out of here before we both throw caution to the winds and consummate the mating bond."

"I can't tempt you a little?" She stretched her arms above her head until her breasts pressed against her tight shirt.

"You tempt me a lot." He rearranged the crotch of his shorts. "But you've already told me no once, and I'll try to remember it. I'll see you tomorrow at the bar."

"Not tonight?"

He shook his head. "No, take some time off. You deserve it after last night, and I definitely shouldn't be around you until I can make my choice public. I'm barely holding back as it is. In fact, it might be wise if you took the next two days off."

She sighed in disappointment, and he gave her a rueful smile.

"I'm right there with you, but now that you've passed the tests and the full moon's only a week away, my control is shot. I won't be able to hold back my Brother. Hell, I don't want to now. So I'll see you at my dad's place at seven o'clock on Friday night. The attire is formal."

She picked up the towels and threw them in the laundry hamper, telling herself she'd be fine without seeing Jeff for two days.

*Yeah, right. And I'm really a were-poodle.*

His fingers on her shoulder reminded her he hadn't left her room.

"Be sure to wear this." He lifted her wrist where she'd tied the wolf's head token. "It's supposed to be displayed prominently during the ceremony."

She shivered with the sense of restrained power emanating from his body. The growl in his voice called to her and seduced her. She wanted him, and she wanted him now.

*This is your Mate. Take him.*

*Soon,* she promised, tearing herself away.

"I'll remember to make sure it's visible."

He nodded, his eyes flaring with the same lust coursing through her. Blowing her a kiss, he strode out the door.

# CHAPTER SIXTEEN:
## Truth and Consequences

Julianna texted Eloise, and the blonde woman met her outside her place in the early afternoon.

"You ready to do a little shopping?"

Juliann shook her head with a grimace. "No, not really, but I need something to wear to the ceremony on Friday. Did you hear I've passed the Luna tests?"

Eloise whooped. "I hadn't. Congratulations!"

"Thank you." She sighed. "I'm glad to know I've passed. Takes the pressure off."

"I bet." Eloise pulled onto the highway and headed out of Callowwood. "You know, I was thinking about our earlier conversation about Ms. Solaris, and I had a thought."

It took Julianna few moments to reorient. "Oh?"

"While it appears Ms. Solaris is responsible, I think there may be another player we have to consider." Eloise grimaced.

"Who's that?"

She bit her lip. "Think about it. Who'd gain if you're disqualified for making an error during the tests and Ms. Solaris is caught striking out at you? Ms. Cutter and Ms.

Wolensky have already been dropped. Who'd be the only one fit to be Luna?"

Julianna scowled. "Ms. Cameron Winthrop."

"Yes."

"And we don't have any proof that she's done anything wrong. No one has heard anything about her, good or bad." *I knew I was missing something.* "She's kept her head down, done what she needed to do to pass the tests. She let the drama between me and Ms. Solaris unfold while she walked the straight and narrow in the background."

"Exactly. To the pack, she'd look like the perfect candidate in all ways. No drama, just perfection." Eloise shook her head. "Like she's always been throughout her life."

"Really?" Julianna raised her eyebrows.

"Oh yeah. She's little Miss Perfection. Her parents have groomed her for this opportunity, ruthlessly, and she took to it like a duck to water." Eloise snorted. "To be honest, her ego is bigger than Ms. Solaris'."

Julianna nodded slowly. "So, if I fail the tests by revealing my true Nature or reacting badly, I'm no longer a threat to her. Pinning it on Ms. Solaris, my chief rival, is the easiest solution. Kill two birds with one stone."

"Of course, there's nothing to tie Ms. Winthrop to the attacks. There's just the scent of apricots, and the thugs who appear to be from Los Angeles, Ms. Solaris's home turf."

"Yeah, but I can't really believe Brenda would waste her energy on petty rivalries. She's already a high-ranking alpha in this pack." Julianna shook her head. "Ms. Winthrop is the only one who'd gain anything if both Brenda and I were disqualified for any reason."

"It infuriates me that Cameron might get away with it and no one will know." Eloise's hands tightened on the steering wheel.

"I can't think of a better way to infuriate her than

winning the post of Luna without underhanded actions."

Eloise laughed. "Yeah, that would definitely get her tail in a twist."

Julianna shook her head. "I probably shouldn't be so snarky about it in front of you. After all, I'm supposed to be an upstanding bitch representing the pack, even when faced with problems like this."

Eloise snorted. "No one is perfect, no matter what Cameron is trying to project. And we all need time to vent, especially to our friends."

"Thank goodness. I really need loyal and trusted friends to get me through this, especially if I become Luna."

Silence filled the car for a couple of miles, Eloise wearing a pensive expression. Julianna hoped she hadn't changed their friendly dynamic. She wanted to keep Eloise as a real friend. Intellectually, she understood she already had the blonde woman's respect and loyal service as an alpha. *The* Alpha.

*Yay me.*

"Have you chosen your cadre yet?" Eloise asked out of the blue.

Julianna frowned. "My what?"

"Your cadre. Your inner circle of advisors and confidantes to help you as Luna."

She rubbed her chin. "Is that the group that hangs around Jeff all the time? I think Zach and Kyle are part of it?"

The mention of Kyle made Eloise grimace, but she nodded.

"I hadn't thought about it." *Is Eloise attracted to Kyle?* "How many can belong to the cadre, and do they have to all be in the same rank?"

"You can choose as many or as few as you want. They don't all have to be of the same rank. They just can't belong to someone else's cadre."

Julianna bit her lip. "Who all has cadres?"

"Just the Alphas."

"Since I'm female, does my cadre have to be all female as well?"

"No, but they should be packmembers that you know and trust."

Julianna nodded. "That makes sense. I guess I've been around long enough to trust a few folks." She shot Eloise a look. "Too bad Kyle's spoken for."

"What? Why?" Eloise's eyes widened.

"He's a good man, and I've worked with him at the bar. And he likes you." Julianna winked.

"What?"

"You haven't noticed?" Julianna grinned. "He always watches you when you come in."

"Really?" Eloise scowled. "He never says anything to me."

"That might be because he knows you're engaged to Scatterstone." Julianna tilted her head. "Why are you engaged to Scatterstone if Kyle is so hot for you? Kyle's a good guy."

"I *know* Kyle's a good guy." Eloise frowned. "But Tommy asked me first and he's an alpha. It's a good opportunity for a beta like me."

Julianna raised her eyebrows. "Is that you talking or your parents?"

Eloise growled. "Me? I think. I don't know. Accepting his proposal seemed like a good idea at the time."

"It must have made your parents pretty happy, an alpha asking you to marry him."

Eloise nodded, her expression bleak. "It did. And it was flattering to me. But recently he's been such an ugly jerk, almost heartless at times. And he's terribly jealous of my friendship with Kyle."

Julianna nodded. "Did you know that I was married before?"

Eloise shook her head.

"Yeah, it didn't work out. But one of the things I learned was that anything that annoyed me before we married only got worse and worse the longer we were together." Julianna shrugged, not wanting to waste time on her past. "If Scatterstone is heartless and jealous now, he's only going to get more so as time goes on."

Eloise bit her lip and nodded. "I don't doubt you're right."

"Let me ask you one question and I'll leave it alone. You don't even have to answer me aloud."

"What's that?"

"Is Kyle your True Mate?"

Eloise swallowed hard. They lapsed into silence as they arrived in Leland and found a place to park. It was remarkably busy for a random Wednesday in the middle of the day. Tourists visiting the large gold mines in the area filled the shops and sidewalks.

"Ready for this?" Julianna eyed the crowds.

"I am if you are. We can watch each other's backs." Eloise winked and Julianna grinned.

"Deal."

Despite the large number of people, they took their time shopping.

*Choosing dresses, shoes, and jewelry for the party on Friday is serious business.*

Eloise relaxed and became jovial, making wry observations that had Julianna laughing. She hid her sharp wit around the other packmembers, especially Scatterstone, but was very aware of her surroundings.

Julianna considered what Eloise had told her about the cadre as she pulled a black sheath dress onto her body. *Not bad.* She needed to choose women and men she could trust to be honest and loyal to her.

*Someone who'd tell me I look terrible in this dress, for instance.* She turned around in the mirror. *I thought black is supposed to be slimming.*

Who had been in her corner? Only a few people came to mind, but Eloise Farkas stood at the top of the list. Julianna pulled the sheath dress off and hung it back on the hanger. She'd make an excellent First. *Or is that Second? Well, whatever.*

Julianna lifted a light gray sleeveless gown and unzipped the back, pulling it over her hips.

*Who else?* Sebrina, certainly, but she probably couldn't choose someone of higher rank. Which left the other betas who weren't a part of someone else's cadre. She reached behind her to pull the zipper up. *Which beta would have the courage to tell me that gray makes me look dead?* She grimaced and removed the dress.

By the time Julianna found a dress she liked, she'd made up a short mental list of male and female packmembers. She met Eloise outside the shop, and they piled their purchases in the back of the car for the drive home.

"Did you find something you liked?"

"Yes." Eloise nodded. "I can hardly wait to put it on."

"And show it off to Kyle, I imagine."

She smirked. "Maybe."

"But not Scatterstone?"

She lost her smile. "No. I thought about what you said and I think…well, I still have a lot to think about."

"Fair enough. I also have been doing some thinking about the cadre, and I wanted to ask you if you'd be willing to be in mine." She waved her hand in the air. "If I'm chosen, that is."

"Are you serious?"

"Yeah, completely. You're quick-witted, observant, and you know all the little quirks of the pack that I don't. Would you consider it?"

Another silence filled the car. Julianna wondered if she'd said something wrong.

*Maybe there's some sort of formal pledge or something.*

Eloise gave her a blinding smile. "Yes, Mistress Julianna."

"Oh, good glory, don't go all formal on me. We're not even in Callowwood yet."

She laughed. "Sorry. It's a big deal for me to be asked. Goddess, it's a great honor to be asked to be in the Luna's cadre."

"So, is that a yes?"

"Nope. It's a Hell Yes."

Julianna laughed. "I like that response."

Eloise grinned. "It's the only one I got."

The tension bled away as they drove back to town. Eloise shared funny anecdotes about the pack and her friends in it as if she no longer worried about rank. Julianna enjoyed the camaraderie with her, feeling confident about being Luna for the first time since the party.

"Hey, thanks for the company while shopping. And for accepting my invitation for my cadre." Julianna squeezed Eloise's arm before she got out of the car. "I really appreciate it."

"My pleasure. And thanks for the advice on my fiancé. I'll think about it."

"You're welcome. Call me later if you want to talk."

"Will do." Eloise nodded before Julianna shut the door and unloaded her packages. The blonde woman waved as she headed back down the driveway.

Julianna watched her leave as excitement zinged through her. Eloise's acceptance gave her the courage to choose others. She gathered her purchases and hauled them up to her apartment, humming.

She spent the rest of her afternoon deciding whom to ask, weighing the pros and cons of each. She wrangled her courage and took a few deep breaths before she picked up her phone. She left messages for most of the people she'd selected, hoping she didn't sound too desperate. Had anyone ever turned down a place in an Alpha's cadre?

Two of her choices happily accepted her invitation. One squealed so loudly she had to hold the handset away from her head for long seconds. By the time she crawled into bed, three others in addition to Eloise had agreed to be in her cadre. She burrowed under the covers on her bed and sighed with satisfaction. She only wished Jeff could have crawled in beside her.

**** 

By Thursday afternoon, Julianna was ready to bribe someone to make time go faster. The morning had been fruitful. The last of the packmembers she hadn't talked to the night before agreed to join her cadre and she felt on top of the world.

But it quickly diminished as the day wore on, with nothing on her schedule except laundry and chores. She'd managed to finish four full loads and was scrubbing the grease off of her stove top when someone knocked on her door. *Oh thank goodness for the distraction.* Julianna removed her rubber gloves and strode into her living room, but paused. Gut instinct warned her to be careful, and she inhaled deeply.

Emotional scents of fear, sorrow, and regret flowed around the edges of the door, and a flicker of unease shot through her body. She opened it slowly. Sebrina stood waiting nervously outside with her hands knotted in her skirt until the knuckles showed white.

"Hello, Sebrina." Julianna eyed her carefully. "Are you all right?"

"I must speak with you, daughter." The other woman's voice rasped in the silence.

"All right. Won't you come in for some tea?"

Sebrina stared at Julianna for a long, solemn moment then nodded and stepped across the threshold. She glanced around the small living room, but dismissed the mess as she shuffled into the kitchenette to stand beside the table.

"Please, sit down." Julianna pulled out a chair. "You look worried, Sebrina. Is everything all right?" She took her time preparing a tea ball while the kettle boiled, hoping the horrible tension in the kitchen would fade a little.

"I must tell you a story, daughter, before tomorrow night, so you understand who you are," Sebrina whispered. The stench of miserable fear filled the small space.

"Okay." Julianna sat down across the table. "What story?"

Sebrina studied Julianna's face, saying nothing for long moments. Julianna felt like she'd jump out of her skin. Silence stretched between them, and the tension increased to a screaming pitch. When the teakettle began to whistle, Julianna jumped, scrambling to fill her teapot. She tried to keep her unease from pushing her off center, but Sebrina's continued silence ate at her calm.

"Tea?" She presented Sebrina a mug.

The Paiute woman nodded and took the cup, wrapping her hands around it as if she felt cold.

"Many years ago, now," Sebrina said as Julianna sat down, "I met a man who made my heart shiver. He was tall, strong, and handsome, with midnight black hair and blue, blue eyes. He looked at me like I was the most beautiful woman in the world, and though he was younger than me, he seemed oblivious to the markings of age on my body. He wasn't so young by human standards, but his body was strong and unbroken, and I wasn't as I am now."

She rubbed the wrinkles on her hands meditatively.

"At that time, Indians were considered less than whites in this country, and this man wasn't supposed to be interested in females like me." Sebrina followed the grain of the wood in Julianna's table with her fingers. "But he'd been teaching at a reservation school when I visited family who lived nearby. When I saw him, he captivated me with his beauty and strength, even if he seemed old in human terms."

Julianna could relate. "How old was he?"

"I think he'd reached his sixties."

"Wow."

"Yes, it seems old to one as young as you, but there was nothing weak or feeble about this man. He caught my eye one day while I was walking through town. He offered to buy me a meal, and I couldn't say no. He began to court me in a very old-fashioned way, unusual for a man with white heritage. He called at my family's house and offered gifts to my relatives in honor of their hospitality."

A small smile fluttered across Sebrina's lips, but the sadness thickened.

"He did this for over a year, and I was flattered and enthralled with his tenacity and efforts. How could such a beautiful male want me, as old as I was? But after his courtship, he asked me to become his wife, and I could only agree because I knew him to be my True Mate, however strange it seemed for a Moon Singer to mate with a human.

"We married a month later, and we celebrated in the best way." Sebrina's smile broadened. "He was as hearty and strong as I always knew he'd be, and I rejoiced to be his wife."

Despite this happy news, Sebrina's face slid back into solemnity. Julianna's congratulations died in her throat.

"Not everyone felt that way about our mating. Several humans in this town had no love for the Indians, and to them, I was not a person, not a Moon Singer, not even a woman. I was an Indian and no white man should pollute the race with a mongrel child from a squaw."

Julianna's anger kindled as Sebrina paused to sip her tea as if her throat had dried. Old prejudices infuriated her, but Sebrina's memories couldn't be changed.

"One night when I visited family, those humans took my husband and beat him nearly to death then left him in our small house and set it afire. He burned to death before I could get to him. I burned along with him, and only my family kept me out of the flames. I felt lost without him."

Julianna blinked back tears as Sebrina's grief crystallized before her. Sweet glory, how would it feel to lose Jeff? She couldn't even imagine.

"I'm so sorry, Sebrina."

Sebrina came back to herself out of the mists of time and waved her hand dismissively. "It was long ago." Again her face took on the stoic expression Julianna had learned meant she was uncomfortable with a topic. "But he left a piece of himself behind with me."

Julianna frowned when Sebrina didn't go on.

"What?"

"I realized I was pregnant."

Julianna's blood froze, and dread hit her gut.

"Without my husband, I felt so alone and lost. A Moon Singer surrounded by humans who cared not for our ways." Sebrina gripped her mug like a lifeline. "I left that town and moved to the land around Callowwood to find a place to settle where no one knew me. The baby came when it should, but not as I expected."

Sadness suffused her face, and she took a deep breath to continue. "The baby was human. Such a thing had never happened among our people in my experience, despite the Stories. I thought the baby would be a Moon Singer and born in its natural form. When it came out human, I panicked and left it on the front steps of a human temple of worship in Leland." She dropped her gaze to her hands around her mug as an interesting grabbed her attention.

"I left the baby there and didn't look back. I thought it was best for the child."

Julianna felt her stomach sink.

"What sex was the child?"

Sebrina closed her eyes. "It was a girl."

"And this was, what? Thirty-six years ago?"

"Yes."

Julianna let that news settle, her guts churning.

"Are you saying you're my blood mother and you didn't want me?"

Sebrina jerked as if she'd been slapped. "I was alone, and afraid, and you looked human. I didn't know what to do with a human child."

That didn't make Julianna feel better.

"What would you have done if your husband had lived and I had been born a wolf?"

"I would have had time to tell him, to make him understand my true nature, and what to expect." Sebrina shrugged with one shoulder. "But it didn't happen that way."

"No, it didn't." Julianna's anger seethed.

"When I saw you in your true form, I realized you belonged to my family, to my line. Our family had been given a special marking to identify us as part of the First Canid's family—"

"Wait, wait, wait." Julianna held up her hand. "You're part of the First Canid's family?"

"Yes."

"Why didn't anyone say anything about it? Why didn't you tell me?"

Sebrina shrugged again uncomfortably. "Most do not know. I have never mentioned it to anyone. Especially after my shame of abandoning my husband's child. I only saw it on you when you changed. I'd given up my husband's most precious gift and here you were, before me once again. I'm sorry."

Through Sebrina's recitation, Julianna's throat tightened. Her disbelief gave way to vitriolic rage, and she rose to her feet, her mug clenched in her fist.

"How could you?" She closed her eyes, trying to find calm, but the fury won out. "How could you abandon me like that? I was so lost and alone at that orphanage. I got in trouble for wanting to play with my human littermates. It frightened me and I had to hide my lupine side to find a family. To find someone who'd love me, who wanted me. I had to deny my entire being so I wouldn't be discarded!"

She stopped, and her eyes narrowed.

"Is that why you've been helping me? Because you feel guilty for leaving me on the church steps?"

"No, daughter, I've been helping you because you seemed so lost when you returned to Callowwood." Sebrina regarded her solemnly.

"Why would that be? I'd been abandoned!" Julianna hurled the mug into the sink, and it shattered in a spray of pottery and amber liquid.

A thunderous silence filled her kitchen. Julianna burned with her anger, and she squeezed her eyes tightly shut, trying to find some serenity.

"Forgive me, daughter, for not understanding what a gift you were to the People, to me," Sebrina begged softly. "I've seen you grow and learn and understand faster than I ever thought our People could. You make me proud, my daughter, and you make me grieve for what I gave up when I left you. I'm sorry."

Julianna wanted to shout and scream at Sebrina, but it wouldn't change the past or heal the hurt ripping at her heart. She tipped her head back and forced herself to breathe, just breathe.

When she'd gained a foothold on her fury, she opened her eyes and turned back to the silent Paiute woman. Sebrina seemed to have aged several years in those few moments. She looked small and vulnerable, and Julianna's Sister wanted to go for the throat.

Incongruously, Julianna remembered Sebrina's advice before she opened her mouth, and she made herself speak calmly, rationally, if not warmly.

"Did you live here in Callowwood the whole time I grew up with the Morrises?"

"No. I returned to my family for a time."

"Why did you come back here?"

"I'd become friends with the previous Luna, and she offered me a place of honor within the pack."

"You never thought about me? Wondered what had happened to me?"

Sebrina's face crumpled, and she bit her bottom lip. "I couldn't change the past and worrying about it only brought me pain." She shrugged. "I assumed you'd been given to a human family and I'd made the right decision."

Julianna felt ready to choke. "You never recognized me? Not even when I grew up?"

"No."

Betrayal punched her in the gut, and tears pricked behind her eyes. She swallowed hard and nodded in defeat.

"I appreciate you coming by to tell me, but I'd like to be alone now. I need to get a lot done this evening."

Sebrina rose to her feet and looked at Julianna for a moment before she nodded. Then she shuffled to the door, her shoulders hunched and her head down. In the doorway, she turned to offer another look of resignation. Julianna kept her face impassive, and Sebrina tightened her lips before retreating down the stairs. Julianna closed the door on her birth mother and stood for several long minutes, staring at nothing.

She felt like she'd been kicked in the teeth.

"I'm gonna go take a shower," she mumbled out loud, just to hear something in the oppressive silence.

Sebrina's story had shaken everything she thought she understood about herself. Someone had played 52-Pickup with her life and left her to reassemble the mess into order. How appropriate. *My life was nothing but a house of cards, gone with one deep breath.*

Emotions swirled in a kaleidoscope of color. Anger, hurt, and betrayal swarmed around surprise and disbelief. Frustration splashed its own brilliant streak across them all, and she gave up trying to analyze which took priority. How did she feel about Sebrina being her mother?

*About the same as I felt when I figured out I'm a werewolf.* She leaned her forehead against the tiled wall, letting the water cascade around her, soothing the hurts in heated waves. She hardly noticed the tears blending with the droplets on her face.

It made sense why she was a Moon Singer and her parents weren't. But her birth father was human. *Maybe that's another reason I was able to suppress my Sister form as long as I did. Woo-hoo for me.*

She shook her head. *Why did you come out when you did, Sister? Why didn't you just remain hidden?*

*Because it was time to be yourself. That stupid human had hurt you. You needed me. And you needed your Mate.*

*How did you know Jeff hadn't mated by then?*

Her Sister mentally shrugged. *You needed your Mate.*

She slid down the wall and dropped her head onto her upraised knees, letting the water pound over her head. She desperately wished it would wash away the maelstrom of sentiment raging within her. She stayed there until the water turned cold.

She stopped shivering when she toweled herself dry and wrapped her silk robe around her, but her insides remained frozen. She'd been unwanted.

So much for being part of the First Canid's family. *Sebrina is a descendent, and I'm the next generation.* She sat down at her mirror. *Holy shit, I'm the next generation.* How very DaVinci Code. Like the female cop learning she was related to Jesus. *Only I'm related to Ho'a'tote.* She stared at the mirror for a long time, studying her face critically.

Her brown-black hair glistened in the light, and her slightly almond-shaped green-hazel eyes looked out over a pert and full lips. Julianna studied her wide cheekbones and found similarities between her face and Sebrina's. But someone else's genetics shaped her brows and pointed chin.

Julianna stared at herself, trying to find truth in her reflection. The phone rang, but she didn't feel like talking to anyone, and all her important phone calls had already been made.

She trudged across the room to the bedside table and stared at the offensive contraption. The phone continued to ring impatiently, demanding her attention. She snorted and pressed a button on the side, silencing the ringer. The ensuing quiet settled around her shoulders like a hood, and the sense of betrayal returned. Her tears rolled again, and she wiped ineffectually at them with her sleeve.

Dropping her robe to the floor with disgust, she crawled into her bed and let her tears soak the pillowcase instead.

\*\*\*\*

Jeff frowned and shoved his cell phone back into his pocket. Julianna usually answered when she was home. Maybe she went out for the evening. He'd given her the night off, after all. He knew it was for the best, but he missed her. He hadn't realized how much he enjoyed her company at the bar. Last night had been excruciating without her presence, and tonight wasn't any better. He'd wanted to hear her voice.

Probably better that she didn't answer. Exhaustion from holding back his arousal and his Brother form nipped at the edges of his awareness. Even the sound of her voice had him harder than steel, and he didn't need that tonight. He thumped his fist on the bar and turned his attention to cleaning up the used dishes.

"Hey, Mr. Jeff, how are you this evening?" The soft feminine voice made the customary mask slide over his expression. Cameron Winthrop settled onto a stool at the bar.

"Good evening, Ms. Winthrop. I'm doing good and you?"

"Very well, thank you, Jefferson." She tilted her head coyly. "Did you hear? I passed all the tests as of yesterday."

*Didn't know. Don't care.*

"Congratulations." He gave her a wider smile. "That's great news."

"It is, isn't it? Goddess, I'll be so glad when all this is over." She sighed, her breasts pressing up against her shirt. "I'm looking forward to tomorrow night."

"It should be quite a party."

"Mmm-hmm." She reached up and pulled her ponytail over her shoulder. "Are you looking forward to it?"

He nodded as he added soap to the dishwasher. "I am, actually."

"It's so great for the pack. Not even my parents saw the last Luna chosen, and now I'm a candidate. It's really exciting."

He nodded, but his interest in her words had waned. He wanted to talk to Julianna and share his observations of the last few weeks with her, not with Cameron Winthrop. Cameron smelled cloyingly sweet, and it damn near suffocated him. He didn't know why she stank so badly to him. He hadn't Mated yet, but the urge to find something, anything, to do to get away from the younger female skittered around his skull.

His walkie-talkie beeped imperatively at him, and he pulled it out with a shot of relief. "Yeah?"

"Hey, boss," Kyle's voice said. "We got a problem in the back room."

"On my way." Jeff glanced up at Cameron as he put the walkie-talkie away. "Excuse me, Ms. Winthrop."

"Of course."

He strode away and tried to ignore the wistful expression on her face. *Chewed bones, can't tomorrow night get here any faster?* He hoped Kyle's problem was big enough to distract from the hours creeping by because nothing else had done the trick.

# CHAPTER SEVENTEEN:
### Forgive and Remember

Morning came before Julianna wanted to face it. Sunlight teased her awake and gilded her entire bedroom with cheerful light. *Damn, why is it so friggin' bright?*

She groaned and hauled herself into a sitting position, scrubbing her face with her hands. She was groggy and sleepy, but the clock told her she'd slept about twelve hours. How could she be tired after all that rest?

"Ugh." She rolled her feet to the floor and stood up. Maybe a hot shower would revive her.

The shower did help, but it also woke her up enough to remember the ending to her previous day, and the sad betrayal crashed over her again.

"Oh, Goddess," she moaned. When did I start praying to the Goddess? She didn't remember, but it felt right given her ancestry.

Cooking breakfast for herself required too much energy, so she dressed and trudged down to her car, hoping the grumble of the Camaro's engine would soothe some of her hurts. The burgundy beast happily growled to life, and she smiled. It reminded her of Jeff's growly laugh when her head had rested against his chest, and happiness surged through her, taking the edge off her pain.

Julianna drove to Cindy's Café and tried to immerse herself in the scents of artery-hardening bliss and the cheerful proprietor. Always happy to see her, Cindy gave her one of the booths near the windows, despite her solitude. Julianna thanked her and ordered mint green tea. She couldn't bear drinking Sebrina's favorite. When the tea arrived, she curled her hands around her mug and stared out at the morning, hoping the sunshine and hot steam would tickle the answers to her questions out of the ether.

"May I join you, or is this a one-person party?"

Julianna looked up to see her mother standing beside the table, dressed in a dove gray silk blouse and somber black slacks.

"Oh, hey, Mom." She rose and gave Beth a hug. "Sure, have a seat. What are you doing up so early?"

"I was out walking and saw your car." Beth seated herself across the table while Julianna settled down. She took in Julianna's somber expression and cocked her head. "Are you all right?"

"Oh, yeah, I think so." She leaned back against the booth. "Just been a rough couple of days, and I'm just trying to sort everything out. Would you like some tea?"

"You're drinking tea? I thought you preferred coffee."

"Usually I do." She bit her tongue before she said more. "I don't really need the caffeine right now. Mint tea is soothing for the stomach, and I need all the soothing I can get."

"All right, what's going on?"

Julianna looked at her mother, and tears gathered in the corners of her eyes again. Sebrina might be her birth mother, but Beth would always be Mom, the one who made things better when the shit hit the fan.

"Oh, glory, Mom, I don't know." She stared out the window, hoping to stall her tears. "I just feel like everything is caving in on me, and I can't seem to stop it."

"Hey now, dear one," Beth crooned. She reached across the table to squeeze Julianna's hand. "Is it your father?"

Julianna shook her head and laughed humorlessly. "No, ironically enough, it's not Dad." She took a deep breath. "I met my birth mother yesterday."

"What?" Beth sat back hard.

"Yes, she came by to tell me where I came from and why I ended up…where I did." Julianna sipped her tea to try to calm herself down. "I don't know how to feel, Mom. I'm hurt and angry and confused and betrayed. Why didn't she want me when I was a baby? I feel…"

"Abandoned?"

"Yeah."

Beth nodded, her gaze turning thoughtful. Emotions swept across her face, and Julianna could smell the conflicting effects. Beth's scent alternated between tangy fear and acrid, protective anger.

"How did she know you are her daughter?"

Julianna bit her bottom lip. "She recognized me from my resemblance to…an old family photograph." She hated lying, but she couldn't reveal the Moon Singers, even now.

Beth nodded and sighed. She smiled and squeezed Julianna's hand again.

"I understand your confusion and hurt over your birth mother's disclosure." Beth's voice filled with compassion. "But here's the way I've had to look at it. Your birth mother must've had a reason for giving you up, whether she was alone, or too afraid to deal with a baby, or just too young. Maybe she knew she didn't have the resources to adequately take care of you." She shrugged. "Whatever her reasons, you came to your father and me, and we were so grateful that God had granted us a little child to raise as our own. It felt like a gift from Heaven. You were perfect, and we loved you with all our hearts."

Beth smiled lovingly. "I'm so pleased to have been

your mother. To watch you grow up and learn and become the woman you are today. I'm so proud of you, and I love you, even if I didn't give birth to you. In her own way, I suspect your birth mother loves you, too. She just didn't know how to deal with the awesome responsibility of raising a child."

"But why tell me now, after thirty-six years?" Julianna asked plaintively.

Beth shrugged. "Maybe she saw how beautiful you've become and regrets losing the time with you. Maybe she just wanted you to know a little more about your family history. I don't know her reasons for telling you, but she gave me the opportunity to raise you and be the mother to comfort you. For that, I'll always be grateful."

Beth paused, straightening her shoulders. "Don't be angry with her or hate her. She gave you to the best family she could without knowing it. Dwell on that, rather than her decision to give you up. And remember that I love you, and your dad loved you. She gave you the gift of us."

Julianna took a shuddering breath as her emotions leaked out of her eyes. She closed them, holding onto her teacup for dear life.

"Oh, now, don't cry, dear one." Her mother took her hand. "It'll be okay, no matter what. What did she come to tell you, that she was sorry?"

Julianna nodded again while tears fell.

"Well, then, take her apology at face value and let it go." Beth patted her hand. "These decisions were made long ago, and they can't be changed, only regretted. She can do no more than apologize, and she did. Take it as her sincere regret and be happy you had a home and a family who loved you."

"But she's in town." Julianna wiped her face with hands, hating the whine in her voice. "I see her all the time. She's been teaching me the history...of Callowwood and its families, for the last couple of months. How can I face her again?"

Beth studied Julianna for a few moments, her expression thoughtful. Then she shrugged as if letting something go.

"Is anything really different? Has her role in your life changed now that you know she's your birth mother?" Beth spread her hands. "You say she's been teaching you history. That's part of a parent's job. She's been teaching you about yourself in her own way. Now she gave you another piece of information to go with what you knew. She obviously cares about you, even before she recognized you as her lost child. Take it as that and let the rest go."

Julianna let the words sink into her consciousness, and some of her confusion eased.

"Is that what you'll do, Mom?"

Beth smiled ruefully. "Yes, I'll try. I admit I was concerned she wanted to take you back as her daughter, but in reality, it's too late for that. She can only start to build that kind of relationship with you. I already have it."

Julianna chuckled, wiping away her tears. "Yes, you do. Thanks, Mom."

"You're welcome, dear one. Now, are you having breakfast?"

"Yeah, I didn't feel like cooking this morning."

"I can imagine." Beth picked up the menu. "What are your plans for the weekend? Do you have to work the whole time?"

Thinking about the choosing ceremony scheduled for that evening, Julianna suspected neither she nor Jeff would be working much at all. She wanted to tell Beth everything about the pack and the discovery of Jeff Lightfoot as her True Mate, but Beth's humanity made it impossible.

"Not tonight. Jeff Lightfoot invited me to a party."

Beth dropped the menu to the table.

"Jeff Lightfoot."

"Yes."

"He invited you to a party? Do you think he's getting serious?"

"Yes." Julianna couldn't hide her smile.

"Are you going as his special guest?"

"Yes." Julianna blushed as her mother's smile widened.

"Is it a formal party?" Beth's eyes sparkled.

"Yes, why?"

"This must be a dream come true for you. As I recall, you mooned over him for years."

*Mooned. How accurate.* Julianna nodded and grinned.

"It must be all that time you spend working with him. He's finally figured out you're a beautiful and accomplished young woman." Beth nodded confidently as she picked up the menu again. "I was surprised at his ignorance when it came to you. But he was young and male, and young men can be very blind when their hormones are running. Now that he's a man, and still unmarried, he's able to see the extraordinary woman you are. About time."

Julianna snorted, amused, and Beth winked.

"By the way, he stopped by yesterday."

Julianna choked on her tea. "What?"

Beth looked far too smug. "Apparently, he wanted to see how I was doing after your dad's passing, and offered any help I might need."

"Really?"

"He also mentioned that he thinks you're wonderful and asked if it would be okay to court you."

Julianna gaped, her jaw hanging. "Court me? He actually said the word 'court'?"

Beth tried to look innocent, but her eyes twinkled. "Yes, he did. I said I'd think about it."

"You did not."

Beth laughed. "No, I didn't. I said 'go right ahead, young man.'" She smiled broadly. "Oh, dear one, I'm so happy for you. You do want him to court you, right? Even after Terence?"

Julianna grinned. "More than anything."

"Excellent." Beth nodded with satisfaction.

Cindy arrived to take their orders and chatted a short time with Beth. Julianna settled herself in her mother's words about Sebrina and Jeff, and felt her unhappiness lift. Sebrina's past choices couldn't be changed. Holding on to anger over them wasted precious energy. Besides, Jeff had come to her mom and asked for her blessing. Life had shifted from sad to awesome.

"Now, what time is the party tonight?" Beth asked as Cindy took their orders to the kitchen.

"Seven o'clock."

"Have you decided what you're going to wear?"

"Yes. Eloise Farkas and I went shopping on Wednesday."

"Eloise? That nice young woman at the clinic?"

"You know Eloise?" Julianna raised her eyebrows.

"Oh yes. She helped a lot when your father got so sick. She was always kind and patient. Funny, too. I'm glad you've made friends with her."

Julianna sipped her tea, marveling at how small the world could become.

"Do you want some help with your hair for the party?" Beth gave her a bright smile.

"Yes, please. Can you help me?"

"I'd be happy to."

"Thanks, Mom." Julianna hoped all her gratitude showed in her voice.

"You're more than welcome. You'll knock his socks off tonight."

*I sincerely hope so.*

\*\*\*\*

Julianna thanked her mom for the breakfast and headed

out into the morning sunshine, feeling lighter than she had in weeks. The waiting and posturing and competing were done. She could relax a little.

She still had a lot to think about, but for the moment, she let the thoughts go and enjoyed the sunshine flickering through the trees before the day's heat took off. She inhaled deeply, trying to let her tension flow out of her when she caught a familiar scent. She paused and scanned the world around her.

Across the street, sitting on a bench with a cup of coffee in his hand, sat Leslie Dunmore, her Fresno neighbor. He met her gaze and raised the cup in greeting, a sardonic smile curling his lips as she trotted across the street. He waited for her, appearing relaxed. But she could smell some of his unease under his personal fragrance of wild mountain penstemon and pine.

"Leslie? I thought that was you. What are you doing here in Callowwood?" Julianna stopped in front of him.

"Hey, darlin'. How've you been?" He gazed at her, his expression showing nothing beyond friendly interest.

"Good. Busy, but good." She frowned, tilting her head. "What are you doing here?"

"I'm visiting family." He met her gaze without flinching.

"You have family in Callowwood?" Unease zipped up her back.

He nodded slowly. "I do." He paused and patted the bench. "Sit for a minute. I have something to tell you."

"Okay." She settled beside him, wondering why he smelled so familiar to her. *Probably because I lived next to him for over a year.*

"I don't think there's an easy way to break this to you so I'll just show my cards and let the chips fall where they may." Leslie shook his head. "I'm your uncle, on your mother's side."

"What?"

The words didn't make any sense. Her parents had been only children despite their Irish roots and family gatherings had been small affairs. She didn't have any aunts or uncles or cousins.

"I don't understand. My parents were only children."

Leslie kept his gaze on her, steady and patient, waiting for her to catch on. *Just like Sebrina.*

"Oh my glory. You're Sebrina's brother, aren't you?"

He nodded. "Yes, her younger brother."

"Does she know you're here?" Julianna shot a look around the town as if Sebrina was waiting just out of sight.

"No. I haven't visited her yet." He sipped his coffee before he swung his gaze away. "She doesn't know I know who you are. That I always knew."

"How long? How long have you kept an eye on me?" Julianna's anger grew.

"Since after you were adopted." Leslie rubbed his hands together around the cup. "Sebrina didn't know I knew she was pregnant. But she'd had the baby and gave you up before I caught up to her. It took me a while to find you again."

Julianna shook her head. "Why didn't you adopt me or take me in when you did find me?"

"Because the Morrises had already done so." He grimaced. "I was going to steal you away one night, but then I saw how much they doted on you and you responded. And you didn't smell like a Moon Singer at that point. I thought maybe you'd gotten too much of your father's genetics and wouldn't turn when you hit puberty. So, I waited. And you didn't change."

She coughed a half-sob. "I didn't change because I *had* to be human. No one came for me. No one wanted me to be a Moon Singer. So, I suppressed that side of me. If you'd come for me, I would've been able to change."

"I'm sorry, Julianna. I should've shown you who I was much sooner." He shook his head, his lips drawn tight. "I didn't know you had the ability, but I couldn't stay away from you. I had to keep an eye on you because you're family."

"Family?" She narrowed her eyes. "Family watches out for each other."

"I did—"

"Family is there to hold each other when the shit hits the fan. Family doesn't hide." She raised her chin. "I didn't need a guardian or babysitter. I needed someone who cared enough to be honest and there for me."

Leslie never looked away, but he remained silent for so long, she didn't think he'd respond.

"You're right. I let you down. I did what I thought was best, but honestly, I was a coward and did what was best for me." He nodded. "You're right to be angry with me and I accept that I made mistakes. If you ever need to know more about our family, I'll be happy to tell you." He fished something out of his back pocket. "This is my card with my cell number on it. Feel free to text or call anytime."

He handed her the card and stood. "I wish you the best tonight. I understand you're a candidate for Luna in this pack, and I think you'll make an excellent one." He nodded to her and sauntered away, his ponytail swinging against his back.

# CHAPTER EIGHTEEN:
## Pick of the Litter

Jeff stood between his father and sister in the entryway of their home and fidgeted. Three days without Julianna had become torture. Thank the Goddess he wouldn't have to repeat her absence anytime soon.

The black tuxedo tailored for him fit just fine, but with the nearness of the full moon, it felt like a suit of armor. He tried to keep a mellow expression on his face, but he couldn't stop himself from scanning the doorway.

Seven o'clock had come and gone, but Julianna still hadn't stepped through the doors.

He greeted the Winthrops as they passed by, nodding to Cameron. She a sweet and demure smile. A gold sequined sheath dress rippled over her form like molten metal, molding over her breasts tight enough to show her nipples. Her wolf's head Token dangled from her left wrist and winked in the light of the foyer like a warning.

"Have you talked to Ms. Morris, Tawny?" He tried to shake off the odd unease.

"Yes, and she promised to be here, Jeff. Don't worry."

"I'm not worried."

Tawny snorted.

He wasn't worried, not really. He told himself he shouldn't see her before the party, but his flimsy assurances couldn't stem the flood of desire.

*Dammit, sit! We'll see her soon enough.*

*I want to see her now,* his Brother whined.

Jeff nodded and shook hands with most of the guests coming in through the doors, but he barely remembered what he said and to whom. Eloise Farkas entered with her parents, but without Tommy Scatterstone. Jeff wondered if she'd finally realized Scatterstone's jackassery. They still hadn't heard anything about Nora Farkas.

Jeff nodded to Zach, Kyle, Leo, Thomas, and Henry, his cadre of betas. They struck a resplendent picture in matching tuxedos made for this kind of event. To his surprise, Gary and Woody came in together, also wearing tuxedos.

Jeff nodded to them, recognizing a difference in both males. They carried themselves with more confidence than they had a few days before. He scented their excitement and pleasure at attending the event.

*I'd be excited and pleased, too, if Julianna would just show up.*

Brenda Solaris entered the house like a queen surveying and receiving her subjects' blessings. Her fiery red evening gown with an ankle-length skirt slit to the hip certainly caught the attention of everyone around her, particularly the unattached males.

*Fortunately, I am attached.*

Brenda sparkled and charmed, as if she knew she'd be the next Luna. She took the Alpha's hand and smiled, her eyes flashing coquettishly for Jeff. Jeff replied with his amused half-smile and caught the scent of apricots again. Mixed with her overwhelming anticipation, the scent struck him as cloying and thick.

"So good to see you again, Alpha, Jefferson." All her graceful moves seemed calculated to impress.

"Welcome back, Ms. Solaris." He nodded dutifully.

"It's my pleasure to be back in your house. I hope to be here more often in the future."

Jeff dipped his chin but said nothing and she was forced to move on. Relief swelled as the night air pushed away her scent. *Thank the Goddess.*

Sebrina entered and his unease tripped another warning. The old Paiute woman shambled slowly without her usual smile. She appeared tired and worn down, older than he'd ever seen her. Everything about her screamed sorrow and resignation, and Jeff found himself reaching to take her hands.

"Ah, Jefferson." She offered him a warm smile that didn't reach her eyes. "Good to see you. How are you this evening?"

He laughed lightly. "Excited and anxious all at once. But tell me how you're doing, Mistress Westwind. I scent sorrow on you tonight."

She gave him a thoughtful look. "That story isn't mine to tell, Jefferson, but perhaps it'll become clear when the Lady Moon shines full. Tonight, I'm simply here to enjoy the company of other Moon Singers and see the next generation of the pack's leadership develop."

"Yes, of course." He squeezed her hands. "Please, let me know if there's anything I can do to help. Perhaps we can share stories later with a friend. Have you seen Ms. Morris yet this evening?"

Sebrina shrank into herself. Sorrow suffused her expression, and Jeff wondered what had happened between the two females.

"I have not." Sebrina shook her head, her mouth tightened in pain. "I'm sure she'll arrive when she's ready to do so. Please excuse me. I don't want to hold up the others. I'll speak with you after."

She shuffled away, her head down. Jeff watched her go with concern, but he had to turn back to the guests coming in. What could be bothering Sebrina? Nothing ever fazed her. What had happened in the last few days to make her so sad?

He continued greeting the guests, including the Cutters and their sullen daughter, Tammy. She no longer wore a wolf's head token and her eyes seethed with resentment. She stank of frustration and indignation. She said enough to the Alpha and Jeff to be dutiful, but teenage angst suffused her body language.

*Yet another reason why you wouldn't make a good Luna.*

"Wow." Tawny grasped his elbow. He glanced at her then lifted his gaze to the doors to see what had caught her attention.

His heart just about stopped in his chest.

Julianna stood in the doorway, glowing like a shining star against the black sky. She wore a long velvet gown that clung to her curves like a second skin, and Jeff's Brother howled with lustful joy. The rich teal of the velvet and the tastefully low neckline drew attention to the smooth skin of her breasts. He immediately wanted to drag his tongue over them to discover if they were indeed as smooth as they looked.

Julianna's beauty hit him like a punch in the gut, and her pure scent filled his nose until he staggered with pleasure. His cock surged, and he wanted nothing more than to pounce on her, kiss her into submission, and take her hard and wild. He held himself still, awestruck by the beautiful female who sauntered toward him.

When she stopped in front of the Alpha, Richard took her hand and kissed her knuckles. Jeff gritted his teeth to keep from ripping her hand out of his father's.

"Thank you for coming tonight." Richard nodded.

"I'm honored to be here, Alpha." She smiled as she turned to Jeff. "Good evening, Jefferson. How are you?"

*Horny, desperate, and rock hard for you.* "I'm great,

thank you. We're very glad you could come tonight."
*Fucking ecstatic.*

"Thank you." Her eyes blazed with her desire as she caught the scent of his arousal. "I'm very happy to be here."

She took his hand and shivered at the exact moment excitement and lust shot through him. He clenched his jaw and sternly reminded himself to let her go so he didn't appear to be favoring her.

*Fucking appearances. I'm so done with this charade.*

Julianna licked her lips, and his blood boiled through his veins. He had to think about changing the oil in his Camaro when she turned to Tawny and greeted her as well.

"I'll see you at dinner." She dipped her chin.

"Yes, right." *Smooth, jackass. Roll that tongue back into your mouth.*

Jeff watched her walk away, and his breath caught. The back of her dress rested modestly low, and a slit in the skirt stopped three inches short of her ass. A train of a gauzy material just like her scarf filled the slit and he wanted to sift through it with his fingers. His cock tried to stand up and sing.

*Down!* He groaned under his breath. *How the hell am I going to make it through tonight?*

Jeff knew his duty, but he desperately wanted to escort his Mate to her seat in the garden. And stay by her side, forever. Declaring her his favorite and skip all the rigmarole. Forcing his shoulders to relax, he stayed, but his smile felt strained by the time he escorted his sister to the garden. Tawny looked over at him and grinned, but said nothing.

Her smile remained in place until she caught sight of Zach standing beside Theo. Tawny's attention sharpened, and her body tensed. Zach suddenly straightened up and stared at her with the same intense focus, making Tawny blush.

*Is Zach checking out my sister?* Jeff raised an eyebrow at his First, who coughed with chagrin and nodded, his expression smoothing into its usual impassiveness.

Tawny sighed, but smiled when he shot her a look. They arrived at the table where Julianna spoke with MaryBeth and JenniLynn Grayhound. Julianna kept up her conversation with the twins, but she sent him a glance, acknowledging his presence. His insides turned to mush, and his pants tightened once more. Tawny elbowed him, and he realized he'd been standing there, staring at Julianna like an idiot.

"Uh, right, okay." He pulled out Tawny's chair for her. "I'll leave you then." He kissed his sister on the cheek and turned away, trying to get his arousal under control.

\*\*\*\*

Julianna savored Jeff's presence, letting the scent of his desire wash away some of her unease. After discovering Sebrina was her birth mother and Leslie her blood uncle, she needed Jeff as her north star, the one constant in her life. She'd wanted to throw herself into his arms when she came in but told herself she could wait until after the ceremony. Her body didn't agree, but she'd managed to walk away.

*Think about something else or everyone is going to scent your arousal.*

Like the first time she'd sat here in this garden under the twinkling lights of the tents. She'd stood, dressed up, waiting for her future to bloom before her. But this time, she'd chosen the outcome. She'd come full circle.

"Are you sure you want us in your cadre if you're chosen?" Jennilynn asked for the sixth time. "We're only low-level betas. There're many other betas with more experience who favor you."

"You're both, what, twenty-eight years old?"

The women nodded.

"You're the only betas other than Tawny Lightfoot who spoke to me the first evening I became a packmember. I value that kind of friendly kindness."

"Well, we liked you the moment we scented you." Marybeth blushed. "You smelled right."

"What do you mean, 'smelled right'?"

"Uh, well…" Marybeth's blush deepened.

"What she means is she can scent when someone is suited for something." Jennilynn rolled her eyes at her sister.

"Really?"

Marybeth shrugged. "It's just this weird sense of rightness about people. Everything just smells 'good' or 'settled'. It's hard to explain."

Julianna nodded, impressed. "That's a very useful talent."

"It would be if it worked for me, but it only works for other people." MaryBeth grimaced. "I have to muddle along on my own like everyone else. Except they have me."

"Yet another reason to have you in my cadre. Perhaps you could help determine if someone might help or hurt the pack."

MaryBeth looked thoughtful. "I guess. I've never tried that before."

"I'd give you the opportunity if I'm chosen Luna." Julianna sipped her water. "Interested?"

"I don't know. It seems like a big responsibility."

Julianna nodded. "Regardless, I'd still like you both in my cadre." She took one of each woman's hands and squeezed gently.

"We'd be honored, Mistress Julianna," they said together without hesitation.

"Thank the Lady Moon."

They both grinned.

"Ladies and gentlemen, it's time to begin." Richard's

voice boomed out over the assembly.

She found Sebrina seated on her left, and unease flickered. The Paiute woman looked old. She wore sadness like a mantle over her shoulders. Julianna's ego wanted to shout, *it's her own damn fault*, but her heart knew better.

*Holding on to anger over something that can't be changed is the epitome of stupidity.*

Could she forgive Sebrina?

*Yes,* her Sister said.

Putting her words into action, Julianna reached out and grasped the older woman's hand under the table as she sat down. Sebrina looked over at her in surprise, and Julianna gave her a compassionate smile, squeezing her hand to convey her forgiveness.

Sebrina studied her a long time. After several seconds, she squeezed back. Relief filtered through her scent of sorrow, and she took a deep breath.

Julianna let out her own inner sigh of relief.

"Tonight is a great night for us all." Richard gestured to the crowd. "To our honor and delight, we have three Luna candidates who have passed all Seven Leadership Tests. Please join me up here for all to see. In alphabetical order: Brenda Tiffany Solaris, Cameron Elizabeth Winthrop, and Julianna Sarah Morris."

Julianna rose with the others, her heart swelling with excitement. Sebrina gave her an encouraging smile as she strode to the dais. She stood to Cameron's left with her head up. She'd earned her place, and dammit, she'd take it. *Whatever happens after Jeff chooses me, it'll be exciting.*

"Your candidates for Luna." Richard stepped back, and polite applause washed through the audience. "Now, as is the custom, the Successor will choose the best female for his mate from the three candidates."

Richard stepped down from the dais, and Jeff strode into his place, his expression tense and watchful. Julianna's awareness riveted on him, and she rolled her shoulders to loosen them, keeping her eyes trained on her male. Jeff's primal virility sang through her mind, and her body reacted to his presence by tightening.

Everywhere.

The crowd hushed, and a shriek boiled in her chest in response to the tension building in the garden. She clenched her jaw and tried to breathe normally, but her heart raced as Jeff stalked toward them, his eyes hot and feral. Wetness coated her nether lips and she hoped no one would notice in all the excitement.

Jeff paced around them, orbiting them to inspect every physical aspect. Julianna heard him breathing deeply, taking in their scents for comparison. He never paused in his measured strides, constantly circling them.

Julianna tried to keep calm, but her heart thundered, and her nipples hardened to tight little points. His eyes snapped to hers, and he growled low in his throat, but he didn't stop his circuit.

Brenda smiled at him expectantly and wiggled a little with her excitement. Cameron's smile became seductive, and she whined softly, her body undulating as if her dress encased her body too tightly. Julianna wanted to snap at the other two. *He's my Mate, and I'll be damned if either of you bitches touch him!*

She heard another low growl and realized it had come from her. The sound was full of warning, and Jeff's gaze returned to her, his eyes flaring with lust and dominance. Her canines elongated in her mouth, but she kept her lips firmly shut in a tight smile. She raised her chin in challenge, and his shoulders tensed, but he kept up his mesmerizing revolutions.

When he stopped directly in front of them, he scrutinized them with his blazing golden eyes. All of them panted as if they'd been the ones circling their prey. Julianna shivered with every stroke of his gaze. Brenda's body froze in anticipation and Cameron gave a soft excited exhalation. Julianna could barely hold herself still.

The tension had wound up so tight Julianna was ready to jump out of her skin. Jeff's hot gaze stopped on each female, but when he met her eyes, satisfaction filled his expression. He shifted his body until he faced her alone.

He reached for her hands and excitement, electricity, and hot desire shot through her. Her nipples felt like they'd cut through her bodice, and she desperately wanted to rub them against his chest until they relaxed.

His nostrils flared, and his smile heated.

"I, Jefferson Eric Lightfoot, Successor of the Callowwood Pack, choose you, Julianna Sarah Morris, as my Luna." His eyes smoldered with his burning passion. "I choose you to be my strength in times of conflict, my compassion in times of strife, my wisdom in times of uncertainty. I choose you to be the mother of my pups and the pack's Guardian of the Stories."

Energy swirled around them, fed by the anticipation of the crowd and the vows Jeff had spoken. Julianna let herself be buoyed up by it, and her response burst from her with a brilliant grin, exposing her long canines.

"I, Julianna Sarah Morris, daughter and last descendent of Ho'a'tote, the First Canid, accept the position of Luna of the Callowwood Pack, to stand beside you in strength, compassion, and wisdom, to bear your pups and to keep the stories alive in the pack's memory."

Amazement rippled through the crowd. Mouths gaped and eyes widened while whispers floated in the still air. The tension reached a crescendo. Julianna's blood thundered through her veins, and her hands tingled. Jeff stared at her hungrily, his eyes full of triumph, and he trembled in an effort to keep his motions smooth. His jaw clenched as he dragged her away from the others and turned to face the audience.

"I give you Julianna Sarah Lightfoot, future Luna of the Callowwood Pack!" Jeff's joy rang clear for all to hear.

The pack exploded into cheers and applause, the excitement and jubilation rising in a roar. Dishes and cutlery jangled as people pounded on the tables like in old Viking times, and howls split the night.

The sharp scent of disappointment filled Julianna's nose as the other two candidates left the dais to return to their seats. Brenda tore off her wolf's head token and threw it to the floor. Cameron quietly removed her token and solemnly handed it to Richard. Julianna caught the scent of unbridled fury, but when she turned her head to chase it, the scent faded. She shrugged it away.

She did catch sight of Leslie standing at the back of the tent, a proud smile on his lips. He inclined his head with respect and warmth settled in her chest. She'd have to get to know him again, learning who he really was, but for now, this was enough.

Jeff brushed her back with his hand and she shot him a grateful smile.

"Jeff, can I choose my cadre right now, or should I do it in private?"

He looked at her, and lust flared in his eyes. She shivered with the promise of pleasure to come, but he reined it in with effort.

"You're Alpha now, my sweet Lupine. You can do anything you wish."

"Well, not anything." She grimaced. "You're the Alpha, and you weren't allowed to touch me until tonight, remember?"

"I seem to remember touching you a little." He winked, his gaze full of wicked humor.

She bit her bottom lip and blushed.

"Go ahead and name your cadre tonight."

"Thanks."

He chastely kissed her cheek and stepped behind her, his hands resting on her hips as she turned to face the audience. Pleasure zinged through her from the heat in his hands, but she focused and raised her hands to catch the audience's attention.

"I thank you all for your acceptance and approval of me as your Luna." A whistle broke the silence, and she grinned a triumphant smile. "It's a great honor for me, and I'm grateful. In particular, I must thank Sebrina Westwind for patiently teaching me all the stories of our People, especially those of my family. She taught me there's more to being a Moon Singer than the family that raised me or the hardships that influenced past choices."

Julianna inclined her head deeply to Sebrina, and the older woman's expression filled with gratitude. Applause thundered around them, and Jeff patted her back as he stepped away. She missed the heat of his touch, but focused on her moment.

"I recently learned the value of having loyal friends at my back, and I chose my cadre based on that lesson. I want you all to be aware of the exceptional packmembers who have won my gratitude and friendship."

Julianna paused and thought carefully. The order of the names would correspond to the rank the cadre members held for the rest of her tenure as Luna.

"Eloise Farkas, for her wisdom and honesty in all things."

Applause sounded, along with whispers within the members of the pack. Eloise rose and picked her way to the dais where Julianna stood, her eyes sparkling. She stopped before Julianna and bowed her head to her Luna. Julianna nodded in return, accepting Eloise's wink and grin before returning her attention to the crowd.

"Marybeth and Jennilynn Grayhound, for their friendship and unswerving loyalty."

The twins rose and strode to where Eloise stood, their faces showing their unabashed pleasure at being named part of the new Luna's cadre. They, too, bowed their heads to Julianna then faced the crowd.

"Woody Scatterstone, for his cool head under pressure and his complete honesty."

Silent surprise greeted her announcement as Woody sauntered out of the crowd and stopped before Julianna, his eyes bright and full of feral joy. He bowed his head, but never dropped her gaze, before he spun in place and stood beside Jennilynn. His scent radiated sheer triumph and satisfaction.

Julianna suspected her choice of an omega member turned tradition on its ear and would elevate Woody to a low-level beta. She didn't care. He deserved the honor. Unlike his younger brother, Tommy, he had a much better attitude.

"Gary Howler, for his historical knowledge of the pack and his medical skills in the field."

Shock rippled through the crowd. Gary's advanced age made his inclusion a surprise. Julianna guessed the Lunas of the past generally chose women to be in their cadres, but Julianna valued Gary's perspective and his ability to stay calm in stressful situations.

He paused next to Woody with a half-smile on his face and swept his body into an elaborate bow from bygone times. Then he spun to face the pack, and Julianna had to hide a grin. *Show-off.*

Julianna gestured to her friends. "Ladies and gentlemen, the cadre of the Luna-elect."

She stood back and let her cadre take the attention. Richard nodded to her as she retreated to stand beside Jeff. He grasped her hip and squeezed, showing his approval.

"In accordance with our traditions," Richard shouted over the applause, "the Successor and Luna will take the leadership when they have whelped their first child. When that occurs, I will step down as Alpha, and Jefferson Lightfoot will take up the reins of leadership. To the future Alpha and Luna!"

"To the future Alpha and Luna!" Howls once more

echoed under the tents. Julianna grinned when Jeff squeezed her with his arms, laying a soft kiss to the back of her neck.

"I have to talk to my cadre, Jeff," she whispered through the rising lust.

"That's fine. But if those males touch you, I'll tear them apart."

"Aw, come on. Just one hug? I promise it'll be short."

Jeff's jaw bunched, and his eyes narrowed as his gaze fixed on Gary and Woody.

"Just. One. Hug."

She winked and stepped off the dais to join her cadre. Eloise hugged her immediately.

"I knew it would be you." She grinned fiercely.

Julianna laughed. "Thanks for believing in me."

Eloise snorted but stepped back to let the others close. Marybeth and Jennilynn shared their hug, but Julianna didn't mind. Gratitude for the love and loyalty she sensed from both of them filled her heart. They each winked the opposite eye at her and said together, "See you back at the table."

Then she turned to Gary and Woody. "I'm into hugs, gentlemen, but this is the only time I'll be able to offer you one."

Gary stepped into her embrace and squeezed her gently. "You're magnificent, Ms. Julianna, and I'm very pleased to have you as my Luna. It's an honor to be in your cadre, and I will serve you to the best of my ability."

"Thank you, Gary." She smiled as he stepped back. "I'm grateful you agreed."

He gave her a mock-horrified expression. "Turn down a chance to serve the prettiest female in town? Hell no."

Julianna laughed as she turned to Woody, and he hugged her like a brother.

"Thank you, Ms. Julianna," he whispered. "I don't know what more I can say. It's an honor."

"I liked you the minute I met you, Woody." She stepped back so Jeff could relax. "You have a strength that most of the others don't see, and I wanted you to know I see it." She tilted her head. "This elevates you from omega rank, doesn't it?"

"Yes, it does." Triumph filled his smile. "You made me beta tonight, and I can't thank you enough for that." His smile melted in to solemnity. "And I'll always have your back."

"That's what I need."

He nodded and retreated to join Gary. The two males walked away together, and she admired them in their tuxes, amazed she'd never noticed how handsome they were. They'd give the ladies of the pack a show tonight.

She grinned and shook her head before she looked around for Jeff. He stepped up close and inhaled deeply through his nose as he pressed a kiss against her nape. Her pulse quickened, and goosebumps rose on her skin.

He settled his hands on her hips and drew her close to his body, rubbing his own arousal against her ass with a subtle motion of his hips. She sucked in a startled breath as liquid flooded between her legs. An excited whimper burned in her throat.

"Those males are lucky I know you're mine." He growled against her ear. "If they touch you again, I'll tear out their throats."

Julianna shivered at the possessive fury in his voice. "They know it. No one will touch me but you. I promise."

"Good." He nuzzled her ear, nipping the skin below the lobe. "Holy Mother, I'm dying for you. The last three days have been hell on me." He drew back and moved to her side. "Unfortunately, we have to stay here, socializing until after dinner." He smirked. "But as soon as our duty is done, I'm paying you back for that little stunt you pulled two days ago."

"I thought you paid me back in the shower."

He chuckled darkly. "Not nearly enough, my dear Luna."

He jerked her against his chest and bent his head to place a soft kiss on her lips. The force of his desire burning in the tender touch stole her breath. He pulled back and clenched his jaw, releasing her reluctantly.

"Now, let's go eat, and I'll let you sit with your cadre, but after the meal, you'll stay by my side as my Luna and my Mate."

She smiled up at him wickedly. "And if I refuse your demands, my Alpha?"

He growled at her under his breath, but she felt it all the way down to her pussy. "Then I'll spank your ass and torture you until you're screaming with pleasure, minx."

Julianna laughed, and he grinned as he took her arm. They strode to the front of the buffet line, just behind his father.

"I feel like I'm at a wedding."

Jeff nodded. "In the eyes of the pack, we are married." He glanced at her raised eyebrows. "Why else would everyone dress up so much?"

A small pang of sorrow for her human mother bit the pit of her stomach, but she nodded and filled her plate. He watched her as if he thought she might disappear. She winked at him and sauntered away, wiggling her hips. She heard him catch his breath, and joy screamed through her.

She settled into her seat and forced herself to start eating before the others joined her. Her mother would be appalled. She'd have to get over her human tendencies.

Julianna barely tasted the food. The knowledge that she'd be in Jeff's bed that night sent butterflies dancing in her gut. Her awareness centered on the male sitting with his own cadre a few tables away. How would she make it through dinner?

At last her table filled up with her cadre, and she thanked her lucky stars for the company to distract her.

Despite the conversation, she couldn't stop sneaking glances over to the table where Jeff sat with Zach and Kyle. Eloise followed her gaze and elbowed her.

"It'll be over soon, I promise," she whispered.

"What will?"

"Dinner." Eloise smirked. "None of us will keep you longer than necessary. We all know how long you've been waiting to be together."

Julianna moaned. "Is it that obvious?"

"Uh, yeah." Eloise snorted. "We could scent both of you when you stood close to each other."

"Sorry. We tried not to touch each other, but no one said we had to stop feeling arousal. At least we no longer have to pretend we're only mildly interested."

"Yeah, lucky you." Eloise's gaze returned to where Kyle chatted with Zach.

"Don't wait. Tell him."

"Tell who what?"

Julianna dropped her chin. "Tell Kyle you choose him. It's not like you're the Alpha pair and have to wait for test results."

"But I agreed to marry Tommy."

"Don't saddle yourself to misery if you don't have to." Julianna squeezed her hand. "There are no points for martyrdom."

She would've said more, but her thoughts splintered when Jeff rested his hands on her shoulders. Excitement sizzled through her body as she took his hand. He pulled it to his lips and kissed her knuckles. Delicious pleasure shot straight to her crotch. *How does he stay so cool?*

Her gaze dropped to the front of his slacks. He wasn't nearly as unaffected as his expression appeared.

"Shall we make our rounds?" He cleared his throat to remove the hoarseness in his voice.

"Oh, yes, let's do that." Julianna glanced at her dinner companions. "Please excuse me."

Eloise and the others nodded with smug smiles. Julianna didn't care. Jeff smelled too good, and he radiated warmth and strength. She wanted to explode from the need burning through her, but he continued to be the perfect gentleman as they made the rounds through the pack.

The eyes of the other candidates' families echoed disappointment, but they remained gracious in defeat. Brenda watched Julianna with narrowed eyes, but the threat had no teeth. Despite her little tantrum on the dais, Brenda responded courteously when they spoke with her.

"I never got the chance to thank you for coming to my father's respects party." Julianna inclined her head. "It was kind when you didn't know me at all."

"I didn't go for you." Brenda shrugged. "I went to pay respects to the future Alpha."

Julianna nodded. "I assumed as much. Thank you anyway. I hope you find your Mate, Ms. Solaris, and I hope he's as Alpha as Jeff."

Brenda stared at her for a long time, the icy blue eyes calculating and evaluating Julianna's statement. Julianna met her gaze frankly, and Brenda tilted her head. The woman smelled like surprise and uncertainty.

"Thank you, Luna. I appreciate that."

"You're welcome. Enjoy the rest of your evening."

Julianna beamed and turned with Jeff to move on to another table of guests, her thoughts racing. *Brenda isn't the one who set me up.* She might have been disappointed at Jeff's choice, but her scent hadn't been choked with seething fury or malice. She'd been a formidable opponent, but she didn't smell like an enemy.

When they approached Cameron's family, the Winthrops broadcasted cold, forbidding formality. Julianna eyed Cameron for any sign of maliciousness, but the younger female only exuded disappointment and responded graciously to the conversation.

Maybe she'd been jumping at shadows. *But I was so*

311

*sure she'd set Brenda and me up.* Relief followed Julianna's departure from the Winthrops.

She hardly remembered what she said to everyone. She smiled and thanked people for their congratulations, but her awareness centered on her Mate and the feeling of his hand on her body. She caught sight of Tommy Scatterstone conversing with a group of young males on the far side of the garden. He kept shooting looks at Eloise, but her First ignored him beautifully.

"Hey, now. You've been chosen as Luna. You don't need to be scoping out the competition." Jeff drew her away from the last table of betas.

"Heh. Not even remotely."

"Good." Jeff buried his nose in her hair. "Holy Goddess, you smell wonderful."

"Not as good as you. Have we done our duty to the pack?"

"Yes."

"Good. Now take me to bed."

"Yes, ma'am."

Jeff pulled her into the house faster than propriety demanded, but Julianna laughed with elation. Her heartbeat sped up when he stopped her at the staircase and looked around for observers. When he saw no one, he grabbed her hand and bolted up the stairs, pulling her along with him.

# CHAPTER NINETEEN:
## Mark of the Wolf

"Now it's my turn, my lovely Lupine."

Julianna spun to face Jeff as he kicked the bedroom door closed and reached up to loosen his bow tie with a quick jerk. He branded her with a look of hungry determination as he toed off his shoes.

A frisson of excitement shot up her back, and she gave him a challenging grin. "Bring it on, wolf-boy."

"Oh, I'm so much more than a boy." He growled as he unhooked his cummerbund and dropped it to the floor. He stalked toward her while he shrugged out of his jacket and tossed it to the bureau. Then he slid behind her, dropping a deceptively gentle kiss on her neck. "And tonight, you'll learn just how much more I am."

He pulled on one end of her gauzy scarf, and it slid off her shoulders with a sensual hiss. He licked the back of her neck and placed another small kiss at her nape. She shivered a little as his hands slid down her arms, pulling the wide straps of her dress with them. The stretchy material glided down off her breasts, exposing them to his hands as he released the straps.

He growled in appreciation. "No bra."

"You think I'd wear a bra in this dress?"

"I'm not thinking right now. I'm enjoying." His fingers gently plucked at her nipples. She moaned as sensation zinged straight through her, pinging her brain and pooling between her legs.

"Holy Mother, you smell good."

Jeff moved around until he stood in front of her, never releasing her breasts from his hands.

"I love how the wolf pendant looks against your naked skin." He bent down and nuzzled the pendant before he took one hard nipple into his mouth, suckling it gently. She gasped and pushed her breast deeper into his mouth.

He dropped to his knees before her, releasing her nipple with a soft pop and worked the remainder of her dress down over her hips. It slid off easily, revealing the tiny gold Lycra thong covering her trimmed mound. He let out a sound of excited surprise and buried his nose against the little triangle of fabric covering her pussy.

"Oh, sweet Goddess." He moaned as he pulled her to him, holding her tightly against his face with his hands on her buttocks. "You wore that just to tease me."

Julianna laughed darkly. "Of course, my handsome lover. You think I have no experience in seduction?" She wiggled her hips back and forth within his grip. "Oh, you have no idea what I've learned about eroticism in the eighteen years I've been gone. I only held back for the last few months because I wanted you bad enough to be patient."

She spun in his grip until his face pressed between the cheeks of her ass, and she bent forward with her hands on her knees. He froze in surprise and took a deep breath, inhaling the scent of her arousal.

"Is this a toy?"

The heat from his tongue licking the little drop crystal on her thong just above the cleft of her ass stopped her laugh short. She shivered and arched her back, offering her hips to him in wanton abandon.

Jeff growled, and he gripped her hips tighter to keep her from moving away from his mouth. He slid one hand around her thigh and pushed between her legs, rubbing her clit. Electric pleasure shot through her, and she keened with surprised delight, demanding more with every breath. Pressure and excitement built until she writhed against his tongue and his hand, reaching for an orgasm.

Suddenly, he took his hand away and stood up behind her, letting all that lovely tension fade. She mewled in disappointment and gave him a puppy-dog look over her shoulder. He shot her a wicked grin and dragged her to the bed.

"Sit."

She stared at him a moment to see if he was serious. He didn't smile, but his eyes twinkled with humor. She settled on the bed and raised an eyebrow.

"Stay," he said with a half-smirk.

She growled but sat still as he continued to undress.

He unbuttoned his shirt, releasing his cufflinks with soft clicks, and pulled it off his shoulders slow enough to tease. Julianna's mouth watered when his chest emerged from his seductive motions. She adored his chest, his hard, full pectoral muscles covered with light brown hair. A slender line of it ran down the center of his cut abdomen over his navel and disappeared down into his slacks. The fabric stretched over his very hard and long arousal.

He pushed the pants and his boxer briefs over his hips. Anticipation dragged a moan from her when his large cock emerged from his clothes with an imperative thrust like the exclamation point.

Despite his beautiful arousal, her eyes slid down to enjoy the deliciously hard muscles of his legs as he rose and stepped out of his discarded pants. Even his feet held beauty, showing strength and power like his hands.

"Goddess in heaven, you're so damn beautiful."

Julianna's pussy creamed with the thought of that lovely male body pressed up against her.

Jeff gave her an arrogant smile as he stepped back up to her, his cock and tight balls at throat height. She inhaled the scent of his arousal. It was a wonderful combination of desert rain and earthy male. She wanted to bury her nose in his balls to sniff it forever.

"I love it when you do that." He stared down his body at her, his eyes glowing nearly gold with his desire. "It turns me on like nothing else." He gave her a rueful half-smile. "Hell, just seeing you tonight turned me on. I've been hard since Wednesday morning."

"I did try to take the edge off, you know." She inhaled his wonderful scent again.

"I know." He lifted her head away from his groin. "That was the only thing that stopped me from finding you and fucking you so hard you couldn't walk tonight."

"We'll see who fucks whom into submission, won't we, my Alpha?" She bared her teeth in a grin.

Jeff snarled at her with lust and pushed her onto the bed. He followed her down as he braced himself over her with his arms, his eyes blazing. He pressed his hard cock against her mound, and Julianna hissed with the hot, hard contact. Flexing his hips, he rubbed his hardness against her, and she writhed beneath him with a little whimper of pleasure.

"Yes, we will, my Luna."

He retreated, dropping to his knees between her legs, and widely spread her thighs with his shoulders.

Shoving his hands under her butt cheeks to lift her, he challenged her with his eyes as he held her open pussy before his mouth. She gasped in surprise when he leaned forward and placed a soft teasing kiss upon her nether lips.

The sensation of his mustache and goatee rubbing softly against the hairs surrounding her pussy robbed her of all coherence. He tickled her, breathing on her sensitive skin, and she moaned. The sensations began to build up her orgasm, but slowly, teasingly. She wanted to shift her hips back and forth, but his hands held her still while he sampled her.

Julianna thought she'd go out of her mind, and she whined her frustration at his touches. He chuckled evilly just before the hot warmth of his tongue hit her clit. She shrieked with delirious pleasure and jerked her hips, but he held them fast and taunted her with little flicks of his tongue on her clit and swollen lips.

"Oh, Goddess, Jeff." She writhed. "Please."

"Please what, Julianna?"

"Stop torturing me."

"I told you it was your turn, my sweet Luna." He growled as she tried to move again, and his hands tightened. "You got to torture me Wednesday morning. It's my turn to do the same to you."

"Ahhhhhhh!" She wailed when he inserted his tongue between her lips and wiggled it back and forth.

She bucked her hips against his lips, and he dug in. He fed off her, licking the entrance to her pussy and sucking on her clit with precise pressure. He groaned with approval as she moved faster.

"Oh glory, please, Jeff. Harder!"

He growled and obliged, shoving his tongue as deep as he could into her hot, wet slit.

The extra sensation of his warm, slick tongue in her pussy pushed her over the edge into ecstatic bliss. She shrieked with joyous release and cascaded with the falling stars behind her eyes.

At last, she came down. "Oh good glory, Jeff."

Julianna panted as she looked down her body at him. He smiled with satisfaction, licking the remaining cream of her release off his lips and chin.

"I needed you so much."

He placed a small kiss on her mound. He rose to his

feet and gestured to her to move further onto the bed.

"I'm happy to give you that anytime you want, Julianna." He crawled over her body. "All you have to do is ask and I'll bow to your glorious pussy."

She laughed, and he closed his eyes with delight.

"I love that."

"What?"

Gold overtook all the brown in his eyes as his lust increased. "Your laugh. I want to make you laugh like that all the time. No more sorrow, frustration, or pain."

"I'll make you a deal." He raised an eyebrow. "I'll laugh more if you smile at me."

His grin filled his whole face. "Like this?"

Julianna nodded and pulled him down for a kiss. It started out soft and sensuous, just lips against lips, until she opened her mouth. When his tongue slid between them, she tasted herself on him. Arousal built inside her again, and she slid her hands over the taut muscles of his back.

Jeff growled with her touches and pressed his chest against hers. The crinkly chest hair rubbing against her nipples pulled them into hard little points. He pulled back to trail kisses down her cheeks and neck until he paused over her breasts. Liquid heat slid through her with each brush of his lips, and she moaned when he skimmed his cock and balls down her inner thigh.

He ground them against her knee for a moment before his lips descended to her aching nipples, and he nipped a swollen little peak. Julianna yipped deliriously with each scrape of his elongated canines against the soft swell of her breast. He tended to one nipple, pulling it into his mouth. He soothed his bites with his tongue while his hand massaged the other peak, flicking it gently.

Waves of ticklish pleasure flooded her senses, and she moaned. When she'd fantasized about making love to Jeff, her imagination hadn't even come close. Even her dream had been a pale shadow of this.

He pulled his mouth away from her breast and descended on the other one, his free hand stroking her side with feather-light touches. The combination of sensations made her shiver and filled her pussy with more cream. She whined and squirmed, but he only renewed his attention to her breast, working the nipple with his tongue before gently nipping it.

"Ah, Julianna, you taste so damn sweet," he purred against her skin.

Rising up on his elbows, he pressed his cock against her mound, grinding it back and forth. It felt like heated steel, and Julianna loved its hardness rubbing against her over-sensitized clit. She brought her hands to his hips, sliding them over his buttocks and grabbing his ass. Hard.

She wanted more.

Rolling her hips, she tried to capture his hardened flesh between her nether lips and engulf it. He laughed smugly at her and grabbed one of her hands to hold it above her head.

"Be patient, little Luna." He captured her other hand. "You'll get my cock when I'm ready to give it to you."

"I'm ready now."

Julianna pushed against the bed with her free hand and one of her feet. He didn't have the leverage to stop her, and she slammed him onto his back with a grunt of surprise. She pivoted around her secured hand and straddled him, his cock pressed between their bodies.

She looked down at him with a triumphant grin, and he huffed a surprised laugh.

"Very impressive, my Luna. But can you keep me here?"

Before she could reply, he wrapped his arms around hers and sat up. Then he flipped her over onto her back and pinned her to the bed.

She squirmed fiercely under his weight, wriggling her hips opposite her shoulders. She tried to get out from his grip, but he held her tight. She snarled at him, but he just growled in reply and nipped her shoulder beside her neck a little, using his weight to hold her down.

"And where do you think you're going, little Lupine?"

"I want to touch you." She twisted beneath him.

"Ah, but you had your turn on Wednesday."

"That wasn't enough. I want to touch you more."

Jeff chuckled but didn't let her go. Instead, he grabbed her hands and pushed them into the bedding over her head, pressing his hips against hers. Julianna wiggled her pelvis until his hot, rigid flesh pressed between her nether lips. When she tried to shove him inside, he held himself away from her, only the tip of his cock teasing her.

She growled in frustration and twisted, trying to buck him off of her, but he dropped more of his weight onto her. He dragged his tongue over the side of her neck, and she keened as pleasure shot through her, making her tremble. He continued to lick her neck and shoulder, nipping gently with his teeth.

Julianna gasped. Would he bite her? *Oh, glory, yes please.*

"Stop teasing me." She thrust her hips at him. She only succeeded in rubbing his tip against her clit, torturing herself more. "Holy First Canid, just fuck me!"

Jeff chuckled darkly against her shoulder and pushed his hips forward, allowing the head of his cock to slide between her lips. Then he stopped.

Julianna writhed, seeking more of him. She narrowed her eyes. Tease her some more, would he? She'd just see about that.

"Is that the best you can do, Jeff?" She gave him a feral grin. "Is that all I've been waiting for? I've held myself away from you all these months, driven myself crazy from wanting you, and that's all you can give me?"

His laughter turned into a fierce growl, and he slammed his cock into her with one rough thrust. She shrieked at the intrusion and arched her back to take more of him. He pulled back and thrust again and again and again until it became one constant motion. The sounds of flesh hitting flesh blended with their erotic snarls and groans. Her pleasure built, and the scent of joyful sex filled her nose.

Julianna bucked against Jeff, and her passion rose like an oncoming storm. Each time his hips met hers, pleasure slammed through her and her body arched. She moaned her excitement and rode him hard, looking up into his golden eyes.

"You're mine, Julianna." He slammed into her. "Mine!"

"Make me yours, Jeff." She wrapped her legs around his, tightening her inner muscles. "Make me your Luna."

He roared as he thrust in a few more times, then he swooped down and snapped his teeth into her shoulder. Tingling power like an electric shock, seared through her in a pulsating connection, pushing her over the edge of bliss. Julianna screamed as her orgasm flooded through her, and her teeth elongated in her mouth. They itched in her gums, and she closed her jaws on whatever body part lay closest, flying over the edge of pleasure once more.

She came back to herself with her teeth buried in Jeff's shoulder and his jaws locked in hers. They lay there panting for long moments, neither willing to let the other go. When Jeff licked the wound he had given her, the energy surged again, reestablishing their connection. It rippled through her in a rush that made her body arch in a taut bow.

"Sweet glory."

"You got that right." He laughed, and she smiled up at him. Then she licked his shoulder playfully, and he shuddered with pleasure. "Holy shit, that's amazing."

To her surprise, Julianna felt some of the pleasure he experienced, and it set off another ricochet within her. Her inner muscles clamped down on Jeff's cock again, and he groaned, flexing his hips.

"Yes, amazing. Promise me we can do that a lot more."

A wicked laugh erupted, and he claimed her mouth in a blistering kiss. She tangled her tongue with his and squirmed against him, feeling his cock stiffen again. Julianna consciously squeezed her internal muscles again, and he thrust his hips a few times.

"Oh, First Canid." His eyes rolled up in his head.

"Don't take my great-great-grandfather's name in vain," she teased, and his eyes opened wide.

"Are you really the last descendent?"

"At least the latest one here in Callowwood. I don't know if I have more family elsewhere." Julianna trailed her fingers over his shoulder and arm. "I only learned that I'm related to Him yesterday afternoon. I don't know anything more than that."

Jeff stared down at her thoughtfully and brushed the fingers of his hand over the side of her face. "How did you find this out?"

Julianna rolled her lips inward and stared at her bite mark on his shoulder. He'd have to know the truth of her connection to Sebrina eventually.

"Sebrina told me."

He studied her for a few moments more then he smiled as if that was a good enough explanation. "Then I'm a very lucky Alpha to have found my True Mate in First Canid's family."

She snorted at his flippancy. "You don't believe me."

"I didn't say that."

"You didn't have to. I can hear it in your voice."

He sighed and rolled off her, taking his luxurious heat with him. "Isn't the First Canid just a creation myth?"

"Not according to Sebrina, and she should know."

"Why?"

Julianna bit her lip. "Because she knows all the stories and kept all the lore. She taught them to me."

Jeff lay silently beside her for a few moments, thinking. "But they're just stories."

"Almost all creation stories are based on some truth. Even Jesus and Buddha were real people at one time."

"So the First Canid was real, too?"

"I think so."

"And you're a descendent."

"Yes."

"How do you know that if you were adopted by human parents?"

"I told you. Sebrina told me."

"How does she know about your ancestry?"

Julianna took a deep breath, closing her eyes. "Because she's my mother."

A stunned silence greeted her words. Julianna opened her eyes and turned her head, needing to see Jeff's face.

He looked astonished, the brown in his eyes overwhelming the gold.

"She's your mother."

Julianna nodded slowly. "And I have an uncle that's kept an eye on me since I was a baby."

Jeff lapsed into silence, and she could tell his mind raced. She waited for him to reach all the conclusions she had earlier that week. She knew he wouldn't like what he'd discover, but she didn't know if she could explain it to him.

"Why?" The scent of anger and disbelief rose between them. "Why did you grow up with human parents when she's been here the whole time? Why did she abandon you? Didn't she want you?"

Julianna sighed. "Her reasons are her own, and she'll have to explain them to you when she's ready. Just remember that it happened in the past, and it can't be changed now. She didn't know who I was until I changed for the first time in front of her. When she saw me in my Sister form, she realized I had to be related to her. Apparently, my looks are mixed enough that I don't look like her or my father."

"Who is your father? Where is he in all this?"

"He's dead."

"Oh. I'm sorry."

"Don't be too hard on Sebrina, Jeff." Julianna squeezed his arm. "She regrets her decision to give me up. We can't punish her any more than she can punish herself. Besides, I grew up in this town, in a good and loving family, and I turned out okay. Her decision wasn't all bad."

"But you're her child." His elongated canines flashed with his distress. "How could she do that to you? And if you're right and you're part of the First Canid's family—"

Jeff stopped short and turned his wide eyes on her. "Sebrina is a descendent, too?"

Julianna just nodded.

"How do you know it's not just a story she told you?"

Julianna stiffened. "I might be an inexperienced Moon Singer, but I can still smell when someone's lying to me, Jeff. She believes the story and I have no reason to doubt her. Besides, being part of the First Canid's family hasn't given her more honor or status than any other alpha female. And she certainly hasn't flaunted it."

"Oh, dear Goddess." He rolled onto his back, his gaze returning to the ceiling as he organized his thoughts.

She touched his chest. "I believe her, Jeff."

He said nothing to that, just kept staring into space.

"Are you sorry you chose me for your Luna and Mate?"

He moved so quickly she couldn't remember if he'd been lying quietly next to her when his body settled on top of hers. She groaned in satisfaction as his warmth surrounded her and his thumbs stroked over her cheeks.

"I'll never be sorry for that." His eyes shifted back to gold with his sincerity. He ducked his head and licked the bite mark on her shoulder, making her tremble with pleasure. "You're my Luna, my Mate, and your parentage doesn't change any of that. So I'm True Mated to the latest descendant of the First Canid. Big deal."

She laughed softly and wrapped her arms tightly around

his ribs. "Glory, I love you."

She felt his chuckle before she heard it. "And I love you."

"Do you know how often I want to hear that?"

"Um, once a week?" He grunted when she thumped his shoulder with her fist.

"Try once an hour. To start." She smiled. "I've waited a long time to be right here."

"I've waited just as long to give you this." He brushed his lips over the mark in her shoulder, and she arched her back with a soft wail. "I wanted you even when I thought you were human. When you showed up at your father's funeral, it was all I could do to stay away from you. You smelled so damn good." He nipped her collarbones. "I wanted to wrap you up in my arms, covering my body with your scent. In fact…"

Jeff's cock stiffened and pushed against her aching nether lips as he took her mouth with a fervent kiss. She melted beneath his heady onslaught and reveled in the sensations his kiss sent through her body.

When he drove into her, she growled and wrapped her legs around him, riding his swift lovemaking with a sense of belonging. He continued his nipping, wet kisses as his cock shuttled in and out of her pussy. Every soft touch combined with the smooth thrusts of his cock built up her pleasure.

Julianna moved with him, reveling in the sweetness of his love and the glorious hardness of his cock in her core. They both toppled over into the well of ecstasy. Jeff stiffened above her, bowing his head until his lips rested on her shoulder once more, and his teeth sank into her with his last stroke. The warm jets of cum spilled into her just like in her dream, and his pleasure slid through her, enhancing her own. Her pussy tightened around him until she couldn't tell where he stopped and she began.

"Goddess above, Julianna." Jeff panted when he

released her shoulder. "You're so damn sweet." He carefully rolled his body off hers, but she missed his weight.

She chuckled. "I hope that means I taste good instead of just being cute and nice."

"Oh, yeah."

"Good."

They rested together for a few moments, and Julianna's satisfaction settled into her heart. She'd True Mated with Jeff, and no one could take that away from her. He belonged to her, and she didn't have to hide it anymore. She thought about Beth's delight in Jeff's invitation and realized she'd have to tell her mother about the changes in their relationship. How would she explain that?

"Jeff?"

"Hmm?"

"If I'm your True Mate and chosen as your Luna, that makes me your wife, right?"

He rolled onto his side to look at her. "Oh, yeah." He breathed into her ear, and she shivered. "Why?"

"Beth won't know what happened tonight."

"Oh, yes, she will."

"She will?"

Jeff smiled so tenderly it brought tears to Julianna's eyes.

"I stopped by to see your mom a few days ago. I asked her if I could court you."

"She told me."

"She did?" He grinned. "Does that mean she approves?"

Julianna laughed. "I think her words were 'it's about time.'"

He joined her then sobered as he brushed her face with his fingers. "So, Julianna Sarah Morris, future Luna of the Callowwood Pack, will you marry me in a conventional wedding so we can announce to everyone in town that you're mine and only mine?"

"Will I get to wear a lovely dress and see you in that tux again?"

He chuckled and tucked her closer to his body, her breasts pressed against his ribs. "Absolutely."

"Yes. Oh, yes."

Jeff leaned down and licked the mark on her shoulder, and she shuddered as the magic slid through her once more.

Julianna reveled in the pinging excitement until the bedroom door crashed open and slammed against the wall. They both shot out of the bed and stood at attention regardless of their state of undress. One part of her mind remarked dryly that a naked woman with her breasts hanging out offered very little menace, but she'd be damned if she'd lie in bed with an intruder in her room.

Jeff slid his body in front of hers, naturally protecting his female.

*Dammit, Jeff.*

She shifted to one side. Cameron Winthrop stood in the doorway, seething. Rage wafted of her as she bared her teeth. Julianna's fury erupted, and she returned the expression, her long canines scraping her lower lip.

*What the fuck is she doing here?*

# CHAPTER TWENTY:
### The Luna of Callowwood

Jeff's anger and frustration unfurled as he took in Cameron's visage. The female's eyes narrowed in fury, and her hair looked like someone had taken a fork to it. Her scent shifted between rage, indignation, and rancid meat. He wrinkled his nose, his lips pulling back from his teeth in a warning snarl. He'd allow no one to interrupt his time with his new Luna. He'd chosen Julianna, and that was that.

"What are you doing here, Cameron?"

"I'm here for what's rightfully mine!" She snarled, her gaze centered on Julianna.

Somewhere deep inside, a voice quipped, *I think you have the wrong room.* He would've laughed if the situation wasn't so dangerous.

"I don't have anything of yours." Julianna shifted farther to the side.

"Yes, you do." Cameron paced closer, her motions stiff with fury. "You took him. You distracted him from the bitches who were better for him than some runaway pretender who wouldn't know a Moon Singer from a mothball. Jeff Lightfoot is supposed to be my mate. I'm supposed to be the next Luna."

*You were never my Mate.* She'd merely been a political conciliation to uphold the traditions. Jeff wanted to shout it at her, to throw it in her face in response to her audacity of barging in on him and his True Mate. His father's training kept his words behind his lips, despite the rage ripping through him with each insult she hurled at Julianna.

Julianna remained icily stoic, wearing nothing but the wolf pendant. Despite her lack of clothing, she looked as regal as a queen. *Holy Mother of All, she's fucking gorgeous.* With her shoulders squared and her head up, Jeff knew he had to start thinking about something else or he'd give away just how sexy he thought her.

"I'm neither a pretender nor a runaway, Ms. Winthrop. I've never pretended to be anything but what I am."

"Really?" Cameron's sneer ripped through the room. "You pretended to be human for all those years growing up. I don't know how you did it. You even smelled human. But now you show up just as he needs a Luna? How convenient for you."

To Jeff's surprise, Julianna laughed. "Do you think I orchestrated my father's death to coincide with the candidacy party? I've been away for eighteen years. I didn't know anything about Jeff's ascendency until I returned to Callowwood."

Jeff bit back a snarl. "You need to go back downstairs to the party and leave us alone, Cameron."

"Oh, I'll leave as soon as I get what I came for."

Shrieking in rage, Cameron leapt forward, swiping at Julianna's chest with one hand. Jeff pivoted to stop her, but she ducked under him. Julianna snarled as Cameron's fingers raked across her bare chest before the younger female shot out the door, crowing her triumph.

"Give that back!" Julianna launched herself after Cameron.

Jeff tried to catch her, but she flew out the door before

he could stop her.

*Dammit, what the hell is wrong with me tonight?*

He grabbed his pants and shoved his legs into them before he snagged his shirt and tore after them. He'd be damned if every male in the pack would enjoy the naked glory of his lovely Luna.

Jeff reached the ground floor just as Cameron's voice carried from the backyard, shrieking her right to be Luna and the proof in the form of the previous Luna's pendant. Julianna demanded its return as he bolted down the hall. *Dammit, I have to get the shirt on her.* He gritted his teeth and raced for the doors.

What greeted his eyes when he arrived alternately fueled his fury and set his blood alight with arousal. Cameron paced in the center of the space before the podium with her hand in the air, his mother's pendant dangling from it. Wild eyes filled with righteous anger swept the crowd, and her whole body vibrated as she fixated on her rival.

Julianna stood at the edge of the circle of packmembers closest to the house, her own body regal and calm. Jeff sensed her dampened anger as she stared the other woman down. His pride for his True Mate surged, and he strode toward her, intent on wrapping his shirt over her glorious beauty.

"You selfish, blind, stupid son of a bitch!" Cameron's face twisted up into a hideous scowl when she saw him. Julianna stiffened, and Jeff threw the shirt over her shoulders.

"I've been here the whole time. Right here!" Cameron jabbed herself between her breasts with a hard finger. "I know how the pack needs to be run. I know the families, the problems, our goals, and needs. I know what's happened with the pack for the last eighteen years while she's been absent." The hard finger flung itself at Julianna. "But who did you choose? The rookie. And who did you bring in as part of the candidates? An outsider from LA. You never once looked at me. I was right here the whole time. A local and better than all the others. Hell, I even passed all the tests without a hitch. I was perfect. But did you notice? No-O-ooo. You were too busy sniffing after Ms. Morris' tail to notice!"

Jeff raised a disdainful eyebrow at Cameron in disbelief. The best choice?

"Who did you choose? The little girl who dogged your footsteps for years. The newbie who just showed up in time for you to start looking for a Luna. The one bitch who knew nothing about the Callowwood Pack, not even how to shift shape."

Gasps echoed around the clearing, and Julianna tilted her head curiously.

"Oh, yes, Miss Morris, I was there." Cameron's lip curled with disdain. "I was there when you learned how to shift into your Sister form from Sebrina. I watched you struggle to become what you were supposed to be. You didn't even know how to do the simplest things our people know. You're not worthy of being Luna.

"I was the best candidate, and I still am!" She brandished the pendant, her eyes blazing. "I passed all the tests. I should be Luna." Her zealous gaze fixed on Jeff once more. "But you never saw me. All she does is attract trouble, Jeff." Cameron's voice filled with a wheedling whine. "You saw what those thugs from LA did to her. You know that whore from LA hired them to take her out. She brings trouble to our pack and our town."

A snarl ripped from the crowd, and Brenda Solaris pushed into view, her face an icy mask of fury.

"Watch what you say, little bitch. I never hired anyone from LA. I have family here, who invited me to come and be a candidate for Luna. I had nothing to do with any attacks on the future Luna."

"I'm the future Luna!" Cameron raged, her face

flushing. "And it's so obvious you hired those thugs. They were from LA, and we all know it pays to have friends in low places. Hell, they even smelled like your apricot perfume. It doesn't take a genius to figure that out."

As Brenda bristled, suspicion wound through Jeff. *How does Cameron know all the details of the men who attacked Julianna?* They hadn't been publicized. No one knew about the apricot perfume until the morning after the attack in the bar. Where did Cameron learn about it?

Anger coalesced inside him once more. Had Cameron been endangering Julianna from the beginning? She'd admitted to spying on her when Sebrina trained her. What else had she been up to? He'd taken a step toward the younger female to beat her into submission when a hot, feminine hand pressed against his chest and he turned his furious gaze to his True Mate.

Julianna wore his shirt buttoned over her chest, and it hung low enough to just cover the tops of her thighs. Snarled tendrils of hair draped around her face, appropriate for a sexually satisfied female, but her expression showed only serenity. Pride and awe stilled his fury, and he halted at her command.

In that moment, he loved her far deeper than just the lustful pull of the mating bond. Julianna represented the perfect female for him, strong, calm, and femininely powerful. He wanted to shout out his love for her, but she turned her attention back to the raving bitch still pacing, and he had to swallow the words.

His cadre wove through the crowd, and Jeff caught Zach's eye as his First moved into position behind Brenda. Jeff nodded in acknowledgment, and Zach replied in kind, signaling that he and the others would keep everyone else from interfering. Kyle and Thomas already stood behind the Winthrops, and Leo shadowed the Alpha as Richard stepped to the edge of the circle.

Jeff tested the air, drawing in the scents of the pack

around him. Most felt a mixture of surprise and excitement for the conflict approaching. He sensed his father's unease, and righteous anger from the Winthrops, but the rest broadcast anticipation.

Gary and Woody appeared at the edges of the circle, their expressions wary and angry. He sensed their protective instincts and their intent to defend their Luna. They weren't alone. Eloise Farkas and the Grayhound sisters stood there as well. Jeff had never seen the blonde woman look so ferocious, but her stance showed her as a warrior, strong and deadly. Gratitude for her intent fired through him, and he returned his attention to the tableau before him.

The stage was set. They only awaited the play.

\*\*\*\*

Julianna faced her rival with fury and disgust swirling inside her. She sensed Jeff's presence behind her and the blast of his anger as he shifted to one side. She wanted to fling herself at Ms. Winthrop and claw her until her face showed nothing but ribbons of torn flesh. *Ease up there, Sister. This is yet another test of our poise as Luna.* She reined in her emotions and raised her chin in challenge.

"I don't wear perfume," Brenda said. Julianna's gaze returned to the ad exec's face. "No true Moon Singer would. I do wash with apricot-scented soap, but I haven't been in physical contact with anyone from LA. I'll give you my phone to prove it." Brenda's eyes met Julianna's, and the other woman managed to look submissive as she dropped her head. "I swear, Luna, that I know nothing about the attack on you."

"Oh, please." Cameron sneered as she gestured with the pendant. Julianna gritted her teeth with each flash of the aquamarine eyes in the lights of the tent. *I want that back.* "Why should we believe your lies? You'd say anything to save yourself."

Brenda reached into her purse and pulled out her BlackBerry. She tossed it to Tawny, who caught it deftly. "Go ahead, check it. I've got nothing to hide." Her gaze returned to Cameron with a look of pity. "The Successor was wise to choose Ms. Morris. You think you're entitled, and that makes you weak."

Julianna scented Cameron's rage flood over the pack and thanked the Goddess she stood across the clearing. It smelled like a combination of burnt hair and sewage. She idly wondered if her own anger reeked as bad.

"I am not weak!" Cameron's lips drew back from her teeth in a menacing snarl. "I'm perfect!" She focused her wild eyes on Jeff again. "I never stepped out of line. I never drew more attention to myself than was necessary. I wasn't as flashy as those California whores. I was here, I was perfect, and I love you. I'm your perfect mate. How could you pick her?"

"Because she's my True Mate, Ms. Winthrop." His customary half-smile mocked her, but Julianna read the fury burning beneath his golden irises. "Love can't trump nature. The Goddess chose Ms. Morris as my True Mate long before you were groomed as a candidate for Luna."

"That's just a myth. This isn't about the Goddess."

Julianna tensed, reading the subtle shift in the other female's body language.

"It's about who's the best candidate. And that's me. I should be Luna!"

"There's no precedent for this, Ms. Winthrop." The Alpha's voice cut through the echoes of Cameron's tirade. "The tests and the choosing ceremony prove who's the best for the Successor. None of our rules have been broken by the chosen candidate. You can't claim the right to be Luna simply because of a pendant and a story of inexperience. Ms. Morris passed the tests and was chosen by the Successor. His decision stands."

"Then he chose wrong." She dropped the pendant into the grass. "And I'll prove it."

The change overcame Cameron's body too swiftly to track, and a black wolf hurtled toward Julianna without warning.

Julianna's Sister wasn't as slow in reaction.

She met her rival in a crash of claws and teeth, her fury finally unleashed. Cameron jerked aside to avoid her gleaming canines, but Julianna scored the black wolf's shoulder as her forepaws wrapped around Cameron's torso. She came down on top of the other female, but Cameron twisted and broke free, surging to her feet to leap at Julianna again.

She reared up on her hind legs, snapping at her rival's throat. Cameron ducked, and Julianna's teeth caught her ear, tearing through the flesh. Cameron snarled and rolled, pulling her head away as she scrambled to her feet. The ear drooped a little, and blood stained her cheek while her eyes gleamed with feral rage.

Cameron charged her again, her teeth raking at Julianna's chest where she'd grabbed the pendant earlier. Julianna tried to pull aside at the last moment, but Cameron's rage overpowered her, and the sharp fangs tore through the fur, blooding her. Pain shrieked through her awareness, demanding attention, and she yelped involuntarily.

Her anger flared, and her Sister shot forward in a new attack, but Julianna managed to pull her back. The wolf was better at fighting, but Sebrina's advice flickered through Julianna's awareness. She had to think to protect them both.

Taking a deep breath, she tried to center her mind as she'd been taught in tai chi. Her Sister's wrath prowled just outside her calm, but she sharpened her focus and steadied her body until the calm soothed the fury. She watched how Cameron moved, noting any weaknesses or unsteadiness.

*She's running on rage and adrenaline. She probably doesn't feel anything.* That would make her strong but thoughtless. No strategy, only brute strength.

Cameron reminded Julianna of tracking coyotes to their dens. The wily predators had underestimated her intelligence and thought themselves too smart for her abilities. *Make her think she's won. What kind of ruse would sucker her in?* Cameron wasn't thinking, but she had enough intelligence to take victory when she saw it.

The other female growled low in her throat and darted toward Julianna's flank. She spun away, but Cameron's claws raked her hip and tore furrows in the fur. Julianna snarled and snapped at her opponent, but Cameron had already bolted out of reach.

Pain buzzed at the back of her mind as she turned to watch the other wolf circle around her. The eyes of her opponent filled with a killing rage, rolling white with insanity. *How do I lure her into overconfidence?*

Her memory served up a vision of watching killdeer birds teasing a neighbor's dogs each time they went for a run. The birds would feign a broken wing to lure the predators away from their hidden nests, only staying a few steps ahead. *Feign an injury, then take her down. Who says I'm not related to Ho'a'tote?*

She narrowed her eyes and flattened her ears, snarling. She lowered her shoulders to the ground with her butt in the air in the "play" position, tempting her rival to come at her. *Come on, bitch. Come play with me. See if you can take me when I'm down.* Cameron took the bait and pounced, trying to hold Julianna down. Julianna shot sideways, snapping her jaws over Cameron's muzzle and clamping down, hard.

Cameron yelped in surprise but still managed to tear her head away just as she dragged her hind claws down Julianna's belly. Julianna released her opponent and lurched away with a squeal of pain, pretending more injury than she felt. She panted and limped painfully at the edge of the circle, letting her ears droop with feigned exhaustion.

A collective gasp of surprised dismay echoed around them, and Julianna scented Jeff's distress like a breath of fetid air. She didn't dare huff a laugh, but satisfaction in her acting skills trickled through her.

Julianna hobbled around the edges of the clearing, watching her rival carefully. Cameron believed her ruse and strutted, her teeth gleaming in the lights of the garden as blood slid from the large gash in her muzzle. She snarled triumphantly and shook her head, flinging the blood from her eyes. Julianna wheezed as if too tired to make another charge, but she gathered herself for Cameron's next move.

*Come on, you mongrel. Come at me and see how weak I am.*

With a howl, Cameron shot across the clearing at her, and Julianna whimpered for effect, rolling to her shoulder to get her feet up into Cameron's falling belly. She thrust her head forward and closed her teeth over Cameron's throat, using the crazed female's momentum to roll her over and slam her onto her back. Julianna pivoted around her jaws' grip and dropped her weight onto Cameron's struggling body, pinning it to the ground.

Julianna growled, squeezing her teeth together. "Do you yield? Do you admit I'm Luna?"

Cameron froze when she heard Julianna's voice in her head.

"Do you yield to me as your Luna?"

Cameron squealed with frustrated denial and struggled against her.

"Do you yield?"

"Never!"

"Very well."

Jerking her head to the side as her jaws tightened, she tore Cameron's throat out in a rush of hot blood. Her Sister howled at the defeat of her rival, and Julianna embraced her true self, the wolf meant to hunt and defend her pack from all intruders.

Stepping back from the carcass on the ground, Julianna turned her bloodied muzzle toward the current Alpha and awaited his judgment. She'd known Cameron wouldn't let this go. She had challenged the Luna and lost, just as any male could challenge the Alpha for mastery of the pack.

Richard's face appeared calm, but his eyes shone with suppressed excitement. The whole pack waited silently until he nodded in acknowledgment of her victory. The garden erupted with triumphant and mournful howls.

Julianna shifted back into her human form and wiped one hand across her bloody mouth. Jeff's shirt hung undamaged, but stains formed as it touched her healing body. Her chest burned with the marks of Cameron's attack. One butt cheek ached, but victory silenced the pain. She sought her Mate's eyes and found him staring at her with a feral look of lustful joy. She lifted her chin in challenge, and his growl of dominance slithered across the space between them.

"How could you?" Julianna's gaze snapped to Catherine Winthrop struggling against Kyle's grip. "She was just a child."

Julianna growled a warning. "Are you challenging me as Luna, Mrs. Winthrop?"

"She was a better candidate than you ever were. How could you kill her?"

Julianna's Sister wanted to pounce on the older female, but she held her back. "I'm sorry for your loss, Mrs. Winthrop, but Cameron was no longer in control. She let her lust for power and prestige overwhelm what she knew to be right. The pack agreed that the tests and the choosing ceremony would determine the next Luna. She rejected the Successor's choice. If she disregarded the agreements within the pack, then what would've stopped her from ignoring the Alpha or the needs of the pack as a whole?"

"She would've made a better Luna, you murderous slut!" Mrs. Winthrop screeched.

Growls of anger and protest echoed around them. Her cadre converged on Kyle and the struggling female.

"It seems to me you need to choose your loyalties, Mrs. Winthrop." Richard stepped into the circle, his expression hard. "Jeff is the Successor, and your daughter challenged the chosen Luna. She lost. Now you must choose if you're going to follow the future Alpha and Luna or leave the territory of the Callowwood Pack."

"You can't be serious." Catherine's face twisted in fury. "You can't all take her side. She killed my daughter! She killed my little girl. How can you defend her?"

"She's the Luna," Woody said.

"She won the challenge," Eloise added.

"She was stronger," the Grayhound sisters said together.

"She's my Mate and your Luna." Jeff dropped a hand on Julianna's shoulder.

"I'm Luna, Mrs. Winthrop, and I earned my place honorably." Julianna straightened her shoulders. "Jeff Lightfoot and I are Mated before the Lady Moon and the pack. He chose me in the choosing ceremony. Your daughter defied the pack's rules and protocols, challenged me to combat, and lost. I asked her if she was willing to yield." Julianna looked down at the body. "She said no."

Catherine let loose a furious shriek and launched herself at Julianna, but Kyle held her back. She jerked futilely against her own arms.

"You're nothing but a conniving, thieving, murdering whore!" Catherine howled as she struggled. "We all know you mated with Jeff Lightfoot that night he stayed at your house and skewed the choosing ceremony. My daughter would've been Luna if not for your slutty ways. Is that what you learned when you left our town? How to whore yourself to get what you wanted?"

More growls erupted, and Jeff stalked toward the screaming woman with so much menace Julianna feared he'd do damage. She moved to stop him when Richard's voice rang out and silenced everyone.

"Get your mate under control, Mr. Winthrop, or you'll be banished and branded rogues. Be certain what's most important to you. You know the consequences."

Mr. Winthrop blanched white and grabbed his wife, holding her tight against him.

"No, no, Michael. You have to let me go. We have to stop her. She killed our daughter."

"That's enough, Catherine!" Michael Winthrop barked, and Catherine whimpered, dropping her head at his ferocity. "Come on, it's been a long day. Let's go home."

"But Michael, she killed her—"

"It'll be okay, darlin'. Let's go home now."

Mr. Winthrop spun his wife and dragged her away toward the house, protesting each step. Anger, frustration, and grief wafted after them, poisoning the air along with the reek of death. Julianna let her breath out slowly and looked at Jeff. His whole body radiated tension, and waves of anger rippled around him.

As her adrenaline ebbed, she looked down on Cameron's body. The death of a promising young alpha female had fallen on her shoulders. *What a waste.* She grimaced. *I've made enemies of the Winthrops tonight. An auspicious beginning–Not.*

*Very auspicious. You vanquished a deranged intruder and proved your strength.*

"The Luna of the Callowwood Pack is victorious in the Challenge." Richard waved at Julianna. "Does anyone else wish to issue a Challenge?"

*Sweet glory, please let it be no.* She didn't want to fight anyone else tonight. Julianna tensed again, inhaling deeply.

Silence reigned in the garden, and only the wind rustling the pine trees dared to break its spell. Julianna held her breath. *Please, please, nobody Challenge me again tonight.*

"Very well, let's bury the body and go home." Richard gestured toward Cameron's corpse. "Enough excitement for one night."

"Alpha, with your permission." Julianna raised her hand.

Richard's cadre paused and looked at Richard, waiting for him to acknowledge her before touching the dead wolf.

"Yes, Luna?"

"Bury her with full honors, please." She crouched beside the body. "She fought for what she believed in, no matter how wrong it was, and she was an admired member of the pack. She may have lost the Challenge, but she should be honored for her attempt."

"You wish to honor your rival, Luna?" Surprise and something else flashed in his eyes.

Julianna shrugged uncomfortably. "She made a bad decision. She's already paid for it."

Richard looked at her a long time before he nodded slowly.

"Very well. Bury her with honor."

The packmembers shook themselves as if coming awake, their expressions shell-shocked. Jeff nodded to her with approval and offered her his half-smile before turning to his cadre.

Julianna rose and wrapped her arms around her body. Emotion and adrenaline still pumped through her with each heartbeat, but she couldn't decide what she felt. Fear? Anger? Grief? Lust? Excitement? Exhaustion? Part of her just wanted to curl up on her bed and hide her head under her pillow, away from the pack, the politics, and the overwhelming grief of the Winthrops.

She took a deep breath in and closed her eyes. She was Luna now. No more hiding in the crowd. *Welcome to the world of the first lady.* Always the one they'd all look to for etiquette and proper behavior, even in a bloody fight to the death. *Good grief.*

Jeff wrapped his arms around her from behind and laid a soft kiss at the nape of her neck. All the conflicting emotions drained away, and Julianna let herself fall into the warm strength of his body behind her.

"That was beautifully done, my Luna." He handed her the wolf's head pendant Cameron had stolen.

She shivered as she took it. "You think so?"

"Yes. It'll go a long way to mollifying some of the Winthrops' supporters in the pack. They'll see you're fair and honest and didn't add insult to injury. Word will get back to the Winthrops of your request, and they'll have even less to be pissed off about."

"Losing their only daughter isn't something they're just going to forget, Jeff." A cold draft swept over her buttocks and she pressed her body against his, seeking warmth. "I may have won the Challenge, but I've made enemies of them forever. They won't forgive me for that."

"They don't have to forgive you. But they do have to acknowledge you as the winner. You beat their daughter fairly and even had her body buried with honors. They can't argue with that."

Julianna snorted. "Tell that to her mother."

Jeff grimaced. "Let's get you inside and wrapped up in something warm."

He tugged her toward the house, walking a little behind her to literally cover her ass.

She chuckled. "Can I wrap myself up in you instead?"

His teeth flashed in the lights of the garden. "That's the idea." He stopped and pulled her to face him. "I love you, Julianna Sarah Lightfoot."

"Do you?"

"More than words can say." He fumbled to a stop. "Somehow, the words can't convey everything I'm feeling."

She grinned. "Maybe you'd better show me, then." Before he could drag her back into the house, she tugged on his arm. "But how about we don't stay here tonight? I'd rather have no one else barging in on us."

He frowned. "That was a one-time thing."

"Maybe, but I think it's time for you to move out of your parent's house. I have my own apartment." She gave him a significant look. "Tomorrow we can start looking for our own place, but tonight, I don't want to be here."

He nodded slowly. "Can we go back to the room long enough for you to get dressed?"

She smirked. "I'm as dressed as you are." She ran a hand over his hairy chest.

Jeff laughed. "Yeah. I suppose tradition has it that the couple goes off to a place to be alone after the wedding." He tugged Julianna into the house and up the stairs toward their room.

"It wasn't just a wedding, Jeff."

"No, but it's good to regroup alone after that, too."

True enough.

Maybe it would be okay. She had Jeff as her Alpha, and she'd won the Challenge. She had a cadre full of loyal friends, Sebrina's mentoring, and an uncle to watch over her. The Winthrops would never be friends, but she no longer stood alone in the Callowwood Pack. She'd truly come home.

They dressed and packed a bag for Jeff before they headed out to her car.

"Hey, it looks like I get to ride in the sexy Camaro after all."

Julianna grinned. "When we get home, you'll get to ride a lot more than that."

Jeff growled playfully. "Then we better get home fast because you're mine, Luna."

They made it to her house in record time. She dragged him up the stairs and into her little apartment, her arousal ramping up with each step. She turned and locked the door behind him. *No way in hell I'm letting anyone else interrupt.*

Her chin came up and she gave him her best smart-ass grin. "You ready to love your Luna?"

"I'm planning a hell of a lot more than that." He matched her grin and dragged her into the bedroom, making good on his promise.

THE END

# AUTHOR'S NOTE
## ABOUT CALLOWWOOD PACK, BOOK 1

This story is a revised and expanded version of the original tale published by Siren Publishing in 2012. However, there have been some changes to the original manuscript. I've introduced Leslie Dunmore as more than just Julianna's Fresno neighbor. He's now part of her extended family and that means he'll get his own tale when the time comes.

Eloise Farkas was in the original tale as a secondary character, necessary because of her missing sister, but I already have a sequel for her in mind and decided this time she needed more parts in this story. Now she's very important, and her sequel makes more sense.

There are a few new scenes and extended conversations in this new version and I hope they make this story better and clear, and set up for the sequels. I hope you enjoy the changes.

Thanks so much for reading.


Siobhan

# SECOND CHANCE SUCCUBUS
## CAPITOL OF SECOND CHANCES, BOOK 1
### SNEEK PEEK

*Everyone deserves a second chance...*

As an ancient succubus, Lady Aislynn is cursed to survive
off sexual energy for eternity. To live without killing,
Aislynn runs the Underground, a pleasure club in Las
Vegas where she safely feeds on the ample eroticism of her
patrons. A murder inside her club threatens the haven she's
built, even as it brings unwanted attention—and possible
salvation—in the form of two handsome brothers, both in
search of the truth.

Werewolves Chayse and Nik Wolffe haven't seen each
other in five years, and the last place they expect to cross
paths is a strip club. The detective and PI find their cases
intertwining around the enticing Aislynn and her club. Nik
may believe in Aislynn's innocence, but Chayse knows all
too well the destructive power of a succubus. He's
determined to keep himself and Nik free of her spell.

Nik's missed sharing lovers with his brother, but Chayse
seems dead-set against reconciling the past or building a
future. Luckily fate, and the Goddess, may have plans for
the two embattled werewolves and the succubus with love
enough for them both.

# OTHER BOOKS BY SIOBHAN MUIR

*Her Devoted Vampire* (from Three Lakes Books)
*Queen Bitch of the Callowwood Pack* (from Three Lakes Books)
*Second Chance Succubus* (from Three Lakes Books)
*Wildfire's Heart* (from Three Lakes Books)
*Darwin's Evolution* (from Amazon)

**Cloudburst Colorado Series**
*A Hell Hound's Fire* (from Three Lakes Books)
*The Beltane Witch* (from Three Lakes Books)
*Christmas I.C.E. Magic* (from Three Lakes Books)
*Cloudburst Ice Magic* (from Three Lakes Books)

**Rifts Series**
*Take the Reins* (from Three Lakes Books)
*A Centaur's Solstice Wish* (from Three Lakes Books)
*In Death's Shadow* (from Three Lakes Books)

**Bad Boys of Beta Squad Series**
*Bronco's Rough Ride* (from Three Lakes Books)
*The Navy's Ghost* (from Three Lakes Books)
*Rimshot's Hard Target* (from Amazon)
*Bam-Bam's Inked Hart* (from Three Lakes Books)

**The Ivory Road**
*A Walk in the Sand* (from Three Lakes Books)
*Outback Dreams* (from Three Lakes Books)

**Triple Star Ranch Series**
*Rope a Falling Star* (from Three Lakes Books
*Star Light, Star Bright* (from Three Lakes Books)

**Warbler Peninsula Series**
*Order of the Dragon* (from Three Lakes Books)
*The Valkyrie's Sword* (from Three Lakes Books)

**Coming Soon**
*Deli's Take Out* (Bad Boys of Beta Squad #4)
*Loch'd Hearts* (Elemental Hearts #2)
*The Samhain Soldier* (Cloudburst, Colorado #5)

# ABOUT THE AUTHOR

Siobhan Muir lives in Cheyenne, Wyoming, with her husband, two daughters, and a vegetarian cat she swears is a shape-shifter, though he's never shifted when she can see him. When not writing, she can be found looking down a microscope at fossil fox teeth, pursuing her other love, paleontology. An avid reader of science fiction/fantasy, her husband gave her a paranormal romance for Christmas one year, and she was hooked for good.

In previous lives, Siobhan has been an actor at the Colorado Renaissance Festival, a field geologist in the Aleutian Islands, and restored inter-planetary imagery at the USGS. She's hiked to the top of Mount St. Helens and to the bottom of Meteor Crater.

Siobhan writes kick-ass adventure with hot sex for men and women to enjoy. She believes in happily ever after, redemption, and communication, all of which you will find in her paranormal romance stories.

Connect with Siobhan online at:
http://siobhanmuir.com
http://www.facebook.com/siobhan.muir.35
http://twitter.com/SiobhanMuir
http://siobhanmuir.com/siobhans-blog
http://pinterest.com/siobhanmuir.35

www.ingramcontent.com/pod-product-compliance
Lightning Source LLC
Chambersburg PA
CBHW072316020726
47501CB00002B/525

* 9 7 8 1 9 4 7 2 2 1 0 4 8 *